Julia Quinn started writing her first book one month after finishing college and has been tapping away at her keyboard ever since. She is the author of the *New York Times* bestselling *Bridgerton* series which begins with *The Duke and I*. Other titles in this series are: *The Viscount Who Loved Me, An Offer from a Gentleman, Romancing Mr Bridgerton, To Sir Phillip, With Love, When He Was Wicked, It's In His Kiss* and *On the Way to the Wedding*. She is a graduate of Harvard and Radcliffe colleges and lives with her family in Colorado.

Please visit her on the web at www.juliaquinn.com

Dancing at Midnight

Julia Quinn

piatkus

PIATKUS

First published in the US in 1995 by Avon Books,
An imprint of HarperCollins, New York
First published in Great Britain in 2008 by Piatkus Books
This paperback edition published in 2008 by Piatkus Books
Reprinted 2008 (three times), 2009 (twice), 2010, 2011 (twice), 2013

A CIP catalogue record for this book
is available from the British Library.

ISBN 978-0-7499-3913-7

Data manipulation by Phoenix Photosetting, Chatham, Kent
www.phoenixphotosetting.co.uk
Printed and bound in Great Britain by
Clays Ltd, St Ives plc

Papers used by Piatkus are from well-managed forests
and other responsible sources.

MIX
Paper from
responsible sources
FSC® C104740

Piatkus
An imprint of
Little, Brown Book Group
100 Victoria Embankment
London EC4Y 0DY

An Hachette UK Company
www.hachette.co.uk

www.piatkus.co.uk

For my father, who never forgets to tell me how proud he is of me. I'm proud of you, too!

And for Paul, even though he seemed to think the story could be improved by moving the whole thing to the rain forest.

Dear Reader—

"What comes first," someone once asked me, "the characters or the plot?" I find questions like this nearly impossible to answer, since they seem to imply that there is actually some kind of method to the madness that is my writing career. The truth is, it varies from book to book. In the case of *Dancing at Midnight*, my second novel, however, it was definitely the characters.

I began with Belle Blydon, who had played such a prominent role in my first novel, *Splendid*. I already knew who she was—a closet bluestocking who wants nothing more than to find true love. Her hero, however, was a little more complicated. I had already written an out-and-out romp, and I wanted to try something new. And so I created John Blackwood, a war hero haunted by memories of violence, a man who feel he does not deserve a chance at happiness. He is a tortured hero in every sense of the word.

And suddenly I found myself with a new challenge: Could I write a book with dark and serious themes but still make it warm and funny? Could I create characters with very real problems and obstacles to overcome and still make my readers chuckle?

I hope so, and I hope you enjoy *Dancing at Midnight*.

With my very best wishes,

Julia Q.

Chapter 1

Oxfordshire, England, 1816

If, one by one, you weeded all the world—
Arabella Blydon blinked. That couldn't be right. There weren't any gardeners in *The Winter's Tale.* She held the book farther from her face. Even worse. She pulled the book closer. The type on the page slowly focused.

If, one by one, you wedded *all the world—*
Belle sighed and leaned back against a tree trunk. That made a lot more sense. She blinked a couple of times, willing her bright blue eyes to focus on the words that lay before her on the page. They refused to obey, but she wasn't about to read with her face pressed into the book, so she squinted and plodded on.

A chilly wind passed across her, and she glanced up at the overcast sky. It was going to rain, no doubt about that, but if she were lucky she'd have another hour until the first drops fell. That was all the time she'd need to finish *The Winter's Tale*. And that would mark the end of her Grand Shakespearean Quest, the semi-academic endeavor that had occupied her spare time for nearly six months. She'd started with *All's Well that Ends Well* and proceeded alphabetically, wending her way through *Hamlet*, all the *Henrys*, *Romeo and Juliet*, and a host of other plays she hadn't even heard of before. She wasn't exactly sure why she'd done it, other than the simple fact that she liked to read, but now that the end was in sight she was damned if she was going to let a few raindrops get in her way.

Belle gulped and looked this way and that, as if afraid that someone had heard her cursing in her thoughts. She glanced back up at the sky. A beam of sunshine burst through a tiny hole in the clouds. Belle took that as a sign for optimism and plucked a chicken sandwich out of her picnic lunch. She bit into it daintily and picked up her book again. The words seemed just as unwilling to focus as before, so she moved the volume closer to her face, which she contorted in a number of different ways until she found a squint that worked.

"There you go, Arabella," she muttered. "If you can just hold this exceedingly uncomfortable pose for another forty-five minutes, you should have no problem with the rest of your book."

"Of course your facial muscles will probably be quite sore by that point," drawled a voice from behind her.

Belle dropped her book and whirled her head around. Standing a few yards away was a gentleman in casual, yet elegant, attire. His hair was a rich chocolate brown and his eyes were the exact same color. He was looking down at her and her solitary picnic with an amused expression, and his lazy pose indicated that he'd been watching her for some time. Belle glared at him, unable to think of anything to say but hoping that her scornful gaze would put him in his place.

It didn't seem to do the trick. In fact, he looked even more amused by her. "You need spectacles," he said simply.

"And *you* are trespassing," she retorted.

"Am I? I rather thought you were trespassing."

"I most certainly am not. This land belongs to the Duke of Ashbourne. My cousin," she added for emphasis.

The stranger pointed to the west. "*That* land belongs to the Duke of Ashbourne. The boundary is that ridge over there. And thus you are trespassing."

Belle narrowed her eyes and pushed a lock of her wavy blond hair behind her ear. "Are you certain?"

"Absolutely. I realize that Ashbourne's land holdings are vast, but they are not infinite."

She shifted uncomfortably. "Oh. Well, in that case, I am very sorry for disturbing you," she said in a haughty voice. "I'll just see to my horse and be off."

"Don't be silly," he said quickly. "I hope I am not so ill-tempered that I cannot allow a lady to read under one of my trees. By all means, stay as long as you like."

Belle considered leaving anyway, but comfort won out over pride. "Thank you. I've been here for several hours and am quite ensconced."

"So I see." He smiled, but it was a small one, and Belle got the impression that he was not a man who smiled often. "Perhaps," he said, "since you will be spending the rest of the day on my land, you might introduce yourself."

Belle hesitated, unable to discern whether he was being condescending or polite. "I'm sorry. I am Lady Arabella Blydon."

"Pleased to meet you, my lady. And I am John, Lord Blackwood."

"How do you do?"

"Very well, but you still need spectacles."

Belle felt her spine stiffen. Emma and Alex had been urging her to get her eyes examined for the last month, but they were, after all, family. This John Blackwood was a perfect stranger and certainly had no right to offer her such a suggestion. "You can be sure I will take your advice under consideration," she muttered, somewhat ungraciously.

John inclined his head, a wry smile touching his lips. "What are you reading?"

"*The Winter's Tale.*" Belle sat back and waited for the usual condescending comments about women and reading.

"An excellent play, but not, I think, Shakespeare's finest," John commented. "I myself am partial to *Coriolanus.* It's not very well-known, but I quite liked it. You might read that sometime."

Belle forgot to be pleased that she had met a man who was actually encouraging her to read and said, "Thank you for the suggestion, but I've read it already."

"I'm impressed," John said. "Have you read *Othello*?"

She nodded.

"The *Tempest*?"

"Yes."

John searched his brain for the most obscure

Shakespearean work he could recall. "What about *The Passionate Pilgrim?*"

"Not my favorite, but I plodded through it." Belle tried but couldn't stop the smile that was creeping across her face.

He chuckled. "My compliments, Lady Arabella. I don't think I've ever even *seen* a copy of *The Passionate Pilgrim.*"

Belle grinned, graciously accepting the compliment as her previous antagonism toward the man melted away. "Won't you join me for a few minutes?" she asked him, waving toward the empty expanse of blanket spread out beneath her. "I still have most of my picnic lunch, and I would be happy to share it with you."

For a moment it looked as if he would accept. He opened his mouth to say something, then let out a tiny sigh and closed it. When he finally spoke, his voice was very stiff and formal and all he said was "No, thank you." He took a couple of steps away from her and turned his head so that he could stare out across the fields.

Belle cocked her head and was about to say something further when she noticed with surprise that he limped. She wondered if he'd been injured in the peninsular war. An intriguing man, this John. She wouldn't have half minded spending an hour or so in his company. And, she had to admit, he was really quite handsome, with strong, even features, and a body which was lean and powerful in spite of his injured leg. His velvety brown eyes displayed obvious intelligence, but they also seemed hooded with pain and skepticism. Belle was starting to find him very mysterious, indeed.

"Are you certain?" she asked.

"Certain of what?" He didn't turn around.

She bristled at his rudeness. "Certain that you don't want to join me for lunch."

"Quite."

That got her attention. No one had ever before told her that he was *quite* certain he could do without her company.

Belle sat uncomfortably on her blanket, her copy of *The Winter's Tale* lying limply in her lap. There didn't seem to be anything she could say with his back half to her. And it would have been impolite to start reading again.

John suddenly turned around and cleared his throat.

"It was really too bad of you to tell me I need spectacles," she said abruptly, mostly just to get something in before he could.

"I apologize. I've never been very good at polite conversation."

"Perhaps you should converse more," she retorted.

"Were you using a different tone of voice, my lady, one might suspect that you were flirting with me."

She slammed *The Winter's Tale* shut and stood. "I can see that you were not lying. You are not dreadful at merely polite conversation. You are lacking at all forms of it."

He shrugged. "One of my many qualities."

Her mouth fell open.

"I can see that you do not subscribe to my particular brand of humor."

"I cannot imagine that many people do."

There was a pause, and then a strange, sad light appeared in his eyes. It disappeared just as quickly, and the tone of his voice sharpened as he said, "Don't come out here alone again."

Belle shoved her belongings into her satchel.

"Don't worry. I shan't trespass again."

"I didn't say you couldn't come on my property. Just don't do it alone."

She had no idea how to reply to that so she merely said, "I'm going home."

He glanced up at the sky. "Yes. You probably should. It's going to rain soon. I've two or so miles to walk home myself. I shall certainly be drenched."

She glanced around. "Didn't you bring a horse?"

"Sometimes, my lady, it is better to use one's feet." He inclined his head. "It has been a pleasure."

"For you, perhaps," Belle muttered under her breath. She watched his back as he walked away from her. His limp was quite pronounced, but he moved much more quickly than she would have thought possible. She kept her gaze fixed on him until he disappeared over the horizon. As she mounted her mare, however, a compelling thought entered her head.

He limped. What kind of man was he that he preferred to walk?

John Blackwood listened to the hoofbeats of Lady Arabella's mare as she cantered off. He sighed. He'd acted like an ass.

He sighed again, this time loud with sorrow and self-loathing and pure, simple irritation. Damn. He never knew what to say to women anymore.

Belle set off back to Westonbirt, the home of her relations. Her American-born cousin Emma had married the Duke of Ashbourne a few months earlier. The newlyweds preferred the privacy of country life to London and had resided at Westonbirt almost continuously since their wedding. Of course the season was over, so no one was in London anyway. Still, Belle had a feeling that Emma and her husband would probably avoid much of London's social scene even when the next season was underway.

Belle sighed. She'd no doubt be back in London for the next season. Back at the marriage mart, looking for a husband. She was getting heartily sick of the entire process. She'd been through two seasons already and accumulated over a dozen proposals, but she'd rejected every one. Some of the men had been completely unsuitable, but most were decent sorts, well-connected and quite likeable. She just couldn't seem to make herself accept a man she didn't care deeply about. And now that she'd had a glimpse of how happy her cousin was, she knew that it would be very difficult to settle for anything less than her wildest dreams.

Belle spurred her horse into a canter as the rain began to thicken. It was almost three o'clock, and she knew that Emma would have tea ready for her when she returned. She'd been staying with Emma and her husband Alex for three weeks. A few months after Emma's wedding, Belle's parents had decided to take a holiday in Italy. Ned, their son, was back up at Oxford for his final year so he didn't need any watching over, and Emma was safely married. That left only Belle, and since Emma was now a married lady she was a suitable chaperone, so Belle went off to stay with her cousin.

Belle couldn't imagine a more pleasing arrangement. Emma was her best friend, and after all the mischief they'd gotten into together, it was quite amusing to have her as a chaperone.

Belle breathed a sigh of relief as she rode up a hill and Westonbirt rose over the horizon. The massive building was really quite graceful, with long, narrow columns of windows marching across the facade. Belle was already starting to think of it as home. She headed into the stables, handed her mare over to a groom, and made a mad dash for the house, laughing as she tried to dodge the raindrops which had started to fall at a furious rate. She stumbled up the front steps but before she could push open the heavy door, the butler opened it with a flourish.

"Thank you, Norwood," she said. "You must have been watching for me."

Norwood inclined his head.

"Norwood, has Belle returned yet?"

The feminine voice floated through the air, and Belle heard her cousin's footsteps clattering along the floor of the hallway that led to the foyer.

"It's starting to get quite wet out there." Emma turned the corner into the hall. "Oh good! You're back."

"A little wet, but none the worse for the wear," Belle said cheerily.

"I told you it was going to rain."

"Do you feel responsible for me now that you're an old married matron?"

Emma made a face which told her exactly what she thought of that. "You look like a drowned rat," she said plainly.

Belle made an equally unpleasant face. "I'll change my clothes and come down for tea in a moment."

"In Alex's study," Emma advised. "He's joining us today."

"Oh, good. I'll be right down."

Belle headed up the stairs and through the labyrinth of hallways which led to her room. She quickly peeled off her sodden riding habit, changed into a soft blue dress, and headed back downstairs. The door to Alex's study was closed and she could hear giggling, so she wisely knocked before she entered. There was a moment of silence and then Emma called out, "Come in!"

Belle smiled to herself. She was learning more and more about this married love thing by the minute. Some chaperone Emma was turning out to be. She and Alex couldn't manage to keep their hands off each other whenever they thought no one was looking. Belle's smile grew wider. She wasn't exactly sure about the particulars of making babies, but she had a feeling all this touching had something to do with why Emma was already pregnant. Belle pushed open the door and walked into Alex's very large, very masculine study. "Good afternoon, Alex," she said. "How has your day been?"

"Drier than yours, I understand," he said, pouring some milk in his teacup and ignoring the tea entirely. "Your curls are still dripping."

Belle looked down at her shoulders. The fabric of her dress was damp from her hair. She shrugged. "Oh well, nothing to do about it, I suppose." She settled down on the sofa, and poured herself a cup of tea. "And how was your day, Emma?"

"Fairly uneventful. I've been going over various books and reports from some of our lands in Wales. It looks like there may be some sort of a problem. I'm thinking of heading out there to investigate."

"You are not," Alex growled.

"Oh really?" Emma countered.

"You aren't going anywhere for another six months," he added, glancing lovingly at his flame-haired, violet-eyed wife. "And probably not for another six after that."

"If you think I'm going to lay abed until the baby comes, you're mad in the head."

"And *you* have to learn who's in charge here."

"Well then, you—"

"Stop, stop," Belle laughed. "Enough." She shook her head. Two more stubborn people in this universe had yet to be found. They were perfect for each other. "Why don't I tell you how *my* day went?"

Emma and Alex both turned their faces to her expectantly.

Belle took another sip of her tea, letting it warm her up. "I met a rather odd man, actually."

"Oh, really?" Emma leaned forward.

Alex leaned back, his eyes glazing over with a bored expression.

"Yes. He lives near here. I think his land borders yours. His name is Lord John Blackwood. Do you know him?"

Alex shot forward. "Did you say John Blackwood?"

"It was John, Lord Blackwood, I think. Why, do you know him? John Blackwood is probably a fairly common name."

"Brown hair?"

Belle nodded.

"Brown eyes?"

She nodded again.

"About my height, medium build?"

"I guess so. He wasn't quite as broad in the shoulders as you are, but I think he was nearly as tall."

"*Did he limp?*"

"Yes!" Belle exclaimed.

"John Blackwood. I'll be damned," Alex shook his head in disbelief. "And a peer now. He must have been granted a title for military service."

"He fought in the war with you?" Emma asked.

When Alex finally responded, his green eyes were far away. "Yes," he said softly. "He commanded his own company, but we saw each other frequently. I always wondered what happened to him. Don't know why I didn't try to look him up. I suppose I was afraid I'd find out he was dead."

That certainly caught Belle's attention. "What do you mean?"

"It was strange," Alex said slowly. "He was an excellent soldier. There was no one you could depend on more. He was absolutely selfless. Constantly putting himself in danger to save others."

"Why is that strange?" Emma asked. "He sounds like quite an honorable man."

Alex turned his head to the two ladies, his expression suddenly clear. "The strange thing was that for a man who seemed to have such disregard for his own well-being, he behaved quite remarkably when he was wounded."

"What happened?" Belle asked anxiously.

"The surgeon said that he'd have to cut off his leg. And I must say, he was rather callous about it. John was still conscious at the time, and the leech didn't even bother to tell him directly. He just turned to his assistant and said, 'Bring me the saw.' "

Belle shuddered, the image of John Blackwood so ill-treated surprisingly painful.

"He went crazy," Alex continued. "I've never seen anything like it. He grabbed the surgeon by his shirt and pulled him down until they were nose to nose. And considering the amount of blood he'd lost, his grip was remarkably strong. I was going to intervene, but when I heard the tone of his voice, I held back."

"What did he say?" Belle asked, on the edge of her seat.

"I'll never forget it. He said, 'If you take my leg, as God is my witness, I will hunt you down and saw off yours.' The doctor let him be. Said he'd leave him to die if that's what he wanted."

"But he didn't die," Belle said.

"No, he didn't. But I'm sure that was the end of his fighting days. Which was probably all for the best. He was a superb soldier, but I always got the idea that he abhorred violence."

"How odd," Emma murmured.

"Yes, well, he was an interesting man. I quite liked him. Had an excellent sense of humor when he chose to exhibit it. But he was more often than not silent. And he had quite the strictest sense of honor I have ever experienced."

"Really, Alex," Emma teased. "No one could be more honorable than you."

"Ah, my lovely, loyal wife." Alex leaned forward and dropped a kiss on Emma's forehead.

Belle slumped back in her seat. She wanted to hear more about John Blackwood, but there didn't seem any polite way to ask Alex to say more about him. It rather irritated her to admit it, but she couldn't deny that she was incredibly interested in the unusual man.

Belle had always been very practical, very pragmatic, and the one thing she had always refused to do was deceive herself. John Blackwood had intrigued her this afternoon, but now that she knew a bit of his history, she was fascinated. Every little thing about him, from the quirk of his brow to the way the wind ruffled his slightly wavy hair suddenly took on new meaning. And his insistence upon walking made much more sense. After fighting so fiercely to save his leg, it was only natural that he'd want to use it. He struck her as a man of principles. A man you could trust, depend upon. A man whose passions ran deep.

Belle was so surprised by the turn of her thoughts, she actually jerked her head back a little. Emma noticed her movement and inquired, "Are you all right, Belle?"

"What? Oh, just a little headache. More like a twinge, actually. It's gone now."

"Oh."

"It's probably from all my reading," Belle continued, even though Emma seemed perfectly willing to let the subject drop. "I have to try very hard to make the words focus these days. I think that perhaps I ought to have my eyes examined."

If Emma was surprised by her cousin's sudden admission that her eyesight was not quite what it should be, she made no mention of it. "Excellent. There is a very good doctor in the village. We'll see what he can do."

Belle smiled and picked up her tea. It was getting cold. And then Emma said a marvelous thing.

"You know what we ought to do," the duchess said to her husband. "We ought to invite this John Blake person—"

"John Blackwood," Belle interjected quickly.

"Sorry, this John Blackwood person over for supper. With Belle here we'll be evenly matched and we won't have to go out hunting for an extra woman."

Alex put down his glass. "An excellent idea, my love. I think I'd rather like to renew our friendship."

"That settles it, then," Emma said matter-of-factly. "Shall I send him a note or would you rather go 'round yourself to invite him in person?"

"I think I'll go. I'm eager to see him again, and

besides, it would be rude of me not to considering the fact that he saved my life."

Emma paled. "What?"

One corner of Alex's lips tugged upwards in a sheepish smile. "Just once, my love, and there's no point in getting upset over it now."

The look that the couple shared at that moment was so tender that it was almost painful for Belle to look at them. Excusing herself quietly, she slipped out of the study and headed upstairs to her room where the last few pages of *The Winter's Tale* awaited her.

John Blackwood had saved Alex's life? She could scarcely fathom it. It seemed that there was more to their new neighbor than his somewhat churlish exterior.

John Blackwood had secrets. Belle was sure of it. She'd wager that his life story put Shakespeare to shame. All she had to do was a little investigating. This excursion to the country might prove more exciting than she'd anticipated.

Of course, she wasn't going to be able to uncover any of his secrets until she befriended him. And he'd made it rather clear that he didn't much like her.

It was damned irritating, that.

Chapter 2

~~~~~⌒⌒⌒⌒⌒~~~~~

Belle woke up the next morning to the rather unpleasant sound of Emma retching. Turning over in her bed, she opened her eyes to see her cousin crouched over a chamber pot. Belle grimaced at the sight and muttered, "What a lovely way to start off one's day."

"And good morning to you, too," Emma snapped, standing up and walking over to a pitcher of water which had been left out on a nearby table. She poured herself a glass and took a gulp.

Belle sat up and watched her cousin swish the water around in her mouth. "I don't suppose you could take care of this sort of thing in your own room," she finally said.

Emma shot her an annoyed look as she gargled.

"Morning sickness is normal, you know," Belle continued in a matter-of-fact tone. "I don't think it would put Alex off if you got sick in your *own* room."

Emma's expression turned positively peevish as she spit the water out into the chamber pot. "I didn't come here to avoid my husband. Believe me, he's seen me sick plenty of times in the last few weeks." She sighed. "I think I threw up on his foot the other day."

Belle's cheeks pinkened in a sympathy blush for her cousin. "How awful," she murmured.

"I know, but the fact of the matter is I came in here to see if you were awake, and I just got sick along the way." Emma turned a little green and suddenly sat down.

Belle got up hurriedly and pulled on a dressing gown. "Do you want me to get you anything?"

Emma shook her head and took a deep breath, valiantly trying to keep the contents of her stomach down.

"You're not giving me a lot to look forward to about marriage," Belle quipped.

Emma smiled weakly. "It's mostly better than this."

"I certainly hope so."

"I thought I could keep down the tea and plain biscuits I ate for breakfast," Emma said with a sigh. "But I was wrong."

"It's easy to forget that you're expecting," Belle said kindly, hoping to buoy her cousin's spirits. "You're still so slender."

Emma flashed her a grateful smile. "It is very kind of you to say so. I must say, this is a new experience for me, and it is all very strange."

"Are you nervous? You haven't mentioned anything to me."

"Not nervous exactly, more—hmmm, I don't quite know how to describe it. But Alex's sister is due in three weeks, and we are planning to visit her the week after next. I hope to be there for the birth. Sophie has assured me that we are welcome. I am sure I won't feel so nervous once I know what is expected of me," Emma's voice was laced with more hope than certainty.

Belle's experience with birth was limited to a litter of puppies she had seen her brother deliver when she was twelve, but nonetheless, she was not at all certain that Emma would feel more at ease about the procedure after witnessing Sophie having her baby. Belle smiled weakly at her cousin, murmured something unintelligible which was meant to convey her agreement, and then shut her mouth.

After a few moments, Emma's complexion returned to its normal color, and she sighed. "There. I feel much better now. It's amazing how quickly this sickness passes. It's the only thing that makes it bearable."

A maid entered, carrying a tray with morning chocolate and rolls. She set the tray down on the bed, and the two ladies positioned themselves on either side of it.

Belle watched as Emma hesitantly took a sip of her chocolate. "Emma, could I ask you a question?"

"Of course."

"And you'll be frank in your answer?"

One corner of Emma's mouth tipped up. "When have you ever known me not to be frank?"

"Am I not likeable?"

Emma managed to grab her napkin just in time to avoid spitting out her chocolate all over Belle's sheets. "Excuse me?"

"I don't think I'm not likeable. I mean, I think most people like me."

"Yes," Emma said slowly. "Most do. Everyone

does. I don't think I've ever met anyone who *didn't* like you."

"Just so," Belle agreed. "There are probably a few who don't care about my existence one way or another, but I think it's rather rare for someone to actively *dis*like me."

"Who dislikes you, Belle?"

"Your new neighbor. John Blackwood."

"Oh, come now. You didn't speak with him for longer than five minutes, did you?"

"No, but—"

"Then he couldn't have taken you into dislike that quickly."

"I don't know. I rather think he did."

"I'm sure you're mistaken."

Belle shook her head, a perplexed expression on her face. "I don't think so."

"Would it be so terrible if he didn't like you?"

"I just don't like the idea of someone not liking me. Does that make me terribly selfish?"

"No, but—"

"I'm generally considered to be a nice person."

"Yes, you are, but—"

Belle squared her shoulders. "This is unacceptable."

Emma choked back laughter. "What do you plan to do?"

"I suppose I have to make him like me."

"I say, Belle, are you *interested* in this man?"

"No, of course not," Belle replied, rather quickly. "I just don't understand why he finds me so repugnant."

Emma shook her head, unable to believe this rather bizarre turn of conversation. "Well, you'll be able to work your wiles on him soon. With all of the men in London who have fallen in love with you without the least bit of provocation on your part, I can't imagine you won't find success in getting this Blackwood fellow to fall in *like* with you."

"Hmmm," Belle murmured. She looked up. "When did you say he's coming to dinner?"

Lord Blackwood may not have been born a lord, but he did come from an aristocratic, albeit impoverished, family. But John had the misfortune of being the seventh of seven children, a position which almost guaranteed that none of life's favors would come his way. His parents, the seventh Earl and Countess of Westborough, certainly hadn't intended to neglect their youngest child, but there were, after all, five ahead of him.

Damien was the eldest, and as the heir, he was cosseted and given every advantage that his parents could afford. A year later, Sebastian came along, and since he was so close to Damien in age, he was able to share in most of the perks that come with being the heir to an earldom. The earl and countess were nothing if not pragmatic, and given the childhood mortality rate, they were aware that Sebastian had quite a good chance of becoming the eighth Earl of Westborough. Soon after, Julianna, Christina, and Ariana arrived in rapid succession, and as it was apparent at a very young age that all three would become beauties, much attention was paid to them. Advantageous marriages could do much to fill the family coffers.

A few years later a stillborn boy arrived. No one was particularly happy about the loss, but then again, no one grieved overmuch. Five attractive and reasonably intelligent children seemed an abundance of riches, and truth be told, another baby would have been simply another mouth to feed. The Blackwoods may have been living in a magnificent old house, but it was a trial each month just to pay the bills. And it certainly never occurred to the earl to try to *earn* a living.

But then tragedy struck, and the earl was killed when his carriage overturned in a rainstorm. At the tender age of ten, Damien found himself with a title. The family scarcely had time to mourn when much to everyone's surprise, Lady Westborough discovered that she was once again with child. And in the spring of 1787, she produced one last baby. The effort was exhausting, and she never quite regained her strength. And so, tired and irritable, not to mention more than a little worried about the family finances, she took one look at her seventh child, sighed, and said, "I suppose we'll just call him John. I'm too tired to think of anything better."

And after that somewhat inauspicious entry into the world, John was—for the lack of a better word—forgotten.

His family had little patience with him, and he spent far more time in the company of tutors than relations. He was sent off to Eton and Oxford, not out of any great concern for his schooling, but rather because that was what good families did for their sons, even the youngest ones who were irrelevant to dynastic lineages.

In 1808, however, when John was in his final year at Oxford, an opportunity arose. England found herself entangled in political and military affairs on the Iberian peninsula, and men of all backgrounds were rushing to join the army. John saw the military as an area where a man might make something of himself, and he presented the idea to his brother. Damien agreed, seeing it as a way to honorably get his brother off his hands, and he bought a commission for John.

Soldiering came easily. He was an excellent rider and quite handy with both swords and firearms. He took some risks that he knew he should have avoided, but amidst the horrors of war, it became apparent that there was no way he could possibly survive the carnage. And if by some stroke of fate he managed to come through the conflict with his body intact, he knew that his soul would not be so lucky.

Four years passed, and still John managed to surprise himself by escaping death. And then he took a bullet in his knee and found himself on a boat back to England. Sweet, green, peaceful England. It somehow didn't seem real to him. Time passed quickly as his leg healed, but truth be told, he remembered very little of his recuperation. He spent much of the time drunk, unable to deal with the thought of being a cripple.

Then, much to his surprise, he was made a baron for his valor, ironic after all those years of his family reminding him that he was not a titled gentleman. That was a turning point for him, and he realized that he now had something substantial to pass on to a future generation. With a renewed sense of purpose, he decided to get his life in order.

Four years after that he was still limping, but at least he was limping on his own land. The end of the war for him had come a little sooner than expected, and he'd taken the price of his commission and begun investing. His choices proved extremely profitable, and after only five years, he'd saved enough money to purchase a small country estate.

He had finally taken it on himself to walk the perimeter of his property the day before when he'd run into Lady Arabella Blydon. He had been thinking about his encounter with her for quite some time. He probably should go over to Westonbirt and apologize to her for his rude behavior. Lord knew she wouldn't come over to Bletchford Manor after the way he'd treated her.

John winced. He was definitely going to have to come up with a new name for the place.

It was a nice house. Comfortable. Gracious but not palatial, and easily served by a small staff, which was fortunate, as he couldn't afford to employ a fleet of servants.

So there he was. He had a home—one that was his alone, not some place that he knew would never be his owing to the existence of five elder siblings. He had a nice income—a trifle depleted now that he'd bought a house, but he was fairly confident of his financial abilities after his earlier successes.

John checked his pocket watch. It was half past two in the afternoon, a good time to examine some of his fields to the west to see about farming. He wanted to make the soon-to-be-renamed Bletchford Manor as profitable as possible. A quick glance out the window told him that there wouldn't be a repeat of the previous day's downpour and he left his study, heading upstairs to fetch his hat.

He didn't get very far before Buxton, the aged butler who'd come with the house, stopped him.

"You have a caller, my lord," he intoned.

Surprised, John halted in his tracks. "Who is it, Buxton?"

"The Duke of Ashbourne, my lord. I took the liberty of showing him the blue salon."

John broke into a smile. "Ashbourne's here. Splendid." He hadn't realized that his old army friend lived so close when he'd bought Bletchford Manor, but it was an added bonus. He turned around and headed back down the stairs before coming to a bewildered halt in the hall. "Hell, Buxton," he groaned. "Which one is the blue salon?"

"Second door on your left, my lord."

John made his way down the hall and opened the door. Just as he thought, there wasn't a single piece of blue furniture in the room. Alex stood by the window, looking out over the fields which bordered his own property.

"Trying to figure out how you can convince me that the apple orchard is on your side of the border?" John joked.

Alex turned around. "Blackwood. It's damned good to see you. And the apple orchard *is* on my side of the border."

John quirked a brow. "Maybe I've been trying to figure out how to fleece *you* out of it."

Alex smiled. "How have you been? And why haven't you stopped by to say hello? I didn't even know you'd bought this place until Belle told me yesterday afternoon."

So they called her Belle. It suited her. And she'd been talking about him. John felt absurdly pleased about that even though he rather doubted she'd had anything nice to say. "You seem to forget that one is not supposed to call upon a duke unless the duke has done so first."

"Really, Blackwood, I would think we'd be beyond the trivialities of etiquette at this point. Any man who has saved my life is welcome to call upon me any time he likes."

John flushed slightly, remembering the time he had shot a man who had a knife poised to plunge into Alex's back. "Anyone would have done the same," he said softly.

One corner of Alex's mouth tilted up as he remembered the men who had lunged at John as he took his aim. John had taken a knife wound in his arm for his bravery. "No," Alex said finally. "I don't think that anyone would have done the same." He straightened. "But enough talk of war. I prefer not to dwell upon it myself. How have you been?"

John motioned to a chair, and Alex sat down. "The same as anyone else, I suppose. Would you like a drink?"

Alex nodded, and John brought him a glass of whiskey. "Obviously not quite the same, *Lord* Blackwood."

"Oh, that. Got made a baron. Baron Blackwood." John shot Alex a jaunty grin. "Has a nice ring to it, don't you think?"

"A very nice ring."

"And how has your life changed in the last four years?"

"Hadn't changed much at all, I suppose, until the last six months."

"Really?"

"I went and got myself married," Alex said with a sheepish smile.

"Did you now?" John raised his glass of whiskey in a silent toast.

"Her name is Emma. She's Belle's cousin."

John wondered if Alex's wife looked anything like her cousin. If so, he could easily see how she would have caught the duke's attention. "I don't suppose she has also read the entire works of Shakespeare?"

Alex let out a short laugh. "Actually she started to, but I've been keeping her busy lately."

John raised his eyebrows over the double meaning of that comment.

Alex caught his expression immediately. "I've got her managing my estates. She has quite a head for figures, actually. She can add and subtract much faster than I can."

"Brains run in the family, I see."

Alex wondered how John had learned so much about Belle in such a short time but didn't say anything. "Yes, well, that may be the only thing the two of them have in common, besides their uncanny ability to get exactly what they want without your even realizing it."

"Oh?"

"Emma's quite headstrong," Alex said with a sigh. But it was a comfortable, happy sigh.

"And her cousin isn't?" John asked. "She struck me as quite formidable."

"No, no, Belle has quite a strong will, don't get me wrong. But it's not quite the same as Emma. My wife is so stubborn she'll often plunge herself into situations without quite thinking about it first. Belle isn't like that. She's very practical. Very pragmatic. She's got this insatiable curiosity. It's damned difficult to keep a secret around her, but I must say, I quite like her. After seeing some of the hellish situations of my friends, I consider myself quite fortunate in my in-laws."

Alex realized that he was speaking far more openly than he normally would with a friend whom he hadn't seen in years, but he supposed that there was something about war that forges an indestructible bond between men, and it was probably for that reason that he was talking with John as if the last four years had never passed.

Or it also could have been that John was a very good listener. He always had been, Alex remembered. "But enough about my new family," he said suddenly. "You'll meet them soon enough. How are you? You managed to avoid my questions rather neatly."

John chuckled. "Same as ever, I suppose, except now I've got a title."

"And a home."

"And a home. I bought this place by investing and reinvesting the price of my commission."

Alex let out a low whistle. "You must have quite the golden touch in financial matters. We should talk about it someday. I could probably learn a thing or two from you."

"The secret to financial success is not difficult, actually."

"Really? Pray tell, what is it?"

"Common sense."

Alex let out a laugh. "Something I fear I've been lacking these last few months, but I'm afraid that's what love does to a man. Listen, why don't you come over to dine soon? I told my wife about you, and she's very eager to meet you. And of course you already know Belle."

"I'd like that," John said. And in a rare show of emotion, he added, "I think it will be very nice to have some friends in the district. Thank you for stopping by."

Alex looked at his old friend intently, and in a flash he saw just how lonely John really was. But a second later, John shuttered his gaze, and his expression adopted its usual inscrutability. "Very well, then," Alex said courteously. "How about in two days' time? We don't keep town hours out here, so we'll probably dine around seven."

John nodded his head.

"Excellent. We'll see you then." Alex stood up and shook John's hand. "I'm glad our paths crossed again."

"As am I." John escorted Alex out of the house to the stables where his horse was waiting. With a friendly nod, Alex mounted and rode away.

John walked slowly back into the house, smiling to himself as he looked up at his new home. When he reached the hall, however, Buxton intercepted him.

"This arrived for you, my lord, while you were conversing with his grace." He handed John an envelope on a silver tray.

John raised his eyebrows as he unfolded the note.

I am in England.

How strange. John turned the envelope over in his hand. His name was not written on it anywhere. "Buxton?" he called out.

The butler, who had been on his way to the kitchen, turned around and returned to John's side.

"When this arrived, what did the messenger say?"

"Just that he had a note for the master of the house."

"He didn't mention my name specifically?"

"No, my lord, I don't think so. It was a child who delivered it, actually. I don't think he was more than eight or nine."

John gave the paper one last speculative glance and then shrugged. "It's probably for the previous owners." He crumpled it in his hand and tossed it aside. "I certainly have no idea what it's about."

Later that night as John was eating dinner, he thought about Belle. As he nursed a glass of whiskey over the pages of *The Winter's Tale*, he thought about her. He crawled into bed, and he thought about her.

She was beautiful. That much was irrefutable, but he didn't think that was the reason she pervaded his thoughts. There had been a gleam in those bright blue eyes. A gleam of intelligence, and . . . compassion. She'd tried to befriend him before he'd gone and completely foiled her attempt.

He shook his head, as if to banish her from his thoughts. He knew better than to think about women before bed. Closing his eyes, he sent up a prayer for dreamless sleep.

He was in Spain. It was a hot day, but his company was in good spirits; no fighting for the last week.

They had settled into a small town, nearly a month ago. The locals were, for the most part, glad to have them. The soldiers brought money, mostly to the tavern, but everyone felt a little more prosperous when the English were in town.

As usual, John was drunk. Anything to wipe out the screams that rang in his ears and the blood that he always felt on his hands, no matter how often he washed them. Another few drinks, he judged, and he'd be well on his way to oblivion.

"Blackwood."

He looked up and nodded at the man settling across the table from him. "Spencer."

George Spencer picked up the bottle. "Do you mind?" John shrugged.

Spencer splashed some of the liquid into the glass he'd brought over with him. "Do you have any idea when we're getting out of this hellhole?"

"I prefer this hellhole, as you call it, to the deeper one on the battlefield."

Spencer glanced at a serving girl across the room and licked his lips before turning back to John and saying, "Never would have took you for a coward, Blackwood."

John shot back another glass of whiskey. "Not a coward, Spencer. Just a man."

"Aren't we all." Spencer's attention was still focused

*on the girl, who couldn't have been more than thirteen.
"What do you think of that one, eh?"*

John just shrugged again, not feeling especially communicative.

*The girl, whose name he had learned during this past
month was Ana, came over and set a plate of food in
front of him. He thanked her in Spanish. She nodded
and smiled, but before she could leave, Spencer had
pulled her onto his lap.*

*"Aren't you a nice piece?" he drawled, his hand
creeping up and covering her barely mature breast.*

"No," she said in broken English. "I—"

"Leave her alone," John said sharply.

"Christ, Blackwood, she's just a—"

"Leave her alone."

*"You're an ass sometimes, did you know that?" Spencer pushed Ana off of his lap, but not before giving her
backside a vicious pinch.*

John forked a bite of rice into his mouth, chewed, swallowed, and said, "She's a child, Spencer."

Spencer flexed his hand. "Not the way I felt it."

*John just shook his head, not wanting to have to deal
with him. "Just leave her alone."*

Spencer stood up abruptly. "I gotta go piss."

*John watched him leave and turned back to his supper.
He'd not taken more than three bites before Ana's
mother appeared at the table.*

*"Señor Blackwood," she said, speaking in a mix of
English and Spanish she knew he understood. "That
man—he touch my Ana. It must stop."*

*John blinked a few times, trying to rid his mind of its
alcoholic haze. "Has he been bothering her for long?"*

"All week, Señor. All week. She no like it. She frightened."

John felt disgust roiling the contents of his stomach.

"Don't worry, Señora," he assured her. "I'll make sure he leaves her alone. She'll be safe from my company."

The woman bowed her head. "Thank you, Señor Blackwood. Your word comforts me." She returned to the kitchen where, John presumed, she would spend the rest of the evening cooking.

He went back to work on his meal, downing another glass of whiskey along with it. Closer and closer to oblivion. He craved it these days. Anything to wipe his mind free of the death and the dying.

Spencer returned, wiping his hands on a towel as he entered. "Still eating, Blackwood?" he asked.

"You always did have a penchant for stating the obvious."

Spencer scowled. "Eat your slop then, if that's what you want. I'm going off in search of entertainment."

John raised a brow as if to say, "Here?"

"This place is ripe, I think." Spencer's eyes gleamed as he swaggered up the stairs and out of sight.

John sighed, glad to be rid of this man who had always been such an annoyance in his company. He'd never liked Spencer, but he was a decent soldier, and England needed all of those she could get her hands on.

He finished his meal and pushed the plate across the table. The food had been tasty, but nothing seemed to satisfy him anymore. Perhaps another glass of whiskey.

Oh, now he was drunk. Really drunk. There were, he supposed, still a few things for which to thank the Lord.

He let his head slump down toward the table. Ana's mother had been quite nervous, hadn't she? Her face, lined with worry and fear, floated through his mind. And Ana, poor child, she couldn't like having these men around. Especially one like Spencer.

He heard a thump come from the floor upstairs. Nothing out of the ordinary.

Spencer. Oh, yes, that's who he was thinking about.

Pain in the ass, he was. Always bothering the locals, caring for nothing but his own amusement.

Another thump.

What was that he'd said — he was going off in search of entertainment. That was rather like him.

Another odd noise — this one sounded like a woman's cry. John looked around. Didn't anyone else hear this? No one seemed to react. Maybe it was because he was closest to the stairs.

This place is ripe, I think.

John rubbed his eyes. Something wasn't right.

He stood, bracing himself against the table to ease the nausea rocking his body. Why did he have this odd sense that something was amiss?

Another thump. Another cry.

He walked slowly toward the stairs. What was wrong? The noise grew louder as he made his way along the second-floor hallway.

And then he heard it again. This time it was clear. "Noooooooooo!" Ana's voice.

John sobered in an instant. He burst through the door, knocking it off one of its hinges. "Oh, God, no," he cried. He could barely see Ana, her slight form completely beneath Spencer, who was pumping relentlessly into her.

But he could hear her weeping. "Noooo, noooo, please, noooo."

John didn't pause to think. Crazed, he pulled Spencer up off the girl and threw him against the wall.

"What the hell — Blackwood?" Spencer's face was as mottled and red as his member.

"You bastard," John breathed, his hand coming to rest on his gun.

"For God's sake, she's just some Spanish whore."

"She is a child, Spencer."

"She's a whore now." Spencer turned around to retrieve his breeches.

John's hand tightened on his gun.

"That's all she ever would have been."

John lifted his gun. "His majesty's soldiers do not rape." He shot Spencer in the ass.

Spencer howled and went down, letting loose a swift stream of expletives. John immediately went to Ana, as if there was something he could possibly do to erase her pain and humiliation.

Her face was blank. Completely devoid of expression . . .

Until she saw him.

She cringed. She turned away from John in horror. He staggered backward at the force of her terror. He hadn't . . . It hadn't been him . . . He'd meant to . . .

Ana's mother burst into the room. "Mother of God," she cried out. "What is—Oh, my Ana. My Ana." She ran to her daughter, who was now weeping uncontrollably.

John stood in the middle of the room, dazed, in shock, and still drunk with whiskey. "I didn't . . ." he whispered. "It wasn't me."

There was so much noise. Spencer was screaming and cursing in pain. Ana was crying. Her mother was railing at God. John couldn't seem to move.

Ana's mother turned around, her face full of more hatred than John had ever seen in a single person. "You did this," she hissed, and spit in his face.

"No. It wasn't me. I didn't . . ."

"You swore you'd protect her." The woman seemed to be trying to restrain herself from attacking him. "It might as well have been you."

John blinked. "No."

It might as well have been you.

It might as well have been you.

It might as well . . .

John sat up in bed, his body soaked with sweat. Had it really been five years? He laid back down, trying to forget that Ana had killed herself three days later.

Chapter 3

When Belle arrived at breakfast the next morning, she discovered that neither Emma nor Alex were up yet. This was rather surprising because Emma tended to be something of a morning person. Belle guessed that Alex was keeping her abed for his own purposes and wondered if a woman could get pregnant while she was already pregnant.

"For someone who is usually considered quite bright," she muttered to herself, "you know pathetically little about the important things."

"Did you say something, my lady?" a footman immediately inquired.

"No, no, I was just talking to myself," she replied, rolling her eyes at her behavior. If she kept this up, half of Westonbirt would think she was daft.

She helped herself to a bit of breakfast, glancing

through the day-old newspaper that was sitting out
on the table for Alex's perusal. The newlyweds still
hadn't arrived by the time she finished her omelet.
Belle sighed, trying to decide how to occupy herself.

She could raid Alex's library, she supposed, but
for once she didn't feel like reading. The sun was
shining brightly, a rare treat during this exception-
ally rainy autumn, and she suddenly wished that
she weren't alone, that Alex or Emma had decided
not to sleep in that morning, that she had someone
with whom to share the fine weather. But there was
no one. Except—Belle shook her head. She couldn't
just prance over to Lord Blackwood's house and
say hello.

But then again, why couldn't she?

Well, for one thing, he didn't like her.

Which, she countered, was precisely the reason
she ought to pay him a visit. She wasn't going to
be able to rectify the situation if they never saw
each other again.

Belle raised her eyebrows as she pondered the
thought. If she brought along a maid as a chaperone, she wouldn't be so far outside the bounds of
propriety. Well, actually she would, but no one was
about, and Lord Blackwood didn't strike her as
overly high in the instep. Making her decision, she
wandered over to the kitchen to see if Mrs. Goode
could spare some scones. They would make a
lovely breakfast. Perhaps Lord Blackwood hadn't
yet eaten.

She'd be fine. This wasn't London, after all. Forty
gossips would not be wagging their tongues later
that evening at her scandalous behavior. And she
wasn't going to do anything dreadful. She just
wanted to greet their new neighbor properly.
Mostly she just wanted to see what his house

looked like, she told herself. What was it called? Alex had told her the night before. Bletchwood Place? Blumley Manor? Blasphemous Burg? Belle laughed to herself. It was something hideous, that's all she remembered.

She wandered down to the kitchen, where Mrs. Goode was only too happy to arrange a basket. Belle soon departed, laden with fresh jams and homemade scones.

She strode purposefully to the stables where she mounted Amber, her mare. She wasn't quite certain where John's house was located, but she knew it was to the east. If she stuck to the roads and kept heading toward the sun, she'd be bound to run into it eventually.

She set off at an easy trot as she headed down the long drive that led from Westonbirt to the main road. Emma's lady's maid knew how to ride, and she kept pace alongside her. They turned east on the main road, and sure enough, after about a quarter of an hour, they happened upon a drive that looked as if it led to another house. After a few moments Belle found herself in a wide open clearing, at the center of which stood an elegant stone house.

It was small by the standards of aristocracy, but it was stylish and obviously well-built. It suited her. Belle smiled and urged her mare forward. She didn't see any stables, so she saw to her horse herself, tying it to a tree. Emma's maid did the same. "Sorry, Amber," Belle murmured and then took a deep breath and marched up the front steps.

She picked up the giant brass knocker and let it fall with a resounding thud. After a few moments, a white-haired, elderly man answered the door. Belle took him to be the butler. "Good morning,"

she said in cultured tones. "Is this the home of
Lord Blackwood?"

The butler raised an eyebrow. "It is."

Belle offered him her brightest smile. "Excellent.
Please inform him that Lady Arabella Blydon has
come to call."

Buxton didn't doubt for a moment that she was
a lady, not with her fine clothes and aristocratic
accent. With a regal nod of his head, he showed
her to an airy room decorated in shades of cream
and blue.

Belle was silent as she watched the butler disappear up the stairs. Then she turned to Emma's
maid and said, "Perhaps you should, ah, go to the
kitchens and see if there are any, ah, other servants
about."

The maid's eyes widened slightly at being dismissed, but she nodded and left the room.

John was still in bed when the butler arrived,
having decided to treat himself to some much-
needed rest. Buxton entered silently, then put his
mouth very, very close to his master's ear. "You
have a visitor, my lord," he said loudly.

John swatted the butler with a pillow and reluctantly came awake. "A what?" he asked groggily.

"A visitor."

"Good Lord, what time is it?"

"Nine o'clock, my lord."

John staggered out of bed and grabbed a robe to
cover his naked body. "Who the hell comes calling
at nine in the morning?"

"Lady Arabella Blydon, my lord."

John whirled around in shock. "Who?"

"I believe I said Lady—"

"I know what you said," John snapped, his temper shortened by his rather unceremonious awak-
ening. "What the hell is she doing here?"

"I am sure I do not know, my lord, but she did ask for you."

John sighed, wondering when Buxton would realize that every question did not require a response. He sighed again. He didn't doubt for a moment that the sly old butler knew very well that John's remarks had been hypothetical. "I suppose I have to get dressed," he finally said.

"I should think so, my lord. I took the liberty of informing Wheatley that you would require his services."

John turned around and headed to his dressing room. Like Buxton, the valet had also come with the house, and John had to admit that it was not difficult to get used to the luxury. In no time, he was dressed in form-fitting biscuit-colored breeches, a crisp white shirt, and navy blue coat. He deliberately ignored his cravat. If Lady Arabella required a cravat, she shouldn't have come calling at nine in the morning.

He splashed some water on his face then ran his wet hands through his unruly hair, trying to tame the sleep-tossed look. "Damn it all," he muttered. He still looked half-asleep. Hell, who cared? He went downstairs.

Buxton intercepted him on the landing. "Lady Arabella is waiting for you in the green salon, my lord."

John took a breath, trying not to let his exasperation show. "And which one is that, Buxton?"

The butler gave him an amused smile and pointed. "Right over there, my lord."

John followed Buxton's finger and entered the room, leaving the door respectably open. Belle was standing near a blue chair, idly examining a painted vase. She looked utterly charming and damnably awake in her rose-colored gown. "This is a surprise," he said.

Belle looked up at the deep sound of his voice. "Oh, hello, Lord Blackwood." She glanced lightly at his disheveled hair. "I hope I didn't wake you."

"Not at all," he lied.

"I thought that perhaps we didn't get off to a good start when we met."

He didn't say anything.

She took a breath and continued. "Right. Well, I thought I should greet you to the neighborhood. I brought you something to break your fast. I hope you like scones."

John flashed her a wide smile. "I *adore* scones. And they're just in time for breakfast."

Belle frowned at his overly amused tone. She *had* woken him up. "There is some jam to go with them." She sat down, wondering what on earth had possessed her to come over here so early.

John rang for some tea and coffee and then seated himself across from her. He glanced mildly around the room. "I see you have no escort."

"Oh, no, I did bring a maid, but she went off to visit your servants. I would have had Emma accompany me, but she wasn't yet up and about. It's early, you know."

"I know."

Belle swallowed and continued. "It really isn't that important, I don't think. This isn't London, after all, where one's every movement is fair game for the gossips. And it's not as if I'm in any danger."

John's eyes raked appreciatively over her decidedly feminine form. "Aren't you?"

Belle flushed and stiffened in her seat. She looked him straight in the eye and saw honor lurking behind his sardonic facade. "No, I don't think I am," she replied resolutely.

"You shouldn't have come here alone."

"I told you, I didn't come here alone. My maid—"

"Your maid is in the kitchen. You are here in this room. Alone. With me."

Belle's mouth opened and closed several times before she managed to speak. "Well . . . yes, of course . . . but . . ."

John stared at her, thinking that he'd like nothing better than to lean over and kiss those soft lips which were opening and closing with such consternation. He shook his head slightly as if to banish the thought. *Get a hold of yourself, John*, his inner voice warned. "I apologize," he said abruptly. "I certainly did not mean to make you ill at ease. It is just rather uncommon for a young lady to call upon a bachelor unescorted."

Belle smiled archly, his apology somehow relieving her tension. "I am rather uncommon myself."

John didn't doubt it for an instant. He glanced over at her saucy expression and wondered if she had come calling deliberately to torture him.

"Besides," Belle continued, "I didn't think you would be such a stickler for etiquette."

"*I* am not," he pointed out. "Most young ladies, however, are."

A servant brought in tea and coffee, and Belle quickly offered to pour. She handed him a cup of coffee and set about fixing herself some tea, chattering all the while.

"Did you grow up in the area?"

"No."

"Well, then, where did you grow up?"

"Shropshire."

"How lovely."

John made a noise that was perilously close to a grunt. Belle raised her eyebrows and continued. "I am from London."

"How lovely."

Belle pursed her lips at his sarcastic comment. "We have a home in Sussex, of course, but I tend to think of London as home."

John picked up a scone and liberally spread some strawberry jam onto it. "How unfortunate for you."

"Don't you like London?"

"Not particularly."

"Oh." And what else was she supposed to say, Belle wondered. A full minute passed, and she was painfully aware of the speculative and amused glances that John was shooting her way. "Well," she said finally. "I see that you were not lying to me yesterday."

That comment caught John's attention and he looked up questioningly.

"You really are dreadful at making polite conversation."

He let out a bark of laughter. "No one could ever accuse you of being less than astute, my lady."

Belle let that comment pass, not entirely certain that it had been meant as a compliment. As she looked over at him she remembered yesterday's conversation. For a moment, at least, they had enjoyed each other's company. They had discussed Shakespeare, and yes, even teased each other a bit.

He'd been different then, almost boyish. That is, until he had put his guard back up. Belle had a feeling that someone had hurt this man very badly in the past. That didn't, however, mean that she would allow him to abuse her in turn.

She sensed something special in him, something fine and shining and very, very good. And perhaps all he needed was someone to remind him of that. She saw no reason not to throw caution to the wind and try to befriend him despite all of the obstacles he was throwing in her path. Crossing her arms, she said, "You can speak in that arrogant tone if you want, but it won't wash."

John raised an eyebrow.

"You might as well accept it," Belle stated plainly. "You like me."

Much to John's dismay, his coffee cup clattered loudly in its saucer. "What did you say?"

"You like me." Belle cocked her head, looking much like a cat who had just lapped up a very large bowl of cream.

"And how did you reach that conclusion, may I ask?"

"I can just tell."

It was on the tip of his tongue to ask her if she also realized that he wanted her very badly. Could she tell that? Perhaps. He himself was quite surprised by the force of his reaction to her. Yesterday, she'd looked lovely sitting under his tree, but today, to his still slightly sleepy eyes, she was a goddess.

"You needn't look so impressed by my insight," Belle quipped.

A goddess with a very smart mouth.

"You," John said forcefully, "should be whipped."

"I hope you don't intend to search out a crop right now. I've grown rather fond of my backside." Good Lord, Belle wondered, *when* had she grown so bold? She glanced over at his furious visage.

John's traitorous mind decided that it would like to get very, very fond of her backside, and then his even more traitorous body reacted violently to the thought. What on earth was this chit thinking? You only pushed a man so far. Still, he couldn't deny that her words had a ring of truth. He did rather like her. So, trying to steer the conversation out of dangerous waters, he said deliberately, "You are correct. I am not very good at making polite conversation."

Belle took the hint. She smiled prettily and said, "I wouldn't worry overmuch. I still have hope for you."

"Imagine my relief."

"That hope is dwindling by the second," she said between clenched teeth.

John looked over at her as he chewed a bite of scone. Somehow she managed to look sweet and desirable at the same time. God help him, she was already breaking through the protective wall he had erected around himself years ago. She certainly didn't deserve the kind of treatment he'd been dishing out. He swallowed his food, slowly and deliberately wiped his mouth with a napkin, stood up, and took her hand.

"Will you allow me to start over this morning?" he said elegantly, raising her hand to his lips. "I fear I arose on the wrong side of the bed."

Belle's heart did a little flip at the feel of his lips brushing along her knuckles. "It is I who should apologize. I'm afraid that any side of the bed would have been the wrong one at this hour."

John smiled at that and sat back down, reaching for another scone. "These are delicious," he commented.

"Our cook's mother was from Scotland."

"Our cook?" John questioned her choice of words. "Have you become a permanent part of the household, then?"

"No, I shall be heading back to London when my parents return from Italy. But I must admit that

Westonbirt is starting to feel like home."

John nodded and then held up his half-eaten scone. "Ever been to Scotland?"

"No. Have you?"

"No."

There was a moment of silence and then John said, "How am I doing?"

"How are you doing at what?" Belle asked with a perplexed expression.

"Making polite conversation. I've been trying very, very hard for the last few minutes." He flashed her a boyish smile.

Belle couldn't keep down the gurgling laugh which welled up in her throat. "Oh, you're making *great* strides!"

"I shall be ready for a London season in no time." He popped the last bit of scone in his mouth.

Belle leaned forward excitedly. "Are you planning to come to town for the season, then?" The thought thrilled her. She was starting to get bored with the social whirl, and John would certainly liven things up. Besides, she found the idea of dancing in his arms strangely erotic. An electric tingle traveled up her spine just at the thought of being so close to him, and she blushed.

John noticed the color in her cheeks and was wildly curious as to what scandalous thought could make her blush after she'd brazenly come to his home at nine in the morning. He had no desire to embarrass her by asking, however, and so he merely said, "No. I haven't the blunt."

Belle sat back, surprised at his forthrightness. "Well, that's no matter," she tried to joke. "Half the *ton* hasn't the blunt. Most simply manage to get invited to parties every evening and thus never have to pay for their own food."

"I've never been one for parties every evening."

"No, I didn't think you were. Neither am I, as it happens."

"Really? I would have thought you'd be the belle of the ball, if you pardon the pun."

Belle smiled wryly. "I won't be falsely modest and say that I haven't enjoyed a measure of social success—"

John chuckled at her careful choice of words.

"But I must admit, I'm growing weary of the season."

"Is that so?"

"Yes. But I suppose I'll have to go back next year."

"Why go if you find it so dull?"

She grimaced. "One's got to get a husband, after all."

"Ah," was all John said.

"It isn't as easy as you might think."

"I cannot imagine finding a husband would be especially difficult for *you*, Lady Arabella. You must know that you are extremely beautiful."

Belle flushed with pleasure at his compliment. "I had some offers, but none were suitable."

"Not enough money?"

This time when Belle flushed, it was with consternation. "I take offense at that, Lord Blackwood."

"I'm sorry, I thought it was the way of things."

Belle had to admit that for many women, it *was* the way of things, and she accepted his apology with a brief nod. "A few of the gentlemen informed me that they would be able to overlook my appalling bluestocking tendencies on account of my looks and fortune."

"I find your bluestocking tendencies quite appealing."

Belle sighed happily. "How nice it is to hear someone—a man—say that."

John shrugged. "It always seemed silly to me to desire a woman who cannot converse any better than a sheep."

Belle leaned forward, her eyes glittering mischievously. "Really? I would have thought you'd *prefer* such a woman, considering your difficulty with polite conversation."

"Touché, my lady. I cede this round to you."

Belle felt absurdly pleased and was suddenly very, very glad that she'd ventured out that morning. "I'll take that as high praise, indeed."

"It was meant as such." John waved his hand toward the diminishing number of scones. "Don't you want one? I'm liable to eat the whole plateful if you don't intervene soon."

"Well, I already had breakfast but..." Belle eyed the mouth-watering scones. "I suppose one wouldn't hurt."

"Good, I haven't the patience for ladies who try to eat like rabbits."

"No, you prefer sheep, I understand."

"Touché again, my lady." John glanced out the window. "Are those your horses out there?"

Belle followed his gaze and then got up and walked to the window. "Yes, the one on the left is my mare Amber. I didn't see the stables, so I just tied her to the tree. She seems content."

John had stood when Belle had gotten up, and now he walked over to join her at the window. "The stables are in the back."

Belle was intensely aware of his nearness, of the spicy masculine scent of him. The breath seemed to leave her body, and for the first time that morning, she felt robbed of all speech. While he was watching her mare, she stole a quick glance at his profile. He had a straight, patrician nose, and a strong chin. His lips were simply beautiful, full and sensual. She swallowed uncomfortably and forced herself to move her gaze to his eyes. They looked bleak. Belle found herself desperately wishing that she could erase the pain and loneliness she saw there.

Abruptly, John turned and caught Belle watching him. His eyes locked with hers, and for a moment he left his expression unshuttered, allowing her to look into his very soul. Then he quirked a smile, breaking the spell, and turned away.

"She's a lovely mare," he said.

It took a few moments before Belle could catch her breath. "Yes, I've had her for several years."

"I cannot imagine she gets much exercise in London."

"No." And why were they speaking so flatly now, Belle wanted to know. Why had he pulled away from her? She didn't think she could bear being with him for one more moment if they were only going to speak inanities and, God forbid, make polite conversation. "I'd better go," she said abruptly. "It's getting late."

John chuckled at that. It was barely ten in the morning.

In her haste to compose herself and leave, Belle didn't hear his mirth. "You can keep the basket," she said. "It's a gift, after all, along with all the food."

"I shall treasure it always." He pulled the bell-cord to summon Belle's maid from the kitchens.

Belle smiled, and then to her horror and surprise, she felt a tear welling up in her eye. "Thank you for your company. I had a lovely morning."

"As did I." John escorted her to the front hall. She smiled before turning away from him, rocking him to his very soul and sending a fresh wave of desire through his body. "Lady Arabella," he said hoarsely.

She turned around, concern clouding her features. "Is something wrong?"

"It isn't wise for you to keep company with me."

"What do you mean?"

"Don't come here again."

"But you just said—"

"I said don't come again. At least not alone."

She blinked. "Don't be silly. You sound like the hero in a gothic novel."

"I'm not a hero," he said darkly. "You'd do well to remember that."

"Stop funning me." Her voice lacked conviction.

"I'm not, my lady." He closed his eyes, and for a split second an expression of pure agony washed over his features. "There are many dangers in this world about which you don't know. About which you should *never* know," he added harshly.

The maid arrived in the hall.

"I'd better go," Belle said quickly, completely unnerved.

"Yes."

She turned and fled down the steps to her horse. She mounted quickly and set off down the drive to the main road, intensely aware of John's eyes on her back the entire way.

What had happened to him? If Belle had been intrigued by her new neighbor before, now she was ravenously curious. His moods shifted like the wind. She didn't understand how he could tease her so sweetly one moment and be so dark and forbidding the next.

And she couldn't shake the idea that he somehow *needed* her. He needed someone, that much was clear. Someone who could wipe away the pain that surfaced in his eyes when he thought no one was looking.

Belle squared her shoulders. She'd never been one to back down from a challenge.

Chapter 4

$\sim$ $\odot$ $\odot$ $\sim$

Belle was plagued by thoughts of John for the rest of the day. She went to bed early, hoping that a good night's sleep would give her new perspective. But sleep eluded her for hours, and once she fell into slumber, John haunted her dreams with startling persistence.

The next morning she slept a little later than usual, but when she went down to breakfast, she found that Alex and Emma had stayed abed again. She didn't feel like searching out something with which to amuse herself, so she finished her breakfast quickly and decided to go for a walk.

She glanced down at her booted feet, decided that her shoes were sturdy enough for a bit of a hike, and slipped out the front door, leaving a note for her cousins with Norwood. The autumn air was crisp but not cold, and Belle was glad that she hadn't bothered to put on a cloak. Taking quick strides, she found herself heading east. East toward John Blackwood's property.

Belle groaned. She should have known this was going to happen. She stopped, trying to force herself to turn around and head west. Or north or south or north by northwest or anything but east. But her feet refused to obey, and she trudged onward, trying to excuse her behavior by telling herself that she only knew how to get to Blondwood Manor by way of the main road, and here she was going through woods, so she probably wouldn't ever get there anyway.

She frowned. It wasn't called Blondwood Manor. But for the life of her, she couldn't remember what it *was* called. Belle shook her head and kept on walking.

An hour went by, and Belle started to regret her decision not to bring her mare. It was a couple of miles to the edge of Alex's property, and from what John had told her the previous day, she knew it was another couple of miles to his house. Her boots weren't turning out to be as comfortable as she had hoped, and she had a sneaking suspicion that a blister was forming on her right heel.

She tried to keep a stiff upper lip, but the pain soon reached new heights of irritation. With an audible groan, Belle finally gave up and conceded defeat to her blister. She squatted down and patted the grass with her hand, checking to see if it was damp. The early morning dew had already evaporated, so she plopped down onto the ground, unlaced her boot, and pulled it off. She was about to get up and start walking again when she realized that she was wearing her favorite stockings. With a sigh, she reached up under her skirt and slowly rolled one off.

* * *

From his position ten yards away, John could not believe his eyes. Belle had wandered onto his property again, and he was just about to make his presence known to her when she started muttering to herself and then sat down on the ground in a most undignified manner.

Intrigued, John darted behind a tree. What followed was a scene far more seductive than he would have ever dreamed possible. After pulling off her shoe, Belle had lifted her skirts well above her knees, giving him a tantalizing view of her shapely legs. John almost groaned. In a society that considered ankles promiscuous, this was racy, indeed.

John knew he shouldn't look. But as he stood there, watching Belle roll off her stocking, he could come up with no better alternative. If he called out to her, he'd only embarrass her. Better she didn't know that he was there. A true gentleman, he supposed, would have the fortitude to turn his back, but then again, John found that most men who took the time to call themselves gentlemen were fools.

He just couldn't take his eyes off of her. Her innocence only made her more seductive—more so than the most professional of performers. Her unintended striptease was all the more sensual because Belle was lowering her stocking with agonizing slowness not because she had an audience but because she seemed to love the feel of the silk sliding along her soft skin.

And then, much too soon for John's tastes, she was done and muttering to herself again. He smiled. He'd never met anyone who talked to herself quite so often—especially not in such amusing tones.

She stood and looked herself up and down a few

times until her gaze fell on a bow which adorned her dress. She tied her stocking around the frippery, firmly securing it to her attire, and then reached down and picked up her boot. John almost laughed when she started to mutter again, glaring at her shoe as if it were some small, offensive creature as she realized that she could have just stuffed her stocking into the boot for safekeeping.

He heard her sigh, so she must have done so loudly, and then she shrugged her shoulders and trudged away from him. John quirked a brow at her movements because she wasn't walking home, she was heading toward his house. Alone. One would have thought that the chit would have had the sense to heed his warning. He thought he'd frightened her the day before. Lord knew he frightened himself.

He couldn't contain a smile, however, because with one of her boots off, she was limping almost as much as he did.

John quickly turned and headed back into the woods. After his accident, he had exercised his bad leg religiously, and as a result, he could walk quite swiftly—almost as fast as an uninjured man. The only problem was that overexertion meant that his leg would later ache as if he'd walked—no hopped—to hell and back.

But he wasn't thinking about these consequences as he sped through the woods. Foremost on his mind was how to cut through the forest and intercept Belle closer to Bletchford Manor without her realizing that he had been spying on her.

He knew that the path curved to the right up ahead, so he cut diagonally through the woods, cursing every tree stump he no longer had the agility to leap over. When he finally emerged onto the path about a half mile closer to his house, his knee was throbbing, and he was panting from the exertion. He put his hands on his thighs and leaned down for a moment, trying to catch his breath. Pain shot up and down his leg, and it was pure agony just to straighten it. Wincing, he rubbed his knee until the stabbing sensation receded into a dull ache.

He stood up, and just in time. Belle had just limped around the corner. John quickly took a step in her direction, wanting to appear as if he had been strolling down the path all morning.

She didn't see him right away because she was looking down at the ground for pebbles so that she could avoid them with her unshod foot. They were only about ten feet away from each other when she heard the sound of his footsteps. She looked up instantly and saw him approaching. He was wearing that enigmatic little smile of his, as if he knew something that she didn't. Actually, she thought, it was more like he knew something that she never would.

"Oh, hello, Lord Blackwood," she said, curving her lips into a smile that she hoped matched the mystery of his. She rather thought she failed; she'd never had a mysterious day in her life, and besides, she sounded too cheerful by half.

Amidst all of Belle's turbulent thoughts, John nodded.

"I suppose you're wondering what I'm doing on your property again."

John raised an eyebrow, and Belle had no idea whether his gesture meant: You're an annoying little trespasser, You're an amusing piece of baggage, or Your actions aren't worth the time it would take to think about them. So she plodded on.

"I did, of course, realize that this was your property, but I headed east from Westonbirt when I left this morning. I don't know why, but I did, and the eastern border is really much closer to the house than any of the other ones, and so since I like to take fairly long walks, it's only natural that I'd reach the border, and I didn't think you'd mind." Belle clamped her mouth shut. She was babbling. That was unlike her, and she was quite annoyed with herself for doing it.

"I don't mind," John said simply.

"Oh. Well, that's good, I suppose, because I have no wish to be forcibly thrown off your property." That sounded really stupid. Belle shut her mouth again.

"Would it really require force to get you off my property? I had no idea you liked it so much."

Belle smiled impishly. "You're teasing me."

John gave her another one of those small smiles, the kind that would have said so much if the rest of his face weren't so inscrutable.

"You don't talk much, do you?" she blurted out.

"I didn't think there was a need. You seem to be holding up both our ends of the conversation admirably."

Belle frowned. "That was a horrid thing to say." She looked up. His velvety brown eyes, usually so unreadable, were filled with amusement. She sighed. "But true. I don't usually talk this much, you know."

"Really?"

"Really. I think it's because you're so silent that I feel the need to talk more."

"Ah. So we have shifted the blame to my shoulders?"

Belle glanced flirtatiously at his shoulders, which were a little broader than she'd remembered. "They do seem a bit more capable of bearing such a heavy load."

John grinned at her, really grinned, which was something he didn't do very often. He suddenly felt glad that he'd worn one of his better coats; he frequently threw on old ones for his early morning walks. Then he was annoyed with himself for caring.

"Is this a new fashion?" he asked, motioning to the boot in her hand.

"Blister," Belle said, lifting her dress up a few inches. It was risqué, she knew, but she shrugged it off. The two of them had such bizarre conversations, normal rules of etiquette just didn't seem to apply.

Much to her surprise, however, he got down on one knee and took her foot into his hands. "Mind if I take a look?" he asked.

Belle tugged her foot back nervously. "I don't think that will be necessary," she said quickly. Seeing her foot was one thing. Actually touching it was something else altogether.

John held fast. "Don't be a prude, Belle. It could become infected, and then you'll really be miserable."

She blinked a few times, more than a little surprised at his bold use of her first name. "How did you know that I'm called Belle?" she finally asked.

"Ashbourne told me," John replied, examining her pale toes. "Where is this damned thing, anyway?"

"On my heel," Belle answered, dutifully turning around.

John let out a low whistle. "You've got a nasty one there. You ought to get a more comfortable pair of shoes if you intend to hike around the countryside."

"I wasn't hiking, I was walking. And I *do* have better shoes. I just hadn't intended to take a walk this morning until after I was dressed, and I didn't feel like changing my attire." Belle let out a frustrated sigh. Why did she feel the need to explain herself to him?

John stood up, pulled out a crisp, white handkerchief, and took Belle's arm. "There is a pond not too far away from here. I can get some water to clean the sore."

Belle let go of her skirt. "I don't think that's necessary, *John*."

John warmed at her rather pointed use of his given name and was glad that he'd gone ahead and used hers without asking first. He decided he liked this Lady Arabella, even if she was a little too well-connected for his tastes. He couldn't remember the last time he'd smiled so much. She was smart and fun—a little too beautiful for his comfort, but he was certain that with a little effort, he could control his attraction to her.

She did, however, have a rather appalling disregard for her own well-being, as evidenced by her lack of spectacles, her soon-to-be festering blister, and her penchant for unchaperoned excursions. She obviously needed someone to lecture a little sense into her. Since he didn't see anyone else nearby, he decided he might as well be the one to do it, and he started walking toward the pond, practically dragging her along behind him.

"Jo-ohn!" she protested.

"Be-elle!" he countered, imitating her complaining tone perfectly.

"I'm fully able to take care of myself," Belle said, quickening her stride to keep up. For a man with such a pronounced limp, he could move fast.

"Obviously not, or you'd have spectacles perched on your nose."

Belle halted in her tracks with such force that

John actually stumbled. "I only need them when I read," she ground out.

"It warms my heart to hear you admit it."

"I thought I was beginning to like you, but now I'm certain that I don't."

"You still like me," he said, grinning as he started pulling her again toward the pond.

Belle's mouth fell open. "No, I don't."

"Yes, you do."

"No, I—all right, maybe a little," she allowed. "But I do think you're acting rather high-handed."

"And I think that you have a hideous little blister on your heel. So stop complaining."

"I wasn't—"

"Yes, you were."

Belle shut her mouth, aware that she'd been blabbering away far too much. With a sigh, she finally gave in and let him lead her to the pond. When they reached it, she sat down on a grassy patch near the shore while John walked over to the water and dipped his handkerchief into it.

"Is that clean?" she called out.

"My handkerchief or the water?"

"Both!"

John walked back to her side and held up the snowy white cloth. "Sparkling."

She sighed at his determination to treat her blister and poked her bare foot out from under her skirt.

"This isn't going to work," he said.

"Why not?"

"You're going to have to roll over onto your stomach."

"I don't think so," Belle replied, her tone firm.

John tilted his head to one side. "The way I see it," he said thoughtfully, "we have two options."

He didn't say anything more, so Belle was forced to ask, "We do?"

"Yes. Either you roll over onto your stomach so that I can take care of your blister, or I can slide on my back and wiggle under your leg so that I can see your heel. Of course that would probably require my sticking my head under your skirts, and while the thought is intriguing—"

"Enough," Belle muttered. She rolled over onto her stomach.

John took the handkerchief and gently dabbed it against the sore, cleaning away the small amount of dried blood which had crusted around it. It stung a little when he touched the raw flesh, but Belle could tell that he was being extraordinarily gentle, so she didn't say anything. When he pulled a knife out of his pocket, however, she changed her mind.

"Aaaack!" Unfortunately, the first word to fly out of her mouth was not terribly coherent.

John looked startled. "Is something wrong?"

"What are you planning to do with that knife?"

He smiled patiently. "I was just going to make a small incision in your blister so I can drain it. That will allow the dead skin to dry out."

It sounded like he knew what he was doing, but Belle thought she ought to ask a few questions anyway since she was, after all, letting this relatively strange man take a knife to her person. "Why do you want to dry it out?"

"It will heal better that way. The dead skin will fall off, and the skin underneath will toughen up." He narrowed his eyes. "You've never had a blister before, have you?"

"Not like this," Belle admitted. "I don't usually walk so much. I usually ride."

"What about dancing?"

"What *about* dancing?" she countered.

"I'm sure you go to fancy balls and all that when you're in London. You must be on your feet all night."

"I always wear comfortable shoes," she replied disdainfully.

John wasn't sure why, but her sensibility pleased him. "Well, don't worry," he finally said. "I've treated many blisters, most worse than this."

"In the war?" Belle asked, her voice cautious.

His eyes darkened. "Yes."

"I imagine you've treated far worse injuries than mere blisters," she said softly.

"I imagine I have."

Belle knew that she should stop her questioning; the war was obviously a painful topic for him, but curiosity overpowered discretion. "Weren't there doctors and surgeons for that sort of thing?"

There was a noticeable silence, and Belle felt the pressure of his hands on her foot as the knife punctured her blister before he finally answered. "Sometimes there aren't doctors or surgeons available. Sometimes you just have to do what you can, what makes sense. And then you pray." His voice was flat. "Even if you've stopped believing in God."

Belle swallowed uncomfortably. She thought about saying something soothing such as, "I see," but the truth was, she didn't see. She couldn't even begin to imagine the horrors of war, and it seemed shallow to imply that she could.

John dabbed at the blister again with the damp handkerchief. "That ought to do it." He stood up and held out his hand to her, but she ignored it, rolling over so that she could sit on the grassy knoll. He stood there awkwardly until she patted the spot on the grass next to her. He hesitated, and

Belle finally groaned and slapped her hand down on the ground with considerable force.

"Oh, please," she said in a semi-irritated voice. "I'm not going to bite."

John sat down.

"Should I put a bandage on this?" Belle asked, twisting around so that she could examine his handiwork.

"Not unless you're planning to wear another pair of tight shoes. It will heal faster if you leave it bare."

Belle continued to look at her heel, doing her best to preserve her modesty while she did so. "I don't suppose too many people wander through Weston-birt barefoot, but I think I have enough clout to carry it off, don't you?" She looked up suddenly, offering him a sunny grin.

John felt as if he'd been hit, the force of her smile was so strong. It took him several seconds to tear his eyes off her mouth, and when he did, he moved his gaze up to her eyes, which was a big mistake, because they were as blue as the sky. Bluer, in fact, and so obviously perceptive and intelligent. He felt her stare almost physically, felt it sweeping across his body even though she never took her eyes off his, not even for an instant. He shivered.

Belle wet her lips in a nervous gesture. "Why are you looking at me like that?"

"Like what?" he whispered, barely aware that he'd spoken.

"Like you're ... like you're ... " She stumbled over her words, not quite certain *how* he was looking at her. Her eyes widened in shock as it came to her. "Like you're *afraid* of me."

John felt dizzy. *Was* he afraid of her? Did he fear her ability to upset the precious internal balance he'd only recently been able to achieve? Perhaps, but he feared no one more than himself. The things he wanted to do to her . . .

He closed his eyes against the unbidden vision of Spencer on top of Ana. No, that wasn't what he wanted with Belle, was it?

He had to get a hold of himself. To push her away. He blinked, suddenly remembering her question about running through Ashbourne's house barefoot. "I suppose one can do anything one wants if one is related to a duke," he finally replied, somewhat sharply.

Belle drew back, a little hurt by his tone. But two could play at that game. "Yes, I suppose one can," she said, lifting her chin up a notch.

John felt like a cad. But he didn't apologize. It was probably better if she thought him a boor. He had no business getting involved with her, and it would be so, so easy to let himself do so. He knew a dead end when he saw one. He'd looked her up in *Debrett's Peerage* after she had visited the day before. She was the daughter of an extremely wealthy earl and related to any number of important and influential members of society. She deserved someone who had a title that went back further than a year, someone who could offer her the material comforts to which she was no doubt accustomed, someone who was whole, whose legs were as perfect as hers.

Dear Lord, but he'd love to see her legs. He groaned.

"Are you ill?" Belle was looking at him, trying not to appear concerned.

"I'm fine," he said curtly. She even smelled good, a fresh, springtime scent that seemed to envelop him. He didn't even deserve to *think* about her, not after committing such an unforgivable crime against womankind.

"Well, thank you for treating my blister," Belle said suddenly. "It was very kind of you."

"It was no problem, I assure you."

"For you, perhaps," Belle said, sounding as cheerful as she possibly could. "I had to lie on my stomach next to a man I met just three days ago." *Please, please don't say something unkind,* she silently implored. *Please be as funny and as joking and as sweetly stern as you were just a few minutes ago.*

As if her thoughts traveled through the air and landed on him like a kiss, he smiled. "You may rest assured that I enjoyed my view of your backside immensely," he teased, his hesitating smile quickly developing into a rakish grin. It went against his better judgment, but he was quite unable to be unkind to her when she was trying so hard to be friends.

"Oh, you!" Belle groaned, punching him playfully in the shoulder. "That's a terrible thing to say."

"Hasn't anyone ever admired your backside before?" His hand stole up and covered hers.

"I assure you, no one was ever crude enough to mention it." Her voice was breathless. He didn't stroke her, just let his hand rest lightly over hers, but the warmth of his touch seeped into her, traveled up her arm, and was moving dangerously close to her heart.

John leaned forward. "Didn't mean to be crude," he murmured.

"No?" Belle touched her tongue to her lower lip.

"No, just honest." He was close—just a hair's breadth away.

"Really?"

John made a reply, but Belle didn't understand him because his lips were already brushing gently against hers. She moaned softly, thinking she'd wanted this forever, silently thanking the gods and her parents (although not necessarily in that order) for advising her not to accept any of the men who'd offered for her in the past two years. This was what she'd waited for, had barely dared to hope for. This was what Emma and Alex shared. This was why they were always looking at each other, smiling constantly, and giggling behind closed doors. This was—

John gently ran his tongue along the soft skin of her inner lip, and Belle lost all power to think. She only felt, but, oh, how she felt. Her skin tingled—every inch of it even though he was barely touching her. Belle sighed, sinking into him, knowing instinctively that he would know what to do, how to make this wondrous feeling go on forever. She melted against him, her body searching out the warmth of his. And then he abruptly pulled away, muttering a sharp curse, his breathing harsh and uneven.

Belle blinked in confusion, not understanding his actions and feeling utterly bereft. She gulped down her pain and hugged her legs to her body, hoping that he'd say something kind or funny, or at least something that would explain his actions. And if he didn't, she just hoped that he couldn't see how much she was hurting from his rejection.

John stood up and turned away from her, planting his hands on his hips. Staring up at him through her eyelashes, Belle thought that there was something extremely bleak about his stance. Finally, he turned around and offered her his hand. She took it and rose to her feet, softly thanking him as she did so.

John sighed and ran his hand through his thick hair. He'd never meant to kiss her. He'd certainly wanted to, but that didn't mean he'd had any right to touch her. And he'd never dreamed how much he'd like it, or how difficult it would be to stop.

God, he was weak! He was no better than Spencer, mauling an innocent young lady, and the truth was he wanted more. So much more . . .

He wanted her ear and her shoulder and the underside of her chin. He wanted to run his tongue along the length of her neck, trailing moist fire down to the valley between her breasts. He wanted to cup her backside and squeeze, pull her into him, use her as a cradle for his desire.

He wanted to possess her. Every inch. Over and over.

Belle watched him silently, but he'd turned slightly away from her, and she couldn't see into his eyes. When he finally looked back at her, however, she was shocked by the harsh expression on his face. She took a step back, her hand unconsciously coming up to cover the lower part of her face. "Wh-what's wrong?" she gasped.

"You ought to think twice before you throw yourself at men, my little aristocrat." His voice was dangerously close to a hiss.

Belle stared at him, dumbfounded, until horror, hurt, and fury simultaneously rose within her. "You can rest assured," she bit out icily, "that the next man I 'throw' myself at will not be so lacking in breeding as to insult me as you have done."

"I am so sorry that my blood is not blue enough for you, my lady. Do not worry, I will try not to taint you with my presence again."

Belle raised a brow and stared at him disdainfully, her eyes hard. "Yes, well, we cannot all claim a relationship with a duke." Her voice was sharp, and her words were cruel. Satisfied with her performance, she turned on her heel and strode away, carrying herself with as much dignity as her limping body would allow.

Chapter 5

John stood still for many minutes, watching Belle disappear amidst the trees. He didn't move until she was long gone, thoroughly disgusted with himself and his behavior toward her. But, he reminded himself, it was no more than what was necessary. She was furious with him now, but she'd thank him eventually. Well, maybe not him, but when she was cozily wed to some marquess, she'd thank *someone* for saving her from John Blackwood.

He'd finally turned to head home when he realized that Belle had marched off without her boot. He leaned down and picked it up. Damn, now he'd have to go to return it, and he had no idea how he could face her again.

John sighed, tossing her flimsy boot from hand to hand as he began his slow trudge home. He'd have to come up with some excuse for having her boot in the first place. Alex was a good friend, but he would want to know why John had his cousin's footwear in his possession. He supposed he could go by Westonbirt that evening—

John swore under his breath. He'd *have* to go by Westonbirt that evening. He'd already accepted Alex's invitation for dinner. His curses grew more fluent as he pictured the agony ahead. He'd have to look at Belle all night, and of course she would be ravishing in her expensive evening attire. And then just when he couldn't bear to look at her for one minute longer, she'd probably say something utterly charming and intelligent, which would make him want her even more.

And it was so, so dangerous to want her.

Belle's progress home wasn't much swifter than John's. She wasn't used to walking about without shoes, and it seemed that her right foot managed to find every sharp pebble and protruding tree root in the narrow path. And there was also the little problem of her left shoe, which had a slight heel on it, and left her feeling rather lopsided and forced her to limp.

And every limp reminded her of John Blackwood. Horrid John Blackwood.

Belle started muttering every inappropriate word her brother had ever accidentally said in front of her. Her tirade lasted only a few seconds, for Ned was usually quite careful about holding his tongue around his sister. Fresh out of curses, Belle started in with, "Wretched, wretched man," but that just didn't seem to do the trick.

"Damn!" she burst out as her foot landed on an especially sharp pebble. The mishap proved to be her undoing, and she felt a hot tear spill down her face as she squeezed her eyes shut against the pain.

"You are not going to cry over a little pebble,"

she scolded herself. "And you are certainly not going to cry over that awful man."

But she was crying, and she couldn't stop herself. She just couldn't understand how a man could be so charming one minute and so insulting the next. He liked her—she could tell that he did. It was all there in the way he'd teased her and cared for her foot. And while he hadn't been completely forthcoming when she'd asked him about the war, he also hadn't completely ignored her. He wouldn't have opened up to her at all if he hadn't liked her just a little.

Belle leaned down, picked up the offending pebble, and viciously tossed it into the trees. It was time to stop crying, time to think this problem through in a rational manner and figure out why his entire personality had changed so suddenly.

No, she decided, for the first time in her life she didn't want to be calm and rational. She didn't care about being practical and pragmatic. All she wanted to be was mad.

And she was. Furious.

By the time Belle reached Westonbirt, her tears had dried up, and she was quite happily plotting all sorts of vengeful schemes against John. She didn't expect to actually carry any of them out, but the mere act of planning them raised her spirits.

She plodded through the great hall and was nearly to the curved staircase when Emma called out from a nearby parlor, "Is that you, Belle?"

Belle backtracked to the open doorway, poked her head in, and said hello.

Emma was sitting on a sofa with ledgers spread out on the table in front of her. She raised her eyebrows at Belle's disheveled appearance. "Where have you been?"

"Out for a walk."

"With only one shoe?"

"It's the latest rage."

"Or a very long story."

"Not that long but rather unladylike."

"Bare feet usually are."

Belle rolled her eyes. Emma had been known to wade through knee-deep mud to get to her favorite fishing hole. "Since when have you become the model of taste and decorum?"

"Since, oh, never mind, just come and sit with me. I'm about to go insane."

"Really? Now that sounds interesting."

Emma sighed. "Don't tease me. Alex won't let me out of this blasted parlor for fear of my health."

"You could look on the bright side and view it as a sign of his eternal love and devotion," Belle suggested.

"Or I could simply strangle him. If he had his way, I'd be confined to my bed until the baby arrived. As it is, he's forbidden me to go riding by myself."

"Can he do that?"

"Do what?"

"Forbid you."

"Well, no, he doesn't order me about like most men do to their wives, but he made it quite clear that he'd be extremely worried every time I took Boston out for a ride, and blast him, I love him too much to upset him like that. Sometimes it's best just to humor him."

"Mmm," Belle murmured. "Would you like some tea? I'm a bit chilled." She got up and rang for a maid.

"No, thank you, but go ahead and get some for yourself."

A maid entered silently and Emma ordered some tea. "Oh, and will you please tell Mrs. Goode that

I'll come by to discuss this evening's menu within the hour? We'll be having a guest, so I think we ought to do something special."

The maid nodded and left the room.

"Who is dining with us tonight?" Belle inquired.

"That John Blackwood fellow you met a few days ago. Alex invited him yesterday. Don't you remember? I think we discussed it at tea."

Belle felt her heart sink down to her stomach. She'd forgotten all about their dinner plans. "It slipped my mind, I guess," she said, wishing that she already had her tea so that she could hide her face with the cup. Her cheeks were growing unpleasantly warm.

If Emma noticed Belle's blush, however, she made no mention of it. Belle immediately began discussing the latest fashions from Paris, and the two ladies stayed on that topic until long after the tea arrived.

Belle dressed with particular care that evening, knowing full well that John was the reason for her assiduousness. She chose a simply cut gown of ice blue silk which set off her eyes and wore her hair piled loosely atop her head, allowing soft wispy curls to frame her face. A strand of pearls and matching earrings completed the look, and, satisfied with her appearance, she headed downstairs.

Emma and Alex were already in the parlor waiting for John to arrive. Belle barely had time to sit down when the butler entered the room.

"Lord Blackwood."

Belle looked up as Norwood finished intoning John's name. Alex rose and strode to the doorway to greet his friend. "Blackwood, good to see you again."

John nodded and smiled. Belle was irritated by

the fact that he looked extremely handsome in his evening attire.

"Allow me to introduce you to my wife." Alex led John over to the sofa where Emma was seated.

"How do you do, your grace," John murmured politely, placing a swift kiss on the back of her hand.

"Oh, please, I cannot bear so much etiquette in my own home. Please do call me Emma. Alex has assured me that you are a special friend of his, so I don't think we need to be formal."

John smiled at Emma, deciding that Alex had been his usual lucky self when it came to claiming a bride. "Then you must call me John."

"And of course you already know Belle," Alex continued.

John turned to Belle and took her hand in his. A fierce heat traveled up her arm, but she forced herself not to jerk her hand back. He didn't need to know how he affected her. But when he raised her hand to his lips and kissed her softly, she wasn't able to control the blush that stole across her cheeks.

"It is indeed a pleasure to see you again, Lady Arabella," he said, still holding her hand in his.

"Pl-please call me Belle," she stammered, hating herself for her loss of composure.

John finally released her hand and smiled. "I brought you a gift." He held out a box tied with a ribbon.

"Why, thank you." Curious, Belle untied the bow and lifted the lid. Inside she found her slightly mud-died boot. She stifled a laugh as she lifted it out of the box. "I had a blister," she explained, turning to Alex and Emma. "It was really quite painful, and I took off my boot . . . " Her voice trailed off.

John turned to Emma. "I would have brought

one for you, too, but you don't seem to have left any shoes on my property recently."

Emma grinned and reached down toward her feet. "I shall rectify that matter immediately."

John found himself liking Alex's duchess immensely. It was easy and painless to like her, he supposed. Unlike her cousin, she didn't cause his heart to race and his breathing to stop every time he saw her.

"Perhaps I could simply give you one of my slippers now," Emma added, "and then you could give it back to me next time you dine with us."

"Is that an invitation?"

"Of course, Blackwood," Alex put in. "You are always welcome here."

The foursome exchanged pleasantries for a quarter of an hour, awaiting the call to dinner. Belle sat quietly, surreptitiously studying John, pondering why he would do something as sweet as wrapping her boot up as a present after he acted so rudely that afternoon. How was she supposed to react? Did he want to be her friend again? She kept a weak smile pasted to her face, silently cursing him for setting her into such confusion.

John's thoughts were similarly occupied, wondering how on earth Belle would react to him that evening. She couldn't possibly understand all of the reasons he needed to keep his distance, and Lord knew he couldn't explain it to her. Rape, was not, after all, an acceptable topic for polite conversation.

When dinner was ready, Emma whispered something into Alex's ear and then he rose and took her arm. "You'll excuse me if I defy convention and take my wife in to dinner," he said, smiling rakishly. "Belle, we'll be in the less formal dining room. Emma thought it would be more comfortable.''

John stood and offered his hand to Belle as the other couple swept out of the room. "They seem to have left us quite alone.''

"I imagine they did that on purpose.''

"Do you think so?''

Belle took John's hand and rose. "You should take it as a compliment. It means Emma likes you.''

"And do *you* like me, Belle?''

There was a long pause, followed by a decisive, "No.''

"I suppose that I deserve no better.'' He allowed her hand to drop back to her side.

She whirled around. "No, you don't. I cannot believe you even had the nerve to come over here to dine tonight.''

"I was invited, if you recall.''

"You should have declined. You should have sent word that you were ill, or that your mother was ill, or your dog or your horse or anything to avoid accepting the invitation.''

He had nothing to say other than, "You are, of course, correct.''

"You just don't—You don't kiss someone and then speak to her the way you did to me. It isn't polite. It isn't nice, and—''

"And you are always nice?''

His voice wasn't the least bit mocking, which confused her. "I try to be. Lord knows I tried to be nice to you.''

He inclined his head. "You certainly did.''

"I—'' She broke off and looked up at him. "Aren't you even going to argue with me?''

He lifted his shoulder in a tired gesture. "What would be the point? You are obviously in the right, and I, as usual, am in the wrong.''

Belle stared at him incomprehensibly, her lips parted in amazement. "I don't understand you."

"It is most likely for the best that you don't even try. I apologize, of course, for my behavior this morning. It was unpardonable."

"The kiss or your horrid words afterward?" The words flew out of her mouth before she could stop them.

"Both."

"I accept your apology for your insults."

"And the kiss?"

Belle kept her eyes fixed on the crescent moon which shone through the window. "There is no need to apologize for the kiss."

John's heart slammed into his chest. "I am not sure I understand your meaning, my lady," he said cautiously.

"I only have one question." Belle tore her gaze away from the moon and forced herself to look at him. "Did I do something wrong? Something to offend you?"

John let out a harsh laugh, unable to believe his ears. "Oh God, Belle, if you only knew." He raked his fingers through his hair and then planted his hands on his hips. "You couldn't offend me if you tried."

A hundred conflicting emotions raced through Belle's heart and mind in the space of one second. Against her better judgment, she touched his arm. "Then what happened? I need to know."

John took a ragged breath before he faced her. "Do you really want the truth?"

She nodded.

He opened his mouth, but it was several seconds before his lips formed words. "I'm not the man you think I am. I've seen things . . . " He closed his mouth, a muscle working violently in his throat as he fought to control the emotions playing across his face. "I've done things. These hands . . ." He looked down at his hands as if they were foreign objects. His voice dropped down to a low whisper. "I'm a greedy bastard, Belle, just for kissing you this morning. I'm not fit even to touch you."

Belle stared at him, horrified by the pain etched on his face. How could he not see what was so clear to her? There was something within him. Something so good . . . It seemed to glow from his very soul. And he thought that he was worthless. She didn't know what had happened to make him so, but his pain devastated her. She took a step forward. "You're wrong."

"Belle," he whispered, "you're a fool."

Wordlessly, she shook her head.

John looked deeply into her eyes, and heaven help him but he couldn't stop the slow descent of his lips down onto hers.

For the second time that day, Belle felt that unfamiliar rush of desire as her body swayed closer to his. His mouth brushed gently against hers, and Belle daringly ran her tongue along the soft skin of his inner lip, just as he had done to her that morning. John's reaction was instantaneous, and he pulled her roughly toward him, needing to feel the heat of her body pressed up against his.

The intimate contact set off an alarm in Belle's mind, and she gently pulled herself away from him. Her cheeks were flushed, her eyes bright, and there were considerably more wisps of hair framing her face than there had been just a few moments earlier. "Alex and Emma are expecting us in the dining room," she reminded him breathlessly. "We're going to be quite late."

John closed his eyes and exhaled, mentally willing his body to cool down. After a moment he offered her his arm, quirking his mouth into a lopsided smile that didn't quite meet his eyes. "We shall blame our tardiness on my leg."

Belle felt an immediate rush of sympathy for him. He was a proud man and wouldn't like to admit that his injury slowed him down. "Oh, no, that's not necessary. Emma is forever complaining that I walk too slowly. I shall simply tell them that I was showing you one of the paintings in the gallery. Alex has a marvelous Rembrandt."

John placed his forefinger against her lips. "Shush, we'll blame it on my leg. It's about time I got some benefit from this damned thing."

They exited the parlor, and Belle noticed that he moved quite quickly through the long halls to the dining room. "Tell me when we're almost there," he whispered in her ear.

"It's just around the corner."

John slowed down so much that Belle thought they'd stopped. When she glanced down at his legs, she noticed that he was limping far more noticeably than usual. "You're terrible," she scolded. "I know you can bend your leg more than that."

"I'm having a bad day." His expression was positively angelic.

Alex stood when they entered the dining room. "We thought you'd gotten lost along the way."

"I'm afraid my leg has been paining me a bit today," John replied. "Belle was kind enough to accommodate my slow gait."

Belle nodded, wondering how on earth she was able to keep her lips from twitching. She and John joined Emma and Alex around the small table of the informal dining room. They were served asparagus in mustard sauce, and Emma, recognizing that her neighbor and cousin seemed to be better acquainted than time would warrant, immediately began her interrogation.

"I am so glad you were able to come for dinner this evening, John. But you must tell us more about yourself. What part of England are you from?"

"I grew up in Shropshire."

"Really? I've never been there, but I hear it's quite lovely."

"Yes, it is quite."

"And does your family still live there?"

"I believe that they do."

"Oh." Emma seemed slightly flustered by his odd choice of words but continued the conversation nonetheless. "And do you see them very often?"

"I rarely see them at all."

"Emma, darling," Alex said gently. "Pray give our guest time between questions to eat."

Emma smiled sheepishly and speared a stalk of asparagus with her fork. Before she put it in her mouth, however, she blurted out, "Belle is marvelously well-read, you know."

Belle choked on her food, not having expected the conversation to turn her way.

"Speaking of reading," John cut in smoothly, "did you finish *The Winter's Tale*? I noticed you were nearly done the other day."

Belle took a sip of wine. "Yes, I did. And it marked the end of my Grand Shakespearean Quest."

"Really? I'm almost afraid to ask what that was."

"All the plays."

"How impressive," John murmured.

"In alphabetical order."

"And organized, too. The lady is a wonder."

Belle blushed. "Don't tease me, you wretch."

Alex's and Emma's eyes widened over the playful banter that was sailing across the table. "If I remember correctly," Alex injected, "didn't this quest also involve some poetry?"

"I've abandoned the poetry for now, I think. Poetry is so, well, poetic, don't you think? Nobody actually talks that way."

John quirked a brow. "You think not?" He turned to Belle, and when he spoke again, there was a certain fire in his brown eyes that she had never before seen there.

> "What though the radiance which was
>   once so bright
> Be now for ever taken from my sight,
> Though nothing can bring back the hour
> Of splendour in the grass, of glory
>   in the flower;
> We will grieve not, rather find
> Strength in what remains behind."

There was silence at the table until John spoke again, his eyes never leaving Belle's. "I wish I always spoke with such eloquence."

Belle found herself oddly moved by John's short recitation and the warm tones of his voice. Something about his speech held her spellbound, and she completely forgot the presence of her cousins. "That was lovely," she said quietly.

"Wordsworth. It's one of my favorites."

"Does that poem have particular meaning for you? Do you live by its sentiment?"

There was a very long pause. "No," John said bluntly. "I try to, on occasion, but usually fail."

Belle swallowed, uncomfortable with the pain she saw in his eyes, and searched for another topic. "Do you also enjoy writing poetry?"

John laughed, finally breaking his gaze away from Belle and facing the table at large. "I might enjoy writing poetry if I ever wrote some that was even halfway decent."

"But you recited the Wordsworth with such passion," Belle protested. "You obviously have a deep love of poetry."

"Enjoying poetry and being able to write it are two very different endeavors. I imagine that is why so many would-be poets spend so much of their time with a bottle of brandy in each hand."

"I am certain you have the soul of a poet," she persisted.

John merely smiled. "I am afraid that your confidence is misplaced, but I shall take that as a compliment."

"As well you should. I shan't be satisfied until I add a volume of your poetry to my library," Belle said archly.

"Then I had better get to work. I certainly wouldn't want to disappoint you."

"No," she murmured quietly. "I'm sure you wouldn't."

Chapter 6

⌒◯◯⌒

The next day Belle decided that perhaps she had been too hasty in her dismissal of poetry.

After lunch, she changed into a dark blue riding habit and headed to the stables. Inspired by John's recitation the night before, she took with her a slim volume of Wordsworth's poetry. Her plan was to find a grassy hillside and settle down to read, but she had a feeling that she wasn't going to be able to stop herself from steering her mare toward Blemwood Park, no, Brinstead Manor—drat, why couldn't she remember the name of that place? Whatever it was called, it was where John lived, and Belle wanted to go there.

She urged her mare into a trot, breathing in the fresh autumn air as she headed east toward John's property. She had absolutely no idea what she'd say if she ran into him. Probably something stupid; she seemed to ramble on more than usual with him.

81

"Good day, Lord Blackwood," she tested. No, too formal.

"I just happened to be riding east . . ." Too obvious. And hadn't she used something like that the other day?

She sighed and decided to go with simplicity. "Hello, John."

"Hello yourself."

Belle gasped. She'd been so busy rehearsing what she wanted to say to him that she hadn't even noticed that he was right there in front of her.

John raised his eyebrows at her shocked expression. "Surely you can't be too terribly surprised to see me. You did say 'hello,' after all."

"So I did," Belle said with a nervous smile. Had he heard her talking to herself about him? She looked up at him, gulped, and said the first thing that came to mind. "That's a lovely horse."

John permitted himself a small smile at her skittishness. "Thank you. Although I imagine that Thor might take exception to being called lovely."

Belle blinked and looked closer. John was indeed atop a stallion, and a rather powerful one, to boot. "A very *handsome* horse, then," she amended.

He patted his stallion's neck. "Thor feels much better, I'm sure."

"What brings you this way?" Belle asked, not certain if she was still on Alex's property or had already crossed over to John's.

"I was just heading west . . ."

Belle stifled a laugh. "I see."

"And what brings *you* this way?"

"I was just heading east."

"I see."

"Oh, you must know I was hoping to see you," she blurted out.

"Now that you've seen me," John said, "what do you plan to do with me?"

"I hadn't gotten that far in my plans, actually," Belle admitted. "What would *you* like to do with *me*?"

It occurred to John that his thoughts in that direction were not suitable for polite conversation. He remained silent but couldn't prevent himself from leveling an appreciative gaze at the woman facing him.

Belle interpreted his expression correctly and turned beet red. "Oh, you wretch," she stammered. "That wasn't what I meant."

"I cannot imagine what you're talking about," John said, his face a picture of innocence.

"You know very well, and you're not going to make me say it, you—Oh, never mind, would you like to come to tea?"

John laughed aloud. "How I love the English. Anything can be cured with a pot of tea."

Belle offered him a waspish smile. "You're English too, John, and just for the record, anything *can* be cured with a pot of tea."

He smiled wryly. "I wish someone had told that to the doctor who nearly sawed off my leg."

Belle sobered immediately. What was she supposed to say to that? She looked up at the sky, which was beginning to cloud over. She knew that John was terribly sensitive about his leg, and she should probably avoid talking about it. Still, he had been the one to mention it, and it seemed that the best way to show him that she didn't care about his injury was to joke about it. "Well then, my lord," she said, praying that she wasn't making a terrible mistake. "I shall contrive to spill some tea on your leg this afternoon. If that doesn't do the trick, I don't know what will."

He seemed to hesitate a moment before saying, "I suppose you need an escort back to Westonbirt. I see you're out alone again."

"Someday, John," she said in exasperated tones, "you will make a superb parent."

A fat raindrop landed on his nose, and he threw up his arms in mock surrender. "Lead on, my lady."

Belle turned her mare around, and they headed back to Westonbirt. After a few moments of companionable silence, she turned to him and asked, "Why *were* you out and about this afternoon? And don't tell me that you were just heading west."

"Would you believe I was hoping I'd see you?"

Belle turned to him quickly, scanning his face to see if he was toying with her. His brown eyes were velvety warm, and her heart skipped a beat at his intent gaze. "I might believe you, if you are very nice to me this afternoon," she teased.

"I shall be *especially* nice," John said wickedly, "if that means I'll get an extra cup of tea."

"For you, anything!"

They rode on for several minutes until Amber suddenly stopped cold, her ears pricking up nervously.

"Is something wrong?" John inquired.

"It's probably a rabbit in the woods. Amber has always been very sensitive to movement. It's strange, actually. She trots along a crowded London street as if she hasn't a care in the world, but put her on a quiet country lane and she's suspicious of every little noise."

"I didn't hear anything."

"Neither did I." Belle tugged gently on the reins. "Come on, girl. It's going to rain."

Amber took a few hesitant steps and then

stopped again, turning her head sharply to the right.

"I can't imagine what's wrong with her," Belle said sheepishly.

Crack!

Belle heard the explosion of a gunshot from nearby in the woods and then felt the soft rush of air as a bullet whizzed between their bodies.

"Was that—" she started to ask, but she never completed her question because Amber, already skittish, reared up at the loud noise. Belle had to focus all of her attention simply on keeping her seat. She threw her arms around the mare's neck, murmuring, "Easy girl. Steady, now." She was so frightened, however, that she wasn't sure whether her words were meant to soothe the horse or herself.

Just when she was certain that she wouldn't be able to hold on any longer, she felt John's steely arms wrap around her waist and pluck her from the saddle. She landed unceremoniously next to him atop Thor.

"Are you all right?" he asked roughly.

Belle nodded. "I think so. I need to catch my breath. I was more startled than anything else."

John pulled her close to him, unable to believe the depth of his fear when he saw her holding on to Amber's neck for dear life. The mare was now dancing around in nervous circles, breathing loudly but otherwise settling down.

When Belle felt she had regained some composure, she pulled far enough away from John to look into his face. "I heard a gunshot."

John nodded grimly. He couldn't imagine why anyone would want to shoot at them, but it occurred to him that they shouldn't remain rooted to the spot like sitting ducks. "If I keep you here with me as we ride back, will Amber follow?"

She nodded, and they were soon galloping back to Westonbirt.

"I think it was an accident," Belle said once they slowed down.

"The gunshot?"

"Yes. Alex was telling me just the other day that he has been having trouble with poachers. I'm sure it was a stray bullet that spooked Amber."

"It came a little too close for my comfort."

"I know, but what else could it have been? Why would anyone want to shoot at us?"

John shrugged his shoulders. He had no enemies.

"I shall have to discuss this with Alex," Belle continued. "I am certain he will want to see the rules enforced more stringently. Someone could be hurt. We very nearly were."

John nodded, pulled her closer to him, and urged Thor to go a little faster. A few minutes later they rode into the Westonbirt stables, and just in time, for the raindrops were coming down faster and faster.

"There you are, my lady," he said as he set her down. "Will you be able to make it to the house without injury?"

"Oh, but aren't you coming?" Disappointment was clearly written on her features.

He swallowed, and a muscle twitched in his throat. "No, I really cannot. I—"

"But you will be drenched if you try to ride home now. Surely you must come in for some tea, if only to warm you up."

"Belle, I—"

"Please."

He stared into those marvelous blue eyes and wondered how anyone found the fortitude to deny her anything. He glanced out the stable doors. "I suppose it is rather wet."

Belle nodded. "You'll surely catch the fever if you even attempt to ride home. Come along." She took his hand, and together they made a mad dash for the house.

By the time they rushed through the front door into the hall, they were both rather damp, and Belle could feel strands of her hair plastered to her face. "I must look a mess," she said self-consciously. "I ought to go and change."

"Nonsense," John said, pushing a damp lock of her hair behind her ear. "You look lovely—all misty-like."

Belle caught her breath, his touch still tingling on her cheek. "Surely you mean musty-like. I feel like a dishrag."

"I assure you, Lady Arabella, you do not resemble a dishrag." He dropped his arm. "Although I cannot imagine when you would ever have seen one."

Belle stiffened. "I am not the spoiled child you seem to believe me to be."

John gazed hungrily at the breathtakingly lovely woman standing across from him in the hall. Her hair had partially broken free of its topknot, and golden tendrils, curled by the damp air, kissed the sides of her face. Her long eyelashes glistened with raindrops, framing eyes of an indescribable shade of blue. John took a deep breath and didn't allow his eyes to stray below her soft mouth. "Believe me, I don't think you're a child," he said finally.

Belle swallowed nervously, unable to keep her disappointment off her face. Those were not quite the words she'd hoped to hear. "Perhaps we should continue our conversation in the parlor."

She turned and strode across the hall, her back ramrod straight.

John sighed to himself and followed. He always managed to say the wrong thing around her. He wanted to grab her in his arms, tell her that he thought she was simply wonderful—beautiful and smart and kind and everything a man could want in a woman.

If a man deserved a woman, that was. And he knew that he could never marry, never accept the love of a woman. Not after Ana.

When John entered the parlor, Belle was standing at the window, watching the rain sheeting against the glass. He started to shut the door, then thought the better of it, and left it open a few inches. He walked over to her, intending to put his hands on her shoulders, but when he was but a foot away, she suddenly whirled around. "I'm not spoiled," she said stubbornly. "I haven't had a difficult life, I know that, but I'm not spoiled."

"I know you're not," John replied softly.

"Spoiled means that one is willful and manipulative," Belle continued. "And I'm neither of those things."

He nodded.

"And I don't know why you must always make such awful comments about my background. *Your* father is an earl, too. Alex told me."

"Was an earl," John corrected, relieved that she thought that he was pushing her away due to feelings of social inferiority. That was certainly a consideration, but it was the least of his worries. "Was an *impoverished* earl who certainly couldn't afford to support seven children, the last of whom was, posthumously, me."

"Seven children?" Belle asked, eyes widening. "Really?"

"One was stillborn," John admitted.

"You must have had a lovely childhood with so many other children with whom to play."

"Actually, I didn't spend very much time with my siblings. They were usually occupied with their own pursuits."

"Oh." Belle frowned, not at all pleased with the family portrait he was painting. "Your mother must have been very busy having all those babies."

John smiled devilishly. "I imagine that my father was as well."

She blushed.

"Do you think we could start over for the afternoon?" John asked, taking her hand and dropping a feathery light kiss on her knuckles. "I apologize for assuming that you have never seen a dishrag."

Belle giggled. "That's the most absurd apology I have ever heard."

"Do you think so? I thought it was rather eloquent myself, especially with the kiss on your hand."

"The kiss was marvelous, and the apology was very sweet. It was the part about the dishrag that sounded funny."

"Forget about the dishrag," John said, leading her over to a nearby sofa.

"My mind is already completely blank on that measure," she assured him.

He sat down at the opposite end of the sofa. "I noticed that you have a volume of Wordsworth's poetry with you."

Belle looked down at her forgotten book. "Oh, yes. You inspired me, I'm afraid. But what I want to know is when you're going to get to the task of writing some verse yourself. I know that you'd be brilliant at it."

John smiled at her praise. "Look what happened

when I tried to be poetic this afternoon. I called you 'misty-like.' Somehow 'misty-like' does not come to mind when I think of great poetry."

"Don't be silly. Anyone who loves poetry as much as you do must be able to write it. You need only to apply yourself."

John looked over at her shining face. She had such confidence in him. The feeling was new to him; his family, after all, had never shown very much interest in any of his activities. He couldn't bear to tell her that her confidence was misplaced, and he was terrified of how she might react when she discovered what kind of man he really was.

But he didn't want to think of this. All he wanted to think about was the woman. The woman who smelled like springtime. He wondered how long he could push the realities of his past from his mind. Could he do it for more than a few minutes? Could he gift himself with an entire afternoon of her company?

"Oh dear," Belle said, breaking into his tortured thoughts, "I forgot to ring for tea." She stood and crossed the room to pull the bellcord.

John rose when she did, shifting most of his weight onto his good leg. Before Belle even had a chance to sit down again, Norwood entered the room on swift, silent feet. She ordered some tea and biscuits, and Norwood left just as quietly as he had come in, closing the door behind him.

Belle's eyes followed the butler as he exited the room, and then she turned back and looked over to where John was standing near the sofa. As she gazed at him from across the room, she was certain her heart stopped beating. He looked so handsome and strong in his riding clothes, and she couldn't help but see the appreciation in his eyes as he gazed back at her. She remembered his words from the day before.

I'm not the man you think I am.

Was that true? Or was it possible that he was not the man *he* thought he was? It all seemed so obvious to her. It was in the way he had recited poetry and the firm embrace of his arms when he had held her on his horse. He needed someone to show him that he was good and strong. Dare she hope— he needed her?

Nervously, she crossed the room, stopping a foot or so in front of him. "I think that you are a very good man," she said softly.

John caught his breath as a surging wave of desire rocked through him. "Belle, I'm not. When you rang for tea I was trying to tell you . . ." Christ, *how* could he tell her? "I wanted to say . . ."

"What, John?" Her voice was exquisitely soft. "What did you want to tell me?"

"Belle, I—"

"Was it the kiss?"

It was an erotic nightmare. She was standing there before him, offering herself, and it was getting so damned hard to listen to his conscience and do the right thing. "Oh God, Belle," he groaned. "You don't know what you're saying."

"Yes, I do. I remember every moment of our kiss by the pond."

God help him, John leaned a little closer to her. His hand reached out with no direction from his brain, clasping hers in a warm embrace.

"Oh, John," she sighed, looking down at his hand as if it had the power to heal the world of all its ills.

Such devotion, such faith, such pure beauty was too much for him. With a groan that hovered somewhere between pleasure and agony, he pulled her roughly against him. His lips found hers in a frantic kiss, and he drank of her like a man who'd gone years without nourishment. He sank his hands into her hair, savoring the silky soft feel of it as his lips traveled the length of her face, worshipping her eyes, her nose, the line of her cheekbones.

And at some point during the kiss, he began to feel himself healing. The blackness in his heart didn't disappear, but it began to crack and crumble. The weight on his shoulders didn't lift completely, but it seemed to be lessened somehow.

Could she do that for him? Was she so pure and good that she could erase the stain on his soul? John began to feel giddy, and he clutched her to him more closely, raining light kisses along her hairline.

And then she sighed. "Oh, John, I feel so good." And he knew that she was content.

"How good?" he murmured, nipping at the corner of her mouth.

"Very, very good," Belle laughed, returning his kisses fervently.

John's lips trailed across her cheek to her ear, and he nibbled playfully on her lobe. "You have such sweet little ears," he said huskily. "Like apricots."

Belle drew back, a surprised smile on her face. "Apricots?"

"I told you I'm not very poetic."

"I love apricots," she declared loyally.

"Get back over here," he said in a laugh-tinged growl. He sat down on the sofa and tugged her along with him.

"Oooh, as you wish, my lord." Belle did her best imitation of a leer.

"What a lusty wench you are."

"Lusty *wench*? That's certainly not very poetic."

"Oh, hush." True to his words, John silenced her with another kiss, leaning back against the cushions and pulling Belle on top of him. "Have I told you," he said between kisses, "that you're the most beautiful woman I've ever met?"

"No."

"Well, you are. And the smartest, and the kindest, and"—John's hand stole down the length of her body, cupped her buttocks, and squeezed—"you have the cutest derrière I've ever seen."

Belle lurched back in shocked maidenly honor and then collapsed in giggles atop him. "Nobody told me that kissing was so much fun."

"Of course not. Your parents didn't want you running around just kissing *anybody*, after all."

Belle touched the side of his jaw with her hand, rubbing against the sandy stubble of his whiskers. "No, only you."

John didn't think that her parents particularly wanted her kissing him either, but he pushed the thought out of his mind, unwilling to give up the perfection of the moment. "Most people don't laugh so much while they're kissing." He grinned boyishly and tweaked her nose.

Belle tweaked his back. "They don't? How unfortunate for them."

John pulled her tightly to him in a crushing embrace, as if he could bond her to him by strength alone. Maybe some of her goodness would seep into him, cleansing his soul, and . . . He shut his eyes. He was growing fanciful. "You can't possibly know how perfect I feel right at this moment," he murmured into her hair.

Belle snuggled closer. "I know exactly how perfect."

"Unfortunately, your pot of tea is going to arrive any second now, and I don't think that the servants need to know just how perfect we feel."

"Oh my God!" Belle gasped, nearly flying across the room. "Do I look all right? Can you tell that I—that we—?"

"*I* can tell," John said wryly, trying to ignore the ache of unfulfilled need that pulsed through his body. "But if you smooth down your hair, I don't think that anyone else will be able to."

"It's raining," she said shakily. "Norwood will assume that that's why I'm a bit of a mess." For all her forward behavior that afternoon, Belle was not prepared to get caught in an amorous situation by her cousins' butler.

"Sit back down," John ordered. "We'll converse like two reasonable adults, and then Norwood won't suspect a thing."

"Do you think not? I'd be so embarr—"

"Just sit down, please, and we'll make polite conversation until your butler gets here."

"I don't think I can," Belle said, her voice barely a whisper.

"Why not?"

She sank down onto a chair and kept her eyes focused on her feet. "Because every time I look at you I remember you holding me."

John's heart slammed in his chest. He took a deep breath, fighting the increasingly painful need to leap over the settee, grab Belle, and ravish her right there on the spot. Thankfully, he was saved from having to reply to her emotional comment by a discreet knock on the door.

Norwood entered with a tray of tea and biscuits. After thanking him, Belle picked up the teapot and began to pour. John noticed that her hands were shaking. Wordlessly he accepted the cup she held out to him and took a drink.

Belle sipped at her tea, willing her hands to stop

their trembling. It wasn't that she was ashamed of her behavior; she was simply shocked by the extent of her reaction to him. She'd never dreamed that her body could feel so totally warm from the inside out.

"Penny for your thoughts," John said suddenly.

She looked up at him from over her teacup and smiled. "Oh, they're worth far more than a penny."

"How about a pound, then?"

For about one second Belle toyed with the idea of telling him what she was really thinking. But for only one second. Her mother had not raised her to be such a wanton. "I was wondering if you want me to pour the tea on your leg now or wait until it has cooled off a bit."

John stretched out his injured leg as far as he was able and looked down at it assessingly, pretending to give the matter serious thought. "Oh, I think hot, don't you?"

Belle picked up the teapot with a devilish grin. "If this works, we'll change medical science forever." She leaned over him, and for a second John thought she was really going to pour the tea on his leg. At the last possible moment she righted the pot and put it back down on the table. "The rain is coming down quite hard now," she said, glancing out the window. "You won't be able to return home for some time."

"I imagine we'll be able to keep ourselves occupied."

Belle took one look at his face and knew exactly how he wanted to keep them occupied. She didn't deny to herself that she also longed to while away the afternoon in his arms, but there was a good chance that Alex or Emma would happen upon them, and the last thing she needed was to get caught in an indelicate situation by her cousins.

"I think," she said finally, "that we may have to pursue a different activity."

John looked so disappointed that Belle could barely stifle a laugh. "What do you suggest we do?"

She set her teacup down. "Can you dance?"

Chapter 7

∽◦◦◦∽

Jphn lowered his cup very, very slowly. "Belle," he said finally, "you must know that I cannot."

"Nonsense. Everyone can dance. You have only to try."

"Belle, if this is some kind of joke—"

"Of course it isn't a joke," she cut in quickly. "I know that your leg is injured, but it doesn't seem to slow you overmuch."

"I may have taught myself to move with a reasonable degree of speed, but I do so with a complete lack of grace." His hand strayed unconsciously to his leg. Nightmarish visions of himself tumbling clumsily to the floor played out in his mind. "I'm sure we can entertain ourselves without my playing the fool trying to dance. Besides, we haven't any music."

"Hmmm, that is a problem." Belle glanced around the room until her eyes rested on the piano in the corner. "It appears that we have two choices. The first option is that I could ask Emma to come in and play for us, but I'm afraid she has never been accused of possessing musical talent. I wouldn't wish her noise on my worst enemy." She smiled sunnily. "Much less one of my good friends."

The force of her smile hit John squarely in the heart. "Belle," he said softly. "I don't think this is going to work."

"You won't know unless you try." She stood up and smoothed down her dress. "I think it's agreed that Emma at the piano is not an option, so I suppose I'll just have to sing."

"Can you?"

"Sing?"

John nodded.

"Probably about as well as you can dance."

"In that case, my lady, I think we may be in dire straits, indeed."

"I'm only teasing. I'm no diva, but I can carry a tune."

How much could it hurt to pretend—if only for an afternoon—that she could be his, that she *was* his, that he could possibly deserve her? He stood, determined to taste just a bit of heaven. "I hope you will have the courtesy not to wince out loud when I trod on your feet."

"Oh, don't worry, my lord, I shall wince very softly, indeed." On impulse, she leaned up and quickly kissed John's cheek, whispering, "My feet are very sturdy."

"For your sake, I should hope so."

"Now, which dances do you know?"

"None."

"None? What did you do in London?"

"I never bothered with the social whirl."

"Oh." Belle nibbled on her lower lip. "This is going to be more of a challenge than I anticipated. But have no fear, I am sure you are up to the task."

"I believe the more appropriate question is whether or not *you* are up to the task."

"Oh, I am," Belle said with a jaunty grin. "Believe me, I am. Now, I think we should start with a waltz. Some of the other dances might be a bit too taxing for your leg. Although perhaps not. You yourself said that you are able to move with reasonable speed."

John bit back a smile. "A waltz would be lovely. Just tell me what to do."

"Put your hand here like this." Belle picked up his hand and placed it on her slender waist. "And then I put my hand on your shoulder, see? Hmmm, you're quite tall."

"Is that a compliment?"

"Of course it is. Although I wouldn't like you any less if you were shorter."

"That is certainly gratifying to know."

"Are you poking fun at me?"

"Just a bit."

Belle shot him a teasing glance. "Well, just a bit is all right, I suppose, but no more than that. I'm terribly sensitive."

"I shall try to refrain."

"Thank you."

"Although you sometimes make it very difficult."

Belle poked him in the chest and resumed their waltzing lessons. "Hush. Now, take my other hand like this. Wonderful. We're all set."

"We are?" John cast a dubious eye over their position. "You're rather far away."

"This is the correct position. I've done this a thousand times."

"We could fit another person between us."

"I cannot imagine why we would want to."

John slowly tightened his grip around Belle's waist and pulled her to him until she could feel the heat from his body. "Isn't this better?" he murmured.

Belle's breath caught in her throat. John was barely an inch away, and his nearness was making her pulse race. "We would never be allowed in any respectable ballroom," she said huskily.

"I prefer dancing in private." John leaned down and let his lips brush gently against hers.

Belle swallowed nervously. She enjoyed his kisses, but she couldn't help but feel that she was getting herself into a situation she could not handle. So with more than a few regrets she stepped back, loosening John's grip on her until there was a respectable distance between their bodies again. "I can't very well teach you to waltz if we aren't in the proper position," she explained. "Now then, the key to waltzes is that they are in three-four time. Most other dances are in common time."

"Common time?"

"Four-four. Waltzes go 'one-two-three, one-two three, one-two-three.' Common time goes 'one-two-three-four.' "

"I think I see the difference."

Belle glanced up sharply at him. Tiny lines around his eyes crinkled with humor. Her own lips tugged upward at the corners as she tried to suppress a smile. "Good. Therefore a waltz might sound like this." She started humming a tune which had been very popular in London during the last season.

"I can't hear you." He started to pull her closer.

Belle wriggled back into her original position. "I'll sing, then."

John's hand tightened gently around her waist. "I still can't hear you."

"Yes, you can. Stop your games, or we'll never get our waltzing lesson underway."

"I'd rather have a kissing lesson."

She blushed a deep red. "We already had one of those today, and anyway, Emma or Alex could come in any minute. We must get back to work. I'll lead first, and once you catch on, you can take over. Are you ready?"

"I've been ready all afternoon."

Belle hadn't thought it possible to blush any harder but soon found that she'd been mistaken. "All right then, one-two-three, one-two-three." She applied slight pressure to John's shoulder and began the slow twirl of the waltz. She promptly tripped over his feet.

John smiled boyishly. "Imagine my delight that *you* were the first to stumble."

She looked up at him with a peevish expression. "I'm not used to leading. And it certainly is not very gentlemanly of you to point out my flaws."

"I didn't see it as a flaw. In fact, I rather enjoyed catching you."

"I'll just bet that you did," Belle muttered.

"Want to give it another try?"

She nodded and put her hand back on his shoulder. "Wait just a moment. I think we need to switch positions." She slid her hand down to his waist. "Put your hand on my shoulder. There, now just pretend that I'm the man."

John glanced down at the enticing swell of Belle's breasts. "That," he murmured, "is going to be exceedingly difficult."

Belle missed his desire-filled gaze, which was fortunate because her senses were already quite overwhelmed. "Now then," she said blithely, "if I were the man and you were the woman, I'd just put a little bit of pressure on your waist like this, and then we would move like this." As she softly sang out a waltz, they began to twirl around the parlor, John's bad leg moving with grace he'd never dreamed he could possess. "Wonderful!" Belle cried out triumphantly. "This is perfect."

"I agree," John replied, savoring the feel of her in his arms. "But do you think that I could be the man for a while?"

Belle shifted her hand to his shoulder as her eyes caught his in a sultry caress. She parted her lips to speak, but her throat went dry. Swallowing nervously, she nodded.

"Good. I much prefer it that way." John caught her about the waist and pulled her to him. This time, Belle made no protest, captured by the warmth and excitement of his body heat. "Am I doing this correctly?" he asked softly as he led her in the dance.

"I—I think so."

"You only *think* so?"

Belle snapped herself back into reality. "No, of course not. I know so. You're a very elegant dancer. Are you certain this is the first time you've ever waltzed?"

"Actually, my sisters used to force me to partner them when they were learning."

"I knew you weren't a novice."

"I was only nine."

Belle pursed her lips in thought, unaware of the kissable temptation she was presenting for John. "I don't think people even waltzed when you were nine."

He shrugged his shoulders. "We had a very advanced household."

As they twirled around the parlor, John wondered if he was fighting a losing battle. He kept telling himself that he had to stay away from Belle, but his resolve had so far proved useless next to her sunny smile. He knew that he couldn't marry her; to do so would only hurt the woman he wanted to protect and cherish.

He felt like a fraud just standing next to her after what he had done in Spain.

John exhaled slowly, his sigh a mixture of contentment and frustration. He had promised himself this afternoon. Just a few hours of happiness without any memories of Ana.

"We're supposed to make conversation," Belle said suddenly.

"Are we?"

"Yes. Otherwise people would think we don't like each other."

"There isn't anyone here to form an opinion one way or another," John pointed out.

"I know, but I am teaching you how to waltz, after all, and most of the time one waltzes during a party, not in a private parlor."

"More's the pity."

Belle ignored his comment. "That is why I think you ought to learn how to talk while you dance."

"Is it usually so difficult?"

"It can be. Some men need to count while they waltz in order to keep time, and it's difficult to have a conversation with someone when all he says is 'one, two,' and 'three.' "

"Well, then, by all means, talk away."

"All right." She smiled. "Have you written any poetry lately?"

"You were just looking for an excuse to ask me that," John accused.

"Maybe, maybe not."

"Belle, I told you I'm not a poet."

"I don't believe you."

John groaned, and in his frustration he missed a step. "I will try to write you a poem," he said finally.

"Splendid!" Belle exclaimed. "I cannot wait."

"I would try not to expect great things, were I you."

"Nonsense." She positively beamed. "I am breathless with anticipation."

"What is this?" a voice suddenly broke in. "A dance in my own home and I wasn't invited?"

John and Belle halted in mid-twirl as they looked around to see Emma entering the room.

"I was teaching John how to waltz," Belle explained.

"Without any music?"

"I thought it best not to ask for your assistance on the piano."

Emma grimaced. "That was probably a wise idea." She looked over at John. "I have yet to meet anyone whose skill at the piano does not exceed my own. Including the residents of our stables."

"So I've been told."

Emma ignored his wry smile. "Did you enjoy your lesson, John?"

"Very much so. Belle is a superb dancer."

"I've always thought so. Of course I've never danced with her myself." Emma moved over to a chair and sat down. "Do you mind if I join you for tea? I took the liberty of asking Norwood for another pot. I'm sure this is hopelessly lukewarm by now."

"By all means," John said graciously. "This is your house, after all."

Emma smiled knowingly as she noticed that John and Belle were still standing in each other's arms.

"Don't let my presence deter you from your dance," she said with an impish grin.

The pair immediately made their embarrassed excuses, disengaged themselves, and Belle sat down on the sofa. John murmured something about having to get back home, to which Emma replied with alacrity, "Oh, but you *cannot!*"

Belle leveled a suspicious eye at her cousin and immediately realized that Emma had decided that she and John would suit very well, indeed.

"It's pouring," Emma hastily explained. "You must stay until the rain lets up a bit."

John declined to point out the rain actually *had* let up a bit, and if he waited much longer, it was only going to worsen again. He offered the pair of beautiful women an inscrutable smile and sat down across from them on an elegant yet highly uncomfortable chair.

"You mustn't sit there," Emma said. "It's terribly uncomfortable, and I would get rid of it if Alex's mother didn't assure me it was absolutely priceless. Why don't you move over to the sofa next to Belle?"

John raised a single eyebrow at her.

"I hate when people do that," Emma muttered under her breath. Nonetheless, she continued brightly, "I assure you that you'll have a horrid backache on the morrow if you stay in that chair for more than five minutes."

John rose and sat down comfortably next to Belle. "I am your obedient servant, your grace," he said politely.

Emma flushed, hearing the tinge of humor and mockery in his voice. "Oh dear," she said loudly. "I wonder what is keeping that tea. I'll have to go check on it." With remarkable speed, Emma rose and exited the salon.

John and Belle turned to each other, Belle blushing to the very roots of her golden hair. "Your cousin has not mastered the art of subtlety," John pointed out dryly.

"No."

"I'm not exactly certain what she expects to accomplish. She will probably run into a maid with the tea not two steps from this parlor."

Belle swallowed, sheepishly remembering the time she and Alex's sister Sophie had managed to leave Emma and her future husband alone together for a full five minutes under the pretext of going to inspect a nonexistent harpsichord. "I imagine she'll be able to think of something."

"As much as I would love to take you into my arms again, I have no desire to be interrupted by your cousin returning with tea."

"Oh, I wouldn't worry about that," Belle mumbled. "She'll find a way to alert us of her impending presence. She's quite resourceful."

As if on cue, they heard Emma yelp from the other side of the closed door. "What a surprise!"

Belle frowned. "I would have thought she'd have given us a *bit* more time."

The door opened. "Look who I bumped into in the hall," Emma said, holding onto Alex's hand. "I wasn't expecting him back until much later this evening."

"Her carefully-laid plans foiled by an attentive husband," John murmured as he stood.

Belle stifled a laugh and said, "How lovely to see you, Alex."

"I was only out inspecting the fields," he replied, a perplexed frown crossing his features.

"Nonetheless, it is brilliant to have you back," Emma said unconvincingly.

"Did you locate that tea?" John asked.

"The tea? Oh, yes, the tea. Well, no, I didn't actually."

"A-hem."

Emma jumped at the sound of Norwood clearing his throat directly behind her.

"Your tea, your grace?"

"Oh. Thank you, Norwood. Over there on the table, I think."

"Tea actually sounds quite appealing after riding about in that rain all afternoon," Alex said pleasantly. "Although it does seem to be letting up."

Belle wasn't certain, but she thought she heard Emma groan.

Emma fixed a cup for Alex, and after he had taken a healthy gulp, he said, "There's to be a fair tomorrow near the village. I saw people setting it up while I was out."

"Oh really?" Emma responded with delight. "I adore fairs. Shall we go?"

"I'm not sure," Alex said with a frown. "I don't like the idea of your getting jostled about by crowds."

That remark was greeted by a mutinous glare on Emma's part. "Oh, don't be a stodge," she retorted. "You can't keep me locked up forever."

"All right. But you must promise to be careful." Alex turned to John and Belle, who were watching the interchange from the sofa with amused expressions. "Won't the two of you join us?"

A refusal automatically rose to John's lips, but before he could speak an image of Belle in his arms danced through his mind. They were waltzing . . . Her eyes were glowing with happiness. His heart was filled with tenderness and his body with desire. Maybe he *could* have a bit of joy in his life. Maybe five years of hell was payment enough for his sins.

He turned to Belle. She cocked her head and smiled, raising her brows in invitation. "Of course," he said, "I'll stop by after lunch, and we'll depart together from here."

"Splendid." Alex took another gulp of tea and glanced out the window where the skies were darkening ominously. "I don't mean to be rude, Blackwood, but if I were you, I'd head home now while the rain is light. It looks like it is going to pour again soon."

"I was just thinking the same thing myself." John stood and bowed to the ladies.

Belle was, of course, sorry to see him leave, but the humorous sight of Emma, slumped dejectedly in her chair after her husband unwittingly ruined all of her careful orchestrations, more than made up for her disappointment.

When John arrived home that afternoon there was another note waiting for him.

I am in Oxfordshire.

John shook his head. He'd have to find some way of contacting the previous owners of Bletchford Manor. They had seemed a trifle batty to him—just the sort to have friends who would write such odd notes.

It never occurred to him that the note might be in any way connected to the gunshot in the woods.

John poured himself a glass of brandy before climbing the stairs to his bedroom that evening. He started to take a sip, but then set it down on his nightstand. He felt warm enough without it.

Was this happiness? The feeling had been absent

from his life for so long he wasn't sure how to recognize it.

He crawled into bed, content. He never expected to dream.

He was in Spain. It was a hot day, but his company was in good spirits; no fighting for the last week.

He was sitting at a table in the tavern, an empty plate of food in front of him.

What was that strange thumping sound coming from upstairs?

He poured himself another drink.

Thump.

This place is ripe, I think. John rubbed his *eyes. Who had said that?*

Another thump. Another cry.

John walked slowly toward the stairs. What was wrong? The noise grew louder as he made his way along the second-floor hallway.

And then he heard it again. This time it was clear. "Noooooooooo!" Ana's voice.

He burst through the door. "Oh, God, no," he cried. He could barely see Ana, her slight form completely beneath Spencer, who was pumping relentlessly into her.

But he could hear her weeping. "Noooo, noooo, please, noooo."

John didn't pause to think. Crazed, he pulled Spencer up off the girl and threw him against the wall.

He looked back down at Ana. Her hair—what had happened? It had turned blond.

It was Belle. Her clothes were torn, her body ravaged and bruised.

"Oh, God, not this!" The cry seemed to well up from John's very soul.

He turned back to the man slumped against the wall, his hand tightening on his gun. "Look at me, Spencer," he demanded.

The man lifted his head, but he was no longer Spencer. John found himself looking into his own face.

"Oh, God, no," he gasped, stumbling back against the bed. "Not me. I couldn't do that. I wouldn't."

The other John laughed. It was a sick, maniacal sound.

"No, I wouldn't. I couldn't. Oh, Belle." He looked down at the bed, but she was gone.

"No! Belle!"

John was awakened by the sound of his screams. Gasping for air, he clutched his arms to his stomach. He rolled back and forth, his body racked by silent sobs.

Chapter 8

❧

Belle lay propped up in bed, thumbing through the collection of Wordsworth's poetry she had never gotten around to reading that afternoon. She found herself squinting slightly more than normal, so she leaned over to her bedside table and lit another candle. As soon as she had herself settled again, a knock sounded on the door.

"Come in."

Emma burst into the room, her violet eyes flushed with excitement. "Sophie's having her baby!" she exclaimed. "Three weeks early! A messenger just arrived with her husband's note."

"That's wonderful," Belle breathed. "Isn't it?"

"Oh, yes! It's not good for a baby to be early, but three weeks isn't much, and Oliver wrote that Sophie might have miscounted anyway."

"Will you and Alex leave in the morning?"

"First thing. I wanted to leave right away, but Alex would have none of that."

"He's right, you know. The roads are very dangerous at night."

"I know," Emma replied with a disappointed expression. "But I wanted to let you know tonight in case you wanted to accompany us. Or if you didn't, just to tell you our plans because we're sure to be gone before you wake up in the morning."

"I think that I will not go with you," Belle said slowly, measuring her words carefully as she spoke. She had been looking forward to the fair all evening, and she was loathe to give up her outing with John. Especially now that they would be alone. "I don't imagine that Sophie will want a houseful of guests while she's giving birth. I'll visit once the babe is a bit older."

"All right, then, I'll send your regards." Emma frowned. "Although I'm not certain if I should leave you alone here. I don't think it's proper."

"Alone?" Belle asked disbelievingly. "There are over a hundred servants."

"Not quite a hundred," Emma corrected. "And I did promise your mother I'd be a good chaperone."

"I cannot imagine what brand of insanity must have taken hold of my mother when she thought that you would be a proper chaperone."

"You do know more about society," Emma hedged. "If you think that there won't be any sort of uproar—"

"I *know* that there won't. This isn't London, after all. I doubt that anyone will even hear of my being alone. And if they did, it wouldn't create much fuss with a hundred servants standing guard over me."

"All right," Emma agreed finally. "Just don't invite Lord Blackwood over, please. I'd not want word to get out that you were spending time together unchaperoned."

Belle snorted. "That's an about-face after your machinations this afternoon."

"That was different," Emma replied defensively. Still, she had the grace at least to blush. "And don't tell me that you didn't appreciate my so-called machinations. I can see the way you look at him."

Belle sighed and snuggled down into her quilts. "I don't deny it."

Emma leaned forward, intensely interested. "Are you in love with him?"

"I don't know. How can one tell?"

Emma thought for a moment before answering. "One just somehow knows. It creeps up on a person. The poets write of love at first sight, but I don't think it happens like that."

Belle's smile was wistful. "Only in romantic novels, I suppose."

"Yes." Emma suddenly straightened. "I'd best be getting off to bed. I want to make an early start tomorrow."

"Have a safe trip," Belle called out.

"We will. Oh, and please offer our apologies to Lord Blackwood tomorrow as we won't be able to attend the fair with you. Although I imagine you'll enjoy it better without us."

"I'm sure we will."

Emma made a face. "Just don't invite him back here afterwards. And whatever you do, don't go over to Bellamy Park alone."

"I don't think that's what it's called."

"What *is* the name?"

Belle sighed. "I can't remember. Something with a 'B.'"

"Well, whatever it's called, don't go there. Your mother would have my head."

Belle nodded and blew out the candles as Emma exited the room.

* * *

Shortly after noon the next day, John set out toward Westonbirt, reminding himself for the hundredth time that he was going to have to put an end to this infatuation with Belle. It was getting so damned hard to push her away. She seemed to have so much faith in him that he had almost been able to believe he deserved the happiness she offered.

But dreams had a funny way of working themselves into everyday life, and John couldn't shake the image of Belle lying on that bed in Spain, her body ravaged and used.

He couldn't be with her. He knew this now more than ever. He'd tell her today. He swore to himself that he would do it, no matter how painful the task. He'd do it . . . after the fair. One more blissful afternoon surely couldn't hurt.

On horseback it took only fifteen minutes to reach Westonbirt. John left his powerful stallion in the stables, walked up the front steps, and lifted his hand to knock.

Norwood opened the door before his knuckles even connected with the wood. "How do you do, my lord," he intoned. "Lady Arabella is waiting for you in the yellow salon."

"No, I'm not," Belle chirped, popping out of one of the many rooms which bordered the great hall. "Hello, John. I know I'm supposed to wait dutifully for you in the salon, but I was too impatient. You'll never guess what happened."

"I'm sure I won't."

"Alex and Emma had to rush off at the crack of dawn. Alex's sister is having her baby."

"Congratulations," John said automatically. "Does that mean that our outing is canceled?"

"Of course not." Hadn't he noticed that she was

dressed in her best riding habit? "I see no reason why the two of us cannot have a lovely time by ourselves."

John smiled at her artless words but privately thought that he was treading dangerous waters, indeed. "As you wish, my lady."

The couple rode out in companionable silence, enjoying the brisk breezes of the autumn weather. The fair was actually located closer to John's home than to Westonbirt, so they crossed over the border between the two properties and rode past Bletchford Manor on their way. As they passed the stately old home, John commented, as he always did, "Damn, but I've got to come up with another name for this place."

"I heartily agree," Belle replied. "Brimstone Park conjures up images of hellfire and the like."

John shot her an odd look. "It isn't called Brimstone Park."

"It isn't? Oh, of course it isn't. I knew that." Belle smiled weakly. "What is it called again?"

"Bletchford Manor," John replied, wincing as he said the name.

"Good gracious, that's even worse. At least Brimstone Park had some character to it. And 'bletch' rhymes with 'retch,' which conjures up images even more unfortunate than hellfire."

"Believe me, I am well aware of all of the unpleasant aspects of the present name."

"Don't worry, we'll come up with something." Belle patted John comfortingly on his forearm. "Just give me a little time. I'm quite clever with words."

They reached the fairgrounds, and Belle's attention was immediately diverted by a man on stilts a few yards away from them. They were soon swept up into the rhythm of the fair.

"I've always wondered how they do that," Belle pondered as they stopped before a brightly dressed juggler.

"I imagine it's just a matter of throwing the balls up in the air with the right timing."

Belle elbowed him in the ribs. "Don't be such a spoilsport. You take the magic out of everything. Oh, look at those ribbons!" Letting go of John's hand, she hurried over to the ribbon-seller and inspected his wares. By the time John caught up with her, she already had two ribbons in hand and was deciding between them. "Which do you prefer, John? This?" She held a pink ribbon up against her hair. "Or this?" she asked, replacing the pink ribbon with a red one.

John crossed his arms and pretended to give the matter ample thought before reaching out and plucking a bright blue one off the table. "I prefer *this* one. It is the exact color of your eyes."

Belle looked over at him, caught the warm caress of his gaze, and simply melted. "Then I must have the blue one," she said softly.

They stood there locked into place by each other's stare until the ribbon-seller destroyed the moment with a loud, "A-hem!" Belle tore her eyes away from John and reached down into her reticule, but before she could retrieve any coins, John had paid for the ribbon and placed it in her hands.

"A present, my lady." He leaned over and kissed her hand.

Belle felt the warmth of his kiss travel up her arm straight to her soul. "I shall treasure it always."

The romance of the moment was overpowering. "Are you hungry?" John asked suddenly, desperate to turn the conversation over to more mundane matters.

"Famished."

John led her over to the food stalls where they bought spinach pies and strawberry tarts. Plates in hand, they wended their way to a quiet spot on the outskirts of the fair. John laid his coat down on the ground, and they sat on it and ravenously attacked their food.

"You owe me a poem," Belle reminded him between bites of her pie.

John sighed. "So I do."

"You haven't even tried, have you?" Belle accused.

"Of course I have. I just haven't finished what I started."

"Then tell me what you have now."

"I don't know," he hedged. "A true poet wouldn't release his work until he was certain it was finished."

"Pleeeeeeease!" she begged, her face contorting into an expression that would have been more at home on a five-year-old.

John couldn't hold out against such unrestrained begging. "Oh, all right. How about this?

> 'She walks in beauty, like the night
> Of cloudless climes and starry skies;
> And all that's best of dark and bright
> Meet in her aspect and her eyes.' "

"Oh, John," Belle sighed deliciously. "That was lovely. It made me feel so beautiful."

"You *are* beautiful."

"Thank you," Belle said automatically. "But looking beautiful isn't, I think, as important as feeling beautiful, and that's why your poem touched me so deeply. It was so romantic. It was—wait a minute." She sat upright, her brow furrowed in thought.

John suddenly focused all of his attention on the spinach pie in his hands.

"I've heard that before," Belle continued. "I think I've read it. Quite recently."

"Can't imagine how," John murmured, all the while knowing he was well and truly sunk.

"Lord Byron wrote that! I cannot believe you tried to pass off Lord Byron's poetry as your own!"

"You did back me into a bit of a corner."

"I know, but that's no excuse for outright plagiarism. And here I was, thinking you'd written such beautiful words just for me. Imagine my disappointment."

"Imagine *my* disappointment," John muttered. "I was certain you wouldn't have read it yet. It was only published last year."

"I had to get my brother to buy it for me. They don't sell Lord Byron's work in the ladies' bookshop. Too racy, they say."

"You are too inventive by half," John grumbled, leaning back and resting on his elbows. "If you had stayed in your ladies' bookshop where you belong, I wouldn't be in this mess."

"I don't regret one whit of it," Belle said archly. "It seemed quite silly to me that I wasn't allowed to read what all of society was whispering about, and only because I'm an unmarried female."

"Get yourself married," he suggested jokingly, "and then you can do whatever you want."

Belle leaned forward, excitement glittering in her eyes. "Lord Blackwood, that wouldn't be a proposal now, would it?"

John paled. "Now you've *really* backed me into a corner."

Belle sat back, trying to hide her disappointment. She didn't know what had possessed her to speak so outrageously, and she certainly had no idea how she had expected him to react. Still, accusing her of backing him into a corner was definitely not what she'd been hoping for. "I still think you should write a poem," she finally said, hoping her jaunty tone covered the sadness she wasn't able to keep out of her eyes.

John pretended to give the matter great thought. "How about this one?" he asked with an impish smile.

> "There is nothing more dear to my heart
> Than a woman who's covered with straw-
> berry tart."

Belle made a face. "That was dreadful."

"Did you think so? I thought it most romantic, indeed, considering that you've got strawberry tart on your face."

"I do not."

"Yes, you do. Right here." John extended his finger and lightly touched the corner of her mouth. He lingered for a moment, wanting to trace the outline of her lips, but he pulled away quite suddenly, almost as if burned. He was getting too close to temptation. She had only to sit across from him at a makeshift picnic, and his entire body came alive.

Belle's hand flew up to her face, instinctively touching the spot where he had just touched her. Funny how her skin still tingled. Stranger still how the sensation was slowly spreading through the rest of her body. She looked over at John, who was gazing at her hungrily, his dark eyes smoldering with unfulfilled desire. "There—there are so many people about, my lord," she finally stammered.

John could tell she was nervous. She never would have reverted to her automatic use of the title "my lord" otherwise. He drew back, shuttering his gaze, aware that it was his unconcealed hunger which was making her so ill-at-ease. He took several deep breaths, willing himself to cease this insane desire. His body refused, unwilling to ignore the ravishingly beautiful woman seated not three feet away from him.

John cursed under his breath. This was crazy. Utter madness. He was romancing a woman with whom he couldn't hope for a future. He heard his older brother Damien's voice pounding in his head. *"You are not a titled gentleman. You are not a titled gentleman."* John bit back a wry smile. Funny how life turned out. He'd won himself a title, but his soul was black as sin.

"John?" Belle asked softly. "Is something wrong? You're so quiet."

He looked up and caught the concern in her eyes. "No, just thinking, that's all."

"About what?"

"About you," he replied starkly.

"Good thoughts, I hope," Belle said, nervous at the dark tone of his voice.

John rose to his feet and offered her his hand. "Come, let's go for a walk in the woods while the sun is still shining. We'll lead the horses behind us."

Belle rose wordlessly and followed him to where they had left their mounts. They set off slowly on foot, heading back through the trees toward Westonbirt and Bletchford Manor. The horses followed obediently behind, occasionally stopping to investigate one of the many small creatures which darted through the forest.

After about fifteen minutes of ominous silence, John stopped short. "Belle, we need to talk."

"We do?"

"Yes, this—" John fought to find the correct word but came up empty-handed. "This thing that is going on between us—it has to end."

A deep, dark pain slowly formed in the pit of Belle's stomach and began to spread. "Why?" she asked softly.

He looked away, unable to meet her eyes. "It can't go anywhere. You must realize that."

"No," she said sharply, her pain making her brave and just a little bit shrill. "No, I don't realize that."

"Belle, I haven't any money, my leg is useless, and I've barely got a title."

"Why do you say that? Those things don't matter to me."

"Belle, you could have any man in the world."

"*But I want you.*"

Her impassioned reply hung in the air for a long minute before John was able to say anything. "I'm doing this for your own good."

Belle stepped back, nearly blinded by pain and fury. His words rained down on her like physical blows, and she hysterically wondered if she'd ever again know a moment of happiness. "How dare you condescend to me," she finally bit out.

"Belle, I don't think that you've given this matter sufficient thought. Your parents would never let you marry the likes of me."

"You don't know my parents. You don't know what they want for me."

"Belle, you are the daughter of an earl."

"And as I've pointed out before, you are the son of an earl, so I fail to see a problem."

"There is a world of difference, and you know it." He knew he was grasping at straws. Anything to avoid telling her the truth.

"What do you want, John?" she asked wildly. "Do you want me to beg? Is that what this is about? Because I won't do it. Is this some kind of perverse search for a compliment? Do you want me to spell out all of the reasons I wanted you? All of the reasons I *thought* you were so kind and noble and good?"

John winced at her pointed use of the past tense. "I am trying to be noble right now," he said stiffly.

"No, you're not. You're trying to be a martyr, and I hope you're enjoying yourself, because I most certainly am not."

"Belle, listen to me," he implored. "I am—I am not the man you think I am."

The hoarse agony of his voice shocked Belle into silence, and she stared at him openmouthed.

"I've . . . done things," he said stiffly, turning away so that he would not have to look at her face. "I've hurt people. I've hurt . . . I've hurt *women*."

"I don't believe you." Her words came out low and fast.

"Damn it, Belle!" He whirled around and slammed his fist against the trunk of a tree. "What will it take to convince you? What do you need to know? The very blackest secrets of my heart? The deeds that have stained my soul?"

She took a step back. "I-I don't know what you're saying. I don't think *you* know what you're saying."

"I'll hurt you, Belle. I'll hurt you without intending to. I'll hurt you—Christ, isn't it enough just that I'll hurt you?"

"You won't hurt me," she said softly, reaching out to touch his sleeve.

"Don't delude yourself into thinking I'm a hero, Belle. I'm not—"

"I don't think you're a hero," she cut in. "I don't want you to be a hero."

"God," he said with a dark, sarcastic laugh. "That's the first realistic thing you've said all day."

She stiffened. "Don't be cruel, John."

"Belle," he said raggedly. "I have limits. Don't push me past them."

"And just what is that supposed to mean?" she asked irritably.

He grabbed her by the shoulders as if trying to shake some sense into her. Dear Lord, she was so close, he could smell her. He could feel the soft strands of her hair that the wind was whipping against his face. "It means," he said in a low voice, "that it is taking every ounce of my control not to lean forward and kiss you right now."

"Then why don't you do it?" she asked, her voice a quavering whisper. "I wouldn't stop you."

"Because I wouldn't stop there. I'd trail my lips down the soft length of your throat until I reached those annoying little buttons on your riding habit. And then I'd slowly slip each one apart and spread your jacket open." Dear God, was he *trying* to torture himself? "You're wearing some silky little underthing, aren't you?"

Much to her horror, Belle nodded.

John shuddered as waves of desire rocked through his body. "I love the feel of silk," he murmured. "And you do, too."

"H-how do you know?"

"I was watching you when you got that blister on your heel. I saw you roll off your stocking."

Belle gasped, shocked that he'd been spying on her, yet still strangely aroused by the notion.

"Do you know what I'd do?" John asked huskily, his eyes never leaving hers.

Mutely, she shook her head.

"I'd lean down and kiss you through the silk. I'd take your dusky nipple into my mouth and suck it until it was a hard little bud. And then when that wasn't enough, I'd slide your silky little underthing up along your skin until your breasts were free and exposed, and then I'd lean down and do it all over again."

Belle didn't move a muscle, absolutely rooted to the spot by the sensual onslaught of his words. "Then what would you do?" she whispered, acutely aware of the heat of his hands on her shoulders.

"You want to punish me, don't you?" John asked harshly, tightening his grip on her. "But since you asked . . . I'd slowly peel off every article of your clothing until you were gloriously naked in my arms. And then I'd start kissing you, every damned inch, until you were quivering with desire."

Somewhere in the back of Belle's passion-hazed mind, she dimly registered that she was already quivering.

"And then I'd lay you down and cover your body with my own, pressing you down against the ground. And then I'd enter you oh-so-slowly, savoring each second as I made you mine." John's voice broke off, his breath ragged as an image of Belle with her long legs wrapped around him floated through his brain. "What do you say to that?

Belle ignored his crude question, her body flooded with the sensual images he had planted there. She was on fire, and she wanted him, in every way. It was now or never, she knew that, and she was terrified that she'd lose him completely. "I still wouldn't stop you," she whispered.

Disbelief and desire crashed through John's body until he rudely pushed her away from him, knowing full well that he'd be unable to resist temptation if he remained touching her one moment longer. "For God's sake, Belle, do you know what you're saying? Do you?" He raked his hand through his hair, taking deep breaths as he tried to ignore the painful hardness of his body.

"Yes, I know what I'm saying," Belle cried out. "You just won't listen."

"You don't know who I am. You've built up some romantic image of the poor, wounded, war-hero. Wouldn't it be a lark to be married to a real-life gothic hero? Well, I have news for you, my lady, that's not me. And after a few months, you'd realize that I'm no hero, and it isn't much of a lark being married to a lame pauper."

Rage unlike anything Belle had ever known poured through her, and she launched herself at him, beating her fists mercilessly against his chest. "You bastard!" she cried out. "You supercilious bastard. How dare you tell me I don't know my own mind? Do you think me so stupid that I can't see who you really are? You keep saying you've done something bad, but I don't believe you. I think you're making it up just to push me away."

"Oh, God, Belle," he said hoarsely. "It's not that. It's—"

"Do you think it matters to me that your leg is injured? Do you think I care that your title is not centuries old? I wouldn't care if you hadn't one at all!"

"Belle," John said in a placating voice.

"Stop! Don't say any more. You're making me sick! You accuse me of being spoiled, but it is you who are the snob. You're so obsessed with titles and money and social position that you won't allow yourself to reach out for the one thing you really want!"

"Belle, we've barely known each other for a week. I fail to see how you could have decided that I was the right man for you." But even as John spoke the words, he knew he was lying, for he had already reached the same conclusion about her.

"I'm beginning to wonder that myself," Belle said harshly, wanting to wound him as he had done to her.

"I deserved that, I know, but you'll soon realize that I've done the right thing. Maybe not tomorrow, but once you get over your anger, you'll know."

Belle turned her head away, not wanting to let him see her brush away a tear. Her breath was coming in short gasps, and it was several moments before she was able to still her heaving shoulders. "You're wrong," she said softly, turning back around to face him with accusing eyes. "You're wrong. I'll never realize that you're doing the right thing because you're not! You're destroying my happiness!" She gulped down a lump in her throat. "And yours, too, if you'd only stop to look in your heart."

John turned away, unnerved by the unwavering honesty in her eyes. He knew that he could not tell her the real reason he was pushing her away, so he tried to appeal to her innate sense of practicality. "Belle, you've been raised with every luxury. I can't give you all that. I can't even give you a house in London."

"It doesn't matter. Besides, I have ample funds."

John stiffened. "I won't take your money."

"Don't be silly. I'm sure I have a large dowry."

He whirled around, his eyes hard and deadly serious. "I won't have it said that I'm a fortune hunter."

"Oh, is *that* what this is all about? You're worried about what people will *say*? Dear God, I thought you were above all that." Belle turned on her heel and marched back to her mare, who'd been idly munching on some grass. Grabbing the reins, she mounted the horse, harshly brushing away John's offer of assistance. "Do you know something?" she asked, her tone cruel. "You were absolutely right. You're not the person I thought you were." But her voice broke on the last word, and Belle knew that he could see through her false bravado.

"Goodbye, Belle," John said flatly, knowing that if he went to her now, he'd never be able to let her go.

"I'm not going to wait for you, you know," Belle cried out. "And someday you'll change your mind and you'll want me. You'll want me so badly you'll ache from it. And not just in your bed. You'll want me in your home and in your heart and in your soul. And I'll be gone."

"I don't doubt it for an instant." John wasn't sure whether he'd spoken the words or merely thought them, but either way it was clear she hadn't heard him.

"Goodbye, John," Belle said, her voice choked with sobs. "I know that you're friends with Alex and Emma, but I'd appreciate it if you didn't come round Westonbirt until after I've left." Her vision clouded by tears, she whipped her mare around and took off for Westonbirt at breakneck speed.

John watched her depart, then listened to the sound of her horse's galloping hooves after he could no longer see her. He stood still for several minutes, his mind refusing to digest all that had taken place. After years of shame and self-loathing, he had finally done the right thing, the honorable thing, but he felt like the villain in one of Mrs. Radcliffe's novels.

John groaned out loud and then viciously swore as he kicked a rock out of his way. It had been like this his entire life. Just when he thought he had achieved something he wanted, some greater prize was dangled before him—something he knew he could never have. Bletchford Manor had been a dream to him, a dream of respectability and position and honor, a way of showing his family that he could make it on his own, that he didn't need to inherit a title and an estate to become a gentleman. But in coming to Bletchford Manor he'd met Belle, and it was almost as if the gods were laughing at him, calling out, "See, you'll never really make it, John. *This* is what you'll never have."

He squeezed his eyes shut. He had done the right thing, hadn't he?

He knew he'd hurt her. The pain in her eyes had been naked and raw. He could still see her face in his mind. And then Belle was joined by Ana, her eyes silently condemning him. "Noooo," she moaned. "Noooo." And then the voice of her mother—

"It might as well have been you."

John wrenched his eyes open, trying to banish the women from his mind. He had done the right thing. He could never be the pure soul Belle deserved. A scene from his dream flashed in his mind. He was on top of her. She was screaming.

He had done the right thing. His desire for her was too intense. She would have broken under the force of his passion.

A dull, hollow ache formed in his chest, squeezing at his lungs. In one fluid motion, he mounted his stallion and took off at a speed even faster than Belle's. As he crashed through the forest, the leaves whipped viciously at his face, but John ignored them, accepting the pain as penance due.

Chapter 9

Belle had no memory of her breakneck gallop home. She rode without care to her own safety; all that seemed to matter was getting back to Westonbirt and putting as much distance between herself and John Blackwood as possible.

But once she arrived home and raced up the stairs she realized that Westonbirt was not far enough. How could she bear to remain with her cousins when the man who had broken her heart was only a short ride away?

She stormed into her room, pulling off her cloak with a vicious tug, and proceeded to grab three valises from her dressing room. Furiously she began to stuff dresses into them.

"My lady, my lady, what are you doing?"

Belle looked up. Her lady's maid was standing in the doorway, a horrified expression on her face. "I'm packing," she snapped. "What does it look like I'm doing?"

Mary rushed in and tried to grab the valise away. "But my lady, you don't know how to pack."

Belle felt hot tears pricking her eyes. "How difficult can it be?!" she burst out.

"You need trunks for those gowns, my lady, or you'll crush them."

Belle dropped her bags, feeling suddenly deflated. "Fine. Yes. Of course. You're right."

"My lady?"

Belle swallowed, trying to keep her emotions inside, if only until she could get to another room. "Just pack everything as you see fit. I'll leave just as soon as the duke and duchess return." With that, she rushed from the room, running down the hallway until she reached Emma's office, where she sequestered herself, sobbing furiously for the rest of the day.

Emma and Alex didn't return for a week. Belle didn't know what she did during that time to keep herself occupied. Mostly she just stared out the window.

When Emma arrived, she was naturally perplexed at the sight of Belle's bags, packed and neatly stacked in a small storage room off the main hallway. She immediately sought her cousin out.

"Belle, what is the meaning of all this? And why are you wearing my dress?"

Belle looked down at the violet frock she was wearing. "I packed all of mine."

"Exactly. Why?"

"I can't stay here."

"Belle, I have no idea what you're talking about."

"I have to go to London. Tomorrow."

"What? Tomorrow? Does this have something to do with Lord Blackwood?"

Belle's immediate aversion of her head was all Emma needed to know that she was correct. "What happened?"

Belle swallowed nervously. "He humiliated me."

"Oh, my Lord, Belle. He didn't . . . "

"No. But I wish I had. Then he'd have to marry me, and I—" She broke off with a sob.

"Belle, you don't know what you're saying."

"I know exactly what I'm saying! Why is it that no one can credit me with the ability to know my own mind?"

Emma's eyes widened at her cousin's loss of composure. "Perhaps you should tell me what conspired during my absence."

In a shaky voice Belle related her tale. By the time she was finished, her voice was so racked with emotion that she had to sit down.

Emma perched herself on the end table next to Belle's chair and placed her hand gently on her arm. "We'll leave for London immediately," she said quietly.

For the first time in a week Belle felt a glimmer of life within her. Somehow she felt that she might be able to heal herself if she could just get away from the scene of her heartbreak. She looked over at Emma. "Alex won't like your going."

"No, he won't, but you haven't left me much choice now, have you?"

"He could come with us. I wouldn't mind."

Emma sighed. "I think he has some important estate business that he has to conduct here."

Belle knew how much her cousin hated to be separated from her husband, but still, she was desperate to get away. "I'm sorry," she said lamely.

"It's all right." Emma stood and straightened her

shoulders. "We'll make plans to leave tomorrow."

Belle felt tears forming in her eyes. "Thank you."

Belle had been correct about one thing: Alex hadn't liked his wife hightailing it off to London one bit. Belle had no idea what had transpired between them in the privacy of their own chamber, but when the two ladies headed down the steps the next day to their carriage, Alex was not in a good mood.

"One week," he said warningly. "One week, and I'm coming to get you."

Emma placed her hand on his arm and told him to hush. "Darling, you know that my aunt and uncle aren't returning for a fortnight. I can't come home until then."

"One week."

"You can come and visit me."

"One week." And then he kissed her with so much passion that Belle blushed.

Soon the two ladies were comfortably ensconced in the Blydon house in Grosvenor Square. Now that she was some distance away from John, Belle felt herself growing stronger, but she could not shake off the melancholy which pervaded her spirit. Emma was doing her best to be insufferably cheerful, but she obviously missed Alex. He wasn't helping at all, sending notes twice a day telling her that he missed her and would she please come home where she belonged.

Belle made no effort to let anyone know that she was back in town, but on her third day back, her butler informed her that she had a visitor.

"Really?" she asked without much interest. "Who?"

"He asked that he be allowed to surprise you, my lady."

Her heart slammed in her throat. "Did he have brown hair and brown eyes?" she asked frantically.

"He did wish it to be a surprise."

Belle was so nervous she actually grabbed the butler and shook him. "Did he? Please, you must tell me."

"Yes, my lady, he did."

She dropped her hands and sank into a nearby chair. "Tell him I don't wish to see him."

"But I thought Mr. Dunford had always been a special friend of yours, my lady. I shouldn't like to send him away."

"Oh, it's Dunford." Belle sighed, relief and disappointment both flowing through her. "Tell him I'll be right down." After a moment or two, she rose and went to her mirror to check her appearance quickly. William Dunford had been a close friend of hers for several years. They had courted briefly but had quickly realized that they would not suit and decided not to ruin their friendship by pursuing a romance any further. He was also Alex's best friend and had played a considerable role in the not so easy task of helping Alex and Emma find their way to the altar.

"Oh, Dunford, it's so good to see you!" Belle exclaimed as she entered the salon where he was waiting. She crossed the room to give him a quick hug.

"It's good to see you again, too, Belle. Did you enjoy your spell of rustication with the newlyweds?"

"Westonbirt was lovely," Belle answered automatically, sitting down on a sofa. "Although there was an uncommon amount of rain."

Dunford plopped down lazily into a comfortable

chair. "Well, this is England, after all."

"Yes," Belle replied, but her mind was a thousand miles away.

After a full minute of waiting patiently, Dunford finally said, "Hello? Belle? Yoo-hoo."

Belle snapped back into the present. "What? Oh, I'm sorry, Dunford. I was just thinking."

"And obviously not about me."

She smiled sheepishly. "I'm sorry."

"Belle, is something wrong?"

"Everything is fine."

"Everything is not fine, that much is clear." He paused and then smiled. "It's a man, isn't it?"

"What?"

"Aha! I see that I am correct."

Belle knew she had no chance fooling him, but she nonetheless felt she ought to give it at least a weak try. "Maybe."

"Ho!" Dunford chortled. "This is rich. After years of men falling prostrate at your feet out of love and devotion, little Arabella has finally been felled herself."

"This isn't funny, Dunford."

"*Au contraire.* It's most amusing."

"You make me sound like some kind of heartless ice princess."

"No, of course not, Belle," he said, immediately contrite. "I must admit, you have always been uncommonly nice to every pimply-faced boy who has ever asked you to dance."

"Thank you. I think."

"It's probably why so many pimply-faced boys ask you to dance."

"Dunford," Belle warned.

"It's just that after God knows how many proposals, none of which you showed the least inclination of accepting, it's amusing to see you similarly besotted." After his long explanation Dunford sat back. When Belle offered no comment, he added, "It is a man, isn't it?"

"What—as opposed to a woman?" Belle snapped. "Of course it's a man."

"Well, I could have been completely off the mark. Your favorite spaniel could have died."

"I don't have a spaniel," Belle said peevishly. "It's a man."

"Doesn't he return your affections?"

"No." Her voice was heartbreakingly sad.

"Are you certain?"

"I have reason to believe that he"— Belle chose her words carefully—"cares for me, but he feels that he cannot act on that emotion."

"Sounds like a chap with a little too much honor for his own good."

"Something like that."

"Out of curiosity, Belle, just what is it about this fellow that has you so enamored of him?"

Her face immediately softened. "I don't know, Dunford. I really don't. He has this marvelous sense of honor. And humor, too. He teases me, not in a malicious way, of course, and lets me tease him back. And there is something so good in him. He can't see it, but I can. Oh, Dunford, he *needs* me."

Dunford was silent for a moment. "I'm sure that all is not lost. We can make him come about."

"We?"

He shot her a roguish smile. "This sounds like the most fun I've had in years."

"I'm not sure it's worth the effort."

"Of course it is."

"I'm not sure I want him back."

"Of course you do. Were you listening to your own words not thirty seconds ago?"

"I wish I were as confident as you are."

"Look, Belle, you've been telling me for the last two years that you want a love match. Are you really going to throw it all away over a little pride?"

"I could find somebody nice to marry," Belle said, rather unconvincingly. "I'm sure I could. Men ask me all the time. I wouldn't be unhappy."

"Maybe not. But you wouldn't be happy either." Belle slumped. "I know."

"We'll set my plan into motion tonight."

"What exactly does this plan entail?"

"The way I see it, if this man—just what is his name, anyway?"

"John."

Dunford smirked. "Really, Belle, you can do better than that."

"No, really," Belle protested. "His name really is John. You can ask Emma."

"All right then, if this John fellow really does care for you, he's going to be blindingly jealous when he hears that you're planning to get married, even if he is trying to be noble by giving you up."

"An interesting plan, but who am I going to marry?"

"Me."

Belle shot him a look of utter disbelief. "Oh, *please*."

"I didn't mean we would really get married," Dunford retorted. And then he added somewhat defensively, "And you don't have to sound quite so disgusted with the idea. I'm considered a reasonably good catch, you know. I simply meant that we could start a rumor that we were planning to wed. If John really wants you, it should do the trick."

"I don't know," Belle hedged. "What if he doesn't really want me? What then?"

"Why, you jilt me, of course."

"You wouldn't mind?"

"Of course not. It would do wonders for my social life, actually. I'd have scores of pretty little things coming by to offer me consolation."

"I think I'd rather leave you out of it. Perhaps we could just start a rumor that I'm planning to marry and not mention anyone in particular."

"And how far would *that* tale get?" Dunford countered. "Everyone in London is planning to marry. Your fellow would never hear of it, especially not if he's buried out in the country."

"No, but then again, he probably wouldn't hear any rumor no matter how juicy. He doesn't keep up with the comings and goings of the *ton*. The only way he'd find out we were planning to marry is if we put an announcement in the *Times*."

Dunford paled at the thought.

"Just so," Belle replied. "The only way a rumor is going to reach him is if it's not really a rumor but rather a piece of information deliberately sent his way." She swallowed nervously, hardly able to believe that she was considering such a scheme. "Perhaps we could let Emma in on our plan. She could casually mention to John that I was planning to marry. I won't have her use your name. I won't have her mention any name at all—just tell him I'm about to announce an engagement."

"It won't look odd her just happening to drop by?"

"They're neighbors. There is nothing suspicious about her stopping by to say hello."

Dunford leaned back and smiled with glee, his even white teeth gleaming. "An excellent strategy,

Arabella. And it saves me from having to pretend I'm in love with you."

She shook her head. "You're impossible."

"If your beau doesn't appear on the scene complete with white horse and shiny armor to carry you off into the sunset, well, then I'd have to say he probably wasn't worth his salt in the first place."

Belle wasn't completely sure about that, but she nodded anyway.

"In the meantime, we ought to get you out and about. This John fellow—what did you say his last name was?"

"I didn't."

Dunford raised an eyebrow but didn't press her for details. "What I was going to say is that your little lie isn't going to look very convincing if he finds out that you've been holing yourself up in this mausoleum since you arrived."

"No, I suppose not, but hardly anybody is in town now. There isn't very much to get out and about to."

"As it happens I've been invited to what is sure to be an exceedingly dreadful musicale tonight, and as the host is a distant relation of mine I have no way to get out of it."

Belle's eyes narrowed. "This isn't one of your Smythe-Smith cousins again, is it?"

"I'm afraid so."

"I thought I told you that I would never attend another one of their recitals. After the last one, I am convinced that I know exactly how Mozart would sound if performed by a herd of sheep."

"What can you expect when you've been cursed with a name like Smythe-Smith? At any rate, you haven't much choice. We've already decided that you've got to get out and about, and I don't see any other invitations coming your way."

"How kind of you to point that out."

"I'll take that as a yes and come by to escort you tonight. And don't look so glum. I suspect this beau of yours will come sailing into town any day now, and then you'll be saved from all future butcheries of music."

"He won't show up for at least two weeks, actually, because Emma is acting as my chaperone until my parents return from Italy. She can't very well be in two places at once, and anyway, I doubt he'd believe I've fallen in love with someone else so quickly. I'm afraid you're stuck with my company for a fortnight. Provided, of course, that I don't have to attend any more musicales."

"I would never be so cruel. Until tonight, then, Belle." With a rakish smile, Dunford rose, bowed smartly, and left the room. Belle sat on the sofa for several minutes after his departure, wondering why she couldn't have fallen in love with him instead of John. It would make matters ever so much simpler. Well, maybe not that much simpler, as Dunford wasn't the least bit in love with her, at least not above the love of one friend to another.

Belle rose and headed up the stairs, wondering if she had set herself on the right course of action. Failure would be exquisitely painful, but she knew that she wouldn't be able to live with herself if she didn't at least try to carve out a life with John. She'd just have to wait a couple of weeks.

Chapter 10

⌒◯◯⌒

As it happened, Belle did not have to wait two weeks to set Dunford's plan into motion. Precisely one week after she and Emma arrived in London, Alex strode purposefully through the front door with a slightly plump, middle-aged lady scurrying at his heels.

Belle happened to be walking through the hall when he burst into the house. "Oh my," she breathed, observing the commotion with an amused eye.

"Where is my wife?" Alex demanded.

"Upstairs, I think," Belle replied.

"Emma!" he called loudly. "Emma, get down here."

Within seconds Emma appeared at the top of the stairs. "Alex?" she said disbelievingly. "What on earth are you doing here? And who might your, er, guest be?"

"Your one week is up," he stated flatly. "I'm fetching you home."

"But—"

"And this," Alex cut her off forcefully and motioned to the lady at his side, "is my great-aunt Persephone who has kindly agreed to act as Belle's chaperone."

Belle surveyed Persephone's disheveled appearance and decidedly harried expression and wondered if the lady had had any choice in the matter. After shifting her gaze to Alex's determined visage, she decided that Persephone most assuredly hadn't.

"Persephone?" Emma echoed weakly.

"My parents were interested in mythology," the lady said with a smile.

"You see," Alex said, "her parents liked mythology. That explains everything."

"It does?" Belle asked.

Alex shot her such a withering glare that Belle closed her mouth with alacrity. "Emma," he said softly, beginning a slow march up the stairs. "It's time to come home."

"I know, I miss you, too, but I was only going to be another week, and I cannot believe you dragged your aunt halfway across the country."

Persephone smiled. "All the way across the country, actually. I'm from Yorkshire."

Belle swallowed a laugh and decided that she and Persephone would suit each other very well, indeed.

"Pack your belongings, Emma."

Belle and Persephone watched the couple with unconcealed interest until they melted into each other's arms and Alex's lips captured Emma's in a scorching kiss. At that point, Persephone turned away. Belle kept one curious eye on the couple but had the good grace to blush.

But they just kept on kissing and kissing until it grew quite awkward for Belle, Persephone, and all six servants who were standing in the front hall. Trying to make the best of a very strange situation, Belle smiled brightly at Persephone and said, "How do you do? I'm Lady Arabella Blydon, but I expect you know that already."

The older woman nodded. "I am Miss Persephone Scott."

"It is nice to meet you, Miss Scott."

"Oh, please call me Persephone."

"And I am called Belle."

"Good, good. I imagine we will get on very well together." Persephone glanced stiffly over her shoulder and cleared her throat. "Are they still at it?" she asked in a whisper.

Belle looked up and nodded. "It's only for a week you know."

"They're going to do that for a *week*?"

"No," Belle laughed. "I meant my parents are due to return in a week. Then you'll be free to do whatever you want."

"I expect I shall. Alex paid me a king's ransom to get me to come down here."

"Really?"

"Yes. Of course, I'd have come if he'd only paid my traveling expenses. I don't get down to London very often. It's quite an adventure. But before I could say a thing, he came out and offered me a stupendous sum. I accepted immediately."

"Who wouldn't?"

"Who, indeed." Persephone made a few awkward jerking motions with her head.

"Still kissing," Belle said, interpreting her signal correctly.

"Their behavior is not exactly, er, polite. Especially with a young unmarried lady in the vicinity." She looked over at Belle and smiled. "I've never been a chaperone before. How did I sound?"

"Not nearly stern enough."

"Was I not?"

"No, but I much prefer you this way. And don't worry about them." Belle flicked her head over her shoulder at the passionate couple on the second floor landing. "They are usually much more circumspect. I expect it is just that they missed each other. They've been apart for a week, you know."

"Well, I suppose we will have to excuse them. They certainly do love each other."

"Yes, they do," Belle said softly, and then she knew that she was doing the right thing about John because she really wanted someone in her life who loved and desired her so much that he would kiss her for five minutes straight in front of eight witnesses. And it stood to reason, of course, that the man in question would have to be someone she would also want so desperately that she would return the kiss, onlookers be damned.

Belle sighed. It would have to be John. She suddenly realized, however, that she hadn't yet told Emma about the plan. "Oh dear," she blurted out. She had to find a moment alone with her before Alex dragged her off to Westonbirt, and at the rate they were going, they would be joined at the lips the entire way back.

"Is something wrong?" Persephone inquired.

"Oh dear." Belle darted up the stairs and

grabbed Emma's hand out of Alex's hair. "So sorry, Alex, it looked like fun, but I've got to speak with Emma. It's quite important." She gave Emma a rather vigorous tug. Alex had fallen into some kind of passion-induced haze, and it was probably this weakness which allowed Belle to pull Emma out of his embrace. Within seconds, the two women were ensconced in Emma's bedroom. Belle quickly locked the door. "I need you to do something for me," she said.

Emma just stared at her blankly, still quite dazed from Alex's passionate kiss.

Belle snapped her fingers a couple of times in front of her cousin's face. "Hello? Wake up! You're not being kissed anymore."

"What? Oh, sorry. What do you need?"

Belle quickly laid out her plan. Emma wasn't certain that it would work but said that she'd play her part. "Just one thing," she added. "Is he really going to believe that you've gotten over him so quickly?"

"I don't know, but if he does come to London, he'll soon learn that I have not been sitting here like a sad lump. Dunford's been making sure that I've been introduced to any number of eligible bachelors. Three earls last week and one marquess, I think. It's really quite surprising how many people are here in London during the off-season."

"I hope you know what you're doing."

"I have no idea what I'm doing," Belle confessed with a sigh. "But I don't know what else to do."

John threw himself into his work at Bletchford Manor, overseeing renovations on the house, and even helping out on one or two of them. The physical labor was oddly soothing; occasionally he even managed to think about something other than Belle.

The work on his house and the surrounding lands kept him busy during the day, and he tried to devote his evenings to financial matters, eager to rebuild the funds he had used to purchase Bletchford Manor. But as evening melted into night, he found that his thoughts strayed to the blond maiden who was presently residing three hours away in London. She certainly had wasted no time in getting as far away from him as possible.

He couldn't stop himself from recalling every moment he'd spent in her company, and each scene he played out in his head was like a small dagger to his heart. He woke up nearly every night hard and aroused, and he knew that he'd been dreaming about her. He thought briefly about heading to a nearby village to find a woman who could satisfy his ache but gave up the idea, realizing that no woman could make him feel better. No woman besides Belle, at least.

He was surprised when Buxton announced that the Duchess of Ashbourne had arrived. *You will not ask her about Belle*, he told himself as he went to the blue salon to greet her.

"Hello, your grace," he said politely. Emma looked in fine spirits, and her hair seemed especially bright.

"I thought I told you to call me Emma," she scolded.

"Sorry. Habit, I guess."

"How have you been?"

"Fine. How's Belle?" If he could have kicked himself without the duchess noticing, he would have done so. Hard.

Emma smiled slyly as she realized that Belle's plan was going to be a resounding success. "She's doing quite well, actually."

"Good. I'm happy for her." And he was, he supposed, although it would have been nice if she had pined for him just a little bit.

"She's thinking about getting married, actually."

"*What?*"

Emma found herself wishing that she had some way of capturing John's expression, for truly it was priceless. "I said she's thinking about getting married."

"I heard you," John snapped.

Emma smiled again.

"And who is the lucky man?"

"She wouldn't tell me, actually. She just said that it was someone she met in London last week. An earl, I think, or maybe it was a marquess. She's been going to quite a number of parties."

"Obviously." John didn't even make an effort to keep the sarcasm out of his voice.

"She seems to be enjoying herself."

"She certainly wasted no time in finding herself a man," he said peevishly.

"Well, you know how it is."

"Know how what is?"

"Oh, love at first sight and all that."

"Yes," John said darkly.

"Actually," Emma said, leaning forward.

"What?"

I'm brilliant, Emma thought. *Absolutely brilliant.* "Actually," she repeated. "She said he reminded her a little of you."

Fury, jealousy, outrage, and a hundred other nasty emotions raced through John in exceedingly unhealthy proportions. "How nice for her," he bit out icily.

"I knew you'd be pleased," Emma said in a breezy tone. "After all, you two were such good friends."

"Yes, we were."

"I'll make sure that you get an invitation to the wedding. I'm certain that it will mean a lot to Belle to have you there."

"I'll be busy then."

"But you don't know when the wedding will be. She hasn't set a date."

"I'll be busy," John repeated, his voice hard.

"I see."

"Yes, I'm sure you do." John wondered if Alex's wife was uncommonly cruel or just exceedingly naive. "It has been very kind of you to stop by with news of Belle, but I'm afraid I have business I must attend to immediately."

"Yes, of course," Emma said, standing up with a sunny smile. "I shall convey your best wishes to Belle." When he made no comment, she offered him an innocent look and asked, "You do wish her the best, don't you?"

John only growled.

Emma stepped back and smothered a laugh. "I shall tell her you said hello, then. And please do come and call soon. Alex would love to see you, I'm sure." As she walked down the steps to her carriage, it occurred to her that she'd better send Belle a note saying that John would be arriving in London very, very soon.

John watched Emma disappear down the drive from his front steps. As soon as she was gone from view, he swore viciously, kicked the side of his house for good measure, and strode back to his study where he poured himself a tall glass of whiskey.

"Goddamn, good for nothing, fickle female," he muttered, taking a healthy swig. The liquor burned a trail down his throat, but John could barely feel it.

"Getting married?" he said loudly. "Married? Ha! I hope she's miserable." He drained the rest of the glass and poured a new one. Unfortunately the whiskey did not dull the pain that was squeezing at his heart. When he had told Belle that she'd be better off without him, he'd never dreamed that it would be this excruciatingly painful to think of her in another man's arms. Oh, he'd figured that she would get married someday, but the image had been hazy and unfocused. Now he couldn't get the picture of her and this faceless earl or whoever he was out of his mind. He kept seeing her smile in that impish way of hers and then lean up to kiss him. And then once they were married, oh God, it was awful. He could see Belle, nude in the candlelight, holding her arms out to this stranger. And then her husband would cover her body with his and . . .

John drained his second glass of whiskey. At least he didn't know what this man looked like. He certainly didn't need to picture the scene in any more vivid detail.

"Damn, damn, damn, damn, damn," he muttered, punctuating each "damn" with a kick to the side of his desk. The desk won the battle handily, being made of solid oak, and John's foot would no doubt show bruises the next day.

Was it going to be like this for the rest of his life? He had gone into the village the other day, and every woman had reminded him of Belle.

He'd bumped into one who had eyes that were almost as blue. Another had been just about her height. Would his heart lurch every time he saw a blond woman across a crowd?

He sank down to the floor, leaning against the side of his desk. "I'm an ass," he moaned. "An ass."

And that litany sounded in his mind until he finally fell asleep.

He was walking through a house. It was lush, opulent. Intrigued, John walked further.

What was that strange thumping sound?

It was coming from a room at the end of the hall. He walked closer, terrified by what he thought he might find there.

Closer. Closer. It wasn't thumping, after all. John felt the fear begin to drain from his body. It was . . . dancing. Someone was dancing. He could hear the music now.

He pushed open the door. It was a ballroom. Hundreds of couples whirled around in effortless waltzes. And at the center . . .

His heart stopped. It was Belle.

She looked so beautiful. She threw back her head and laughed. Had he ever seen her so happy?

John moved closer. He tried to get a good look at her dance partner, but the man's features were always blurred.

One by one, the other couples dropped from view until there were only three people left in the room. John, Belle, and Him.

He had to get away. He couldn't bear to watch Belle with her lover. He tried to move, but his feet were glued to the spot. He tried to look away, but his neck refused to twist.

The music grew faster. The dancing couple whirled out of control until ... they weren't dancing.

John narrowed his eyes, trying to get a better look. What was happening?

The couple was arguing. Belle looked as if she were trying to explain something to the man. And then he hit her. The back of his hand slammed across her cheek, his rings leaving red welts across her pale skin.

John yelled out her name, but the couple didn't seem to hear him. He tried to go to her, but the feet that had just refused to carry him from the room wouldn't take him in the opposite direction, either.

The man hit her again, and she fell to the floor, her arms rising up to shield her head. John reached out, but his arms weren't nearly long enough. He called her name, over and over, and then, blessedly, the couple faded from view.

The next morning John woke up feeling not quite so sorry for himself, although he did have a headache distinctly worthy of pity, self or otherwise. He wasn't at all certain what he had dreamed about last night, but whatever it was, it had left him with the conviction that he wasn't going to sit around and watch Belle throw her life away on some dissolute earl.

That he did not know for certain that her possible fiancé was an earl or that he was dissolute did not enter the picture. What if he beat her? What if he forbade her to read? John knew that he wasn't good enough for her, but he was no longer certain that anyone else was, either. John, at least, would try to make her happy. He would give her everything he had, give her every piece of his soul that was still intact.

Belle belonged with someone who would appreciate her wit and wisdom as well as her grace and beauty. He could just imagine her having to sneak books into the house behind the back of her disapproving aristocratic husband. He probably wouldn't even consult her on any important decisions, feeling that a woman could not be intelligent enough to offer a worthy opinion.

No, Belle needed him. He had to save her from a disastrous marriage. And then, he supposed, he'd simply marry her himself.

John wasn't unaware that he was about to pull one of the greatest about-faces in history. He could only hope that Belle would understand that he had realized she'd had been right all along. People made mistakes, didn't they? After all, he wasn't some infallible storybook hero.

"No, Persephone, I think you should stay away from lavender."

Belle and her companion had gone shopping. Persephone was eager to part with some of the ample funds given to her by Alex.

"I've always liked lavender, though. It's one of my favorite colors."

"Well, then we shall find a gown with lavender accents, but I fear that the color does not suit you as well as some others."

"What would you suggest?"

Belle smiled at the older woman as she fingered a bolt of dark green velvet and held it up under her chin. She was quite enjoying her time with Alex's maiden aunt, although it did at times seem that their roles were reversed. Persephone constantly asked for her opinion on all matters, from food to fashion to literature. She rarely left Yorkshire, she'd explained, and had no idea how to go about in London. Still, Persephone had a quick wit and an understated sense of humor which entertained Belle to no end.

But it wasn't Persephone's companionship which was bringing such a ready smile to Belle's face that afternoon. She had just received an urgent message from Emma instructing her to be ready for John's arrival any day now. Apparently he had not taken the news of her impending marriage well.

Good, Belle thought with not a little smugness. She shuddered to think how she would have reacted had someone brought her similar news of John. She probably would have wanted to scratch the offending woman's eyes out. And she was not normally a violent person.

"Do you really think this green will do the trick?" Persephone asked, frowning at the fabric.

Belle snapped out of her reverie. "Hmmm? Oh, yes. You've got such nice green flecks in your eyes. I think it'll bring them out."

"Do you think so?" Persephone held up the bolt of velvet and looked in the mirror, tilting her head in a decidedly feminine manner.

"Oh very much, and if you are so partial to lavender, perhaps you would be willing to substitute this deep violet color. I think it will look lovely on you."

"Hmm, maybe you're right. I do adore violets. I've always worn violet scented perfume."

Persephone's interest sufficiently engaged, Belle wandered over to Madame Lambert, the not entirely French proprietress of the shop.

"Ah, Lady Arabella," she gushed. "Eet eez so

good to see you again. We have not seen you for many months."

"I've been out in the country," Belle replied congenially. "But if I might ask you a private question?"

Madame Lambert's blue eyes sparkled with excitement, and, undoubtedly, the prospect that Belle's request would somehow make her a mint of money. "Yes?"

"I need a gown. A very special gown. Two very special gowns, actually. Or perhaps three." Belle frowned as she contemplated her forthcoming purchase. She needed to look ravishing when John came to London. Unfortunately, she had no idea when he would arrive, or even—banish the thought—if he would arrive.

"Zat should not be a problem, my lady."

"I need a different sort of gown than I usually purchase. Something more . . . alluring."

"I see, my lady." Madame Lambert smiled knowingly. "You perhaps wish to attract a particular gentleman. I will make you ravishing. Now when do you need zese gowns?"

"Tonight?" Belle's answer was more of a question than a reply.

"My Gawd!" Madame Lambert shrieked, completely forgetting her accent. "I am good but I cannot perform miracles!"

"Will you be quiet?" Belle whispered urgently, looking nervously around. She liked Persephone, but she didn't think that she needed to know that her charge was planning a seduction. "I only need one of them tonight. The rest can wait. At least until tomorrow. It shouldn't be that difficult. You have all my measurements. I assure you I haven't grown fat since our last meeting."

"You ask a great deal, my lady."

"If I weren't absolutely convinced that you could do it, I wouldn't have asked. After all, I could have gone over to Madame Laroche." Belle smiled and let the words hang in the air.

Madame Lambert sighed dramatically and said, "I have a gown. Eet was for another lady. Well, not a lady exactly." At Belle's horrified expression, she hastened to add, "But she had exquisite taste, I assure you. She, er, lost her source of funds and could not pay for eet. With a few minor alterations, I think eet will fit you."

Belle nodded and called over to Persephone that she was going to the back room for just a moment. She followed Madame Lambert, who led her to a closet door. "Eef you want to attract a man without appearing vulgar," the dressmaker said, "then zees is what you need." With a flourish, she pulled out a gown of midnight blue velvet which was startling in its simplicity. Free of adornment, it let its elegant cut show its style.

Belle fingered the soft velvet, admiring the way the bodice was shot through with silver thread. "It's lovely," she said. "But it isn't very different from what I already own."

"From zee front, eet ees just like the rest, but from zee back . . . " Madame Lambert turned the dress around, and Belle realized that most of her back would be revealed. "You will need to wear your hair up," Madame continued, "so you will not obscure zee effect."

Belle reluctantly tore her gaze from the gown and looked at the dressmaker. "I'll take it."

John made excellent time to London, especially considering that he hadn't given Wheatley much notice. The efficient valet had packed up his clothing with remarkable speed. John hoped that it would not take long to win back Belle's favor, for he doubted that he had enough elegant clothing to last much more than a fortnight. He had always been a stickler for quality, but quality was expensive, and as a result he didn't have much of it.

He took a deep breath as he climbed the steps to his older brother's town house. He hadn't seen Damien for years, although he had received a brief congratulatory note on his being raised to the peerage. Damien would probably not be thrilled to see him, but one couldn't very well turn out one's own brother, could one? And besides, John didn't have any other options. He certainly didn't have time to find a suitable residence to rent. For all he knew, Belle could be engaged already.

Taking a deep breath, he picked up the heavy brass knocker and let it slam down against the door. A butler appeared almost instantly.

"Is the earl available?" John inquired politely.

"Who may I say is calling?"

John handed him a crisp white calling card. The butler took note of his last name and raised an eyebrow.

"His brother," John said simply.

The butler ushered John into a spacious sitting room off of the main hallway. A few minutes later Damien entered the room, surprise evident on his face. As always, John was struck by the family resemblance between them. Damien was an older and slightly softer version of himself and did not look his thirty-nine years. He had always been quite handsome, classically so, whereas John's face was a bit too lean and angular to fit the guidelines of aristocratic elegance.

"It's been an age," Damien finally said, holding out his hand. "What brings you to town?"

John took his brother's hand and shook it in a firm grasp. "I have urgent business in London, and I fear I did not have time to procure lodgings ahead of time. I was hoping that I could impose upon your hospitality while I conduct my affairs."

"Of course."

John had known Damien would agree. He doubted that his brother was enthusiastic, or even remotely pleased about the request, but Damien had always placed great stock in good manners and breeding and certainly would not refuse hospitality to his own brother. As long, of course, as his brother did not abuse this privilege.

"I thank you," John replied. "I assure you that should it become apparent that my business cannot be completed in a fortnight, I shall look elsewhere for lodgings immediately."

Damien graciously inclined his head. "Have you brought anyone with you?"

"Just my valet."

"Excellent, then I may assume that you have brought evening clothes?"

"Yes."

"Good. I have been invited to a small party this evening, and the hostess sent me a note not an hour ago asking if I might bring an extra man. Someone has gone ill, it seems, and now she has too many women."

The thought of going out in society did not appeal to John in the least, but he agreed because he might ascertain just who Belle was thinking about marrying.

"Excellent," Damien replied. "I shall send a note round to Lady Forthright immediately. Oh, and you shall be able to meet the woman I am thinking of courting. It is high time I got myself a wife, you know. I really do need an heir."

"Of course," John murmured.

"I think she is an excellent choice, although I do need to interview her further. Good breeding and quite lovely. Intelligent, but not ingratiatingly so."

"She sounds a paragon."

Damien turned to him quite suddenly. "Perhaps you know her. She recently spent a month or so visiting relatives out near your new home. What is it called? I can't remember."

John felt an evil, sick sensation form in the pit of his stomach and then spread rapidly to his every extremity. "It's called Bletchford Manor," he said coldly.

"Terrible name. You really must change it."

"I intend to. You were about to say ..."

"Oh yes. Her name is Lady Arabella Blydon."

Chapter 11

⌒◯◯⌒

John felt as if he'd been hit. The air grew stifling, and Damien's face took on an undeservedly sinister expression. "I am familiar with Lady Arabella," he finally managed to get out. He took bittersweet pleasure in the fact that his voice sounded almost normal.

"How nice," Damien said mildly. "She'll be at the party this evening."

"I shall be pleased to renew her acquaintance."

"Good. I shall let you get settled in. Lightbody here will show you to your room. I'll stop by later to fill you in on this evening's details." Damien smiled blandly and left the room.

The butler entered with quick and silent efficiency and informed John that his belongings had been removed to a guest chamber upstairs. Still in a daze, John followed the butler to his room, where he proceeded to lie on the bed, stare at the ceiling, and let fury take over his entire being.

His brother? *His brother?* He'd never dreamed that Belle had this kind of malicious streak. He willed himself to clear his mind of her; he was getting far too upset, and she obviously wasn't worth it.

He wasn't successful. Every time he managed to steer his thoughts to food or horses or anything neutral, a familiar blond head and bright smile intervened. Then the smile melted into a sneer as he watched her cavort off with his brother.

Damn that woman!

When it was time to get ready for the party, John dressed with exceptional care in evening clothes of stark black relieved only by the crisp whiteness of his shirt and cravat. He and his brother exchanged polite conversation in the carriage, but John was much too preoccupied by the thought of seeing Belle again to pay very much attention to Damien. He didn't fault his brother for falling for her; he was only too familiar with her charms. But he was furious with Belle for deliberately seeking out such a vicious revenge against him.

When they arrived at the Forthright mansion, John allowed the butler to relieve him of his great coat and immediately scanned the room for Belle. She was over by the corner, animatedly talking to a tall, handsome man with dark hair and eyes. She had certainly been busy in the two weeks since their last meeting, he thought bitterly. Damien's attention was immediately captured by a friend of his, and since their hostess was nowhere to be found, John managed to avoid long, belabored introductions. He made his way over to Belle, willing himself to keep his raging anger in check. When he was just behind her, he said, "Good evening, Lady

Arabella," not quite trusting himself to say anything more.

Belle whirled around, so excited to see him that she missed the coldness in his voice. "John!" she said breathlessly, her eyes lighting up with unconcealed happiness. "What a surprise." He had come. He had come. Relief and joy washed over her, then were replaced by irritation. Damn, she hadn't worn that daring blue dress. She'd never dreamed he'd arrive in London so quickly.

"Is it?"

Belle blinked. "Excuse me?"

"Perhaps you should introduce me to your friend." John wanted nothing other than to speak to her alone, but he saw no way to ignore the man at her side.

"Oh, of course," Belle said, stumbling on her words. "Lord Blackwood, this is my good friend Mr. William Dunford."

Dunford smiled at her in a manner that was much too familiar for John's taste. "Didn't know you knew my first name, Belle," he teased.

"Oh, hush, Dunford. Next time I'm going to call you Edward, just to be contrary."

A fresh spurt of jealousy raced through John at Belle and Dunford's familiarity. Nevertheless, he automatically extended his hand. Dunford shook it, murmured a greeting and then politely excused himself. Once Dunford left, however, John allowed his true emotions to come to the surface.

Belle gasped and actually stepped back from the sheer fury she saw radiating from his eyes. "John, what is wrong?"

"How could you, Belle?" he spat out. "How could you?"

She blinked. She had expected jealousy, not this barely leashed rage. "How could I what?"

"Don't play the innocent. It doesn't suit you."

"What are you talking about?" Belle repeated, her voice growing nervous.

He only glared at her.

Then she remembered the lie that Emma had told him in order to get him to come to London. Maybe he thought that she and Dunford... "Is this about Dunford?" she asked quickly. "Because if it is, then there is nothing to worry about. He's quite an old friend of mine, but that is all. He's Alex's best friend, too."

"This isn't about him," John hissed. "It's about my brother."

"*Who?*"

"You heard me."

"Your brother?"

John nodded curtly.

"I don't even know your brother."

"If you keep up your lies, Belle, they're going to trip you up. And believe me, I'm not going to be around to catch you when you fall."

Belle swallowed. "I think we had better continue this conversation in private." Head held high, she swept out of the room and onto a balcony. By the time she reached her destination, some of her confusion had metamorphosed into anger, and when she turned to face him, her eyes were flashing wildly. "All right then, Lord Blackwood. Now that we are no longer performing before an audience, suppose you tell me just what that little scene was about."

"You are in no position to make demands on me, my lady."

"I assure you, I was not made aware of any such limitations on my behavior."

John seethed. He wanted to grab her by the shoulders and shake her. Shake her and shake her and shake her and then he . . . Oh Christ, he wanted to kiss her. But John was not in the habit of kissing people in anger so he simply stared her down and said, "I realize that my behavior toward you has not always been impeccable, but setting your cap after my brother is petty and childish. Not to mention disgusting—he's almost twice your age."

Belle still wasn't certain what precisely he was talking about, but she was in no mood to offer him any explanations so she lifted her chin and replied, "It's quite common for women of the *ton* to marry older men. I believe women mature faster, and thus we find men our age, *or sometimes as much as eight to ten years older*"—she said that part quite pointedly—"childish and bothersome."

"Are you calling me childish and bothersome?" His voice was low and deadly serious.

"I don't know. Was I? Now, if you'll excuse me, I am finding this *conversation* exceedingly childish and bothersome, and I have much better ways to spend my time."

John caught her in an iron grip. "I don't excuse you, thank you very much, and I have no better way to spend my time. I have one question for you, and I want it answered." He paused, and his silence forced Belle to look up into his eyes. "Have you always been this deliberately cruel?"

Belle yanked her arm back. "I'd slap you," she hissed. "But I'm afraid your cheek might contaminate my hand."

"I'm sure you'll be happy to know that you hurt me. But, my lady, it was only for a minute. Because then I realized that I want no part of any woman who would stoop to consorting with my brother just to have revenge against me."

Belle finally let her exasperation show. "For the

last time, John, I have no idea who your brother is."

"Well, that's interesting, because he knows who you are."

"Lots of people know who I am."

John put his face very close to hers. "He's thinking about marrying you."

"What?"

"You heard me."

Belle blinked in surprise as some of her anger dissipated in the confusion of the moment. "Well, I suppose that a number of men have thought about marrying me," she said thoughtfully. "But that doesn't mean that they have all asked me. And it certainly doesn't mean that I have reciprocated their feelings."

For a moment John wanted to believe her but then he remembered Emma's words. *She's thinking of getting married . . . An earl, I think . . . Actually, she said he reminded her of you.* "Don't try to talk your way out of this one, little girl," he warned.

"Little girl? Little girl! Contamination be damned, I think I will slap you!"

Belle raised her hand but John caught it easily. "You haven't my instincts, Belle," he said silkily. "You could never win a battle between us."

His air of condescension was just the spark to set Belle's anger into full-fledged fury. "Let me tell you a thing or two, Lord Blackwood," she raged, pulling her hand back. "First of all, I don't know who your brother is, and second of all, even if I did want to marry him, I fail to see why that would have anything to do with you, since you have made it abundantly clear that you want nothing at all to do with me. Thirdly, I see no reason why I would ever have to explain my actions to you of all people. So, fourthly—"

"Stop at three, Belle," John smirked. "You're losing my interest."

Belle shot him her best attempt at a sneer and raised her hand as if she were going to try to slap him again. His interest sufficiently engaged, she stomped mightily on his foot. John didn't even wince. She hadn't thought he would; her slippers were not made out of especially hard material. Still, her spirits were buoyed by her small victory, and she scoffed, "Your instincts are getting old, John."

"If you want to inflict real damage, get some sturdy shoes, Belle. And they might save you from another blister next time you go for a hike."

Belle swallowed as she remembered how gently John had cared for her foot. It was difficult to reconcile that tender man with the sardonic and insulting one standing in front of her now. With a deliberately impatient sigh, she looked him in the eye and said, "I would like to go back to the party. So if you would kindly step aside . . ."

John didn't budge. "Who are you thinking about marrying?"

Belle groaned to herself as her lies came back to haunt her. "None of your business," she snapped.

"I said, who are you thinking about marrying?"

"And *I* said, it's none of your business."

John leaned forward. "Not the Earl of Westborough by any chance?"

Belle's eyes bugged out. "*He's* your brother?"

She really didn't know they were related. No one could fake that expression. But John wanted to be absolutely certain, and so he said, "His surname didn't clue you in?"

"I only met him last week. I don't know his surname. He was simply introduced to me as the Earl of Westborough. And before you accuse me of any other heinous crimes, let me tell you that I only knew that your father was an earl because Alex told me. I had no idea which one."

John didn't say anything, just stood there silently judging her. Belle found his behavior extremely irritating and said, "Although now that you mention it, he does look a bit like you. Slightly more handsome, perhaps, and he doesn't limp."

John ignored her insult, recognizing it for what it was: a mindless jibe from one wounded animal to another. "You really didn't know he was my brother?"

"No! I swear to you!" And then Belle felt as if she were acting like she was begging his forgiveness when she hadn't done anything wrong, so she said, "But that doesn't change any of my plans."

"Plans? To marry him?"

"I'll inform you of my plans when I see fit." *I hope I inform myself of my plans when I see fit,* Belle thought wildly, *because I haven't any idea what I'm saying.*

John's hands clamped down on her shoulders. "Who are you planning to marry?"

"I'm not telling."

"You sound like a three-year-old."

"You're treating me like one."

"I'm only going to ask you one more time," John warned softly, his face approaching hers.

"You have no right to talk to me like this," Belle whispered. "Not after you—"

"For God's sake, Belle, don't throw that in my face again. I've already admitted that I've treated you badly. But I have to know. Don't you understand that? I have to know!" John's eyes blazed with passion. "Who are you planning to marry?"

Belle saw the desperation in his face and her resolve shattered. "No one!" she burst out. "No one! It was a lie! Just a lie to get you to come to London because I missed you." John's grip slackened with surprise, and she quickly jumped away and turned her back to him. "Now I'm completely humiliated. I hope you're satisfied."

John stared openmouthed at her back as her words sunk in. She still cared for him. The knowledge was a balm on his aching heart. But he did not for one moment appreciate the torture she'd put him through, and he fully intended to tell her that. "I do not like being manipulated," he said in a low voice.

Belle spun around, completely infuriated. "You don't like being manipulated? That's all you can say? You don't like being manipulated. Well, let me tell you something. I don't like being insulted. And I have found your behavior extremely insulting." She swept past him, her back ramrod straight, and her head held with a dignity she did not feel.

John was still so stunned by her unbelievable confession that her movement caught him by surprise, and he just barely caught hold of her fingertips when he tried to stop her. "Belle," he said, his voice ragged with emotion. "Please don't go."

Belle could have easily left the balcony; his grip on her was tenuous at best. But something in his hoarse voice compelled her to turn around, and once she did, she was spellbound by the fierce longing in his eyes. Her mouth went dry, and she forgot how to breathe. She had no idea how long she stood there, her gaze captured by this man who had come to mean so much to her. "John," she whispered. "I don't know what you want."

"I want you."

His words hung heavily in the air as Belle's heart begged her head to let herself believe him. What did he mean—he wanted her. Did he just want to touch her, to kiss her? She already knew that he was strongly attracted to her; he'd never been able to hide that, just as it had been quite obvious that she felt the same way.

Or did he want her in his life? As his friend, companion, or even his wife. Belle was terrified to ask the question. He'd already broken her heart once; she was not especially eager to let him do so again.

John saw the hesitation in her clear blue eyes and hated himself for having made her so wary. It was time to tell her how much he cared for her, he knew that. But his own fears held him back, and instead he said softly, "May I kiss you?"

Belle slowly nodded and stepped forward as John reached out and took her other hand in his. An overwhelming shyness washed over her, and she dropped her gaze.

"Don't look away," he whispered, moving his hand to her chin. He gently tilted her face up as he closed the distance between them. "You're so, so beautiful. And so kind and good and smart and funny and—"

"Stop!"

His nose was now resting on hers. "Why?"

"It's too much," she replied tremulously.

"No. No, it's not. It will never be too much."

He tilted his face so that his lips could gently brush over hers, and Belle felt a shiver of excitement rush through her. They continued in that way for a long minute, their lips just barely touching, until John could bear it no longer, and he crushed her to him.

"Oh God, Belle, I've been so, so stupid," he groaned. He didn't kiss her, just held her next to him as if he could somehow imprint her body on his. He clutched her tightly, hoping that some of her gentle goodness and courage would infuse into him. "I'm so sorry. I never meant to hurt you," he whispered raggedly. "It was the one thing I'd never meant to do."

"Shhh," Belle broke in. She couldn't bear to listen to him torture himself. "Just kiss me. Please. You see, I've been thinking about it for days, and I—"

John needed no further urging, and this kiss was as fierce as the first had been gentle. He devoured her hungrily, drinking her in as he murmured nonsensical words of love and desire. His hands were everywhere, and Belle wanted them everywhere, wanted him more than she'd ever imagined, more than she could ever understand. She sank her hands into his thick hair, marveling at the texture of it even as his lips slid down her neck to the base of her throat.

"I can't believe this," she moaned.

"What?" he managed to ask between nips.

"This. Everything. The way you make me feel. The—Oh!" Belle let out a whispered shriek as his mouth traveled to the sensitive skin just behind her ear.

"What else can't you believe?" he asked devilishly.

"That I want you to keep on kissing me," she answered in a feverish voice. "And that there is a party still going on in the next room."

Belle's words had an unintended effect, and with great effort John pulled away from her and let out a low curse. "I'd almost forgotten," he muttered. "Someone could discover us any minute."

Belle felt unbelievably cold without his arms around her, and she couldn't stop herself from reaching out to him. "Please," she whispered. "I've missed you so."

She was a mighty temptation, but John held firm.

"I didn't come all the way to London just to ruin your reputation."

"I wish you would," she muttered under her breath.

"I beg your pardon?"

"Nothing."

"We'll have to go back in separately."

Belle smiled at John's concern. "Don't worry. I'm certain Dunford is covering for us splendidly." At John's raised eyebrow, she added, "I told him a little about you."

He shot her such a look that she was compelled to further explain, "Just a little, though, so don't worry that I've spilled all your secrets."

John pushed down the guilt that bubbled within him. She didn't know his biggest secret, and he'd have to tell her eventually. But not now. He didn't have to tell her now. "Your hair is mussed," he said instead. "You might want to do something about that. I'll go back to the party first. I'm sure my brother is looking for me."

Belle nodded, and together they walked into the darkened hall. Before they parted ways, however, she took his hand. "John," she said softly. "What happens now? I have to know."

"What happens now?" he repeated with a jaunty grin. "Why, I court you. Isn't that what's supposed to happen next?"

She answered him with a smile and ran off.

When John reentered the drawing room he was not surprised to find his brother regarding him with a curious expression.

"Where did you disappear to?" Damien inquired.

"Just wanted to get some fresh air." If Damien had noted that Lady Arabella had left the room at the same time, he didn't mention it. "Why don't you introduce me to a few of your friends?" John suggested.

Damien nodded politely. Sometime while he was busy introducing John, Belle reappeared and made a beeline for Dunford.

"That was some exit," he said with a grin.

Belle flushed. "Nobody noticed, did they?"

Dunford shook his head. "I don't think so. I was just keeping an eye on you in case you needed any sort of rescuing. In the future, however, I'd keep my trysts to under five minutes were I you."

"Oh dear. How long was I, er, were we gone?"

"Longer than you'd intended, I'm sure. I set it about that you'd gotten something on your dress. All the ladies were properly sympathetic."

"You're priceless, Dunford." Belle grinned.

"Ah, there you are, Lady Arabella."

Belle turned to see Lord Westborough walking toward her. John was at his side, a knowing smile on his face.

"How nice to see you again, my lord," she murmured politely.

"And I believe you have already met my brother," Damien added. "Lord Blackwood."

"Yes, of course. We are well acquainted." Belle winced inwardly at her double-entendre and refused to look up at John, certain that she would be rewarded with a devilish grin. She was saved, however, from any potentially embarrassing conversation by the arrival of their hostess, Lady Forthright.

"Ah, Westborough," she shrilled. "I did not see you come in. And Lady Arabella, it is always a pleasure."

Belle smiled and bobbed a polite curtsy.

"And this must be your brother," Lady Forthright continued.

Damien nodded and introduced them. He then saw another friend and excused himself, leaving John and Belle in the clutches of their none too gentle hostess.

"Lord Blackwood? A baron, are you?" she queried. "Hmmm. I'm not familiar with the title."

Belle's insides clenched in anger. Lady Forthright had always been a meddlesome woman who tried to cover her lack of self-confidence by insulting others.

"It's a relatively new title, my lady," John said, his expression deliberately even.

"Just how new is 'relatively'?" She smiled coyly at her little joke and then looked to Belle to see if she also disdained this newcomer to their ranks. Belle answered her with a scowl that intensified when she realized that the room had grown a bit quieter in the last few moments. Dear Lord, didn't anyone have anything better to do than listen to Lady Forthright's inane babblings? And where had Damien gone? Shouldn't he defend his brother?

"A few years," John replied quietly. "I was honored for military service."

"I see." Lady Forthright drew herself up and squared her shoulders, preening for her audience. "Well, I'm sure you're very brave, but I cannot approve of this reckless handing out of titles. It wouldn't do for the peerage to get too—shall we say—undiscriminating."

"Lord Blackwood is the son of an earl," Belle said quietly.

"Oh, I do not fault his bloodlines," their hostess replied. "But we mustn't get like those Russians who give out titles to just about everybody. Did you know that if one is a Russian duke, all of one's sons get to be dukes as well? Before long the entire country is going to be overrun with dukes. It will be anarchy. Mark my words—that country is going to collapse, and it will be because of all those dukes."

"An interesting supposition," Belle said, her tone frosty.

Lady Forthright didn't seem to notice Belle's irritation. "I find all these new titles somewhat gauche, don't you?"

Belle heard indrawn breaths all around her as all her eavesdroppers waited for her reply. Damien wandered back to her side, and she gave him a tight smile. "I'm sorry, Lady Forthright," she said sweetly. "I am afraid I do not follow your meaning. Your husband is the *fifth* Viscount Forthright?"

"The sixth," she replied sharply. "And my father was the eighth Earl of Windemere."

"I see," Belle said slowly. "So then neither of them did anything to earn their titles other than simply being born?"

"I am certain that I misunderstand your implications, Lady Arabella. And may I remind you that your family's earldom goes back for several centuries?"

"Oh no, I assure you that I am well aware of that fact, Lady Forthright. And we regard the earldom as an important family honor. But my father is a good man precisely because he is a good man, not because he possesses an ancient title. And as for Lord Blackwood, I find his title all the more appealing because it represents the nobility of the man standing before you, not of some long-dead ancestor."

"A pretty speech, Lady Arabella, especially for one who obviously enjoys all the perks of her position. But not entirely appropriate for a gently-reared lady. You have become something of a bluestocking."

"At last! A compliment. I never thought to hear one from your lips. Now if you will excuse me, I am growing weary of this party." Belle purposefully turned her back on her hostess, well aware of the scandal such bad manners would create. "John, it was lovely seeing you again. I hope you call on me soon, but I must find Dunford and have him escort me back home. Good evening."

And while John was still reeling from her passionate defense, she honored him with her most radiant smile and swept past him. He was left facing a furious Lady Forthright who simply "harumphed" at him and bustled away.

John couldn't help himself. He started to laugh.

Later that evening, while the Blackwood brothers were on their way home, Damien brought up the subject of Belle's now obvious friendship with John. "I did not realize that you and Lady Arabella knew each other so well," he said with a frown.

One side of John's mouth twisted up in a wry smile. "She said we were well acquainted, didn't she?"

"Her passionate defense of your position would indicate that you are *quite* well acquainted."

"Well, we are quite."

Damien let the matter drop for a few minutes, but eventually his curiosity got the better of him. "Do you intend to court her?"

"I have already said as much to the lady in question."

"I see."

John sighed. He was behaving rather sharply with his brother, and Damien really didn't deserve it. "I apologize if this puts a crimp in your plans. I assure you I did not know that you had tender feelings for Belle before I arrived. If you must know, she was the reason I came to town in the first place."

Damien pondered that slowly. "I wouldn't say I have *tender* feelings for her. I merely thought she would make me a good wife."

John looked at him oddly. He wondered if his brother's emotions ever ventured beyond appreciation or mild dislike.

"It is obvious, however," Damien continued, "that we would not suit at all. She is a great beauty, to be sure, but I cannot have a wife who spouts out such radical notions in public."

John's lips twitched. "Surely you, too, don't begrudge me my title."

"Of course not." Damien appeared affronted by the accusation. "You earned that title. And our father was, of course, an earl. But you must admit, too many cits are making their way into the aristocracy, whether by purchase or marriage. Lord only knows what's to become of us."

"Belle likes to read," John blurted out, just to make absolutely sure that his brother's interest in her would not resurface. "She's read the complete works of Shakespeare."

Damien shook his head. "I cannot imagine what I was thinking. Bluestockings can be such a nuisance, no matter how beautiful. They're so demanding."

John smiled.

"She wouldn't do, at all," Damien continued. "But you should try for her if you want. She'd be a great catch for a man of your position. Although I must warn you, her parents probably wouldn't approve of the match. I should think she could get a duke if she wanted."

"I imagine she could," John murmured. "If, of course, that was what she wanted."

The carriage came to a halt in front of Damien's town house. When they entered the main hall, Lightbody greeted them with a note which he said had been left expressly for Lord Blackwood. Curious, John unfolded the paper.

I am in London.

John frowned as he remembered the two similar messages he'd received a few weeks earlier. He'd thought that they had been meant for Bletchford Manor's previous owners, but now he realized that he was mistaken.

"Someone you know?" Damien inquired.

"I'm not sure," John replied slowly. "I'm not sure at all."

Chapter 12

John arrived at Belle's house the next morning, arms laden with chocolates and flowers. It amazed him how easy this was—to simply allow her to lighten his heart. He'd been smiling all morning.

Belle was unable to keep the delight from her eyes when she came downstairs to greet him. "To what do I owe the pleasure of your company?" she asked with a bright smile.

"I said I was going to court you, didn't I?" John responded, thrusting the flowers into her arms. "Consider yourself courted."

"How romantic," she said, not without a twinge of sarcasm.

"I hope you like chocolates."

Belle suppressed a smile. He was trying very hard. "I love them."

"Excellent." He shot her a jaunty grin. "Mind if I have one?"

"Not at all."

Persephone chose that moment to sail down the stairs. "Good morning, Belle," she said. "Won't you introduce me to your guest?"

Belle did the honors, and while John was deciding which chocolate to pop in his mouth, Persephone leaned over and whispered, "He's very handsome."

Belle nodded.

"And he looks quite virile."

Belle's eyes widened. "Persephone," she whispered. "I feel I must inform you that this is not the normal type of conversation between a chaperone and her charge."

"Is it not? It ought to be, I think. Ah well, I fear I will never get this chaperoning business right. Pray do not tell Alex of my shortcomings."

"I like you just the way you are," Belle said honestly.

"Isn't that sweet of you, dear? Well, I'm off. The coachman has promised to take me on a tour of London, and I want to make sure we get to all the dangerous parts before dark."

Considering that it wasn't yet noon, Belle could only wonder as to the length of Persephone's route, but she didn't say a word as the older lady fluttered out the door.

"Not exactly the sternest of chaperones," John commented.

"No."

"Shall we retire to a parlor? I'm desperate to kiss you, and I'd rather not do it in the hall."

Belle blushed but led the way to a nearby drawing room.

John kicked the door shut and hauled her into his arms. "Chaperone-less for the entire day," he murmured between kisses. "Was ever a man so blessed?"

"Was ever a *woman* so blessed?" Belle countered.

"I think not. Come over here to the sofa so I can ply you with chocolates and flowers." He took her hand and pulled her along with him as he crossed the room.

Belle giggled softly as she let him lead her to the sofa. She had never seen him so lighthearted, so carefree. There was still a thin veil of sadness and hesitation in his eyes, but it was nothing compared to the haunted look she'd seen back in Oxfordshire. "The only person you're plying with those chocolates is yourself. You've already had three."

John sat and pulled her down next to him. "There is no point in bringing a lady an edible gift unless you like it, too. Here, have one. They're quite good." He picked up a sweet and held it in front of her mouth.

Belle smiled and bit away half of it, licking her lips with deliberate seductiveness as she chewed. "It's exquisite," she murmured.

"Yes, it is." He wasn't talking about chocolate.

Belle leaned forward for the rest of the candy and took it in her mouth, daringly licking his fingers as she did so. "A little bit melted on your skin," she said innocently.

"A little bit melted on *your* skin, too." He moved toward her and licked the corner of her mouth, sending shivers of desire right to the tips of her toes. Leaning forward, he ran his tongue along the soft edge of her upper lip. "I missed a bit here," he murmured. "And here." He moved to her lower lip, which he teased between his teeth.

Belle had quite forgotten how to breathe. "I think I like being courted," she whispered.

"Haven't you ever been before?" John took a little nip of her ear.

"Not like this."

"Good." He smiled possessively.

Belle arched her neck as he ran his lips along her tender skin. "I hope you haven't conducted any other courtships with this particular brand of, er, persuasion."

"Never," he promised.

"Good." Belle's smile was equally possessive. "But you know," she said, taking a quick gasp of air as his hand stole around and cupped her breast. "There is more to courting than flowers and chocolate."

"Mmm-hmm. There is kissing." He squeezed her breast through her dress, causing Belle to squeal with wonder.

"Of course," Belle sighed. "I wasn't forgetting that."

"I'll do my best to keep that at the forefront of your mind." John was busy figuring out the best way to free one of her perfect little breasts from the confines of her attire.

"That's fine. But you must remember, I won't let you forget that you owe me a poem."

"You're a stubborn wench, aren't you?" John finally decided that the best course of action was simply to push the dress down and thank God that the fashions of the day did not require endless streams of buttons.

"Not particularly." Belle laughed softly. "But I still want that poem."

John momentarily diverted her attention by carrying out his plans. He smiled and moaned with pure masculine pleasure as he looked down on her dusky nipple, puckered with desire. He licked his lips.

"John—you're not going to . . . ?"

He nodded and did.

Belle felt all her limbs go weak, and she melted into the sofa, pulling John along with her. He worshipped her breast for a full minute and then moved on to the other one. Belle was helpless against his sensual onslaught and couldn't control the soft cries of desire escaping through her lips.

"Say something," she finally moaned.

"Shall I compare thee to a Summer's day?" he quoted. "Thou art—"

"Oh, please, John," Belle said, pulling his head off of her breast so that she could look into his laughing brown eyes. "If you're going to plagiarize, at least have the sense not to choose something so famous."

"If you don't stop talking this instant, Belle, I shall be moved to drastic action."

"Drastic action? Now that sounds interesting." She pulled his mouth back down onto hers and kissed him eagerly.

Just then they heard an agonizingly familiar voice coming from the hallway.

"What a ninny I am to forget a warm pair of gloves," Persephone said. "It's so nippy out."

Belle and John jumped away from each other instantly. When Belle was not hasty enough in righting her appearance, John took charge of the situation and yanked her dress back up, practically to her chin. As they frantically tried to remedy their mussed appearances, they heard the soft murmur of another voice, probably that of the servant to whom Persephone had been speaking.

"Isn't that kind of you?" Persephone said. "I'll just wait in the drawing room with Belle and her friend while you fetch them for me."

Belle had just managed to throw herself in a

chair opposite the sofa when her chaperone entered. "Persephone, what a surprise."

Persephone leveled a rather shrewd look in her direction. For all her flittering about, she was no dullard. "I'm sure."

John stood politely at Persephone's entrance. "Would you like a chocolate?" he asked, holding the box out toward her.

"I rather would, actually."

Belle fought a blush as she remembered what had happened when John had offered *her* a chocolate. Luckily, Persephone was too busy choosing between the sweets to notice.

"I do like the ones with nuts," she said, plucking one out of the box.

"Is it so very cold out?" Belle inquired. "I heard you saying that you needed warmer gloves."

"Well, it certainly has cooled off since yesterday. Although I must say it's quite hot inside."

Belle bit back a smile. When she looked over at John she noticed that he had started to cough.

"Your gloves, madam."

"Excellent." Persephone stood and walked over to the footman who had just entered the room. "I'll be on my way, then."

"Have a good time," Belle called out.

"Oh, I shall, my dear. I certainly shall." Persephone walked out and started to close the door behind her. "Actually," she said, blushing slightly. "I believe I'll just leave this door, er, open, if you don't mind. Better circulation of the air, you know."

"Of course," John said. And then when Persephone was gone, he leaned forward and whispered, "I'm shutting the door just as soon as she's out of the house."

"Hush," Belle admonished.

The minute they heard the front door close, John got up and shut the door to the drawing room. "This is ridiculous," he muttered. "I'm almost thirty years of age. I have better things to do than sneak around behind some chaperone's back."

"You do?"

"It's damned undignified, I tell you." He made his way back over to the sofa and sat down.

"Is your leg bothering you?" Belle asked, concern clouding her eyes. "You seem to be limping a bit more than usual."

John blinked at the change of subject and looked down at his limb. "I guess so. I hadn't noticed. I've grown used to the pain, I imagine."

Belle crossed over to the sofa and sat back down. "Would it help if I rubbed it?" She placed her hands on his leg and began to rub the muscle just above his knee.

John closed his eyes and laid back. "That feels marvelous." He let her continue her ministrations for several minutes until he said, "Belle . . . about last night."

"Yes?" She continued massaging his leg.

John opened his eyes and stilled her hand by placing his own over her fingers. She blinked, sobered by his serious expression.

"No one has . . . " His mouth opened and closed as he searched for words. "No one has ever defended me like that."

"What about your family?"

"I didn't see very much of them when I was growing up. They were quite busy."

"Were they?" Belle said, disapproval evident in her voice.

"It was always made clear to me that I would have to make my own way in the world."

Belle stood abruptly and walked over to a vase,

nervously rearranging its flowers. "I would never say something like that to my child," she said, her tone strained. "Never. I think a child should be loved and cherished and—" She whirled around. "Don't you?"

He nodded solemnly, entranced by the passion and fire in her eyes. She was so . . . good. No flowery word could possibly be more descriptive.

He could never be worthy of her. He knew that. But he could love her, and protect her, and try to give her the kind of life she deserved. He cleared his throat. "When are your parents returning?"

Belle cocked her head at the abrupt change of subject. "They were supposed to get back any day now, but Emma recently forwarded me a letter from them saying that they were having such a good time that they were staying a bit longer. Why do you ask?"

He smiled up at her. "Would you mind rubbing my leg again? It hasn't felt this good in years."

"Of course." She returned to his side. When he didn't pick up the conversation, she prodded him with, "My parents . . ."

"Oh, yes. I just want to know when I can ask your father for your hand and be done with it." He shot her a cheeky grin. "Ravishing you in dark corners does have its excitements, but I'd much rather just get you to myself and have my way with you in the privacy of my own home."

"Have your way with me?" Belle asked unbelievingly.

John opened his eyes and shot her a rakish grin. "You know what I mean, love." He pulled her to him and nuzzled her neck. "I'd just like to have some time alone with you without fearing that someone is going to walk in on us at any moment."

He started to kiss her again. "I want to be able to finish what I start."

Belle was having none of that, however, and wriggled away. "John Blackwood, was that a proposal of marriage?"

Still leaning back, he looked up at her through his lashes and smiled. "I rather think it was. What do you say?"

" 'I rather think it was. What do you say?' " Belle mimicked. "I say that that is just about the least romantic proposal I have ever heard."

"Have you had so many proposals, then?"

"As a matter of fact, I have."

That wasn't quite what John had expected to hear. "I thought you were supposed to be the practical and pragmatic one in your family. I thought you wouldn't want weepy words of love and all that."

Belle swatted him on the shoulder. "Of course I do! Every woman does. Especially from the man she actually wants to accept. So devise some weepy words and I'll—"

"Aha! So you accept!" John grinned victoriously and pulled her on top of him.

"I said I want to accept. I didn't say I did accept."

"A minor technicality." He started to kiss her again, barely able to believe that she would soon be well and truly his.

"A major technicality," Belle said in an annoyed voice. "I can't believe what you just said to me. You want to marry me and *be done with it*? Good gad, that's awful."

John realized that he had blundered but was too relieved to make amends. "Well, what my proposal lacked in grace, it made up for in sincerity."

"It better have been sincere." Belle shot him a disgruntled look. "I'll say yes just as soon as you ask me properly."

John shrugged his shoulders and pulled her back to him. "I want to kiss you some more."

"Don't you want to ask me something first?"

"No."

"No?"

"No."

"What do you mean?" Belle tried to squirm away from him, but he held firm.

"I mean to kiss you."

"I know that, you oaf. What I want to know is, why don't you want to ask me something right now?"

"Ah, women," John said, sighing melodramatically. "If it's not one thing, it's another. If—"

Belle punched him in the arm.

"Belle," he said patiently. "You must realize that you have thrown down the gauntlet. You're not going to say yes until I do it right, right?"

Belle nodded.

"Then allow me a short grace period at least. These things take time if one wants to be creative about it."

"I see," Belle said, the corners of her mouth tugging up into a smile.

"If you want romance—true romance, mind you, you're going to have to wait a few days."

"I think I'll manage."

"Good. Now will you come over here and kiss me again?"

She did.

John came by later in the week. As soon as he had Belle alone, he pulled her into his arms and said,

"Twice or thrice had I loved thee,
Before I knew thy face or name;
So in a voice, so in a shapeless flame—"

"Angels affect us oft, and worshipped be,"
Belle finished. "I'm afraid it's your bad fortune
that my governess was mad about John Donne.
I've got most of it memorized." At his disgruntled look, she added, "But I must commend you
on your passionate recitation. It was quite moving."

"Obviously not moving enough. Out of my way,
if you please, I've got work to do." Head down, he
tromped out of the room.

"And stay away from the Donne!" Belle called
out. "You'll never fool me with one of his."

She couldn't be certain, but she thought she
heard him mutter a rather inelegant word as he
shut the front door behind him.

John made no mention of his impending proposal during the entire next week, even though he
escorted Belle to a few affairs and called on her
nearly every morning. She didn't bring up the
topic, either. She knew he would deny it, but he
was enjoying his plans, and she didn't want to
spoil his fun. Every so often he would give her a
sidelong assessing kind of glance, and she knew he
was up to something.

Her suspicions proved correct one morning
when he arrived at the Blydon mansion with three
dozen perfect red roses, which he promptly laid at
her feet right in the middle of the great hall. He
sank down on one knee and said,

"Drink to me only with thine eyes,
And I will pledge with mine;

> Or leave a kiss but in the cup,
> And I'll not look for wine.
> The thirst that from the soul doth rise,
> Doth ask a drink divine:
> But might I of Jove's nectar sup,
> I would not change for thine."

He almost got away with it. Belle's eyes misted up, and when he said the part about the kiss in the cup, her right hand strayed involuntarily to her heart.

"Oh, John," she sighed.

Then disaster struck.

Persephone descended the stairs.

"John!" she cried out in a delighted voice. "That is my absolute favorite! How did you know?"

John lowered his head and clenched his fists at his sides. Belle shifted her hand from her heart to her hip.

"My father used to recite that to my mother all the time," Persephone continued, her cheeks rosy. "It never failed to make her swoon with happiness."

"I can imagine," Belle muttered.

John looked up at her, his expression sheepish.

"And it was especially appropriate, you know," Persephone added, "as her name was Celia, God rest her soul."

"Appropriate?" Belle asked, her eyes never leaving John's. As for him, he wisely kept his mouth shut.

"It's called 'Song: To Celia,' after all. By Ben Jonson," Persephone said with a smile.

"Is it now?" Belle said wryly. "John, who is Celia?"

"Why, Persephone's mother, of course."

Belle had to admire him for keeping a straight

face. "Well, I'm glad that Jonson wrote the verse. I'd hate to think that you were writing poetry to someone named Celia, John."

"Oh, I don't know, Celia's a fine name, I think."

Belle offered him a sickly sweet smile. "I think you'll find that Belle is far easier to rhyme."

"I'm sure it is, but I prefer a challenge. Now then, Persephone—that would be a poem worthy of my intellect."

"Oh, stop," Persephone laughed.

"Persephone . . . Hmmm, let's see, we could use cacophony, but that's not very elegant."

Belle couldn't help but be swept away by John's good humor. "How about lemon tree?" she offered.

"That has definite possibilities. I shall have to get to work on it immediately."

"Enough teasing, my dear boy," Persephone said, taking John's arm in a maternal fashion. "I had no idea you were such an admirer of Ben Jonson. He is a particular favorite of mine. Do you also enjoy his plays? I adore *Volpone*, although it is rather wicked."

"I've been feeling rather wicked myself lately."

Persephone giggled beneath her hand and said, "Oh good. Because I saw an advertisement for a performance. I was hoping to find someone to escort me."

"I would be delighted, of course."

"Although perhaps we ought not bring Belle. I'm not sure it's fit for unmarried ladies, and Belle tells me that I'm not quite stern enough as a chaperone."

"Belle tells you *that*?"

"Not in so many words, of course. I doubt she wants to spoil such a good thing. But I know which way the wind blows."

"You're not going to the theater without me," Belle put in.

"I suppose we shall have to take her," John said with an affected sigh. "She can be quite stubborn when she puts her mind to it."

"Oh, be quiet," Belle returned. "And get to work. You have some writing to do."

"I suppose I do," John replied, nodding at Persephone as she disappeared down the hall. " 'Persephone in the Lemon Tree' is sure to be my masterwork."

"If you don't get to work soon it's going to be 'Belle sends you to hell.' "

"I'm quaking in my shoes."

"As well you should be."

John saluted her and then stepped forward and stretched out his arm, assuming a dramatic pose. "Persephone in the lemon tree—Sings to me indomitably." He quirked a boyish grin. "What do you think?"

"I think you're marvelous."

John leaned down and kissed her on the nose. "Have I told you that I have laughed more in the last few weeks than I have in my entire lifetime?"

Wordlessly, Belle shook her head.

"I have, you know. You do that to me. I don't know quite how you've done it, but you've stripped away my anger. Years of hurt and pain and cynicism made me brittle, but now I can feel the sun again."

Before Belle could tell him that that was poem enough for her, he kissed her again and was off.

A few nights later Belle was cuddled up in her bed, several anthologies of poetry strewn around her. "He's not going to fool me with another

'Song—To Celia' again," she said to herself. "I'll be ready for him."

She was a little worried that he might be able to trip her up with one of the newer poets. Her governess had gone over only the classics with her, and it was only because Lord Byron was so notorious that she'd known "She Walks in Beauty."

A quick trip to the bookshop that afternoon had supplied her with *Lyrical Ballads*, by William Wordsworth and Samuel Taylor Coleridge as well as *Songs of Innocence and Experience* by a rather obscure poet named William Blake. The proprietor assured her that Blake would someday find great fame and tried to sell her *The Marriage of Heaven and Hell* in addition, but Belle had put her foot down, figuring that there was no way John would be able to find something romantic in *that*.

A smile on her face, Belle opened up *Songs* and began to flip through the pages, reading aloud as she went along.

> "Tyger! Tyger! burning bright
> In the forests of the night,
> What immortal hand or eye
> Could frame thy fearful symmetry?"

She pursed her lips and looked up. "This modern stuff is very strange." Shaking her head, she turned back to the book.

Thump!

Belle caught her breath. What was that?

Thump!

No doubt about it, someone was outside her window. Terror gripped her and she slid out of bed to the floor. On her hands and knees, she crawled across the room to her dressing table. With a quick glance to the window, she grabbed a pewter candlestick from Boston that Emma had given her as a birthday present a few years earlier.

Remaining close to the ground, Belle scooted over to the window. Careful to stay out of the intruder's line of vision, she climbed up onto a chair which was placed against the wall right next to the window. Shaking with fear, she waited.

The window creaked and then she saw it start to rise. A black gloved hand appeared on the windowsill.

Belle stopped breathing.

A second hand found its place next to the first, and then a firm body tumbled in soundlessly, somersaulting when it hit the floor.

Belle raised the candlestick, setting her aim for the prowler's head when he suddenly turned and looked up at her.

"Good God, woman! Are you trying to kill me?"

"John?"

Chapter 13

❦

"**W**hat are you doing here?" Belle gasped. "Would you put that thing down!"

Belle finally lowered the candlestick and offered John her hand. He took it and got to his feet. "What are you doing here?" she repeated, her heart starting to flutter strangely at the sight of him in her bedroom.

"Isn't it obvious?"

Well, he might be here to kidnap her and spirit her away to Gretna Green, or he might be here to ravish her, or he might just be here to say hello. "No," she said slowly. "It isn't obvious."

"Do you realize that in the past week I have seen you four times with Persephone, twice with my brother, once with your chum Dunford, and thrice at social functions where I'm allowed to talk with you only in the presence of women over the age of sixty?"

Belle bit back a smile. "We've had some time together here when you've come to call."

"I don't count it as being alone when I must worry about Miss Lemon Tree barging in at any moment."

His expression was so petulant that Belle had a vision of him as an eight-year-old stamping his foot at some horrid injustice. "Now, now," she chuckled. "Persephone's not that bad."

"She's supreme as far as chaperones go, but that doesn't eliminate the fact that she's got bloody repellent timing. I'm damned near afraid to kiss you half the time."

"I hadn't noticed any decline in the frequency of your attempts."

John shot her a look which said he did not entirely appreciate her humor. "All I'm saying is that I'm damned sick and tired of sharing you."

"Oh." Belle thought that was just about the sweetest thing she had ever heard.

"I just climbed up a tree, shimmied along an unsteady branch, and then vaulted through a window at an extremely unsafe height. All, might I add, with a bum leg," John said, pulling off his gloves and brushing himself off. "Just to be alone with you."

Belle swallowed as she stared at him, dimly registering the fact that he had actually referred to his injury without bitterness or despair.

"You wanted a romantic proposal," he continued. "Believe me, I'm never going to get more romantic than this." Out of his pocket he pulled a crumpled, red rose.

"Will you marry me?"

Overcome with emotion, Belle blinked away the tears pooling in her eyes. She opened her mouth but no words came out.

John stepped forward and took both of her hands in his. "Please," he said, and that single word held such promise that Belle started nodding furiously.

"Yes, oh yes!" She threw herself in his arms and buried her face in his chest.

John held her tightly for several minutes, savoring the feel of her warm body next to his. "I should have asked you so long ago," he murmured into her hair. "Back at Westonbirt. I tried so hard to push you away."

"But why?"

His throat tightened.

"John, are you ill? You look as if you've eaten something that's gone off."

"No, Belle, I—" He fought for words. He wouldn't deceive her. He wouldn't enter into a marriage based upon lies. "When I told you that I wasn't the man you thought I was—"

"I remember," she interrupted. "And I still don't understand what you mean. I—"

"Hush." He placed his finger on her lips. "There is something in my past I must tell you about. It was during the war."

Wordlessly, she took his hand and led him to her bed. She sat and motioned him to do likewise, but he was far too restless.

He turned abruptly and strode over to the window, bracing himself against the sill. "A girl was raped," he blurted out, thankful that he couldn't see her expression. "It was my fault."

Belle paled. "Wh-what do you mean?"

John recounted the details, finishing with, "That's how it happened. At least that's how I remember it. I was drunk." He let out a short, hollow laugh.

"John, it wasn't your fault." Her words were

soft, but they were filled with love and faith.

He didn't turn around. "You weren't there."

"I know you. You wouldn't have let something like this happen if you could have prevented it."

He whirled to face her. "Weren't you listening to me? I was drunk. If I'd had my wits about me I would have been able to fulfil my promise to Ana's mother."

"He would have found a way to get to her. You couldn't have guarded the girl every minute of the day."

"I could have— I—" He broke off. "I don't want to talk about it."

Belle stood and crossed the room, placing a gentle hand on his arm. "Perhaps you should."

"No," he said quickly. "I don't want to talk about it. I don't want to think about it. I—" He choked on his words. "Will you still have me?"

"How can you even ask?" she whispered. "I lo—" She stopped, too scared of upsetting the precious balance they'd achieved to voice her true feelings. "I care for you so much. I know what a good and honorable man you are, even if you don't."

He reached for her, pulling her roughly into his arms. He clung to her, covering her face with kisses. "Oh, Belle, I need you so much. I don't know how I survived without you."

"And I you."

"You are such a treasure, Belle. Such a gift to me." He suddenly whirled her around, spinning her in a dazzling waltz. They twirled about, turning circle after circle until they both collapsed on the bed, laughing and out of breath.

"Look at me," John gasped. "I cannot remember the last time I allowed myself to be so happy. I smile all day long without knowing why. I climbed a bloody tree, vaulted through your window, and here I am—laughing." He jumped to his feet, pulling her along with him. "It's the middle of the night, and yet here I am with you. Dancing at midnight, holding perfection in my arms."

"Oh, John," she sighed, unable to think of any words to express her feelings.

He touched her chin with his fingers and drew her closer, ever closer.

Belle's breath caught in her throat as his lips swooped down to claim her own. The kiss was different than any other they had shared. There was a fierceness to it that hadn't been there before, a sense of ownership. And Belle had to admit that this possessiveness was not one-sided. The way she kissed him with all her passion, clutched at the sinewy muscles of his back—all this was meant to show him that he belonged to no one but her.

John's hands roamed down her back, spreading warmth through the thin material of her nightgown. He strayed down to her bottom and cupped it, pulling her tightly to him so that she could feel the hard, physical evidence of his desire. "Do you realize how much I want you?" he rasped. "Do you?"

Belle couldn't speak, for his lips had covered her own. She couldn't nod because one of his hands had stolen back up to her thick hair and was holding her head immobile. She responded in the only way she could, which was to reach around to his buttocks and pull him even closer to her. A harsh moan was his answer, and Belle felt a feminine thrill at her power over him.

He sank to his knees, his lips burning a hot path through her nightgown, descending through the valley between her breasts and settling over her navel.

"John?" she asked breathily. "What . . . ?"

"Shhh, just let me take care of everything." He sank down even lower, until his hands could wrap around her ankles. "So soft," he murmured. "Your skin is like moonlight."

"Moonlight?" she said in a strangled voice. The powerful sensations streaking through her body had rendered her voice barely usable.

"Soft and gentle, yet with a touch of mystery." His hands made the slow trip up her calves, pushing her nightgown up along with them. When he was halfway up, he twisted around her to deposit twin kisses on the backs of her knees. Belle cried out and nearly fell over, and she had to clutch on to his head for support.

"You like that, do you? I'll have to remember that." He continued moving upward, marveling at the delicate skin of her thighs. With a devilish laugh, he darted his head under the now rather high hem of her nightgown and planted a kiss in the crook between her leg and her hip.

Belle thought she might faint.

The nightgown moved even higher, past her hips, and Belle felt a vague relief that he had moved from her thighs straight to her stomach, bypassing her most private area.

As John pushed the material further, he rose to his feet, pausing briefly before he bared her breasts. "Did I remember to tell you the other day that they're perfect?" he murmured huskily into her ear.

Belle shook her head mutely.

"Round and ripe with two precious pink buds. I could suckle at them all day."

"Oh God." Belle's knees went completely and totally weak again.

"I'm not done yet, love." He held the hem of her gown just below her breasts and then pressed it to her skin. As he lifted it up, Belle could feel the pressure traveling up the underside of her breasts. Spasms of pleasure shot through her as the hem caught her nipples and then freed them with a bounce. And then before she knew it, she was completely naked, her skin glowing soft and white in the dim light of the candles.

John sucked in his breath. "Never in my life have I seen a sight so glorious," he whispered reverently.

Belle flushed with delight at his words, and then all of a sudden she seemed to realize that she had on not a stitch. "Oh my God," she croaked. Shyness swept over her like a cool wind, and her hands snaked forward to cover herself.

As best she could.

Which wasn't, after all, very well.

John chuckled and lifted her into his arms. "You, love, are perfect. You shouldn't feel ashamed."

"I'm not," she replied softly. "Not with you. It's just very strange. I'm not . . . used to this."

"I should hope not." He pushed the books off of her bed and laid her down on the soft white sheets. Belle stopped breathing momentarily as she watched him begin to undress. His shirt came first, baring a firmly muscled chest that spoke of years of hard exercise. The sight of him caused warm, tingly feelings to pool in her belly. Without thinking she reached a hand out, even though he was much too far away to touch.

John both smiled and groaned at her curiosity. It was getting harder and harder for him to maintain his control, especially when she was lying there looking up at him with huge blue eyes. He sat down on the edge of the bed and yanked off his boots, then stood up again to peel off his breeches.

Belle gasped when she saw his manhood, huge

and . . . no this wasn't going to work. He must be bigger than normal, or maybe she was smaller than normal, but—she gasped again.

His knee.

"Dear God," she whispered. It was covered with scars, and it looked as if a large chunk of flesh had been removed from just above the joint. The taut skin was discolored and without hair, its mere presence an angry reminder of the horrors of war.

John's mouth twisted. "You don't have to look at it."

Belle's gaze shot quickly up to his face. "It's not that," she assured him. "It's not ugly at all." And to prove her point, she slid out of bed and knelt before him to kiss the scars. "It makes me sick to think of how this must have hurt you," she whispered. "And how close you came to losing your leg. You're so vital, so strong. I can't imagine what that would have done to you." She began to kiss him again, raining a soft stream of love onto his skin.

Emotions John had never expected to feel, never dreamed he could feel, surged powerfully within him, and he pulled her roughly to her feet. "Oh God, Belle," he rasped. "I want you so much."

They tumbled onto the bed, landing so that John's hard frame covered hers. The breath was squeezed from Belle's body, yet the weight of him was glorious, unlike anything she'd ever experienced. He kissed her and kissed her until she was certain she would melt, and then suddenly he lifted his head and looked deeply into her eyes.

"I'm going to pleasure you first," he said. "So you know that there is nothing to fear, that there is only beauty and wonder."

"I'm not afraid," she whispered. Then she remembered how large he had looked. "Well, maybe a little nervous."

John smiled reassuringly. "I haven't any experience with innocents, but I want this to be perfect for you. I think it might be easier if I give you release first."

Belle had no idea what he was talking about, but she nodded anyway. "You sound as if you've given this considerable thought."

"Believe me," he said hoarsely. "I've thought of little else." His hand gently slid down the length of her body.

She reached up, touched his cheek, and softly said, "I trust you."

John brushed his lips against hers to distract her when his fingers sought out her very essence. She'd be nervous, and he didn't want it to be too much of a shock.

It was. She nearly flew off the bed. "Are you sure this is what you're supposed to be doing?" she asked breathlessly.

"I'm sure."

And then his mouth joined his fingers. Belle was certain that she'd died. Nothing could possibly feel that wicked . . . or that good.

"Oh John!" she gasped, unable to stop her soul from spiraling out of control. "I don't think . . . I can't . . . "

And then she did. It felt as if every nerve ending in her body suddenly converged in her abdomen. She tensed, then exploded. It took her several minutes to float back down to earth, and all she could say was, "Merciful heavens."

She heard John laugh, and when she opened her eyes saw that he was looking down at her with an amused expression. He leaned down and kissed her nose.

"Was that normal?" she asked in a small voice.

He nodded. "Better."

"Really?"

He nodded again.

"Did you . . . ?" She let her words trail off. She was new to this and hadn't much idea how to go about it.

He shook his head gently. "When I find my release you'll know it."

"Will it be as good as what I . . . ?" She couldn't finish the sentence.

John's eyes darkened with desire, and he nodded.

"Good." Belle sighed. "I wouldn't like it if you didn't feel as good as I do. But if you don't mind, I'd like to cuddle up against you for a minute or two."

His straining manhood disagreed with his words, but John said, "There is nothing I'd rather do."

He'd only held her in his arms for a few seconds when they heard an awful noise.

Persephone's voice.

There was a knock at the door. "Oh Belle?" she said in a stage whisper. "Belle?"

Belle shot up straight. "Persephone?"

"May I come in for a moment?"

Panic gripped her. "Uh, just one moment!" Thank God her door was locked. "Hide!" she hissed at John.

"I'm trying," he hissed back. He hopped out of the bed, cursing the cold night air. He gathered up his clothes, praying he'd got them all, and stumbled into her dressing room.

Belle grabbed her dressing gown, covered herself, and went to the door. She turned the key and opened it, marveling that her quivering legs were actually holding her upright. "Good evening, Persephone."

"I'm sorry to bother you, but I couldn't sleep, and I knew that you had gone to the bookshop today. I was wondering if I could borrow something to read."

"Of course." Belle rushed back into the room and gathered up some of the books. "It's all poetry, but I'm done with it for the evening."

Persephone noticed Belle's bare calves peeking out from under her dressing gown and said, "Don't you wear a nightgown?"

Belle blushed and silently thanked the dark cloak of night for hiding her embarrassment. "I was hot."

"I can't imagine why. The window is wide open. You'll catch a chill."

"I don't think so." Belle thrust the books into Persephone's arms.

"Thank you." Persephone wrinkled her nose and sniffed. "What is that smell? It's most peculiar."

Belle prayed that Persephone's maiden aunt status was entirely accurate because the room reeked of lovemaking. One could only hope that she wouldn't recognize the smell. "Umm, I think it's coming in from outside."

"Well, I can't imagine what it is, but you ought to remember to shut the window before you go to sleep. And if you'd like I could give you some of my violet-scented perfume. I'm sure that smell will go away if you spray a bit of it around."

"Perhaps in the morning." Belle led the way back to the door.

"Good night, then. I'll see you in the morning."

"Good night." Belle shut the door and locked it quickly, leaning back against it with a sigh.

The door to the dressing room swung open. John emerged, his upper body tangling in Belle's dresses. "Good God, woman, you have a lot of frocks."

Belle ignored him. "I was so scared."

"And I felt damned foolish. I'm warning you, I'm not going to put up with this for long." He viciously thrust his bad leg into his breeches.

"You're not?" Belle asked weakly.

"Not a chance. I'm a grown man. I've fought a bloody war, nearly got my leg shot off, played the market for five years and amassed enough money to purchase a damned house. Do you think I like creeping around in closets?"

Belle didn't really think that a reply was necessary.

"Well, I don't, I tell you. I don't like it at all." He sat down in a nearby chair so that he could put his good leg into his breeches. Belle surmised that his injured leg wasn't quite strong enough to hold him up for long.

"And I'll tell you something else," he added, working himself up into a fine bout of annoyance. "As far as I'm concerned, you're mine. Do you understand that? And I don't like being made to feel like a thief for enjoying what is mine."

"What are you going to do?"

He grabbed his shirt. "I'm going to marry you right away. And then I'm going to take you back to Bletchford Manor and toss you into bed and keep you there for a week. All without having to worry about Miss Lemon Tree barging in to spoil the mood."

"You really need to find a new name for your home."

"Our home," he corrected, scowling at her attempt to change the subject. "And I've been too busy chasing after you to give the matter much thought."

"I'll help you." Belle smiled. He loved her. He might not have said as much, but it was right there in his eyes.

"Good. Now if you'll excuse me, I've got to jump back out your window, slide down that tree, return to Damien's, and get some sleep. Then I've got to see about getting a special license."

"A special license?"

"I'm not putting up with this nonsense any longer than I have to. With any luck we'll be married by the end of the week."

"By the end of the week?" Belle echoed. "Are you mad? I can't get married this week. I can't even get officially engaged until my parents return."

John groaned as he picked up his boots and uttered a curse which was completely unfamiliar to Belle. "When are they getting back?" he asked in a very low voice.

"I'm not certain."

"Would it be possible for you to offer an estimate?"

"No more than a couple of weeks, I would imagine." Belle forbore to point out that they would have to wait at least another month or two after her parents returned before they could actually marry. Her mother would insist upon a large wedding. Of that she was certain.

John swore again. "If they're not home within a fortnight Alex can give you away. Or call your brother down from Oxford. I don't care which."

"But—"

"No buts. If your parents ask questions, you can simply tell them that we *had* to get married."

Belle swallowed and nodded. What else could she do? "I lo . . . " She lost her courage, and the rest of the sentence remained on her tongue.

He turned around. "Yes?"

"I—nothing. Be careful getting down that tree. It's rather tall."

"Three stories, to be precise."

His wry grin was infectious, and Belle felt the corners of her mouth tugging up as she followed him to the window.

He leaned down and murmured, "A kiss goodbye." His lips touched hers in one last, passionate caress.

Belle barely had time to kiss him back before he moved away, pulled on his gloves, and disappeared outside. She rushed to the window and looked out, watching him with a smile as he made his way down the tree.

"He could have just gone out the door," she muttered to herself. "Persephone's room is in the opposite direction." Oh well, it was more fun this way, and certainly more romantic. As long as he didn't break his fool neck on the way down. Belle leaned out the window a little further and sighed with relief when she saw his feet touch the ground. He leaned down to rub his bad knee, and she winced in sympathy.

She watched him until he disappeared from sight, leaning against the windowsill with a dreamy expression on her face. London could be beautiful on ocassion, she mused. Like now, with its deserted streets, and—

A movement caught her eye. Was that a man? It was hard to tell. Briefly she wondered what someone would be doing up and about and on foot this time of night.

She giggled. Maybe all of London's gentlemen had decided to do some unconventional courting that evening.

Taking a deep breath, she shut the window and made her way back to bed. It was only when she was snuggled up under her mountain of covers that she remembered that he had never found his fulfillment.

She smiled wryly. No wonder he was so cranky.

John made his way back to his brother's house, his hand on his pistol the entire time. London was getting more and more dangerous these days, and one really couldn't be too careful. Still, he hadn't wanted to bring a carriage by Belle's house. Someone might have seen it, and he didn't want her subject to any vicious rumors. Besides, it was only a few short blocks to Damien's home. It seemed that all of the *ton* was squeezed into one tiny section of London. He doubted that most of them knew that the city continued past the borders of Grosvenor Square.

He was about halfway home when he heard footsteps.

He turned around. Was someone behind him?

Nothing but shadows. He continued on his way. Surely he'd imagined it. He was still paranoid from the war, when every sound could mean death.

He turned the last corner when he heard the footsteps again. And then a bullet whined past his ear. "What the hell?"

Another bullet whizzed by, this one grazing his arm and drawing blood. He whipped out his pistol and spun around. He saw a shadowy figure across the street, furiously reloading a gun. John lost no time in firing, and the villain went down as he took a bullet in the shoulder.

Damn! His aim was off. Gun still in hand, he started after his would-be assassin. The man saw him coming, grabbed his shoulder, and got to his feet. He shot John an apprehensive look, but his face was covered by a half-mask, so John had no way of recognizing him. With one last fleeting glance, the villain rushed off.

As John made his way across the street, he cursed his leg for slowing him down. Never had he been so furious at the fates for maiming him this way. There was no way he'd be able to catch up with his attacker. Accepting defeat, John sighed and turned around. This was trouble.

And he had no right dragging Belle into it.

His hand strayed to his arm as he finally realized that he was bleeding. He could barely feel the pain, however. His fury blocked out all other feeling. Someone was after him, and he didn't know why. Some lunatic was sending him cryptic notes and wanted him dead.

And whoever it was, he probably wouldn't hesitate to involve Belle if he realized how much she meant to John. And if he had been following him at all during the past week, he would know that John had spent every free minute in her company.

John swore as he mounted the front steps to Damien's house. He would not put Belle in danger, even if that meant he had to postpone his marriage plans.

Bloody hell.

Chapter 14

"**P**ardon me, my lady, a message has arrived for you."

Belle looked up as a servant entered the room. She'd been sitting in a dreamlike haze, replaying the previous night with John—for about the fiftieth time. She took the letter, carefully opened it, and read the contents.

Belle,

I apologize for giving you such short notice, but I will be unable to accompany you and Persephone to the theater this evening.

Sincerely,
John Blackwood

Belle looked down at the note for a minute or so, puzzling over the formal tone. With a shrug, she just decided that some people always wrote formally, so she shouldn't be upset that he had signed the note "sincerely" rather than "love." And it didn't really matter that he had felt the need to include his surname in addition to his given name. She tucked the note away, telling herself not to be so fanciful.

She shrugged. Maybe Dunford would be interested in escorting her and Persephone.

Dunford did want to go to the theater, and he had a fine time escorting Belle and Persephone. However, Belle's thoughts frequently drifted off toward the man who had sneaked into her bedroom the night before. She wondered what had kept him from joining her that evening, but supposed that he'd explain everything to her the next day.

Except he didn't come by the next day. Or the one after that.

Belle was more than puzzled. She was damned irritated. She'd been warned about men who used women for their own pleasure and then discarded them, but she just couldn't bring herself to place John in that category. First of all, she refused to believe that she could have fallen in love with a man who was so fundamentally dishonest, and second of all, it had been she who moaned with pleasure the other night, not him.

After two days of waiting and hoping for a glimpse of him, Belle finally decided to take matters into her own hands and sent him a note of her own, asking him to stop by.

There was no reply.

Belle grumbled in irritation. He knew very well that she could not call on him. He was staying with his brother, and both were bachelors. It was entirely unsuitable for an unmarried lady to call on such a household. Especially here in London. Her mother would have her head if she found out about it, which she very well might, considering that she was due back any day now.

She sent him another message, this one more carefully worded, asking him if she had done anything to displease him, and would he please be kind enough to reply. Belle smiled wryly to herself as she wrote the words. She wasn't very good at keeping the twinge of sarcasm from her tone.

A few streets away, John groaned as he read her note. She was getting annoyed, that was clear. And how could he blame her? After a fortnight of flowers, chocolate, poetry, and then finally passion, she had a right to expect to see him.

But what else was he to do? He had received another anonymous note the day after his attack which had simply read, "Next time I won't miss." John had no doubt that Belle would take it upon herself to see to his protection if she knew that someone was trying to kill him. And as he didn't see how Belle possibly *could* protect him, such an endeavor could only lead to her getting hurt.

He sighed with despair and let his head fall into his hands. Now that happiness was finally within his grasp, how could he spend the rest of his life worrying that a bullet was going to catch him unawares? He grimaced. The words "rest of his life" suddenly took on new meaning. If that assassin kept trying, sooner or later he was going to get lucky. John was going to have to come up with a plan.

But in the meantime, he had to keep Belle at a distance—and away from the bullets that were aimed at his back. With an unbearably heavy heart, he picked up a quill and dipped it into an inkpot.

Dear Belle,

I will not be able to see you for some time. I cannot explain why. Please be patient with me. I remain

Yours,
John Blackwood

He knew that he ought to have simply broken things off, but he just couldn't do it. She was the one thing in his life that had brought him true joy, and he wasn't about to lose her. Carrying the offending piece of paper as if it might give him a disease, he made his way downstairs and gave it to a servant. Belle would receive it within the hour.

He didn't even want to think about it.

Belle's response upon reading his brief letter was to blink. This couldn't be real.

She blinked again. The words did not disappear.

Something was terribly wrong. He was trying to push her away again. She didn't know why, and she didn't know why he thought he might be able to succeed, but she couldn't allow herself to believe that he really didn't want her.

How could he not, when she wanted him so badly? God couldn't be so cruel.

Belle quickly pushed those depressing thoughts aside. She had to trust her instincts, and they told her that John did care for her. Very much. As much as she cared for him. He had said to please be patient with him. That seemed to indicate that he was working through whatever problem ailed him. He must be in some kind of trouble, and he didn't want to involve her. How like him.

She grumbled. When was he going to learn that love meant sharing one's burdens? She crumpled the paper into a hard little ball and flexed her fist around it. He was going to get his first lesson that afternoon, because she was going to see him, propriety be damned.

And that was another thing. Her mental cursing had grown by epic proportions during the past few days. She was beginning to shock even herself. Belle tossed the note aside and brushed her hands against each other. She took a small pleasure in blaming her foul language on him.

Not bothering to change into a fancier dress, Belle grabbed a warm cloak and stalked off in search of her maid. She found her in her dressing room, examining her gowns for small rips and tears.

"Oh, hello, my lady," Mary said quickly. "Do you know which gown you wish to wear this evening? It needs to be pressed."

"Doesn't matter," Belle said briskly. "I don't think I'm going to go out this evening after all. But I do want to take a short walk this afternoon, and I'd like you to accompany me."

"Right away, my lady." Mary fetched her coat and followed Belle down the stairs. "Where are we going?"

"Oh, not very far," Belle said cryptically. Her mouth shut in firm determination, she opened the front door and strode down the steps.

Mary scurried to catch up with her. "I've never seen you walk so fast, my lady."

"I always walk quickly when I'm irritated."

Mary had no reply for that, so she simply sighed and quickened her pace. After they had walked a few blocks, Belle stopped short. Mary nearly crashed into her.

"Hmmm," Belle said.

"Hmmm?"

"This is the place."

"What place?"

"The Earl of Westborough's home."

"Earl who?"

"John's brother."

"Oh." Mary had seen John several times during the past few weeks. "Why are we here?"

Belle took a deep breath and lifted her chin stubbornly. "We've come to pay a visit." Without waiting for Mary's reply, she marched up the steps and slammed the knocker down three times.

"What?" Mary nearly screeched. "You can't come calling here."

"I can and I am." Impatient, Belle slammed the knocker down again.

"But—but—only *men* live here."

Belle rolled her eyes. "Really, Mary, You needn't speak of them as if they're a separate species. They're just like you and me." She blushed. "Well, almost."

She had just lifted her hand up again to grab the knocker when the butler answered the door. She gave him her calling card and told him that she was there to see Lord Blackwood. Mary was so embarrassed she couldn't lift her gaze above the level of Belle's knees.

The butler ushered the two ladies into a small salon just off the main hallway.

"Persephone's going to throw me into the street," Mary whispered, shaking her head.

"She will not, and you work for me, anyway, so she can't fire you."

"She won't be happy about it, though."

"I don't see any reason she needs to know about it," Belle said resolutely. But inside she was quaking. This was highly irregular, and if there was one thing her mother hadn't raised her to be, it was irregular. Oh, she had called on John alone in the country, but etiquette was looser there.

Just when she thought her nerves had quite reached their limit, the butler returned.

"Lord Blackwood is not receiving, my lady."

Belle gasped at the insult. John had refused to see her. She swept to her feet and strode out of the room, her carriage held erect by the dignity that had been instilled in her since birth. She didn't stop until she was halfway down the street, and then, unable to help herself, she looked back.

John was standing in a third-story window, staring down at her.

As soon as he saw her turn, he stepped away and let the curtains fall back into place.

"Hmmm," Belle said, still looking at the window.

"What?" Mary followed her gaze but didn't find anything of interest.

"That's a nice tree in front of the building."

Mary raised her brows, convinced that her employer had gone daft.

Belle stroked her chin. "It's uncommonly close to the outer wall." She smiled. "Come along, Mary, we've got work to do."

"We do?" But Mary's words went unheard, for Belle was already several steps ahead of her.

When she got home, Belle marched straight up to her room, pulled out some stationery from her desk and penned a note to Emma, who had been much more of a tomboy while growing up than Belle.

Dearest Emma,
How do you climb trees?

Fondly,
Belle

After Belle sent the note off to her cousin, she dealt with her grief and her anger the best way she knew how. She went shopping.

For this outing she took Persephone with her. The older lady never tired of browsing through the elegant London shops. Much more of a selection than anywhere in Yorkshire, she explained. And besides, it was great fun spending Alex's money.

Neither woman really needed new clothing after their last outing, but the holiday season was approaching, so they browsed through trinket shops, looking for gifts. Belle found an odd little telescope for her brother and a lovely music box for her mother, but she couldn't stop her heart from wishing that it were John for whom she was shopping. She sighed. She would just have to believe that all would work out in the end. She couldn't let herself believe anything else. It would simply be too painful.

It was probably because she was so lost in her thoughts that she didn't notice the two rather unsavory looking characters lurking in an alleyway as she passed by. Before she realized what was happening, one of them had grabbed her arm and started pulling her deeper into the alley.

Belle yelled out and fought with all her might. The thug had pulled her far enough into the alley so that the passersby on the main street did not see her. And London had grown so loud, it was understandable that no one paid her cries any mind. "Let go of me, you cur," she cried out. Her arm felt as if it were being torn from the socket, but she blocked out the pain, intent only on escape.

"She's the one, I tell ya," she heard one of the villains say. "She's the one the fancy cove wanted."

"Shut up and get 'er over here." The other man stepped forward and Belle's terror increased tenfold. There was no way she'd be able to hold out against the strength of both of these men.

But just when it seemed that all was lost, salvation came in the unlikely form of Persephone. She had been distracted by a particularly attractive window display when Belle had disappeared into the alleyway and was quite baffled when she looked back up and her charge was gone. When she called out Belle's name and got no response, she grew worried and began to look about frantically.

"Belle?" she called out again, this time loudly. She scurried forward, her head turning in all directions. Then, as she was passing the alleyway, she saw a blur of movement and Belle's familiar blond hair.

"Good God!" she screamed, loud enough to make most of the people on the sidewalk stop and stare. "Let go of her, you beasts!" She rushed forward, raising her parasol above her head. "Let go, I tell you!" With a furious whack, she slammed her weapon down on the head of one of the assailants.

"Shut up, you old bitch!" he yelled, howling in pain.

Persephone's response was a horizontal swing which clipped him neatly in the middle. The breath knocked out of him, he fell to the ground.

The other thug was caught between utter panic and sheer greed, lusting after the money he'd been promised if he captured the yellow-haired lady. He gave it one last desperate try, barely aware that a number of people had rushed into the alleyway upon hearing Persephone's cries of distress.

"I said let go of her!" Persephone boomed. She changed her attack tactics and started viciously poking him with the end of her parasol. When she stabbed him neatly in the groin, he finally let go of Belle and ran away, painfully hunched over the entire way.

"Persephone, thank you so much," Belle said,

tears of terror belatedly forming in her eyes.

But Persephone wasn't listening. All of her attention was focused on the man still lying on the ground. He made a motion as if to get up, but she jabbed him in the belly. "Not so fast, mister," she said.

Belle's eyes widened. Who would have dreamed that dear old Persephone would have such a tough streak?

The villain saw the growing crowd of people forming around him and closed his eyes, surmising that escape was impossible. Much to Belle's relief, a constable quickly arrived on the scene, and she relayed her story to him. He started to question her attacker, but the man remained closemouthed. That is, until the constable reminded him of the possible punishments for attacking a lady of Belle's position.

The man sang like a canary.

He'd been hired to grab her. Yes, just her. No, not any pretty blond lady, this one in particular. The gentleman who had hired him spoke with uppity accents—definitely highborn. No, he didn't know his name, and he hadn't seen him before, but he had straight blond hair and blue eyes, if that helped any, and his arm was in a sling.

After finishing the interrogation, the constable hauled him away and told Belle to be extra careful. Maybe she ought to hire one of those Bow Street Runners for added protection.

Belle shivered with fear. She had an enemy. One who probably wanted her dead.

As the crowd began to disperse, Persephone turned to her and asked solicitously, "Are you all right, dear?"

"Yes, yes," Belle replied. "I'm fine." Her eyes strayed down to her arm where that awful man had grabbed her. There had been a dress and a coat between her skin and his, but still she felt dirty. "I think, however, I'd like a bath."

Persephone nodded. "I couldn't agree with you more."

Late the next morning a footman brought Belle a reply from Emma.

Dearest Belle,

I cannot imagine why you suddenly want to learn how to climb trees since you never professed any love for it when we were small.

The first step is to find a tree with some reasonably low branches. If you cannot reach the first branch, you'll never get anywhere . . .

The letter continued for two pages. Emma was nothing if not detailed. She was also a little suspicious, as the end of the letter showed.

I hope you find this helpful, although I must say I wonder where you are going to climb trees in London. I profess that I think this has something to do with John Blackwood. Love does strange things to women, as I well know. Be careful, whatever you do, and I can only breathe a sigh of relief that I am no longer your chaperone. God save Persephone.

Fondly,
Emma

Belle scoffed. If Emma were still her chaperone, she'd probably insist upon going along with her. Emma had never been known for prudent behavior.

Belle reread the letter, carefully going over the part about how to climb trees. Was she really going to do this? When she'd stopped outside of Damien's house and assessed that tree, she hadn't really thought that she would do anything about it. She wasn't the sort of daring female who would climb a tree and break into an earl's house through a third-story window. For one thing, she had no head for heights.

But, as Emma so wisely pointed out, love did strange things to a woman. That, and danger. Her nasty experience with those two thugs in the alleyway had convinced her that it was time to act decisively.

Or perhaps rashly was a better word for it.

Belle shook her head. No matter. She'd made up her mind. She was scared, and she needed John.

But those thugs did complicate her plans a bit. She couldn't very well go over to Damien's house in the middle of the night by herself when someone was out to kidnap her. And Mary, of course, would not be sufficient protection. Persephone and her perilous parasol were another story, but Belle doubted that Persephone would agree to go with her. She might be rather lenient as far as chaperones went, but she would certainly put her foot down at Belle breaking into a man's room.

What to do, what to do?

Belle smiled mischievously.

She picked up a quill and wrote a note to Dunford.

"Absolutely not!"

"Don't be stodgy, Dunford," Belle said. "I need your help."

"You don't need help, you need a harness. And I'm not being stodgy, I'm being a sensible. A word of which you appear to have forgotten the meaning."

Belle stubbornly crossed her arms and sank back into her chair. Dunford was up and pacing, his arms flying as he spoke. She'd never seen him so out of sorts.

"This is a damn fool thing you're thinking of, Belle. If you don't break your neck—and that's a pretty big If, considering that all of your tree-climbing experience can be located in a letter from your cousin—you'll probably be arrested for trespassing."

"I won't be arrested."

"Oh, really? And how do you know that you'll just happen to tumble into the correct room? With your luck you'll end up in the earl's bedroom. And I've been watching him watching you. I think he'd appreciate his good fortune."

"He would not. He knows I'm interested in his brother. And I'm not going to 'tumble into his bedroom' as you so delicately put it. I know which room is John's."

"I'm not even going to ask how you know that."

It was on the tip of Belle's tongue to defend her reputation, but she kept silent instead. If Dunford thought that she'd already been in John's bedroom he might be less reluctant to help her get there again.

"Look, Belle, my answer is still no. Absolutely not! With three exclamation points," he added.

"If you were my friend . . . " Belle muttered.

"Exactly. I am your friend for not letting you do this. An amazingly good friend. There is nothing you could say that will make me help you."

Belle rose. "Well, thank you, then, Dunford. I had hoped for your assistance, but I see that I'm just going to have to go about this alone."

Dunford groaned. "Except that. Belle, you really wouldn't go over there by yourself."

"I don't have any choice. My need to see him is most urgent, and he won't receive me. I suppose I'll hire a hack to take me the short distance from here to there so I won't have to walk alone so late at night, but—"

"All right, all right," Dunford conceded with an exasperated expression. "I'll help you, but I want you to know that I completely disapprove."

"Don't worry, you've made that quite clear."

Dunford sank into a chair and his eyes closed in mental agony. "God help us," he groaned. "God help us all."

Belle smiled. "Oh, I think He will."

Chapter 15

"**W**here on earth did you come up with a crazy idea like this, anyway?"

"No matter." Belle glanced over at her reluctant partner in crime. Dunford was not at all pleased to be standing next to her in front of John's brother's house at three in the morning, and he certainly had no qualms about showing his ire.

He scowled as he gave her a leg up into the tree. "I'm not leaving until I see you depart from this house. Preferably through the front door."

Belle didn't look down at him as she grabbed the first branch. "I wish you would. There's no telling how long I might be inside."

"That's what I'm worried about."

"Dunford, even if he detested me, John would insist upon seeing me home. That's just the sort of man he is. You needn't worry about my welfare when I'm with him."

"Perhaps, but what about your reputation?"

"Well, that's my problem, isn't it?" Belle hoisted herself up onto the next branch. "This is much easier than it looks. Have you ever climbed a tree, Dunford?"

"Of course I have," he replied in an irritated voice. She was now even with the second-story windows. Not for the first time, he cursed himself for letting her talk him into this insane scheme. But then again, if he didn't help her, she'd probably have come alone, which was even more insane. He'd never seen Belle like this before. For her sake, he hoped this Blackwood fellow felt the same way about her.

"I'm almost there, Dunford," she called out softly, testing the sturdiness of the branch which would have to bear her weight as she moved horizontally toward the window. "Will you promise me that you'll leave once I'm inside?"

"I'll promise no such thing."

"Please," she pleaded. "You'll freeze out here."

"I'll leave only if Blackwood comes to the window and gives me his word as a gentleman that he'll see you safely home." Dunford sighed to himself. He'd not be able to protect Belle's virtue—if there was anything left to protect, which he sincerely hoped there was—but at least he could make sure she got home safely.

"All right," she agreed, and started inching her way along the thick branch toward the window. After about three seconds on her hands and knees, a better idea offered itself to her, and she straddled the branch, thankful for the breeches she had swiped out of her brother's closet. Using her arms for support, she slowly pushed her way along. When she reached the window, the branch sagged perilously, and Belle quickly climbed onto the wide ledge. Below her she could hear Dunford's footsteps as he scurried toward the building, obviously certain that he was going to have to catch her as she plunged toward the ground.

"I'm fine," she called out softly. She started to push the window up.

John was awakened by the sound of the window scraping against its frame. Years of soldiering had left him a very light sleeper, and the recent attack against his life had honed his senses even further. With one fluid motion he grabbed his pistol from his nightstand, rolled onto the floor, and crouched next to the bed, his leg screaming against the sudden movement. When he realized that the intruder was having a bit of trouble getting the window open, he took advantage of the delay and grabbed his dressing gown. His back to the wall, he made his way around the perimeter of the room until he was standing right next to the window. He would not be surprised this time.

With considerable exertion Belle managed to hoist the window up. Once there was enough space for her to squeeze through, she waved down at Dunford and wormed her way in.

The minute her feet touched the floor, a steely arm grabbed her from behind, and she felt the cold butt of a pistol pressed up against her neck. Fear froze her body and her mind, and she went stiff as a board.

"All right," she heard a furious voice behind her hiss. "Start talking. I want to know who you are and what you want with me."

"John?" Belle croaked.

She was instantly spun around. "Belle?"

She nodded.

"What the hell are you doing here?"

She swallowed nervously. "Could you put the gun down?"

John realized that he was still holding his weapon and dropped it on a nearby table. "For the love of God, Belle, I could've killed you."

She managed a tremulous smile. "I'm glad you didn't."

He raked a hand through his thick hair and then finally took a good look at her. She was dressed in black from head to toe. Her bright hair, which would have undoubtedly glowed in the moonlight, was stuffed under a cap, and the rest of her appeared to be stuffed into a pair of men's breeches. Or rather, a pair of boy's breeches. Her shapely form was shown off quite nicely by her unconventional attire, and he doubted that there were men's breeches small enough to compliment her backside so delightfully.

"What are you wearing?" He sighed.

"Do you like it?" Belle smiled at him, determined to brazen this out. She pulled the cap from her head, allowing the mass of her hair to tumble down her back. "I got the idea from Emma. From something she did once. She, umm, dressed as a boy, and—"

"Spare me the story. I'm sure Ashbourne was as furious as I am now."

"I think he was. I wasn't there. But the next day—"

"Enough!" He held up a hand. "How in hell did you get up here?"

"I climbed the tree."

"Where'd you get a damn fool idea like that?"

"Do you have to ask?"

John shot her a look which told her that he was not amused at having his own behavior thrown back at him. "You could have broken your neck, woman."

"You didn't leave me much choice." She reached forward to place her hand on his arm.

John jerked back. "Don't touch me. I can't think when you touch me."

That was encouraging, Belle thought, and reached forward again.

"I said stop it! Can't you see I'm furious with you?"

"For what? For taking a risk in coming up here to see you? This wouldn't have been necessary if you hadn't been such an addlebrained idiot and refused to see me."

"I had a very good reason for refusing to see you," John snapped.

"Oh, really? And what was that?"

"None of your damned business."

"I can see you're just as childish as ever," Belle sneered. "Ouch!" She jumped back as a rock hit her in her arm.

"What was that?" John hissed, grabbing his gun again and pulling her back from the window.

"When did you grow so paranoid? It's only Dunford, growing irritated at me, no doubt, for waiting so long to tell him that I made it in safely." Belle wriggled from his grasp and moved to the open window. Dunford was looking up at her. She couldn't see his face clearly, but she knew that concern was etched into his expression.

"I'm fine, Dunford," she called down.

"Is he going to see you home?"

"Yes, fine. Don't worry."

"I want to hear it from him."

"Stubborn man," Belle muttered. "Umm, John? Dunford won't leave until you give him your word that you'll see me home safely."

John scowled and crossed over to the window. "What the hell were you thinking?"

"I'd have liked to have seen you stop her," Dunford growled back. "Are you going to escort her home or do I have to remain here and—"

"You know damned well I will, and the two of us are having a talk tomorrow. You're either stupid or drunk or both to let her—"

"*Let* her? *Let* her? Oh, Blackwood, you're going to have a fine time of it as her husband. I didn't *let* her do anything. Napoleon himself couldn't have stopped her. I wish you the best of luck. You're going to need it." Dunford spun on his heel and walked back to the carriage he'd left a block away.

John turned back to Belle. "You'd better have a very good reason for pulling a stunt like this."

Belle gaped at him. "I told you, I needed to see you. What better reason is there? And could you possibly shut the window? It's cold in here."

John grumbled, but he shut the window. "All right. Start talking."

"You want me to start talking? Why don't you start talking? I've been wondering why a man would creep into my bedroom one day and make love to me and then refuse to see me the next."

"It's for your own good, Belle," he said through clenched teeth.

"Now where have I heard that before?" she asked, sarcasm dripping from every word.

"Don't throw that back at me now, Belle. It's an entirely different situation."

"So I *might* understand—if you told me what was going on. And while you've been off and immersed in your affairs, I've been having quite a little adventure."

"What the hell does that mean?"

"It means that someone tried to kidnap me two

days ago." Belle had turned away, so she didn't
see the blood drain from John's face. Taking a deep
breath, she risked everything and said, "And if you
really cared about me, I would think you'd want
to see about protecting me. I'd rather not go about
this alone, you know."

John grabbed her harshly by the shoulders and
turned her around. The expression on his face told
her that he still cared for her, and she would have
been overjoyed if he hadn't looked so completely an-
guished. "Tell me what happened," he insisted, his
face pinched with concern. "Tell me everything."

She quickly told him about the incident in the
alley.

"God*damn*!" he exploded, pounding his fist into
the wall.

Belle gasped as she saw a crack snake through
the plaster.

"And you're sure they said a highborn gentleman wanted you? You in particular?"

She nodded and winced as he shook her. "And
also that his arm was in a sling."

John let out a foul expletive. He'd shot his attacker just a few nights ago in the shoulder. With
a ragged sigh he limped over to a table with a bottle of whiskey and a glass. He picked up both and
then discarded the glass, taking a healthy swig of
the liquor directly from the bottle. He swore again
and then held the bottle toward Belle. "Want
some?"

She shook her head, unnerved by his stark expression. "No, thank you."

"You may change your mind," he said, laughing
harshly.

"John, what is wrong?" Belle rushed to his side.
"What is going on?"

He looked her straight in the eye, straight into

those perfect blue eyes that haunted him every night. There was no point in keeping the truth from her any longer. Not after his enemy had already decided that she was a valuable commodity. He was going to have to keep her close to him now if he wanted to keep her safe. Very close. At all times.

"John?" Belle implored. "Please tell me."

"Someone is trying to kill me."

The words fell on her like an avalanche. "What?" she gasped. She swayed and would have fallen to the floor if he hadn't reached out and caught her. "Who?"

"I don't know. That's the damned part about it. How in hell am I supposed to watch my back if I have no idea what I'm watching for?"

"But do you have any enemies?"

"None that I know of."

"Merciful heavens," Belle breathed, and John had to crack a smile at her extremely ladylike attempt at cursing.

"Whoever wants me dead has realized that you are very, very important to me and isn't above using you."

"Am I?" Belle asked softly.

"Are you what?"

"Very, very important to you?"

John let out a harsh breath. "For God's sake, Belle. You know that you are. The only reason I haven't been following you like a lapdog for the past few days is that I had hoped that my assailant hadn't yet made the connection between us."

Amidst her terror over John's safety, Belle felt a warm glow of happiness at his words. She hadn't misjudged him. "What are we going to do now?"

John sighed raggedly. "I don't know, Belle. Keeping you safe is my first priority."

"And yourself, too, I should hope. I couldn't bear

it if something were to happen to you."

"I'm not going to spend my life running, Belle. Or rather, limping, as the case may be," he added wryly.

"No, I can see that you wouldn't like that."

"Damn it!" His fingers tightened around the bottle of whiskey, and he very likely would have thrown it against the wall if Belle hadn't been there to temper his fury. "If I only knew who was after me. I feel so goddamned helpless. And useless."

Belle rushed to comfort him. "Please, darling," she implored. "Don't be so harsh with yourself. No man could do more than you're doing. But I think the time has come for us to seek out help."

"Oh?" he asked derisively.

Belle ignored his tone. "I think we should go to Alex. And Dunford, too, perhaps. They're both quite resourceful. I think they could help."

"I'm not going to involve Ashbourne. He's got a wife now to worry about and a child on the way. And as for your friend Dunford, I don't precisely respect his judgment after tonight."

"Oh, please don't blame Dunford for that. I didn't leave him much choice. It was either come and watch over me or know that I was going to do it on my own."

"You're a fine piece of work, Belle Blydon."

Belle smiled at what she decided to interpret as a compliment. "And as for Alex," she continued. "I know that you saved his life once."

John looked up sharply.

"He told me all about it," Belle said, stretching the truth just a tad. "So don't think you can deny it. And I know Alex well enough to know that he'll have been wanting to repay his debt to you for a long time."

"I don't see it as a debt. I did what any man would have done."

"I disagree. I know many men who won't even go out in the rain for fear of ruining their cravats, much less risk their lives for another. For God's sake, John. You can't do this alone."

"There is no other way to do it."

"That's not true. You're not alone anymore. You have friends. And you have me. Won't you let us help you?"

John didn't answer right away, and Belle let out another panicked rush of words. "It's just pride stopping you. I know that, and I won't forgive you if you . . . if you die, and only because you were too bullheaded to ask for help from the people who care about you."

He moved away from her and walked over to the window, unable to turn his thoughts from the man who was stalking him. Was he out there, just through the thin curtain? Was he just waiting, biding his time? And would he hurt Belle?

God, don't let him hurt Belle.

A long minute passed, and then Belle finally spoke, her voice quavering. "I . . . I think you should know that I'm counting on you to protect me. I'll face whatever lies ahead, but I won't do it alone."

John turned back around, his face stark with emotion. He opened his mouth but did not speak.

Belle stepped forward and touched his cheek with her hand. "And if you'll let me," she said softly, "I want to protect you, too."

John placed his hand over hers. "Oh, Belle, what did I ever do to deserve you?"

She finally allowed herself a smile. "Nothing. You didn't have to do anything."

With a groan, John pulled her into his arms. "I'm

never going to let you go again," he said fiercely, burying his hands in her thick hair.

"Please say you mean it this time."

John pulled away and took her face in his hands, his brown eyes firmly focused on her blue ones. "I promise you. We will face this together."

Belle wrapped her arms around his waist and let her cheek sink against his firm chest. "Can we possibly ignore this until morning? Or at least for the next few hours? Just pretend that everything is perfect?"

John leaned down and gently brushed his lips against the corner of her mouth. "Oh, darling, everything *is* perfect."

Belle turned her face so that she could return his kisses with all of her unschooled eagerness. Her passion only served to inflame his, and before she knew it, he had lifted her into his arms and carried her the short distance to his bed.

He laid her down and smoothed her hair from her face with such reverence that tears came to Belle's eyes. "I'm going to make you mine tonight," he said, his voice fiercely tender.

Belle only uttered one word. "Please."

His lips trailed hot kisses down the side of her neck as his nimble fingers quickly divested her of her clothing. He touched her like a starving man, caressing, rubbing, squeezing. "I can't . . . go slow," he said harshly.

"I don't care," Belle moaned. She felt the now familiar tendrils of excitement creeping up her legs and down her arms all the way to the center of her very being. She wanted release, begged for it, pleaded for it. She'd never dreamed that desire could come upon her this quickly, but having tasted it once before, she couldn't fight the urge to quench its hot flame. Her hands clawed at his dressing gown, driven by her need to feel his skin against hers.

John seemed to be feeling the same urges, and he nearly tore his robe in his haste to feel her breasts pressed up against his chest. "God, how I want you," he growled, sliding one hand down her torso to nestle in her crisp thatch of hair. She was wet, and the knowledge nearly drove him out of his mind.

He didn't know how much longer he could hold out without plunging himself into her, but he wanted to be absolutely certain that she was ready for him, so he gently slid one finger inside of her. He could feel her muscles clenching around him, and he was stunned by the rawness of her desire.

"Please," Belle begged. "I want . . . " Her voice trailed off.

"What do you want?"

"I want you," she rasped. "Now."

"Oh, darling, I want you, too." With gentle urging, he parted her legs and positioned himself above her, ready to enter but not quite touching her. His breath was uneven, and it took everything in him to say, "Are you sure, love? Because once I touch you I'm not going to be able to stop."

Belle's answer was to place her hands firmly on his hips and pull him toward her. John finally allowed himself to do what he'd been dreaming about for weeks and slowly entered her. She was small, though, and he was terrified that he would hurt her, so he went very slowly, pushing forward and pulling back to allow her body to get used to his. "Does it hurt?" he whispered.

It was a teeny bit uncomfortable when he pushed forward, but Belle could feel her body relaxing so she shook her head, not wanting to worry him. Besides, she knew where all this was leading, and she wanted very badly to get there.

John groaned to himself when he reached the thin barrier of her maidenhead. It had taken every ounce of his self-control not to pound into her the way his raging body demanded. "This may hurt you a bit, love," he said. "I wish it could be otherwise, and I wish I could take the pain for you, but I promise you it will only be this once, and—"

"John?" Belle interrupted softly.

"What?"

"I love you."

It felt as if his throat were about to close. "No, Belle, you don't," he gasped. "You can't. You—"

"I do."

"No, please. Just don't say it. Don't say anything. Don't . . ." He couldn't speak. He couldn't breathe. She was his, but he might as well have stolen her. She was more than he deserved, and if he was greedy enough to want her in his life, he wasn't enough of a bastard to ask for her heart.

Belle saw the tortured look in his eyes. She didn't understand it, but she wanted so desperately to make it go away. Words couldn't heal him so she demonstrated her devotion by pulling his head down to hers.

He was undone by her soft and gentle movements, and he plunged forward, sheathing himself completely within her. She felt so good, unlike anything he'd ever experienced, but he forced himself to lie still for a minute as he felt her passage stretching to accommodate him.

Belle smiled tremulously. "You're so big."

"Just the same as any man. Although I don't intend that you should ever have basis for comparison." He began to move within her, softly thrusting and enjoying the sweet friction between their bodies.

Belle gasped as she felt him. "Oh my."

"Oh my, indeed."

"I think I like this." Without thought, Belle began to move her hips beneath him, rising to meet him as he plunged within her. Her legs snaked around him, and her new position allowed him to come even further within her, so far that Belle was sure that he was touching her heart.

His movements grew faster and harder, and Belle was swept along with him as they traveled on that raging sea toward release. She plunged her fingers into his skin, raking him with her nails as she tried to get even closer to him. "I want it now!" she gasped, feeling her body begin to spiral out of control.

"Oh, you shall have it, I promise." His hand slipped between their bodies and touched her most sensitive nub of flesh. She exploded the moment he touched her, crying out her passion as every muscle in her body tensed and then seemed to shatter.

The feeling of her clenching around his hard shaft was more than John could bear, and he thrust into her one last time, grunting harshly as he poured himself into her. Together they collapsed into a dazed, sweaty tangle of arms and legs, heat radiating from their bodies.

After John's breathing had returned to normal, he brushed a damp tendril from her face and asked, "Well?"

Belle smiled up at him. "You have to ask?"

He breathed a sigh of relief. She wasn't going to ask him about his refusal to accept her declaration of love. He felt his body relax and even managed a teasing smile as he said, "Indulge me."

"It was wonderful, John. Like nothing I've ever known. And I have you to thank."

He tweaked her nose. "You played a pivotal role yourself."

"Mmmm," Belle replied noncommittally. "But you were holding back for me, making sure that I was . . . all right," she finished, unable to think of better words. When John made a move to protest, she placed her hand over his mouth and said, "Shh. I could see it in your face. You're such a gentle, caring man, but you try so hard not to let people see that side of you. Look at everything you did to make this perfect for me. Even pleasuring me before so I wouldn't be scared by my feelings tonight."

"It's because I—because I care about you, Belle. I want everything to be perfect for you."

"Oh, it is, John," she said with a contented sigh. "It is."

"I'm going to protect you," he vowed fiercely. "I'm going to keep you safe."

Belle snuggled into the crook of his arm. "I know, darling. And I'm going to keep you safe, too."

John smiled as an image of her wielding a broadsword floated through his mind.

"I'm not helpless, you know," Belle said.

"I know," he said indulgently.

His tone annoyed her, and she twisted around to face him. "I'm not," she protested. "And you'd better get used to it, because I'm not going to let you try to deal with this monster all by yourself."

John looked down at her and raised one eyebrow. "Surely you don't think I'm going to let you put yourself in danger?"

"Don't you see, John? If you put yourself in danger, you might as well be putting *me* in danger? It's the same thing."

John didn't see, but he didn't want to deal with it while she was lying all warm and soft in his arms. "Didn't you say that you wanted to forget about our problems for a few hours?" he reminded her softly.

"Yes, I guess I did. But it's hard, isn't it?"

John's hand strayed to the abrasion on his arm where a bullet had grazed him earlier in the week. "Yes," he said darkly. "It is."

Chapter 16

Morning came all too quickly, and Belle soon realized that she was going to have to return home. She pulled on her clothes quickly, still not quite able to believe that she had sneaked into John's room the night before. She'd certainly never thought of herself as the reckless, daring type. She sighed to herself, supposing that women did desperate things when in love.

"Is something wrong?" John immediately inquired, pulling a white shirt over his arms.

"What? Oh, it's nothing. I was just thinking that I never want to climb a three-story tree again."

"Amen to that."

"Not that getting up the tree was so dreadful. But inching along the branch to your window—"

"It doesn't matter," John cut in firmly. "Since you won't be doing it again."

His concern for her was so plain that Belle forgot

to be outraged over his high-handed behavior.

As they quietly made their way through Damien's house, Belle wondered at the wisdom of their walking back to her home by themselves while their enemy remained at large. She mentioned her worries to John when they reached the front steps.

John shook his head. "He strikes me as the cowardly type. More likely to move under the cloak of darkness."

"He attacked me during the day," Belle reminded him, stubbornly halting in her tracks.

"Yes, but he used hired thugs, and also you're a woman." John could see that Belle was about to make a protest at being dismissed so casually, so he added diplomatically, "Not that I think you're less than capable, but you must know that most men wouldn't see you as much of a threat. Besides, there is no reason he'd be up and about this early in the morning. Why should he wait out here if I'm probably going to be in bed for several more hours?"

"But he might have seen me last night. And then he'd know that you would have to take me home."

"If he had seen you last night, he would have grabbed you." The thought sent a shiver of fear through John and strengthened his resolve to put an end to this episode as soon as possible. His chin set determinedly, he took Belle's hand and led her down the steps. "Let's be on our way. I'd like to get you home before noon."

Belle took a deep breath of the crisp air. "I don't think I've ever been out this time of the morning. At least not on purpose."

John offered her a rakish grin. "And would you say it was on purpose that you're out now?"

"Well, maybe not exactly." She blushed. "But I had been hoping . . . "

"You're shameless."

"Perhaps, but you'll note that this story has a happy ending."

John's thoughts turned to the mystery man who had attacked them both. "Unfortunately, this particular chapter has not reached a conclusion."

Belle sobered. "Well, a happy middle, then. Or whatever it is one calls the part right before the climax."

"I rather thought we climaxed last night."

Belle's cheeks reached unparalleled heights of pinkness. "I was speaking in literary terms," she muttered unnecessarily.

John decided to stop torturing her and shut his still smiling mouth. After a suitable interlude, he asked, "Do you think Persephone will have risen yet?"

Belle frowned and looked at the sky, which was still pink and orange with the last stripes of dawn. "I'm not certain. She's a strange bird. I never know quite what to make of her. Besides, I'm rarely up at this hour, so I wouldn't know if she's an early riser."

"Well, for your sake I hope she's still abed. The only thing she could really do is insist that I marry you, which wouldn't be a problem because I plan to do exactly that and with all possible haste. All the same, I'd like to avoid screaming and swooning and all that female nonsense."

Belle gave him a sharp look at the "female nonsense" comment and muttered, "I imagine that Persephone and I will manage to comport ourselves in a manner so as not to offend your masculine sensibilities."

John's lips twitched. "See that you do."

Belle was spared from further comment by their arrival at her front steps. She had had the foresight to bring a key with her the previous night, and they slipped silently inside. John immediately made as if to leave, not wanting to create a scene.

"Please don't go yet," Belle said quickly, placing a gentle hand on his arm. Amazingly, none of the servants had witnessed their clandestine entrance. "Wait for me in the library. I'll run up and change into something more suitable."

John regarded her masculine attire with a smile and nodded as Belle scurried up the stairs. She stopped on the landing, looked back down with an impish grin, and said, "We have much to discuss."

He nodded again as he saw himself into the library. He trailed his fingers along the spines of the books until he found one with an intriguing title and plucked it off the shelf. He browsed through it lazily, not paying much attention to the words. His thoughts rested stubbornly on the fair-haired angel just upstairs from him. What on earth had possessed her to climb a tree to his third-story window? Not that he was displeased with the results, but still, he'd kill her if she tried something like that again. He sighed as his body grew warm, not with desire but with contentment.

She was his. He still wasn't certain how it had all come about, but she was his.

Belle reappeared dressed in a pale pink frock which brought out the natural rosiness of her cheeks. Her hair had been hastily pulled back into a loose knot which, while no one would mistake the style for fashionable, was at least presentable.

John raised a brow at her speedy transformation. "Only five minutes, my lady. I am stunned . . . and impressed."

"Oh, come now, it's not that difficult to get oneself dressed," Belle said.

"My sisters could never accomplish it in less than two hours."

"I suppose it all depends on how badly one wants to get where one is going."

"And did you want to get where you were going very badly?"

"Oh, yes," Belle breathed. "Very badly." She took a step toward him, and then another and another, until they were quite close. "I think you've made a wanton out of me."

"I certainly hope so."

Belle noticed that his breathing had grown slightly ragged and smiled. It was nice to know that she could affect him the way he did her. "Oh, by the way," she said offhandedly. "It usually *does* take more than five minutes for a lady to get changed."

"What?" John's eyes had glazed over with desire, and his mind absolutely refused to comprehend her statement.

Belle turned around. "The buttons."

He sucked in his breath as he gazed at her smooth white back, laid bare by her gaping dress.

"Would you mind?" she asked softly.

Wordlessly, John slipped her buttons into their buttonholes, his fingers straying to her warm skin at every possible occasion. When he reached the top one, he leaned down and dropped a tender kiss on the fragrant skin of her neck.

"Thank you," Belle said softly as she turned around. Every nerve ending on her neck and back felt as if it had suddenly come alive. Aware that she was going to have to behave with a bit more propriety—they were in her father's library, after all—she moved over to an overstuffed leather chair and sat down. "We do have a few matters to discuss," she said after making herself comfortable.

"Tomorrow." John lowered himself into the chair next to hers.

"I beg your pardon?"

"We're getting married tomorrow."

Belle blinked. "That's a bit soon, don't you think?" She had resigned herself to the fact that she was not going to have the wedding of her dreams, but she rather thought she deserved something a little special. She doubted that any of her relatives would be able to make it to London to witness her nuptials if John had his way.

"I'd do it today, but I think a lady ought to have a bit of time."

Belle eyed him warily, hoping that he was being sarcastic. "We don't need to be quite so hasty."

Her words did not worry him; John knew that she wasn't trying to back out of the marriage. Still, he had no desire for a long engagement. Not after what he had tasted the night before. "I should think we need to be extremely hasty. I want you near me where I can see to your safety. Not to mention the fact that you could be carrying my child."

Belle paled. She had been so swept away by passion she hadn't even given a thought to the possible consequences. She supposed that was why so many people ended up having rather inconvenient babies. "I wasn't proposing that we wait for months. I was merely hoping for a week or so. Besides, you will need time to obtain a special license."

"Got it."

"Already?"

"Last week. When I gave you a fortnight to wait for your parents to get home."

"My fortnight is not up." Belle smiled triumphantly and leaned back. She had won herself a few days, at least.

"Sorry, but that offer was extended before I realized that we had a rather inconvenient enemy.

I'm no longer willing to wait that long. I'll say it again—I want you near me where I can keep an eye on you."

Belle sighed to herself. He was really being quite romantic, and she was certainly not immune to a little romance. Still, she doubted that she could even get herself a new dress for her wedding if it were held tomorrow. The thought of getting married in one of her old frocks was decidedly *not* romantic. She looked up at him, trying to deduce whether there was any use in pleading her cause. He looked implacable. "All right. Tomorrow it is. In the evening," she added quickly.

"I thought weddings were held in the morning."

"This one won't be," she muttered.

John nodded graciously. He could grant her that. He rose and smoothed down his coat. "If you'll excuse me, I have some arrangements to make. Have you a favorite clergyman? Someone whom you would especially like to perform the service?"

Belle was touched that he had thought to ask but told him that there was no one in particular of whom she was especially fond. "But you'd better take some of my footmen with you," she added. "I don't want you going out alone."

John assented. He was of the opinion that his enemy would choose to attack at night, but there seemed no reason not to take precautions. "And I want you to stay here," he warned.

She smiled at his concern. "You can be assured that if I do go out, I shall take along no less than eight companions."

"I shall personally throttle you if you do not," John grumbled. "I'll call later today once I know when a clergyman is available."

Belle followed him out into the hall and arranged for two of her footmen to spend the day with him.

She accompanied him to the front door, where he took her hand and placed a light kiss on her palm. "Oh, John," she sighed. "Will I ever get enough of you?"

"I certainly hope not." He smiled cheekily and slipped out the door.

Belle shook her head and wandered up the stairs. Good God, was she really getting married tomorrow?

She sighed. She was.

She made her way to her bedroom and crossed over to her desk and sat down. She pulled out some of her writing paper and a quill. Where to start? She decided to write to her brother.

Dearest Ned,

I am getting married tomorrow evening. Won't you come?

Belle

She smiled and slipped the cryptic note into a creamy envelope. That ought to get him down to London in a hurry. Her note to Dunford was identical except that she included John's name. Not that it would come as much of a surprise to him.

Emma wouldn't stand for anything quite as mysterious, so Belle decided to be frank. Besides, her cousin already knew quite a bit about her relationship with John.

Dearest Emma,

To my great joy, John and I have decided to marry. Unfortunately, we must do so with great haste.

Belle frowned as she wrote that. Emma would certainly think the worst. Of course, she would be correct, but Belle was not inclined to think of the recent events in her life as the "worst" anything. Nevertheless, she continued on in her missive.

> I realize that this is terribly short notice, but I hope that you and Alex will be able to come to London tomorrow for my wedding. Unfortunately, I do not yet know the exact time of the ceremony, but it will be held in the evening.

Belle's frown turned into a grimace. That was a lot of "unfortunatelys" for what was supposed to be a joyous event. She was really making a mess of this. Giving up all pretense of elegant writing, she quickly finished up the note.

> I imagine you're surprised. I'm a little surprised myself. I'll explain it all to you when you arrive.
>
> > Much love,
> > Belle

She was just about to take the letters downstairs and ask a servant to summon three swift messengers when Persephone walked by her open door.

"Goodness, you're up early," the older lady exclaimed.

Belle smiled and nodded, suppressing the devilish urge to point out that she had never precisely gone to bed.

"Any particular reason?" Persephone persisted.

"I'm getting married tomorrow." No reason not to be blunt.

Persephone blinked like an owl. "Excuse me?"

"Married."

The blinking continued. Belle revised her opinion slightly and decided that her chaperone resembled an ordinary owl not so much as a somewhat deficient one. After a few moments, however, her birdlike friend regained her voice. "Is it someone we know?"

"Why, Lord Blackwood, of course," Belle snapped irritatedly. "Who else?"

Persephone shrugged her shoulders. "He has not come by for some time."

"I'd hardly call a few days 'some time,' " Belle said defensively. "And anyway, that is much beside the point as we are reconciled and getting married tomorrow evening."

"Indeed."

"Aren't you even going to congratulate me?"

"Of course, dear. You know that I think he is a very fine man, but I feel that I have somehow failed in my duties as your chaperone. However will I explain this to your parents?"

"You don't even know my parents, and furthermore, they haven't the slightest clue that I've got a chaperone." Belle looked over to Persephone and immediately realized that she had said the wrong thing. The older lady seemed to have metamorphosed from an ill owl to an agitated ferret. "Try to think of it this way," Belle offered hopefully. "The aim of all young ladies is to get married, or so we're told. Correct?"

Persephone nodded, but she looked dubious.

"I'm getting married. Therefore I have achieved a noble goal, and this reflects well on you, as my chaperone and companion." Belle smiled weakly, unable to think of the last time she had uttered such complete nonsense.

Persephone shot her a look which seemed to say, "Oh, really?" in the most sarcastic of tones.

"All right," Belle gave in. "It's an uncommon situation, I admit. And people will probably talk about it for weeks. We've simply got to make the best of it. And besides all that, I'm happy."

Persephone's lips curved into a romantic half-smile. "Then that's all that matters."

Belle was certain that she would never be able to sleep that night, but she awoke the next morning feeling rather refreshed. John had come by again the day before to tell her that he had found a priest who would marry them at seven o'clock the following evening. Belle had smiled, insisted that he keep her footmen for the rest of the day, and then politely pushed him out of the house. She had things to do.

Determined not to have a completely untraditional wedding, she arranged to have dozens of flowers sent to her house and then dragged Persephone out shopping for a dress. Needless to say, they brought along several male servants as escorts. Belle did not like to think of herself as panicky, but then again, she had no wish to be dragged off into another filthy alleyway.

Madame Lambert shrieked at the idea of producing a wedding dress on such short notice but nonetheless managed to provide Belle with an extremely flattering green silk gown which needed only minor alterations. The dress was simply cut, with the skirt falling gracefully to the floor from a high empire waistline. The neckline left her shoulders slightly bared and was adorned by layers of gauzy white material. The dress was more appropriate for warmer weather, but Belle decided that under the circumstances she really couldn't complain.

The rest of the day passed with surprising slowness. Belle had always thought of weddings as requiring mountains of preparations but quickly found that these mountains melted away when one's marriage was to be performed in one's home with less than a half dozen guests.

And now it was the day of her marriage, and she had absolutely nothing to do except sit around and be nervous. She'd feel better when Emma arrived, she decided. What she needed was some female company. Persephone was lovely, but she'd never been married and wasn't much help. She'd tried to have a "little talk" with Belle the night before, but it soon became painfully apparent that she had far less to "talk" about than Belle did. And Belle was quite determined to keep her mouth shut.

The conversation disintegrated rather quickly.

Unfortunately, Emma seemed to be taking her own sweet time in getting to London. Belle wandered aimlessly about the house all day, quite unable to concentrate on anything. She nibbled at breakfast, picked at her lunch, and then finally settled into a window seat in her mother's drawing room and stared out at the street.

Persephone came by and poked her head into the room. "Is everything all right, dear?"

Belle didn't turn around. For some inexplicable reason, her gaze was completely fixed on a small black dog yapping along the sidewalk. "I'm fine. Just thinking."

"Are you certain? You look a bit . . . strange."

Belle tore her eyes off of the cityscape and turned to face Persephone. "I'm fine, really. I just haven't anything to do, that's all. And if I did, I doubt I'd be able to concentrate on it."

Persephone smiled and nodded. Wedding jitters. She left the room.

Belle turned back to the window. The dog had departed the scene, so she decided to watch the leaves on the tree across the way. How many would fall off in such a strong wind?

Good God, when had she grown so melodramatic? She now knew why people made such a fuss about weddings. It was to keep the bride's mind occupied, lest she fall into strange mental chasms.

Strange mental chasms? Where had that come from? Now she knew she was really in trouble. She went back to her bedroom, laid herself down on her bed, and by sheer force of will made herself go to sleep.

She only realized that she'd drifted off when Persephone began to shake her by her shoulders. "My heavens, girl," she was saying. "I cannot believe you've been napping on your wedding day."

Belle rubbed her eyes, marveling that she had actually been able to force herself to sleep. "There seemed naught better to do," she said groggily.

"Well, Lord Blackwood's downstairs with the Reverend Mr. Dawes, and he's looking rather anxious to get on with the proceedings."

"What time is it?" Belle asked, coming awake rather quickly.

"Half past six in the evening."

Good Lord, how long had she been asleep? "Have any of my relatives arrived yet?" All three of them, Belle thought ruefully.

"No, but I hear that the roads out of town have been muddy of late."

Belle sighed. "Well, I suppose we can't wait all night for them. Please tell Lord Blackwood that I'll be down just as soon as I can. Oh, and if you don't mind, don't tell him that I was sleeping."

Persephone nodded and left the room.

Belle got to her feet and crossed over to her dressing room where her slightly too casual wedding dress was hanging. She supposed she ought to ring for her maid to help her dress. She'd always dreamed that she'd have her mother and Emma and perhaps a few friends with her to help her into her wedding gown. They would be laughing and joking and giggling over every little thing. It would be a grand affair, and she would feel like a queen. But there was no one. She was alone.

Alone on her wedding day. What a depressing thought.

Her thoughts strayed to John, who was undoubtedly waiting impatiently downstairs. She could see him in her mind's eye, pacing in the drawing room, his gait punctuated by the limp which had become so dear to her. Her lips tilted up into a smile. She wasn't alone. And she never would be.

She had just reached for the dress when she heard a commotion in the hallway. Her head swiveled instinctively toward the door as it burst open. Emma quite literally flew into the room.

"Good God, cousin!" she burst out, gasping for breath. Belle had no doubt that she'd taken the steps two at a time coming up the stairs. "Do you think you might have given me a little notice?"

"It was all somewhat sudden," Belle hedged.

"I suspect that that is something of an understatement."

Their attention was distracted by an even louder commotion in the hall.

"Oh dear," Emma muttered. "That would be Alex."

The man in question nearly kicked the door in.

"It certainly would," Belle returned dryly.

Alex's chest was heaving with exertion. Belle rather thought he'd taken the steps *three* at a time. He fixed his deadly green gaze on his wife, who had the grace to look at least a little uncomfortable.

"If I ever see you jump out of a carriage like that again, so help me God, I'm going to strangle you."

Emma chose the path of least resistance and avoided talking to her husband altogether. "He's a little overprotective due to my delicate condition," she said to Belle.

"Emma . . ." he said warningly.

John chose that moment to appear in the doorway. "What the hell is going on here?"

Belle shrieked, threw her arms up in the air, and ran into her dressing room. "You can't see me!" she yelled.

"Oh for God's sake, Belle. This isn't exactly a normal wedding."

"It's going to be as normal as I want it. So get out. I'll see you downstairs." Her voice was muffled, emerging through several layers of fabric and a rather thick wooden door.

Alex rolled his eyes and muttered, "Women," which caused his wife to glare at him most vigorously. "I need a drink." He stalked out of the room. John followed without a backward glance.

Emma shut the door quickly behind them and scurried over to the dressing room door. "They're gone," she said quietly, not at all sure why she was whispering.

"Are you certain?"

"For heaven's sake, Belle. I have eyes, don't I? I tell you, they're gone."

Belle poked her head around the side of the door, and when she was satisfied that the room was devoid of male creatures, ventured out.

"I *used* to think you were the most sensible person I knew," Emma muttered.

"I lost my sense," Belle said, meaning it.

"Are you sure you're ready to do this?"

Belle nodded and a tear welled up in her eye. "I

just thought it'd be different. My mother isn't even here!" She sniffled loudly.

Emma touched her arm, deeply moved by her cousin's tears. "You can wait, Belle. There is no reason you have to go through with this today."

Belle shook her head. "I can't wait, Emma. Not another day." And then she told her the entire story.

Chapter 17

Once Emma was convinced that Belle was truly in love with John, she helped her cousin into her wedding gown and proclaimed her the most radiant bride she'd ever seen.

"I suppose that means my eyes aren't bloodshot any longer," Belle joked. She'd let loose quite a torrent of tears.

Emma solemnly shook her head. "Do you want Alex to give you away?"

Belle frowned. "I had hoped that Ned would be here by now. If I cannot have a father of the bride, I was hoping for at least a brother. As it is, Father is going to be furious that he didn't get to give me away."

"Well, he got to give me away," Emma said efficiently. "That will have to do. Did Ned send a reply?"

"There wasn't time."

Emma nibbled at her lower lip. "Why don't I go downstairs and stall the proceedings? I'll be right back."

She slipped out the door and made her way to the drawing room. John was pacing back and forth, not so much with nervousness as with impatience. "What's taking so long?" he snapped.

Emma pursed her lips and looked up at the clock. "It's only ten minutes past seven. That's perfectly punctual for a wedding that is supposed to begin at seven."

"Women." This came from her husband, who was sprawled on a sofa which was much too small for his large frame. Dunford was sitting across from him, smirking.

Emma shot both of them a rather nasty look before turning back to her future cousin-in-law. "We only need a bit more time," she hedged.

"Emma, darling," her husband said in an unbelievably smooth tone. "Could you come here for a moment?"

Emma eyed him suspiciously but walked over to the couch.

"Do you see the priest over there?" he whispered.

She nodded.

"Do you see anything, er, shall we say, *odd* about him?"

Emma tilted her head as she surveyed the portly gentleman. "He does seem to be leaning a little to the left."

"Just so. He's been here thirty minutes, and that's his fourth glass of brandy. I think we ought to get this ceremony underway while we are still able."

Wordlessly, Emma exited the room and went back upstairs. When she reached Belle's bedroom, she said, "I don't think we can stall very long."

"Not even a few minutes?"

"Not if you want to get married tonight."

Belle had no idea what *that* meant but decided she'd rather not find out. She picked up a piece of white Spanish lace and fixed it on her head. "I suppose we cannot wait any longer for Ned. You had better summon Alex to give me away."

Emma darted back down the stairs, grabbed her husband by the hand, and asked Persephone to begin at the piano. She and Alex met Belle at the top of the landing just as Persephone began thumping away.

"Good God," Alex said as the cacophony assaulted his ears. "Is that Beethoven?"

"I could have sworn I asked for Bach," Belle said, furrowing her brow.

"I don't think it's Bach, either," Alex said. "I don't think it's anything."

"We can only hope she doesn't start to sing," Emma said. She shot her cousin one last smile before she headed down the stairs as matron of honor.

"She could hardly do worse than you," Alex jibed.

Belle looked at her cousin who was already halfway down the stairs. "I don't think she heard you," she whispered.

"That's probably a blessing. Shall we go?" Alex offered her his arm. "I believe it's our turn."

As they floated down the stairs, past all of the pink and white roses Belle had specially ordered, her nervousness and disappointment over the hastiness of her wedding melted away, and all that was left was a deep sense of contentment and joy. Each step took her closer to the man she loved, the man whose life would soon become inextricably linked with her own. When she turned into the drawing room and saw him standing next to the priest, his eyes glowing with pride and desire, it was all she could do not to run headlong into his arms.

She and Alex finally reached the front of the room, and he placed her hand on John's arm and stepped away.

"Dearly beloved!" Mr. Dawes barked. Alcoholic fumes swept across Belle's face. She coughed discreetly and took a tiny step back.

Persephone missed her cue and kept banging away at the piano, enjoying herself immensely. Dawes turned to her with obvious irritation and yelled, "I said, 'Dearly Beloved!' "

Persephone's musical thumps died a slow and painful death.

Belle took advantage of Dawes's momentary distraction to whisper to John, "Are you sure he's a man of God?"

John bit back a smile. "Quite sure."

Dawes turned back to the couple. "As I was saying—Dearly beloved." He blinked a few times and surveyed the scant crowd. "Or rather," he muttered, "perhaps I should say the three of you."

Belle couldn't help herself. "There are four guests, if you please."

"I beg your pardon."

"I said," she ground out. "There are four guests. I realize that this is an irregular wedding, but I'd like to be credited with all four of my guests." She could feel John next to her, shaking with silent laughter.

Dawes was not the type to give in easily to what he saw as a mere slip of a girl, especially after he'd been fortified with five glasses of fine brandy. "I see three."

"There are four."

His finger jabbed at Alex, then Emma, then Dunford. "One—two—three!"

"Four!" Belle finished with a triumphant motion toward Persephone who was watching with obvious fascination and mirth from the piano.

At this point Dunford exploded with loud laughter, which set off Emma and Alex, who had heretofore managed to keep themselves under control. Dawes grew quite red in the face and said, "*She* is the piano player."

"She's my guest."

"Oh, all right, you impertinent little chit," he grumbled, mopping his brow with a limp handkerchief. "Dearly beloved, we are gathered here before *four* witnesses . . . "

The ceremony continued with blessed uneventfulness for several minutes. John could hardly believe his luck. Just a few more minutes, he thought, and they'd exchange vows and rings, and then she'd be his for all of eternity. Fairly bursting with joy and impatience, he forced himself to resist the urge to shake the voluble priest and get him to speak faster. He knew that he was supposed to be savoring every moment of the ceremony, but what he really wanted was to be done with it all and retreat to some hideaway where he could be alone with his bride for the next week.

John's hopes for a speedy ceremony, however, were dashed when he heard the front door to the house slam open with a resounding crash. Dawes looked at him in askance, and he nodded curtly, signaling that the ceremony should proceed.

Dawes fumbled forward even as heavy footsteps came crashing toward them through the hall. Determined not to interrupt again, Belle kept her eyes scrupulously forward, but John was unable to keep himself from turning around as a dark-haired young man burst into the room. His eyes were so blue that he could only be Belle's brother.

"Good God!" Ned Blydon exclaimed, jumping over a sofa. "Have you gotten to the part about objections yet?"

"Er, no," Dawes said, his bulbous nose glowing red in the candlelight. "We haven't."

"Good." Ned grabbed Belle's free hand and dragged her away from the makeshift altar. "Do you know what you're doing?" he hissed. "Who is this man? Do you know anything about him? What is going on? And how dare you send me a note saying only that you're getting married the next day? What were you thinking?"

Belle waited patiently throughout his tirade. "Which question do you want me to answer first?"

"Look here!" Dawes boomed. "Is this marriage going forward or not? I've got—"

"It's on," John said in a deadly voice.

"I'm a busy man," Dawes spluttered. "I've got—"

"Mr. Dawes," Dunford interrupted smoothly, flaying him with a devastating smile. "I must apologize for this interruption. It is scandalous that a man of your stature should be treated thus. Won't you join me in a glass of brandy while this matter is cleared up?"

Belle didn't know whether to thank Dunford or throttle him. At this rate Dawes would be too drunk to perform the ceremony. She rolled her eyes and turned back to her brother, who was looking at her with concern. "Are you certain you want to do this?" he was saying. "Who *is* this man?"

Alex stepped forward and tapped Ned on the shoulder. "He's a good man," he said softly. Beside him, Emma nodded vigorously.

"Do you love him?" Ned asked.

"Yes," Belle whispered. "With all my heart."

Ned looked her in the eye, trying to gauge the depth of her feelings. "Very well, then. I apologize for the interruption," he said loudly. "But we're going to have to start over from the beginning, because I want to give my sister away."

"See here, young man! We're already more than halfway through," Dawes barked. "I'm a busy man."

"You're a red-faced drunk," Belle muttered to herself.

"Did you say something?" Dawes said, blinking vigorously. He turned to Dunford, whom he now perceived as an ally, and grabbed him by the shoulder. "Did she say something?"

Dunford carefully disengaged himself from the priest's grasp. "Don't worry, good fellow, you'll get paid extra for your troubles. I'll see to it."

Belle and Ned hurried up the stairs and had just reached the top when they heard Dawes say, "Is she going to play the piano again?" A loud whacking sound followed, the origin of which Belle didn't want to know.

Within seconds, Persephone began playing the piano with a vengeance, and Belle began her second procession of the day down the stairs to get married.

"You look beautiful," Ned whispered.

"Thank you." Belle smiled at his words, deeply touched. She and her brother loved one another dearly, but it was a bickering sort of love, not a complimenting one. When Belle reached the drawing room again, John's eyes were still shining at her with love and pride, but this time she also saw a trace of humor. She smiled back at him, a silly little half-smile to tell him that she didn't care that her wedding had fallen into a shambles. She only wanted him.

The ceremony proceeded remarkably smoothly considering the earlier mishaps. Persephone even stopped pounding the piano promptly when Dawes groaned, "Dearly beloved."

In due time John and Belle were man and wife.

There was much cheering when they kissed, although Dunford later remarked that he clapped more for the fact that the ceremony had actually made it through to the end than he had for the couple's happiness.

After the customary congratulations and requisite kissing of the bride by all the male guests (there were only three; it didn't take very long), Ned looked brightly at his sister and asked, "Where is the reception? I'm famished."

Belle's face fell. She'd forgotten all about a reception. And to think that she'd been complaining to herself because she hadn't anything to do. But then again, even though she was aglow with happiness over having finally married the man of her dreams, she felt that a celebration tonight would feel more like a dinner party than a wedding reception.

"Belle decided to put off a reception," John cut in smoothly, "until your parents get home. She felt that your mother would prefer it that way."

Ned thought that his mother would have preferred it if Belle had also held off on the wedding ceremony, but he held his tongue. He smiled blandly at his new brother-in-law and then finally asked the question which had been foremost on his mind all evening. "Just exactly how did you and my sister meet?"

"I've recently bought property near Ashbourne's holdings at Westonbirt," John replied. "We met there."

"And he fought with Alex on the Peninsula," Belle added. "They were good friends."

Ned looked at John with new respect.

"Speaking of the war," Alex suddenly put in, "you'll never guess who I saw from my carriage as we arrived."

John turned to face him. "Who?"

"George Spencer."

Belle felt John's fingers tighten on her arm. He appeared as if he were about to say something, but no sound emerged from his mouth.

"Surely you remember him," Alex said.

"Who is George Spencer?" Belle asked.

"Just an old acquaintance," John said quickly.

Alex leaned down and dropped a fraternal kiss on Belle's cheek. "I believe we were about to leave the newlyweds to their own devices." He smiled at Emma, who immediately made motions as if to leave.

John waylaid him, however, placing a firm hand on his arm. "Actually, Ashbourne," he said in a low voice. "Could I have a word alone with you before you leave?"

Alex nodded, and the two men went off into the library.

John shut the door behind them. "I'm not certain if you ever knew the full story about George Spencer."

Alex cocked his head. "I know you forced him to desert the army."

"*After* I shot him."

"Excuse me?"

"In the ass."

Alex walked over to a nearby table, poured himself a glass of whiskey, and then downed it in one gulp. "Any particular reason?"

"He was raping a young Spanish girl. A girl I had sworn to protect."

Alex swore softly, and his knuckles grew white around the glass.

"If it really was George Spencer loitering outside," John said caustically, "I don't think it was because he wanted to offer his best wishes to the bride and groom."

Alex raised a brow. "Is there more to this story?"

John weighed out the advantages and disadvantages of telling Alex about his plight. The last thing he wanted to do was drag a man with a wife and a baby on the way into a potentially deadly situation. But then again, he had a wife, and given his plans for the near future, he rather thought a baby might be forthcoming fairly soon. The weight of these new responsibilities bore down on him, and he remembered Belle's words from just a few days earlier.

You can't do this alone.

John hadn't really known how to follow her advice. He'd been on his own for so long that he had no idea how to ask for help, no idea how to accept it. Alex was his family now—twice removed by marriage, but family nonetheless. John already felt a greater sense of kinship with him than he did with any of his brothers or sisters. Damien hadn't even been able to make it to the wedding.

Yet Alex and Emma had rushed in from the

country. The unfamiliar warmth of family began to wash over John. He looked over at Alex, who had been watching him carefully. "I have a problem," John said softly.

Alex tilted his head.

"George Spencer is trying to kill me."

There was the soft whoosh of indrawn breath before Alex replied, "Are you certain?"

"I am certain that *someone* is trying to kill me," John replied. "And I cannot accept that his presence outside this house is a coincidence."

Alex raked his hand through his hair. He remembered Spencer's rage when John had forced him to desert. "No. It's not a coincidence. We're going to have to do something about him."

John was surprised by how reassured he felt by Alex's use of the word "we."

"Where are you staying tonight?"

It wasn't an unintelligent question. John had, after all, gotten married less than an hour before. Under normal circumstances, he and Belle would have left for a honeymoon or headed back to Bletchford Manor for some time alone. But he didn't feel that they would be safe in the country; there were too many windows and doors at his home that Spencer might be able to sneak into. London would probably be safer, if only because there were so many people around who might witness Spencer's attacks. "I don't know," John finally said. "I've been busy. I hadn't even thought about it. I don't particularly want to take Belle back to my brother's."

"Stay here," Alex suggested. "I'll take Persephone back to my house for the night. Belle certainly doesn't need a chaperone any longer." He offered John a sideways smile. "You took care of that in rather short order."

John couldn't help but grin.

"I'll send over a few extra servants," Alex added. "This place is already crawling with them, but it can't hurt to have a few more. The more people here, the safer you'll be."

"Thank you," John said. "I was also considering hiring a bodyguard for the next few weeks."

"A good idea. I'll see to it."

"That's really not necessary."

"For God's sake, man, you just got married. Let me worry about the damn bodyguards."

John nodded in assent, thinking that he could get used to the idea of having a family who cared.

"Emma and I will remain in town until we have this sorted out," Alex continued. "Contact me in the morning, and we'll decide what to do about Spencer."

"I'll do that."

"And in the meantime, have yourself a splendid wedding night."

John grinned. "I'll certainly do *that*."

A knock sounded at the door, and Belle poked her head in. "Are you through with him, Alex?" she asked. "Because it's my wedding night, you know, and I think I've a right to my groom."

"Actually we were just discussing that very topic," Alex said with a rakish smile. "And as a result I think I want to go find my wife and go home."

Belle shook her head as he left the room. "What on earth were you talking about?" she asked her husband.

He put his arm around her shoulders as they followed Alex out. "I'll tell you all about it tomorrow."

The handful of guests left soon thereafter. As

Emma departed, however, she took Belle's hand in hers and pulled her aside.

"Do you, er, need to have a talk with me?" she whispered.

"I don't think so," Belle whispered back.

"Are you certain?"

"About what?"

"That you don't need to have a talk with me?"

"Emma, what are you talking about?"

"Married love, corkbrain. Do you need to have a talk with me?"

"Oh, er, no. No, I don't."

Emma drew back, a light smile touching her features. "I had a feeling you didn't." She let go of her hand and took a few steps away before turning back to say, "Well then, have a good night."

Belle smiled. "Oh, I shall. I shall."

"What was that all about?" John asked, leaning down to kiss his wife's neck now that all of their guests had departed.

"I'll tell you tomorrow."

"Fine. I have other things on my mind tonight." He steered her up the stairs.

"So have I." She followed with alacrity.

"What are you thinking?" John asked when they reached the landing. "Right . . . now."

"I was thinking that I'm glad that we're staying here tonight."

"Mmmm, me too. It would have taken far too long to make it home."

"To your brother's?"

"No, goose. To Bletchford Manor."

Belle smiled. "It seems so long since I've been there. It hadn't even occurred to me that I have a new home."

"It's not very grand," John said quietly.

"It's grand enough for me."

"It has a terrible name."

"That can be fixed."

"Not very many servants."

"I don't need many. And stop trying to put down Bletchford Manor. It has several excellent attributes."

"Really?" They were at the top of the stairs.

"Oh yes." Belle smiled flirtatiously. "The rose bushes are quite beautiful."

"Is that all?"

"There is a stunning Aubusson carpet in the drawing room."

"Is that all?"

"Well," Belle said with a smile as they turned into her bedroom. "There is the master."

"The master?" John's eyes lit with delight.

"He's very attractive."

"Do you think so?" He kicked the door shut.

"Oh yes, very."

John's hands stole around to the cloth-covered buttons which marched down the center of her back. "I have a secret for you."

"You do?" Belle could feel her heart quickening at the touch of his warm hands on her skin.

"Mmm. This master you're speaking of . . ."

"Yes?"

"He likes you, too."

"Does he?"

John undid the last of her buttons and let the dress slide down her body, leaving her clad only in a silky little thing which drove his every sense wild. "He'd like to begin mastering you tonight."

"Mastering me?" Belle questioned, with just a hint of playful scolding in her voice for his choice of verbs.

"Well, he's done it once before, and he liked it quite a bit."

"Did he now?" Belle could barely get the words out, for John's hands were now moving up her legs, pushing her chemise over her thighs.

"Very, very much."

"Enough to spend a lifetime doing it?" she asked.

"Mmm-hmm. Enough to let you master him."

She cocked her head and smiled. "Really?"

"Oh, yes." His lips found the hollow where her neck met her shoulder.

Belle felt herself moving backwards until she felt the bed behind her. John's mouth had moved down to cover one of her breasts, and she was finding it very difficult to stand. They sank down onto the bed together.

The heat of his body seared her into the mattress for only a moment before he lifted himself up and tore his shirt off. "God, Belle," he said raggedly. "If you only knew . . ."

"If I only knew what?" she asked quietly, her eyes sliding over his bare chest with feminine appreciation.

His hands, which had been undoing the buttons on his trousers, stilled. "How much . . . What you . . . " He gave his head a little shake, as if to dislodge the words from his throat. "My life was . . . " He swallowed. "I don't know how to say it."

Belle reached out and took his hand. "Then show me."

He flattened her palm against his stomach and slid it up to his heart. "It beats for you," he whispered. "Only you."

He moved toward her slowly, as if pulled by some invisible thread connecting them. The rest of his clothing fell to the floor, and then he was with her, the heat of their bodies separated only by the thin silk of her chemise.

Belle could feel the urgency bursting within him. His hands roamed her skin with an energy that was almost frantic. Desire curled through her body, whipped up into white hot heat by his hands and lips and the incoherent whisperings of his mouth.

She tore at her chemise, trying to move it up her body, but he pushed her hands back down. "Leave it," he said. "I like it."

"But I want to feel you," she gasped.

"You can." He splayed his hand over her midriff. "I can feel you. And I feel silk, and heat, and desire."

Belle felt something quickening in her abdomen. Her breath was coming in short little pants. His hips were pressing against hers, the evidence of his desire nestled between her legs. "John, I—"

"What, love?"

"I want to feel you."

A shudder went through his body, and Belle could feel the tension in his muscles as he fought to control his desire.

"You don't have to go slowly," she whispered. "I want it, too."

His eyes flew to hers. "Belle, I don't want to hurt you."

"You won't. You could never hurt me."

His hands moved to her legs, and he slowly separated them, pushing up her silky chemise in the process. The tip of his manhood found her, and he began to move forward.

Belle caught her breath as she felt him entering her. It was the most intimate of kisses, and she arched her hips to bring him even closer. His movements grew faster, more furious.

It was building within her. A force. A tension. It was growing, filling her.

John's breathing grew ragged. He sank his fingers into her hair, gasping her name as he pushed forward and back, his body lost in primal rhythm.

Belle was spiraling toward ecstasy. She clawed at his back, trying to reach something that was so close . . . and then she was there. Pleasure gripped her, and she screamed out his name.

But John didn't hear her. Her shouts were drowned out by his own as he surged forward one last time and exploded within her. He collapsed on top of her, his entire body heaving with exertion.

Many minutes later he rolled onto his side, pulling her along with him. Their bodies were now separated, but John held her close. "I want to fall asleep with you in my arms," he whispered. "I want to feel you, and to smell you. I want to know you're here."

Belle snuggled closer. "I'm not going anywhere."

John sighed, a smile forming on his lips. He nuzzled his face against her hair, dropping a kiss on top of her head. "My wife," he said, unable to keep a touch of wonder from his voice. "My wife."

Chapter 18

❧᎒᎒❧

It wasn't until the next morning that Belle remembered to ask John about his conversation with Alex. He briefly considered hiding the truth from her, but one look into her inquisitive blue eyes reminded him that he respected her far too much to resort to subterfuge.

"I know who is trying to kill me," he finally said, his voice low.

Belle sat up in bed, pulling the covers over her breasts. "Who?"

"George Spencer." He cleared his throat. "The one I told you about."

The blood drained from Belle's face. "But I thought he'd left the country."

"I thought so, too. Ashbourne saw him outside the house before the wedding."

"Are you certain that he'd want to kill you?"

John closed his eyes as his memory took him

271

back to Spain. The stench of sex and blood. The agony in Ana's eyes. The fury in Spencer's. "I'm certain."

Belle put her arms around him and pulled herself close to his side. "Now at least we know who he is. Now we can fight him."

He nodded slowly.

"What are we going to do?"

"I'm not sure yet, love. There is much to consider." But he didn't want to think about any of that yet, not when he was still lying in bed with his wife of less than twenty-four hours. Abruptly changing the subject, he kissed her again and asked, "Did you have a good wedding?"

"Of course," Belle replied loyally.

"Are you certain?" John hated to think that his haste might have spoiled one of the most magical days in her life. "You seemed somewhat distraught before the ceremony."

"Oh, *that*," Belle said, a light blush creeping across her cheeks. "I was just a touch edgy."

"Not having second thoughts about me, I hope." He *hoped*? He prayed.

"No, of course not," Belle said, playfully swatting him on the shoulder. "I never, never even once thought I was making a mistake. I was just a bit at odds with myself because my wedding wasn't exactly how I dreamed it was going to be."

"I'm sorry," John said softly.

"No, no, don't be. Just because it wasn't what I thought I wanted doesn't mean it wasn't absolutely perfect. Oh, dear, am I making any sense at all?"

John nodded solemnly.

"I thought that I needed a church and hundreds of guests and music that actually sounded like music, but I was wrong. What I needed was a drunken

priest, irreverent guests, and a companion who
learned to play piano from a goat."

"Then you got exactly what you needed."

"I suppose so. But then again, all I really needed
was you."

John leaned down to kiss her again, and they
remained thus occupied for the next hour.

As the day wore on, John realized that he was
going to have to take some action about George
Spencer. He certainly had no desire to sit around
and wait for Spencer to finally lodge a bullet in his
chest. He'd go crazy if he had to wait patiently for
his enemy to make a move. For the sake of his san-
ity, then, he would need to come up with a plan.
The idea of skulking in shadows was distasteful,
and he resolved to face the situation head-on and
meet with Spencer in person.

Of course that required knowledge of Spencer's
whereabouts. John had no doubt that such information would not be difficult to obtain. News traveled fast in London, even in the off-season, and
Spencer was from a good enough family to insure
that his arrival would have been noted. One simply
had to ask the right people.

John retired to the library and penned a note to
Alex right away, requesting his help. A reply arrived not twenty minutes later.

Spencer is staying in rented rooms at 14
Bellamy Lane. He has returned to London
under his own name and is enjoying a
lukewarm reception. Apparently he tried to
return to England directly after the war and
was scorned as a deserter. His situation has
improved since then, although not by much.

He does not receive many invitations, but I

do not think that it would be difficult for him
to gain acceptance to large parties and balls.
He has the right accent and the right clothing.
You and Belle will have to be careful.

Please keep me informed of your plans.

Ashbourne

Alex had been busy since the night before. John
shook his head in admiration. He sat down with a
quill and paper. After several drafts, he finally decided on simplicity and sent this letter:

Spencer,

I understand that you are in London. We
have much to discuss. Won't you please come
by for tea? I am staying at my in-laws' house
in Grosvenor Square.

Blackwood

John sent the note off with a messenger and gave
him instructions to wait for a reply.

He wandered out into the hall, looking for Belle.
He still didn't really know his way around the
mansion, which was quite large for a town house.
He felt damned strange staying in someone else's
home, especially since the owners were off in Italy
and had no idea that he'd just married their only
daughter. If the Blydons were in residence, he'd
feel more like a proper guest, but as it was, he felt
like he was playing the master in another's home.
The awkward situation only served to make him
more determined than ever to put an end to his
problems with Spencer. He'd spent five years saving money to buy a home of his own, and now he
couldn't even use it.

If he hadn't just gotten married, he'd have been
in a really foul mood.

He finally found Belle asleep on a sofa in her sitting room. He smiled to himself, thinking that she deserved her nap. He'd certainly done his best to keep her up the night before. Not wanting to disturb her, he tiptoed out of the room and headed back to the library where he settled into a chair with a copy of *The Passionate Pilgrim*. If Belle could read it, he figured, so could he. It irked him that he had to sit around and read while someone was plotting to do him in, but given his current strategy, there didn't seem anything to do other than wait.

He was well into the second act when Belle knocked on the door.

"Come in!"

She poked her head in. "Am I disturbing you?"

"On my first day as a married man? I think not."

She walked in, shut the door behind her and headed over to the chair next to John's.

"Hmm-mmm," he said, catching her by the hand. "Over here." One deft tug, and she toppled onto his lap.

Belle laughed all the way down and planted two kisses along the line of his jaw, marveling at how comfortable she'd grown with this man. "What are you reading?" she asked, peeking at his book. "*The Passionate Pilgrim*? Whatever are you reading that for?"

"You read it."

"And?"

He tweaked her nose. "And I remembered how adorable you looked when we were talking about it the day I met you."

Belle's reply was another kiss.

"I've figured out what was wrong with our wedding," John mused.

"Oh?"

He leaned forward and brushed his lips against the corner of her mouth. "Most couples," he murmured, punctuating his words with little flicks of his tongue, "get to spend an entire week in bed after they get married. We didn't even sleep late."

Belle fluttered her lashes. "We could go back," she suggested.

His hand stole up her midriff and rested on her breast. "An interesting idea."

"Do you think so?" she asked in a breathy voice.

John squeezed her ever so gently, reveling in her response. "Mmm-hmm." He smiled lazily as he watched her arch her back. He could feel her nipple hardening into a tight little bud, and his body hardened in response.

"Will we always feel this way?" she whispered.

"Christ, I hope so." He leaned forward and captured her mouth in a hard, demanding kiss. His lips and tongue were ruthless, demanding everything of her, relentless in their mission to claim her very soul.

Belle's reaction was fast and furious. His brutal kiss inflamed her desire, and she returned his passion in equal measure, raking her hands along his back. His hot mouth moved down her neck, burning a trail of fire along her skin. "Did you lock the door?" he asked raggedly, his lips never leaving her throat.

"What?" Belle was so lost on a sea of passion she could barely hear his words.

"Did you lock the door?"

She shook her head.

"Damn." Reluctantly John tore his mouth from her tender skin and slid out from under her. Belle landed in a soft heap on the chair as he crossed the room to the door, her breath coming in uneven gasps.

John gave the key a decisive twist and turned back to his bride, his eyes gleaming with desire. Unfortunately, he had only taken two steps toward her when he heard a loud knock. He swore under his breath and shot a quick look to Belle to make sure that she was presentable before turning around. Taking his irritation out on the hapless doorknob, he viciously yanked the door open.

"What?" he snapped.

"My lord," came the quavering voice of the footman. "A letter for you, my lord."

John nodded curtly and picked up the paper resting on the footman's silver tray.

"There is usually a letter opener on that desk over there," Belle said, flicking her head toward the desk.

John followed her advice and slit the seal. The letter was written on expensive white paper.

My dear Lord Blackwood,

Do you think I'm stupid?

If you should like to meet I would be more than willing to arrange a time and place on a more neutral ground. I have always had a partiality for the docks.

George Spencer

"Who is it from?" Belle asked.

John crumpled the paper in his hands. "George Spencer," he said in a distracted voice.

"What?" she shrieked. "Why is he writing to you?

"Well, he *is* trying to kill me," John said mildly, his passion sadly diffused by the interruption. "And aside from that, I sent him a letter earlier today."

"What? Why? Why didn't you tell me?"

He sighed. "You're beginning to sound like a nagging wife."

"Well, you took care of the wife part yesterday, and as for the nagging—I think it's my prerogative given our intolerable situation. Now will you answer my question?"

"Which one?"

"All of them," she ground out.

"I wrote him a letter because I thought I might have a better chance of protecting myself if I could meet with him face-to-face and discern the level and nature of his hatred for me. I didn't tell you because you were sleeping. And then you were, er, otherwise occupied."

"I'm sorry for snapping at you," Belle said, somewhat appeased. "But I don't see what you can expect to accomplish by meeting him. You're just giving him an opportunity to kill you."

"I don't plan to take any unnecessary chances, love. I asked him to meet me here. He'd have to be very desperate to try anything in my home, or your home, as the case may be."

As soon as the words left his mouth, John knew they were the wrong ones, for Belle cried out, "But you don't know how desperate he is! If he really, really hates you, he might not care about the consequences of killing you in front of witnesses. Darling, I can't allow you to take such chances." Her voice broke. "Not when I love you so much."

"Belle, don't say—"

"I'll say whatever I damn well please! You take chances with your life, you don't say you love me, you won't even let me tell you that *I* love *you*." She made an inarticulate sound and jammed her fist into her mouth for a moment to still an oncoming sob. "Don't you even care?"

He gripped her upper arms with stunning force. "I care, Belle," he all but growled. "Don't let anyone tell you otherwise."

"No one is trying to. Only you."

A deep and ragged breath racked his body. "Can it be enough to know that I care, Belle? That you've reached depths of my heart I didn't even know existed? Can that be enough for now?"

She swallowed convulsively. Lord, she hated it when she couldn't understand him. Still, she nodded. "For now," she said, her voice low. "Not for long. Certainly not forever."

He took her face in his hands and leaned down to kiss her, but she broke away. "I suppose we have to deal with this monster first. It is difficult to build a marriage when I fear for your life."

John tried to ignore the hollowness that had settled in his heart when she pulled away. "I promise you, darling, that I am taking the safest course of action. I have no wish of dying, but I cannot spend my life hiding away from Spencer. Eventually, he'll find me."

"I know. I know. What did the note say?"

John stood and crossed the room to the window. "He won't meet me here," he said, looking out at the busy street. "I imagine he thinks it's some sort of a trap."

"Is it?"

"A trap? No, although now that I think about it, the idea does have its merits."

"What else did he say?"

"He wants to meet me at the docks."

"I hope you don't plan to meet with him *there*." Belle shuddered. She'd never actually been to the docks, but every Londoner knew that it was a dreadful part of town.

"I'm not stupid," John replied, unconsciously

echoing Spencer's written words. "I'll see if he'll meet me in some other public place. A crowded place," he added, mostly just to reassure her.

"Just so long as you don't go alone. I'm sure Alex and Dunford would be happy to accompany you. And Ned, too, if he's not already back at university."

"I doubt that Spencer will be willing to say what he wants to say to me in the company of others, Belle. But don't worry, I don't plan to meet him without friends nearby. He won't have an opportunity to try anything funny."

"But why would he meet with you other than to try to kill you?"

John scratched his head. "I don't know. He probably wants to tell me *how* he wants to kill me. Or how much."

"This isn't funny, John."

"I wasn't trying to make a joke."

Belle buried her face in her hands. "Oh, John," she moaned. "I'm so scared of losing you. It's almost funny. Part of the reason I fell in love with—" She held up her hand. "No, please don't interrupt. Part of the reason I fell in love with you is because I thought you needed me. I've got hordes of people who like me or love me, but no one has ever *needed* me like you do. But now I realize . . . " She broke off, choking on a sob.

"What, darling?" he whispered. "What do you realize?"

"Oh, John, I need you, too. If something should happen . . . "

"Nothing will happen to me," he said fiercely. For the first time in years he had something to live for. He wasn't going to let a raping bastard take it all away.

Belle looked up at him through teary eyelashes. "What are we going to do?"

"*We* aren't going to do anything," he replied, walking over to her and tousling her hair. Then, for good measure, he crouched down, pried her hands from her face, and kissed her brow. "I, however, am going to write Spencer a note."

He walked over to the table where he'd left the quill and paper he'd used earlier in the day. "What do you suggest I say?" he asked in a mild voice, trying to divert her mind away from her dread and anxiety.

"I think you should call him an idiotic son of a—"

"I don't think that will work," John cut in smoothly, wondering where on earth she'd come up with such a colorful vocabulary. "We don't want to insult him."

"*We* may not, but I certainly do."

"Belle," he sighed, hiding his smile. "You are a priceless gem. Whatever did I do to deserve you?"

"I don't know," she replied, standing up. "But if you want to keep me, I have one important piece of advice: don't die." With that, she took a deep breath and left the room, quite unable to be anywhere near a piece of paper that might eventually cause John's death.

John shook his head as he watched her leave. She wasn't taking this very well. But then, how could he blame her? If someone were trying to kill her, he'd be scouring London like a madman, desperately trying to get to him first.

Pushing such a distasteful thought from his mind, John turned back to the quill and paper before him. How strange to conduct a correspondence with one's assassin.

Spencer,

Do you think *I'm* stupid?

I suggest we meet somewhere slightly more palatable, perhaps Hardiman's Tea and Pastry Shoppe. You may name the time.

Blackwood

He had taken Belle to Hardiman's several times during their hasty courtship. They could get a private table there, but more importantly, the establishment was frequented by enough society matrons and debutantes that Spencer would not dare try anything foolish. Furthermore, it would be easy for Alex to sit nonchalantly a few tables away.

John once again dispatched the messenger to Spencer's lodgings. He expected a quick answer; Spencer would surely be waiting at home for a reply to his invitation.

He sighed and raked his fingers through his hair. He should go talk to Belle. It tore him apart to see her so distraught, but he didn't know what to say to her. He didn't know any words that would make her feel better. He'd been married to her less than twenty-four hours and already she was miserable. He'd failed his bride, and he felt helpless to alleviate her suffering.

His bride.

John's lips quirked into a faint smile. He liked the sound of that. He stood up abruptly, his chair scraping loudly against the hardwood floor.

He strode out into the hall as quickly as his injured leg would let him. "Belle!" he called out, heading up the stairs. "Belle! Where are you?"

She appeared at the top of the steps, panic evident on her face. "John? Is something wrong? What's going on?"

"I just wanted to see you, that's all." He smiled lightly, trying to relieve her tension. "Do you always ask three questions when one would suffice?"

"For heaven's sake, John, you scared the life out of me. Please don't yell like that again. I'm distraught enough as it is."

He crossed the distance between them and put his arm around her. "Please, darling. You're going to make yourself ill. Let's go back to your room and talk."

"Our room," Belle said with a sniffle.

"What?"

"Our room. I'm married now. I don't want a room of my own any longer."

"I don't want you to have one either. Belle, we will have a normal life soon. I promise you that."

Belle let him lead her to their bedroom. She wanted so much to believe him. "I can't help being scared, John," she said softly.

He pulled her to him and breathed in the light fragrance of her hair. "I know, darling, I know. But let's put off that fear for the moment. There is nothing to be afraid of right here, right now."

Her lips quivered into a tiny smile. "This very second . . . ?"

"All there is is me." He traced the line of her jaw with his lips, moving languorously to her ear. And then it wasn't enough.

His hands curved around her backside, pulling her even more intimately against him. He kissed every spot of exposed skin, moving to her hands and wrists once he was through with her neck. He had just moved back to her left earlobe when they heard a voice at the door.

"Ahem."

John didn't even turn, just waved his hand at the offending servant.

"Ahem!"

The voice was more insistent so John reluctantly tore himself away from Belle and twisted his head toward the door. An extremely well-dressed lady was standing there with an odd expression on her face. John had never seen her before, although she did have the most amazing set of blue eyes—really, really blue, rather like . . .

An uneasy feeling crept through him as he slowly turned to Belle, who was still rather firmly pinned against his body. She looked ill. Very ill. Almost green.

"Mother?"

John jumped away from Belle with amazing speed.

Caroline, the Countess of Worth, peeled off her gloves with an efficiency that bordered on fury. "I see you've been very busy since I've been gone, Arabella."

Belle gulped. Her mother's use of her full name was not a sign for optimism. "Well, yes," she stammered. "I have."

Caroline turned to John. "I think you had better leave."

"He can't!" Belle said quickly. "He lives here."

Caroline's only outward sign of perturbation was a strained swallowing motion in her throat. "I'm sure I misheard you."

John quickly stepped forward. "Perhaps I had better introduce myself. I am Blackwood."

Caroline didn't offer him her hand. "How nice for you," she said acerbically.

"And this," he continued, motioning toward Belle, "is my wife, Lady Blackwood."

"Excuse me?" Not even a chink in her calm facade.

"We're married, Mother," Belle said with a weak

smile. "Just yesterday."

Caroline shot a disbelieving look at her daughter, then at the man she had married, then back at her daughter. "Belle, do you think I could speak to you privately for a moment?" She grabbed her daughter's arm with a force that was at odds with her pleasant words and hauled her across the room. "Are you crazy?" she hissed. "Do you realize what you've done? Where on earth is Emma? And how could she let you do this?"

From across the room, John wondered if this propensity to ask questions in rapid succession without waiting for a reply was a family trait.

Belle opened her mouth to say something, but Caroline held her hand up. "Don't!" she warned. "Don't say a thing to me." With a deft movement, she grabbed Belle's arm and deposited her back at John's side.

"Mother," Belle said. "If you'll just..." Her words trailed off at Caroline's quelling stare.

"If you'll both excuse me," Caroline said smoothly. She walked over to the door and called out, "Henry!" Belle and John heard a muffled answer, to which Caroline replied, "*Now*, Henry!"

"I don't like being made to feel like an errant child," John hissed in Belle's ear.

"I *am* an errant child," she whispered back. "At least to them. So please be patient."

Belle's father appeared in the doorway. Henry, the Earl of Worth, was an attractive man with graying hair and an easygoing air about him. His eyes lit up with obvious love when he saw his only daughter. "Belle! Darling! What are you doing in London?"

"Oh, this and that," Belle mumbled.

"She got married," Caroline said flatly.

Henry said nothing.

"Did you hear me?" Caroline burst out, her composed exterior beginning to crumble. "She got married."

Henry sighed wearily and ran his hand through his thinning hair. "Was there some reason you couldn't wait, Belle?"

"I was in a bit of a rush."

Caroline turned pink, not wanting to ponder the implications of that statement.

"Surely you could have waited a few days," Henry continued. "Did you think we wouldn't let you have your choice? You know us better than that. We've let you refuse a dozen eligible men, including young Acton, whose father happens to be my best friend. This fellow looks nice enough. We probably wouldn't have had an objection." He paused. "I presume this *is* the fellow you've married."

Belle nodded, wondering why a lecture from her father always managed to make her feel about seven years old.

"Does he have a name?"

"Lord Blackwood," Belle said clearly.

John took the initiative and stepped forward, extending his hand. "John Blackwood, my lord. I'm pleased to meet you."

"I should hope so," Henry replied dryly. "Have you the means to support my daughter?"

"I just purchased a new home, so I haven't much to spend freely," John replied frankly. "But I am wise and conservative in my investments. She shall not want for anything."

"Where are you from?"

"I grew up in Shropshire. My father was the Earl of Westborough. My brother succeeded him to the title."

"How'd you come about yours?"

John briefly told him about his time in the army. Henry nodded approvingly and finally asked, "Do you care for my daughter?"

"Very much, my lord."

Henry surveyed the younger man, whose hand was now clutched quite firmly in Belle's grasp. "Well, Caroline, I think we're just going to have to trust our daughter's judgment on this score."

"There is little else to do," Caroline said bitterly.

Henry placed a comforting hand on his wife's shoulder. "I'm sure we will have time enough to sort out all of the particulars. For now, I think we should concentrate on becoming acquainted with our new son-in-law, don't you think, Caroline?"

She nodded, loving Belle too much to do anything else.

Belle ran forward and threw her arms around her mother. "You'll see, Mama," she whispered. "He's perfect."

Caroline smiled at her daughter's unbridled happiness, but whispered back, "Nobody's perfect, Belle."

"He's perfect for me."

Caroline gave Belle one last squeeze before putting her at arm's length so that she could get a good look at her. "I expect you're right," she replied. "Now why don't we let your father get to know your, er, husband while you help me get settled in. It has been an uncommonly long journey."

Belle thought that, all in all, her mother was taking this news surprisingly well. She shot a fleeting smile at John and followed her out of the room.

"I don't suppose you've sent a notice to the *Times*," Caroline was saying as she ascended the stairs.

"There hasn't been time."

"Hmmm. Well, I'll have your father see to that

immediately. Where is this new home John has purchased?" Caroline turned around as she reached the top of the stairs, a worried expression on her face. "He did say his name was John, didn't he?"

"Yes, Mama. And it's right next to Westonbirt. I met him while I was staying with Emma."

"Oh." Caroline made her way to her bedroom, where a maid was unpacking her cases. "I suppose I'll arrange a reception for you next spring, when everyone is in town. But I do think that we ought to do something soon, if only to let everyone know you're married."

Belle privately wondered why it was imperative that "everyone" be immediately appraised of her marital status. "Won't the notice in the *Times* suffice?"

"Not at all, my dear. We need to let the *ton* know that you have our approval. No need for everyone to realize that we hadn't even met John until today."

"No, I suppose not."

Caroline suddenly clapped her hands together. "I know! The Tumbleys's winter ball! It's perfect. Everyone always comes in from the country to attend."

Belle gulped nervously. Every year the Earl and Countess of Tumbley held a ball in November. It was one of the few events for which the aristocracy would travel back to London in the winter. Normally, she would have loved to go, but she didn't think it would be safe for her and John to venture out into large crowds at night. "Er, when is it, Mother?"

"Sometime in the next few weeks, I imagine. I'll have to check my correspondence for the exact date. I have such a stack of letters to go through."

"I'm not really sure that we would want to go, Mama. We are newly married, you know, and wanting a bit of privacy."

"If you wanted privacy, you should have high-tailed it back to the country the minute after you said, 'I will.' But as long as you're here, you'll go to this ball, and you'll do it with a smile on your face. And then you can go back to wherever it is that you're living now and rusticate. Where *are* you living now—I mean, what's it called?"

"Bletchford Manor."

"*What*-ford Manor?"

"Bletchford Manor."

"I heard you the first time. It's a dreadful name, Belle."

"I know."

"No, I mean it's hideous."

"I know. We're planning to change it."

"See that you do. After the Tumbley bash, that is, because you're not stepping a foot out of London before then."

Chapter 19

⚜

John sat in Hardiman's Tea Shoppe the next day, his back to the wall as he watched out for a man he hadn't seen in over five years, a man who wanted him dead. He'd secured a table in the rear, with Alex and Dunford discreetly seated four tables away.

John kept his eyes on the door, and ten minutes past the agreed upon meeting time, George Spencer walked into the establishment. John felt the years rush away, and he was back in the Spanish tavern again, watching his countryman violate an innocent girl.

Spencer scanned the room with icy blue eyes until his gaze fell on John. He flicked his head back, propelling his straight blond hair from his eyes. He strode arrogantly through the shop until he reached John's side.

"Blackwood." His voice was cold.

"Spencer. You'll pardon me if I don't offer you the courtesy of rising."

"Not at all. I've heard you're lame. I wouldn't want you to overexert yourself." He shoved the chair back and sat down.

John nodded graciously. "A war wound. Some of us remained with the company through the action. Where did you go, Spencer? France? Switzerland?"

Spencer's hands clutched at the table, and he nearly rose from his seat in his rage. "Damn you, Blackwood. You know that you forced me to desert. Do you know what it's like to come back to England in dishonor? My father had to pay off the authorities just to keep me from getting arrested."

John fought to keep his own rage in check. "And you think you don't deserve to be arrested after what you did?" he hissed. "You should have been hanged."

"Spare me your sensitivity, Blackwood. That girl was nothing. A stupid peasant, nothing more. She'd probably shared her charms with a dozen men before me."

"I saw the blood on the sheets, Spencer. And I heard her screams."

"For the love of God, Blackwood, I did the girl a favor. She was going to have to get that out of the way sooner or later."

John gripped the table in an effort to keep himself from strangling him. "She killed herself three days later, Spencer."

"Did she?" Spencer looked unconcerned.

"Don't you feel any remorse?"

"Damn town was overpopulated, anyway." Spencer held out his hand and idly examined his fingernails. "Those Spaniards breed like rabbits."

"She was an innocent girl," John bit out.

"I am forever impressed by your sense of chivalry. But then again, you always did have a soft spot for the ladies. May I offer you my congratulations on your advantageous marriage? So sorry it's going to be such a short union."

"Leave my wife out of this," John bit out. "You aren't fit to speak her name."

"Oh my, aren't we getting dramatic? I hope love hasn't made you soft, Blackwood. Or perhaps your knee took care of that years ago."

John took a deep breath and forced himself to count to five before speaking again. "Just what is your plan, Spencer?"

"Why, to kill you. I thought you'd figured that out already."

"May I ask why?" he asked, his voice icy with politeness.

"Nobody plays me for the fool, Blackwood, nobody. Do you understand me?" Spencer was growing agitated, and his brow was tense and damp with perspiration. "What you did—"

"What I did was shoot you in the ass." John leaned back and allowed himself his first smile of the day.

Spencer jabbed his finger at John. "I'm going to kill you for that. I've been dreaming about it for years."

"What took you so long?"

John's calm manner only served to enrage Spencer even further. "Do you know what happens when a man deserts? He isn't exactly welcome back in England. His fiancée decides that she might do better elsewhere. His name is dropped from all the lists that matter. You did this to me. You."

"And is England suddenly welcoming you with open arms? I had heard you weren't welcome at the best of parties."

For a moment John thought that Spencer was going to leap over the table and go for his throat. Then, abruptly, the blond man calmed down. "Killing you won't solve all my problems, of course. But it will bring great joy into my life."

John sighed. "Look," he said mildly, "I suppose I don't really need to tell you that I'd rather you didn't kill me."

Spencer let out a short bark of laughter. "Elegantly said, but then again, I'd rather you hadn't ruined my life."

"Why did you come today? Why sit here and make idle conversation?"

"Maybe I was curious. What about you? One would think you'd be hesitant to meet with your killer." He leaned back and presented John with a jaunty grin.

John was beginning to wonder if Spencer was insane. He was obviously obsessed, but at the same time, he seemed bent on maintaining normalcy, sitting here chatting with John as if they were old friends. "Maybe I was curious," he replied. "It's a unique situation. It's a lucky man who gets the opportunity to meet with his killer under such civilized circumstances."

Spencer smiled and inclined his head, graciously acknowledging what he perceived to be a compliment.

"Suppose you tell me what you're planning. You wouldn't want this to be anything less than a challenge, would you?"

"I couldn't care less if it's a challenge. I just want you dead."

John smiled tightly. Spencer certainly didn't believe in indirect speech. "No hints at what I might expect?"

"Something quick and easy, I think. No need to make you suffer."

"How kind of you."

"I'm not a monster, just a man of principle."

While John was pondering that unbelievable statement, Spencer focused on something over his shoulder. "Is that your lovely wife I see, Blackwood? I must commend you on your marital success."

John felt his insides run cold. He twisted in his seat, his gaze swinging around until it fell upon Belle, who had just entered the shop with Emma and Persephone.

John took another deep breath, trying to contain himself. He was going to kill her. He was going to put her over his knee and blister her bottom. He was going to lock her in her room for a week. He was—

"Not very excited to see her, I see."

John swiveled back to Spencer and snapped, "Another word from you, and I will strangle you as I sit."

Spencer leaned back and chuckled, enjoying himself enormously.

"Our conversation is over." John stood up and walked across the room without a backward glance. Alex and Dunford would make sure Spencer didn't attack him. He grabbed Belle's arm before she could even sit down, hissing in her ear, "You are going to be a very unhappy woman."

Belle had the good sense to keep her mouth shut. Or it might just have been that she was dying to get a good look at George Spencer, who had risen to leave just after John. He passed right by them on his way out, tipping his hat at her and murmuring, "My lady."

The only bright spot in John's nightmare was the

enraged expression on Belle's face. He had no doubt that she would have had a fair portion of Spencer's face under her fingernails if he hadn't been holding her firmly by the arm.

Once Spencer was safely out of the shop, John yanked her around to face him and said, "What the hell do you think you're doing?"

Before she had a chance to answer him, Alex showed up at his side, grabbed Emma similarly and hissed, "What the hell do you think you're doing?"

Persephone looked at Dunford and smiled, waiting for her turn, but much to her disappointment, he just stood there and glared at all three women.

"John," Belle said. "I don't really think this is the time." She turned to the rest of their group and gave them a wide but weak smile. "So sorry, but we're going to have to leave."

John growled. Persephone took that as a sign of agreement and waved at him. "Hope to see you soon," she said brightly.

John growled again and this time Persephone said nothing.

Belle looked up at her husband. "Shall we go?"

He walked out, and since her arm was attached to his hand, she went along with him. When they reached the street, John turned to her and said curtly, "Did you bring a carriage?"

She shook her head. "We hired a hack."

This didn't seem to please John, and Belle didn't say anything while he hailed down another one. They rode home in absolute silence. She stole occasional looks at his profile and noticed that a muscle in his cheek was twitching violently.

He was furious. She peeked over at him again. The twitch had speeded up. Beyond furious. He was only waiting until they got home so he wouldn't embarrass her in front of the driver.

She supposed she should be thankful for small favors.

The hack pulled up in front of the Blydon mansion, and Belle scurried out while John paid the driver. She raced up the front steps, through the hall, and into the rear drawing room. She wasn't trying to avoid John—well, perhaps she would have tried if she thought she had any chance of getting away with it. But as it was, she was simply trying to choose a room which was as far away from the servants as possible.

John was only a few steps behind her, so completely enraged he was barely limping. He slammed the door behind him. "What the hell did you think you were doing?"

"I was worried about you."

"So you followed me to my meeting with Spencer? Pardon me if I don't commend your common sense."

"But—"

"Do you understand what kind of man Spencer is?" John exploded. "He *rapes* women. Rapes. Do you understand the meaning of the word rape?"

Belle crossed her arms. "I hate it when you get sarcastic."

"Deal with it."

She clenched her teeth against his harsh tone and turned away.

"Damn it, woman! You put yourself in a dangerous situation. And dragged along Emma and Persephone in the process. Did you think about that?"

"I thought you might need me," she ground out.

"Need you? Of course I need you. Safe and sound and tucked away in the house. Not wandering around in front of killers."

Belle whirled back around. "I'm not some help-less little miss who is willing to sit at home while you gallivant about town. And if you think for one minute that I'm not going to do everything in my power to keep you safe, then your brain is quite broken."

"Listen to me, Belle," John said in a low voice. "We didn't know that much about Spencer. We had no idea what he was going to do. For all I knew, he might have decided that the best way to get to me was through you. He might have grabbed you this afternoon."

"I thought you said you were sure that Spencer wouldn't try anything in a crowded shop. Were you lying to me? Were you? Were you lying just to keep me from worrying about you?"

"Damn it all to hell, of course I wasn't lying to you. I *didn't* think Spencer would do anything at Hardiman's. All the same, I couldn't be one hundred percent certain, and I didn't see any reason to put you in any danger."

"I'm going to help you, John, whether you want it or not."

"Good God, woman, stop being so stubborn. These things take planning and finesse. If you keeping barging into this without looking where you're going, you're just going to get in the way."

"Oh, please, John. I wouldn't have to barge into anything if you would only include me."

"I won't have you put into a situation from which you cannot extricate yourself."

"Do me a favor, John. Worry about yourself. I can run fast. Faster than you."

John flinched as though he'd been hit. "I had no idea my injury made me so much less of a man in your eyes."

"Oh, John, you know I didn't mean it that way."

Belle flung her arms around him and held him close. "I'm just so scared and so angry, yes angry at this man." Belle paused and caught her breath, surprised by the realization that she felt more fury than fear. "I'm angry, and I lashed out at you, and that wasn't fair. It's just that I love you so much, and—"

"Belle, please."

She let go of him and furiously pushed him away. "Please what? Please don't tell you I love you? Please don't *love* you?"

"I can't accept it, Belle."

"What is wrong with you?" she burst out. "Why can't—"

"What is wrong with me," he said in steely tones, his hands gripping her upper arms like manacles, "is that I raped a girl."

"No," she choked out. "No, you didn't. You told me you didn't."

"It might as well have been me," he said, unconsciously echoing Ana's mother's words.

"John, don't say such things. It wasn't your fault."

He let go of her with a chilling abruptness and strode over to the window. "I could have gone up to that room a thousand times before I finally did."

Belle's hand crept up to cover her horrified mouth. "Oh, John, what has this done to you?" she whispered.

"Has it made me less of a man? Yes. Has it blackened my soul? Yes. Has it—"

"Stop!" She covered her ears, unable to bear his words. "I don't want to hear it."

He whirled around. "You're damn well going to hear it." When she didn't move, he stalked back to her and wrenched her hands from her ears. "This is the man you married, Belle. For better or for worse. Don't say I didn't warn you."

"When will you understand that I don't care what happened in Spain? I'm sorry that it did, and I pray for that poor girl's soul, but beyond that, I don't care! It hasn't made you an evil person, and it doesn't make me love you any less!"

"Belle," he said flatly. "I don't want your love. I can't accept it."

Before she even realized what she was about, her hand flew up, and she slapped him across the face. "How dare you?" she breathed, her entire body shaking with rage. "How dare you belittle me this way?"

"What the hell are you talking about?"

"I have never, not even once in my life, given my love to another man. And you throw it back in my face like a trifle."

His hand closed around her wrist. "You misunderstand me. It is because I value your love so highly that I do not accept it."

"You don't accept it because you don't want to accept it. You're mired in misplaced guilt and self-pity. How am I meant to build a life with a man who cannot leave the past where it belongs?"

He dropped her hand, feeling like the lowliest of bastards simply for touching her.

"How can I possibly let myself continue to love a man who can never love me back?"

He stared at her, his entire body suddenly feeling rather queer. "But Belle," he whispered. "I do love you."

John wasn't certain how he expected her to respond, but it was certainly not in the manner she did. She stepped back as if hit, and for a moment she was utterly incapable of speech. She pointed a finger out, jabbing it in his direction while her throat worked violently. "No," she finally gasped. "No. Don't say that. Don't tell me that."

He merely looked at her, every emotion he had ever felt for her clearly written on his face. Love, guilt, hope, longing, fear . . . They were all there.

"You can't do that," she said, each word a hoarse little stab of pain. "You're not allowed. You can't say that and not let me do the same. It isn't fair."

He reached for her. "Belle, I—"

"No!" She jumped back. "Don't touch me. I— Don't touch me."

"Belle, I don't know what to say." He looked down.

"I can't talk to you," she said wildly. "Not now. I can't talk to you. I . . . I . . . I . . . " Her words jumbled in her throat. Her entire body was so overtaken with emotion that she could no longer speak. She swallowed convulsively, pulled open the door, and flew from the room.

"Belle!" John called out. She didn't hear him. He sank into a chair. "I love you."

But the words sounded pathetic, even to him.

Chapter 20

Belle had no idea where she was going when she left the room, but when she bumped into Mary, her maid, in the corridor, she knew what she needed to do.

"Put on your cloak, Mary," she said, her voice uncharacteristically sharp. "I need to go out."

Mary glanced out the window. "It's quite overcast, my lady. Are you certain your errand cannot wait until tomorrow?"

"I don't have an errand. I just want to go outside."

Mary heard the choking sound in her lady's voice and nodded. "I'll be right back."

Belle clutched her own cloak to her body. She'd never even had a chance to take it off after she and John had stormed home from Hardiman's Tea Shoppe.

After a moment Mary came scurrying down the

stairs. Belle didn't even wait for her to reach the bottom before pulling open the front door. She needed fresh air. She needed to be outside.

They strode along Upper Brook Street to Park Lane. Mary immediately made to turn south. "Don't you want to go to Rotten Row?" she asked when Belle kept heading west without her.

Belle shook her head furiously. "I want to get away from the crowds."

"I wouldn't worry about that, my lady." Mary looked about. All of fashionable London was scrambling to leave the park. The heavens looked as if they might open at any moment. "I really think you should consider going home. I'm sure it will rain soon. And it's growing dark. Your mother will have my head. Or your husband."

Belle whirled around. "Do mention him."

Mary took a step back. "All right, my lady."

Belle immediately let out a contrite sigh. "I'm sorry, Mary. I don't mean to be so short with you."

Her maid placed a consoling hand on her arm. They had been together for several years now, and Mary knew her employer well. "It's all right, my lady. He loves you very much."

"That's just the problem," Belle muttered. She took a deep breath and forged further into the park. How far they walked she wasn't sure. Probably not very far, but the wind and the cold tired her. Finally, she turned around. "Let's go home, Mary."

The maid breathed an audible sigh of relief. They trudged for a few moments until Belle suddenly slammed her arm out in front of Mary. "Hold," she whispered loudly.

"What's wrong?"

Belle squinted her eyes at the blond man she saw thirty or so yards up the path. Was that Spencer?

With her eyesight it was impossible to tell. Damn, why had she been so foolish? She never would have come to the park with only a maid for an escort if she'd been thinking clearly. A fat raindrop landed on her nose, jolting her out of her frozen stance.

"Back up," she whispered to Mary. "Very slowly. I don't want to attract attention."

They tiptoed back toward a wooded area. Belle didn't think the blond man saw them, but her nerves were still on alert. It probably wasn't Spencer, she tried to tell herself. If it were, it would certainly be too much of a coincidence to think that he was also out taking a walk in Hyde Park on a cold, windy day, for no other reason than to take in some fresh air. The only reason he'd be out would be to follow her, and the blond man up ahead did not appear to be following her.

Still, she had to be careful. She moved more deeply into the trees.

The air suddenly pounded with thunder, and the rain began in earnest, fast and furious. Within seconds, both Belle and Mary were drenched to the bone. "We must get back," Mary yelled over the din.

"Not until the blond man—"

"He's gone!" Mary tugged on her arm and began to drag her out to the clearing.

Belle yanked her arm back. "No! I can't! Not if he's—" She looked up ahead. No sign of him. Not that she could see much of anything. It had already been growing dark, and the rain had completed the job.

A sudden crack pounded in her ears. Belle gasped, jumping back. Was that thunder? Or a bullet?

She began to run.

"My lady, nooo!" Mary tore after her.

Panic-stricken, Belle ran through the wood, her dress snagging on branches, her hair streaming into her eyes. She tripped, fell, and righted herself. She was breathing hard, disoriented. She certainly didn't see the low-hanging tree branch in front of her.

It slammed into her forehead.

She went down.

"Oh, my good Lord," Mary cried out. She knelt down and shook Belle. "Wake up, my lady, wake up!"

Belle's head lolled from side to side.

"Oh no, oh no," Mary chanted. She tried to drag Belle along the path, but the rain had soaked through her thick garments, making her far too heavy for the maid.

With a cry of frustration, Mary propped Belle up against a tree trunk. Either she stayed with her or went back for help. She didn't like the thought of leaving her lady alone, but the alternative ... She looked around. They were surrounded by trees. No one would ever see them.

Her decision made, Mary straightened, picked up her skirts, and began to run.

John was sitting in the library, nursing a glass of whiskey. He had reached that unique state of anguish which even alcohol cannot obliterate, and so the glass had remained in his hand, untouched.

He sat in excruciating stillness, watching as the sun dipped below the horizon and disappeared, listening as the tiny raindrops which pattered against the windowpane grew into fat rivulets.

He should go to her. He should apologize. He should let her tell him she loved him. *He* knew he didn't deserve it, but if it upset her to hear the truth . . . There was nothing that gripped his heart like a tear in Belle's eye.

He sighed. There were a lot of things he should do. But he was a bastard and a coward, and he was terrified that if he tried to take her into his arms she'd only push him away.

He finally set the glass down. With a fatalistic sigh, he stood. He'd go to her. And if she pushed him away . . . He shook his head. It was too painful to contemplate.

John made his way up to their bedchamber, but there was no sign that Belle had been in the room since their argument. Puzzled, he made his way back downstairs, crossing paths with the butler on the landing.

"Pardon me," John said. "But have you seen Lady Blackwood?"

"No, I'm sorry, my lord," Thornton replied. "I thought she was with you."

"No," John murmured. "Is Lady Worth about?" Surely Caroline would know Belle's whereabouts.

"Lady and Lord Worth are dining this evening with their graces, the Duke and Duchess of Ashbourne. They left over an hour ago."

John blinked. "Very well. Thank you. I'm sure I'll find my wife somewhere."

He descended the last few steps and was about to search Lady Worth's favorite salon when the front door burst open.

Mary was gasping for breath, her brown hair plastered to her face, her entire body heaving with exertion. Her eyes widened when she saw him. "Oh, my lord!"

Icy fear squeezed around John's heart. "Mary?" he whispered. "Where is Belle?"

"She fell," Mary gasped. "Fell. She hit her head. I tried to drag her. I did. I swear it."

John already had his coat on. "Where is she?"

"Hyde Park. She— I—"

He grabbed her shoulders and shook. "Where, Mary?"

"In the wood. She—" Mary clutched her stomach and coughed violently. "You'll never find her. I'll go with you."

John nodded curtly, grabbed her hand, and pulled her out into the night.

Minutes later he was atop his stallion. Mary and a groom followed on Amber, Belle's mare. John sped through the streets, the wind tearing ferociously at his clothes. The rain was coming down hard now, hard and cold, and the thought of Belle out alone in such a vicious storm left him numb.

They were soon at the edge of Hyde Park. He motioned for the groom to bring Amber close. "Which way?" he yelled.

He could barely hear Mary's words over the howling wind. She pointed west, toward a wooded area. John immediately kicked Thor into a canter.

The moon was obscured by the heavy rainclouds, so he had to rely on his lantern, which was flickering nervously in the wind. He slowed Thor down to a trot as he searched the woods, painfully aware of how difficult it would be to spot her in the dark forest.

"Belle!" he screamed, hoping his voice could be heard above the storm.

There was no response.

Belle had lain unconscious for nearly an hour. When she awoke it was dark, and she was shivering uncontrollably, her once-fashionable riding habit sodden. She started to sit up but was overcome by dizziness.

"Dear Lord," she moaned, clasping her forehead

as if she could squeeze away the blinding pain in her temple. She glanced about. Mary was nowhere to be seen, and Belle was completely disoriented. Which way to Mayfair?

"Hell and damnation," she cursed, and this time she didn't feel a single pang of guilt over her foul language. Clutching onto a nearby tree trunk for support, she struggled to her feet, but vertigo quickly claimed her, and she tumbled back to the ground. Tears of frustration welled up in her eyes, spilling down her cheeks and mixing with the relentless rain. Aware that she had no other option, Belle began to crawl. And then, silently begging forgiveness for all of those times she'd finagled her way out of going to church, she began to pray.

"Oh, please God, please God, just let me get home. Just let me get home before I freeze. Before I pass out again, because my head hurts me so. Oh, please, I promise I'll start paying attention to the sermons. I won't stare at the stained glass windows. I won't curse, and I'll mind my parents, and I'll even try to forgive John, although I think You know how hard that will be for me."

Belle's impassioned litany continued as she inched her way through the trees, guided now by instinct, for the sun had completely set. The rain had grown icy cold, and her clothing stuck mercilessly to her, wrapping her in a freezing embrace. Her shivering grew more pronounced, and her teeth began to clatter loudly. Her prayers intensified, and she stopped asking God to get her home and started asking Him just to let her live.

Her hands grew shriveled and prune-like from the wet mud of the path. Then she heard a sharp tear. Her dress had gotten caught on a thorny bush which had spilled out onto the path. She struggled to free herself, but her strength was nearly gone.

Wincing against the pounding pain in her head, she summoned what little power she had left and tore her dress from the thorns.

She had just barely resumed her slow crawl when a bolt of lightning lit up the sky. Terror consumed her, and she wildly wondered how close the bolt had struck. A clap of thunder quickly followed, and Belle jumped in fright, landing on her rear.

She sat in the middle of the muddy path for a few seconds, trying to regain control of her shivering body. With a shaky motion, she pushed away a few locks of hair which were plastered to her face and tried to tuck them behind her ears. But the rain and the wind were merciless, and her hair was soon back in her eyes. She was so God-awful tired. So cold, so weak. Lightning tore through the dark sky again, but this time it lit up the figure of a horse and rider coming up on the path behind her.

Could it be?

Belle caught her breath and forgot all of her anger toward the man riding toward her. "John!" she screamed, praying he could hear her over the shrieking winds because if he couldn't, she'd soon be trampled under Thor's hooves.

John's heart stopped beating when he heard her cry out, and when it resumed, his pulse raced double-time. He could just barely make out her form in the path about ten yards ahead of him. Her hair was so fair it captured what little moonlight hung in the darkness and glowed like a halo. He quickly crossed the distance between them and slid off his horse.

"John?" Belle quavered, barely able to believe that he was right there in front of her.

"Shhh, my love, I'm here now." He knelt down

in the mud and cradled her face in his hands. "Where does it hurt?"

"I'm so cold."

"I know, love. I'm going to get you home." John's relief at finding her quickly turned to fear when he lifted her into his arms and felt her violent shivers. Dear God, she had been out in this freezing rain for at least an hour, and her heavy riding habit was now soaked.

"I was—I was trying to cr-crawl home," Belle managed to get out. "I'm so cold."

"I know, I know," he crooned. Hell, why had she been crawling? But John didn't have time to ponder these questions. Belle's lips were turning a dangerous shade of blue, and he knew that he had to get her warmed up immediately. "Can you sit in the saddle, love?" he asked, seating her atop the horse.

"I don't know. I'm so cold."

Belle started to slide out of the saddle as John was mounting and he had to push her back up. "Just hang on to Thor's neck until I'm up there with you. I promise I'll hold you steady the whole way home."

Teeth clattering, Belle nodded, holding on to the stallion with all her might. In no time, John was seated behind her, his strong arm wrapped fiercely around her waist. Belle sagged into him and closed her eyes. "I c-can't st-stop shivering," she said weakly, feeling like a child who had to explain herself. "I'm so cold."

"I know you are, love."

Mary and the groom rode into sight. "Follow me back," John yelled. He didn't have time to fill them in on the details of Belle's condition. He kicked Thor into a full gallop, and they crashed through the trees.

Nestled firmly against John's torso, Belle slowly let go of the fierce will which had been propelling her before. She felt her mind slipping away from her body, and truth be told, she was so damned tired and cold and sore that she was glad to let it go. She went numb, strangely content now that her aches and pains were receding. "I'm not so cold anymore," she murmured in an eerie voice.

"Oh, Christ," John swore, hoping that he'd misheard her. He gave her a hard jostle. "Whatever you do, don't fall asleep. Do you hear me, Belle? *Don't fall asleep!*" When she didn't respond immediately, he gave her another shove.

Belle didn't even open her eyes. "But I'm so tired."

"I don't care," John said sternly. "You will remain awake. Do you understand me?"

It took Belle a few seconds to process his demand. "If you say so," she said finally.

For the rest of the ride, John alternated between spurring Thor on to keep him riding at top speed and shaking Belle to prevent her from falling asleep. He had to get her home and warmed up. He was terrified that if she went to sleep she wouldn't have the energy to awaken.

After what seemed like hours, they emerged from the trees and picked up speed as they raced across the lawns of Hyde Park and then the streets of London. They came to a halt at the front steps of Blydon House. John quickly slid off the horse, taking Belle along with him. The groom who had been riding with Mary took hold of the reins and led Thor back to the mews. After barking out a quick thanks, John strode into the hall, cradling Belle in his arms.

"Thornton!" he yelled.

Within seconds the butler materialized before him.

"Have a warm bath prepared immediately. Set it in my room."

"Yes, my lord, right away my lord." Thornton turned to Mrs. Crane, the housekeeper who had followed him into the hall. Before he could say a word, she had nodded and hurried up the stairs.

John took the stairs as fast as he could, his good leg taking two stairs with each step. He raced down the hallway, cradling Belle gently against his chest. "We're almost there, love," he murmured. "I promise we'll get you warm."

Belle's head moved slightly. John hoped that she had heard him and was nodding, but he had the sinking feeling that her movement was merely due to his haste going up the stairs. When they reached his room, two maids were hurriedly filling up a tub. "We're heating the water as fast as we can, my lord," one said, hastily bobbing a curtsy.

John nodded curtly and laid Belle down on a towel which had been set atop his bed. Her hair fell back from her face, revealing an ugly purple bruise that stained her forehead. John felt the breath leave his body, and an unspeakable rage poured through him. Rage at what, he wasn't sure—most probably himself.

"John?" she asked weakly, her eyelids fluttering.

"I'm here, love. I'm here."

"I feel strange, very strange. I'm cold but I'm not. I think I'm—I think I'm—" Belle had been about to say the word "dying," but her last rational thought before she drifted into unconsciousness was that she didn't want to worry him.

John swore under his breath, noticing instantly when she slipped away from him. His numb but steady fingers quickly went to work on the frozen buttons of her riding habit. "Don't you leave me, Belle!" he shouted. "Do you hear me? You can't leave me now!"

Mrs. Crane bustled into the room, carrying two more buckets of steaming water. "My lord?" she questioned. "Are you sure you should? That is, perhaps a woman . . . "

He turned to her and said in extremely clipped tones, "She is my wife. I will care for her."

Mrs. Crane nodded stiffly and exited the room.

John turned his attention back to Belle's buttons. When he was finished, he pulled back the sides of the jacket and worked her arms out of the sleeves. Murmuring a quiet apology, he tore her camisole cleanly down the front. The way it was sticking to her body, it would have taken too long to peel it off. Besides, this way she could remain lying down. Mutely, he laid a hand down against her ribs. Her skin was pale and clammy. His fear renewed, John redoubled his efforts and pulled her out of her sodden skirts.

When she was naked in his arms, he carried her over to the steaming tub which was now nearly full. He knelt down and dipped his finger in the water. He frowned. It was a little too hot, but he wasn't sure he had the time to wait for it to cool off. Praying for the best, he lowered Belle into the tub. "There you are, love. I promised you I'd get you warm."

She didn't respond to the heat. "Wake up, Belle," he shouted at her, shaking her slim shoulders. "You cannot sleep until you're warm."

Belle mumbled something unintelligible and swatted him away with her hand.

John took her feistiness as a good sign but nonetheless thought that he ought to get her woken up. He shook her again, and then when that didn't work, he did the only thing he could think of. He dunked her head under the water.

Belle came up spluttering, and for a few moments there was a look of absolute clarity in her eyes. "What on earth?!" she yelled.

"Just warming you up, love," John said with a smile.

"Well, you're not doing a very good job of it. I'm freezing!"

"I'm working as fast as I can."

"The water hurts me."

"There's nothing I can do about that, I'm afraid. It'll sting a bit as it warms you up."

"It's too hot."

"No, love, you're too cold."

Belle grumbled tiredly like a child. Then she looked down, saw John's large hands rubbing gently against her bare skin, and fainted.

"Christ Almighty," John swore. She was a dead weight again, and if he left her for even one moment, she was sure to drown. "Thornton!" he yelled.

Thornton, who'd been hovering solicitously outside the closed door, appeared instantly. He caught one glance of the naked young noblewoman in the tub, gulped nervously, and turned his back. "Yes, sir?"

"Get someone to start a fire in here. It's as cold as a damned morgue."

"Yes, sir, I'll see to it myself, sir." Thornton went to work at the fireplace, scrupulously keeping his back to the tub.

After a few more minutes John was satisfied that the chill had been removed from Belle's skin, but he didn't doubt for a moment that she still felt icy from the inside out. He lifted her from the water, tenderly dried her skin with a towel, and laid her in his bed. He pulled the covers up over her, tucking her in as he would a child. After a few moments, however, she began to shiver again. John placed his hand on her forehead. It was warm, but if he wasn't mistaken, it would be burning within the hour.

He sighed and sank into a chair. It was going to be a terrifyingly long night.

She was so, so cold. Why couldn't she get warm? Belle tossed and turned in the large bed, her body instinctively rubbing against the sheets to create heat.

This was awful. The pain had returned, and every muscle and joint in her body ached with it. And what was that strange clattering sound? Surely that couldn't be her teeth? And why was she so damned cold?

Gritting her teeth against the exertion, Belle forced herself to open her eyes. A fire was burning steadily in a fireplace. A fire. A fire would be warm. She pushed aside her covers and crawled down to the foot of the bed. Still too far away. With agonizing slowness, she swung her legs over the side of the bed. She looked down at herself in confusion. Why wasn't she wearing any clothes? No matter, Belle decided, tossing the thought aside. She just had to concentrate on that fire.

She let her feet touch down on the floor, and immediately her legs wobbled beneath her. She tumbled down, landing on the carpet with a painful thud.

John, who had dozed off in the chair he had positioned at her bedside, came awake instantly. He saw the empty bed and jumped to his feet. "Belle?" He looked around the room frantically. Where could she have possibly gone in her condition? And naked, to boot.

He heard a pained groan from the other side of the bed and hurried over. Belle was lying on the floor in a tangled heap. He leaned down and picked her up. "What on earth are you doing down there, love?"

"Fire," she rasped.

John looked at her blankly.

"Fire!" she repeated a bit more urgently, giving him a feeble shove.

"What about the fire?"

"I'm cold."

"You were trying to warm yourself?"

Belle sighed and nodded.

"I think you should stay in the bed. I'll get you more blankets."

"*No!*" Belle yelled, and John was taken quite aback at her forcefulness. "I want the fire."

"I'll tell you what, why don't I put you in the bed, and I'll bring you a candle to have nearby."

"Stupid."

God help him, he nearly laughed. "Come on, darling. Let's get you back in bed." He laid her down and pulled up the covers, swallowing nervously as he tucked her back in. She had been so funny and adorable that for a moment he had been able to forget just how serious her condition was.

But he couldn't keep kidding himself. Only a miracle would keep a fever from settling into her weary body, and John was not a great believer in miracles. She was definitely going to get worse before she got any better.

Belle was still restless. "Water," she croaked.

John pressed a glass to her lips, using a towel to wipe away the water that dribbled down her chin. "Is that better?"

Belle licked her parched lips. "Don't leave me."

"I won't."

"I'm scared, John."

"I know you are, but there is nothing to worry about," he lied. "You'll see."

"I'm not so cold anymore."

"That's good," he said encouragingly.

"My skin is still a little cold, but my insides—" She coughed, and her entire body shook with spasms. When she finally settled down, she completed her thought. "My insides are hot."

John fought back despair. He had to be strong for her. He had to share this battle with her. He wasn't sure she'd be able to do it alone. "Shhh, darling," he said soothingly, rubbing his palm softly against her brow. "Go to sleep now. You need to get some rest."

Belle drifted away. "I forgot to tell you," she mumbled. "I forgot to tell you this afternoon."

This afternoon? Lord, John thought, that seemed an eternity ago.

"I forgot to tell you," Belle persisted.

"What is it?" he asked softly.

"Always love you. Doesn't matter if you love me back."

And for once, he didn't feel that odd choking feeling.

Chapter 21

From his position next to the bed, John looked down at Belle, worry clouding his expression. It had been several hours since she'd awakened and tried to crawl to the fire. She was still shivering, and her fever had steadily worsened.

She was in a bad way.

There was a perfunctory knock, and then the door to the room opened. Caroline entered, lines of worry etched clearly on her face. "What happened?" she asked in a urgent whisper. "We just arrived home, and Thornton told us Belle is ill."

John reluctantly let go of Belle's hand and escorted Caroline out into the hall. "Belle went for a walk and was caught in the rain. She hit her head." He recounted the rest of the details briefly, leaving out the argument that had prompted her to run outside in the first place. He'd only met his in-laws a day earlier. If Belle wanted to tell

317

her parents of their troubles that was fine. He, a virtual stranger, was not going to do so.

Caroline's hand strayed nervously to her throat. "You look terribly tired. Why don't you sleep? I'll sit with her now."

"No."

"But John—"

"You may remain with me, but I'll not leave her." He turned on his heel and strode back to Belle's bedside. She was breathing evenly. It was a good sign. He put his hand on her forehead. Damn. It was even hotter than before. He doubted she'd be breathing so evenly in an hour's time.

Caroline followed him and stood by his side. "Has she been like this all evening?" she whispered.

John nodded. He reached down, picked up a cloth which had been soaking in cool water, and wrung it out. "There you go, sweetheart," he crooned, laying it on her hot forehead. She mumbled something in her sleep and fitfully shifted positions. She tossed about again and then suddenly opened her eyes wide. Her expression was filled with panic.

"Shhh, I'm here," he said softly, stroking her cheek. Belle seemed to take some comfort in that and slowly let her eyelids flutter shut. John had the impression that she'd never really seen him.

Caroline swallowed nervously. "I think we should send for a doctor."

"At this time of night?"

She nodded. "I'll see to it."

As John sat by Belle's side, carefully and worriedly watching over her, his mind refused to stop replaying the devastating comment she had made several hours earlier.

Doesn't matter if you love me back.

Was it possible that she loved him unconditionally? Even with his past?

Always love you.

And then it suddenly occurred to him—no one had ever said those words to him before.

John lifted the cloth from Belle's forehead and cooled it off in the basin of water. He didn't have time to sit around feeling sorry for himself over an unhappy childhood. It wasn't as if he'd gone hungry or been abused. He just hadn't been loved, and he suspected that thousands of children across Britain had shared similar fates.

Over in the bed, Belle had grown fitful. John immediately turned his full attention to her.

"Stop," she moaned.

"Stop what, love?"

"Stop!"

He leaned over and gently shook her by the shoulders. "You're having a nightmare." Dear God, it tore him up to see her this way. Her face was flushed and feverish, and her entire body was covered by a thin sheen of perspiration. He tried to push her hair out of her eyes, but she batted his hand away. He wished he knew how to use one of those blasted hair things she always had lying around. She'd be more comfortable if he could secure her heavy tresses away from her face.

"Fire," Belle moaned.

"There's no fire here save the one in the fireplace."

"Too hot."

John quickly wrung out the wet cloth.

"No, no, stop . . . " Belle suddenly sat up and screamed.

"No, love, lie back down." John started wiping the sweat from her body, hoping the motion would cool her down. Belle's eyes were open and she was looking at him, but John didn't see even a flicker of recognition in her gaze.

"Stop, stop!" she shrieked, slapping his hands away. "Don't touch me! It's too hot."

"I'm only trying to—"

"What the devil is going on?" Caroline burst into the room.

"She's delirious," John said, trying to cover Belle up with the sheet.

"But there was so much screaming."

"I said she's gone delirious," John snapped, attempting to hold the sheet over Belle's writhing form. "See if we've any laudanum. We need to calm her down." He sighed, remembering that he was talking to his mother-in-law. "I'm sorry, Lady Worth. It's just—"

She held up a hand. "I understand. I'll go look for the laudanum."

Belle started fighting him in earnest, her strength fueled considerably by her fever. She was no match for John, however, whose firmly muscled body had been honed by years in the military. "Wake up, damn you," he said fiercely. "If you wake up the fire will go away. I promise you."

Belle's only response was to struggle harder.

John didn't budge an inch. "Belle," he pleaded. His throat worked violently. "Please."

"Get off of me!" Belle screamed.

Caroline chose that rather inopportune moment to reenter the room with a bottle of laudanum. "What are you doing to her?"

John replied with a question. "Where is the laudanum?"

Caroline poured some into a glass and handed it to him.

"Here you go, Belle," he said softly, trying to pull her into a sitting position and keep her still at the same time. He held the glass to her lips. "Just a little now."

Belle's eyes focused on something behind him and she screamed again. Her hands shot up to her head, knocking the glass from John's hands. It rolled onto the floor, spilling the drug.

"I'll feed it to her this time," Caroline said. "You hold her down." She held the glass to her daughter's lips and forced her to take a gulp.

After a few moments Belle calmed down, and both mother and husband breathed a weary sigh.

"Shhh," John crooned. "You can sleep now. The nightmare is gone. Rest, my love."

Caroline pushed some of Belle's heavy locks from her face. "There must be some way we can make her more comfortable."

John walked over to the bureau and picked something up. "Here is one of her hair contraptions. Perhaps you could pin her hair back from her face?"

Caroline smiled. "It's called a barrette, John." She lifted Belle's hair and secured it into a sloppy bun. "Are you certain you don't want to sleep for a few hours?"

"I can't," he said hoarsely.

Caroline nodded sympathetically. "I will sleep then. You'll be weary in the morning. You'll need help." She moved to the door.

"Thank you," he said abruptly.

"She is my daughter."

He swallowed, remembering when he had been sick as a child. His mother had never come to visit him. His mouth opened and closed, and then he nodded.

"It is I who should thank you," Caroline continued.

John looked up sharply, his expression clearly asking the question, "Why?"

"For loving her. I couldn't ask for more. I couldn't hope for more." She left the room.

Belle soon fell into a deep sleep. John scooted her over to the other side of the bed, where the sheets weren't so sweaty. He leaned down and kissed her temple. "You can fight this," he whispered. "You can do anything."

He walked back over to his chair and slumped into it. He must have dozed off, because when he next opened his eyes, it was past dawn, although one could barely tell for sure through the driving rain. The weather was intensely bleak, and the rain didn't show any sign of letting up. John's eyes searched the scene, trying to find one small piece of the cityscape which might give cause for optimism. And then he did something he hadn't done in many years.

He began to pray.

Neither Belle's condition nor the weather improved for several days. John remained ever vigilant at his patient's bedside, forcing her to drink water and broth whenever possible, and giving her laudanum when she grew hysterical. By the end of the third day, John knew that she would be in serious trouble if the fever did not break soon. She hadn't eaten any solid food, and she was getting thin, much too thin. The last time John had bathed her with the damp cloth he'd noticed that her ribs had become painfully prominent.

The doctor had come every day, but he hadn't been especially helpful. They could do nothing other than wait and pray, he had told the family.

John swallowed down his worry and reached out to touch Belle's forehead. She seemed completely unaware of his presence. Indeed, she seemed unaware of anything other than the nightmares which plagued her fever-ridden mind. John had been calm and purposeful when he began to care for her, but now his even temper was beginning to deteriorate. He'd barely slept in three days, and he hadn't eaten much more than Belle had. His eyes were bloodshot, his face was gaunt, and a look in the mirror told him that he looked almost as bad as his patient did.

He was getting desperate. If Belle didn't pull through soon, he didn't know what he would do. Several times during his vigil he let his head fall limply into his hands, not even bothering to try to stem the tears that ran down his face. He didn't know how he would be able to make it from day to day if she died.

His face bleak, he crossed over to her bedside and perched on the mattress next to her. She was lying there quite peacefully, but John detected a slight change in her condition. She seemed still, unnaturally still, and her breathing had grown shallow. Panic gripped John like a hand around his heart, and he leaned down and grabbed her by the shoulders. "Are you giving up on me?" he demanded harshly. "Are you?"

Belle's head lolled to the side, and she whimpered.

"Damn you! You can't give up!" John shook her even harder.

Belle heard his voice as if it were coming to her through a long, long tunnel. It sounded like John, but she couldn't imagine why he would be with her in her bedroom. He sounded angry. Was he angry at her? Belle sighed. She was tired. Too tired to deal with an angry man.

"Do you hear me, Belle?" she heard him say. "I will never forgive you if you give up on me."

Belle winced as she felt his large hands squeezing her upper arms. She wanted to moan at the pain but she just didn't have the energy. Why wouldn't he leave her alone? All she wanted to do was sleep. She'd never felt this tired. She'd just like to cuddle up and sleep forever. Summoning up all of her strength, she managed to say, "Go away."

"Aha!" John shouted triumphantly. "You're still here with me. Hang on now, Belle. Can you hear me?"

Of course she could hear him, Belle thought irritably. "Go away," she said with a little more force. She shifted restlessly, burrowing back under the covers. Maybe he wouldn't keep on bothering her if she hid underneath the quilts. If she could just keep on sleeping, she'd feel so much better.

John could see the will slipping out of her even though she'd managed to speak. He'd seen that look before, on the faces of men he knew during the war. Not the lucky ones who died in battle, but the poor souls who had fought fever and infection for weeks afterward. Watching Belle slowly letting go of life was more than he could take, and something inside of him snapped. Fury rose within him, and he forgot all of his vows to be tender and considerate while nursing her through her illness.

"Damn it, Belle," he shouted angrily. "I'm not going to sit here and watch you die. It isn't fair! You can't leave me now. I won't allow it!"

Belle made no response. John tried wheedling.

"Do you know how furious I'll be with you if you die? I'll hate you forever for leaving me. Do you want that?" He desperately searched Belle's features, hoping for some sign that she was rallying, but he found none. All his grief and anger and worry converged inside of him, and he finally grabbed her brutally and lifted her in his arms, cradling her as he spoke.

"Belle," he said hoarsely. "There's no hope for me without you." He paused while a tremor shook his body. "I want to see you smiling, Belle. Smiling happily, your blue eyes full of sunshine and goodness. Reading a book, laughing at its contents. I want so much for you to be happy. I'm sorry I wouldn't accept your love. I will. I promise. If you, in your infinite goodness and wisdom, have found something in me worthy of love, well then . . . well, then, I suppose I'm not quite as bad as I thought.

"Oh, God, Belle," he said with a ragged cry. "Please, please hold on. If you cannot do it for me then do it for your family. They love you so much. You wouldn't want to hurt them, would you? And think about all the books you haven't read yet. I promise I'll sneak Byron's next one to you if they won't sell it in your bookstore. There's still so much for you to do, my love. You can't leave now."

Throughout John's passionate soliloquy Belle remained limp, her breathing shallow. Finally, in utter desperation, he broke down and bared his soul. "Belle, *please*," he begged. "Please, please don't leave me. Belle, *I love you*. I love you, and I couldn't bear it if you died. God help me, I love you so much." His voice broke off, and like a man who has suddenly realized the fruitlessness of his situation, he sighed raggedly and laid her gently back down on the bed.

Unable to hold back the lone tear that rolled down his cheek, John tenderly pulled up the blankets and tucked Belle in. Taking a deep breath, he leaned forward. God, it was torture to be so close to her. He lightly brushed his lips against her ear, whispering, "I love you, Belle. Remember that always."

Then he left the room, praying that "always" would last longer than the next hour.

Belle was lying in bed a few hours later when she felt a comforting warmth suffuse her body. Funny how her toes had been cold for so long, even when the rest of her had been going up in flames. But now they felt warm, even—pink. Belle wondered if toes could feel pink, and then decided that they must, because that was precisely the word to describe the way *her* toes were feeling.

In fact, her entire body felt kind of pink. Pink, and cozy, and a little fuzzy, but mostly she just felt good. For the first time in—she frowned, realizing that she had no idea how long she'd been ill.

Gingerly, she hoisted herself into a sitting position, surprised at how weak her muscles were. Blinking her eyes a few times, she took in her surroundings. She was back home in the room she and John had shared on their wedding night. How had she returned? All she remembered was the rain and the wind. Oh, and the fight. Her awful fight with John.

She sighed, bone tired. She didn't care any longer if he didn't want her to say that she loved him. She would take him any way she could have him. All she wanted to do was end this vexing problem with George Spencer and go back to the country, back to Bunford Manor.

Bunford Manor? No, that wasn't right.

Drat. She'd never remember the name of that place. She tilted her head to the side. Sore. She flexed her fingers. Sore. She pointed her toes and groaned. Her entire body ached.

As she sat there testing out various body parts, the doorknob quietly turned and John entered the room. He had finally forced himself to take a fifteen minute break so that he could splash some water on his face and shove some food down his throat. Now he was terrified that he'd find Belle had lost her tenuous hold on life while he was gone.

To his great surprise, when he reached the side of the bed, he saw that the object of his desperate worry was sitting up, shrugging her shoulders. Up, down, up, down.

"Hello, John," she said weakly. "What's the name of your house in Oxfordshire?"

John was so stunned, so completely thrown off balance by her bizarre question, it took him several moments to reply. "Bletchford Manor," he finally said.

"That's an *awful* name," Belle replied, making a face. Then she yawned, for the sentence had taken a lot of energy to get out.

"I've—I've been meaning to change it."

"Yes, well, you should do so soon. It doesn't suit you. Nor me, for that matter." Belle yawned again and snuggled down into the bed. "If you'll excuse me, I seem to be extremely tired. I think I'd like to get some sleep."

John thought wildly of the countless times he had begged her to wake from her nightmares and found himself nodding. "Yes," he said softly. "Yes, you should get some sleep." Dumbstruck, he sank down into the chair that had been his home throughout his prayerful vigil at her bedside.

The fever had broken. Strangely, joyously, amazingly, the fever had broken. She was going to be all right. He was stunned by the force of emotion which thundered through him. For once, his prayers had been answered.

And then a strange thing happened. An odd, warm feeling began somewhere in the vicinity of his heart and began to spread.

He had saved her life.

He could feel a weight being lifted from him. It was a physical sensation.

He had saved a life.

A voice resounded in the room. *You are forgiven.*

He looked quickly over at Belle. She didn't seem to have heard the voice. How odd. It had seemed prodigiously loud to him. A female voice. Rather like Ana's.

Ana. John closed his eyes and for the the first time in five years, he could not picture her face.

Had he finally atoned for his sins? Or, perhaps, was it that his sin had never been quite as eternally condemning as he thought?

He looked back over at Belle. She had always believed in him. Always.

He was so much stronger with her by his side. And so, perhaps, was she. Together they had faced the fiercest enemy of all and won. She would live, and he would never again have to face the future alone.

John took a deep breath, planted his elbows on his thighs, and let his face fall forward into his hands. A crazy smile cracked his face, and he began to laugh. All the stress and anguish of the past few days worked themselves out in this strange, rocking laughter.

Belle rolled over and opened her eyes at the sound. Although his face was covered, she could tell that he looked haggard. The skin on his arms was stretched tight, and the top few buttons of his shirt were carelessly undone. He slowly lifted his head and looked back at her, his brown eyes filled with an emotion she couldn't name. Undaunted, Belle continued her examination. His eyes looked gaunt, and his chin was covered with several days' growth of beard. And his normally thick and shiny hair looked dull. Belle frowned and reached her arm out, covering his hand with her own.

"You look terrible," she said.

It was several moments before John could find his voice to reply. "Oh, Belle," he said hoarsely. "You look wonderful."

A couple of days later, Belle was feeling much better. She was still a little weak, but her appetite was back, and she was entertained by a steady stream of visitors.

John she hadn't seen for over a day. As soon as he was assured she was no longer in danger he collapsed from exhaustion. Caroline gave Belle periodic reports on his condition, but so far the reports had not varied beyond, "He's still sleeping."

Finally, on the third day after her fever broke, her husband entered her room, a slightly sheepish smile on his face.

"I had despaired of ever seeing you again," she said.

He perched on the side of her bed. "I've been sleeping, I'm afraid."

"Yes, so I've heard." She reached out and touched his jaw. "It's so lovely to see your face."

He smiled. "You washed your hair."

"What?" She looked down and pinched a curl between her fingers. "Oh, yes. It was badly needed, I think. John, I—"

"Belle, I—" His words came out at the same time as hers. "You first."

"No, you go ahead."

"I insist."

"Oh, this is silly," Belle said. "We're married, after all. Yet we're so nervous."

"What are you nervous about?"

"Spencer." The name hung in the air for several seconds before she continued. "We must get him out of our lives. Did you tell my parents of our situation?"

"No. I leave that to your discretion."

"I won't tell them. It will only worry them."

"Whatever you say."

"Have you devised a plan?"

"No. When you were ill—" He swallowed convulsively. Just the memory was enough to terrify him. "When you were ill I couldn't think of anything but you. And then I slept."

"Well, I've been thinking about him."

He looked up.

"I think we should confront him at the Tumbley bash," she said.

"Absolutely not."

"Mother has already insisted that we attend. She wants to use the occasion to present us to society."

"Belle, it will be so crowded. How am I to keep an eye on you when—"

"The crowds are what will protect us. Alex, Emma, and Dunford will be able to stay close to our sides without raising suspicion."

"I forbid—"

"Will you at least think about it? We'll face him together. I think that ... together ... we can do anything." She wet her lips, aware that she'd stumbled over her words.

"All right," he agreed, partly because he wanted to change the subject, but mostly because the sight of her licking her lips forced all rational thought from his head.

She reached out and placed her hand on his. "Thank you for taking care of me."

"Belle," he blurted out. "I love you."

She smiled. "I know. And I love you, too."

He picked up her hand, brought it to his mouth, and kissed it fervently. "I still cannot believe that you do, but"—when he saw that she would interrupt, he placed his hand gently over her mouth—"but it gives me more joy than I ever thought possible. More joy than I thought there was in this world."

"Oh, John."

"You've helped me to forgive myself. It was when I knew you weren't going to die, when I realized I had saved your life." He paused, his expression dazed, as if he still couldn't believe the miracle that had taken place in that very room. "It was then that I knew."

"Knew what?"

"That I'd paid my debt. A life for a life. I couldn't save Ana, but I saved you."

"John," she said softly. "Saving my life hasn't made up for what happened in Spain."

His eyes flew to hers, horrified.

"It doesn't *need* to make up for it. When will

you accept that you weren't responsible? You've been torturing yourself for five years, and all because of another man's actions."

John stared at her. He stared hard into those bright blue eyes, and for the first time, her words began to make sense.

She squeezed his hand.

He finally blinked. "Perhaps the truth lies somewhere in between. Yes, I was supposed to protect her, and I failed in that. But I didn't rape her." He shook his head, and his voice grew stronger. "It wasn't me."

"Your heart is free now."

"No," he whispered. "It's yours."

Chapter 22

~~~⌒~~⊙⌒~⌒~~~

John yanked viciously at his cravat. "This is stupid, Belle," he hissed. "Stupid."

Belle tiptoed around his valet, who had let out an agonized groan over the death of his careful handiwork. "How many times do we have to go through this? I told you there was no way to get out of going to the Tumbley bash tonight. Mother would have my head if I didn't show my face before all the *ton* as a properly married lady."

John dismissed his valet with a curt nod, wanting to keep the conversation private. "That's exactly it, Belle. You're a married lady now. You don't have to obey your parents' every order anymore."

"Oh, so now instead of following my parents' orders, I get to follow yours. Pardon me if I don't jump with glee."

"Don't be sarcastic, Belle. It doesn't suit you. All

I'm saying is you don't have to do what your parents tell you anymore."

"Try telling that to my mother."

"You're a grown woman." John made his way over to a mirror and began to refold his cravat.

"I have news for you. Parents don't stop being parents when their children get married. And mothers especially don't stop being mothers."

John pulled the fabric the wrong way and cursed.

"You should have left it the way Wheatley arranged it. I thought it looked quite elegant."

John shot her a look which said he didn't want to hear it.

"Look at it this way," Belle continued, fixing her skirts so they wouldn't wrinkle as she sat down on the bed. "My parents are still getting to know you. They'll be suspicious if we refuse to be seen in public together. You don't want to be at odds with your in-laws for the rest of your life, do you?"

"I don't want to be dead, either."

"That isn't even remotely funny, John. I wish you wouldn't joke about it."

John abandoned his cravat for a moment and turned around so that he could look his wife in the eye. "I'm not joking, Belle. It's going to be a madhouse tonight. I have no idea how I'm going to keep either one of us safe."

Belle bit her lip. "Alex and Dunford will be there. I'm sure they'll be a tremendous help."

"I'm sure they will. But that doesn't guarantee our safety. I don't see why you didn't just tell your parents the truth."

"Oh, *that* would make a good impression," Belle said sarcastically. "They'll just love you once they find out you've put my life in danger." At John's scowl, she added, "Inadvertently, of course."

John finally gave up trying to arrange his cravat and yelled out, "Wheatley!" Then he turned to Belle and said quickly, "I value our lives more highly than your parents' opinions, and you'd do well to remember that."

"John, I really think we'll be fine as long as we stay near Alex and Dunford. Maybe we'll even have a chance to trap—oh, hello Wheatley. His lordship seems to be having a bit of trouble with his cravat. I'm afraid his foul mood has drained the dexterity from his fingers. Do you suppose you could aid him in this endeavor?"

John's countenance turned quite black.

Belle returned his scowl with a bright smile and stood up. "I'm going to see if the carriage is ready."

"You do that."

Belle turned to the door and took a step forward.

John sucked in his breath. "Good God, woman, what are you wearing? Or rather, what aren't you wearing?"

Belle smiled. She had donned the midnight blue velvet gown she had bought a few weeks earlier when she was plotting to seduce him. "Don't you like it?" she asked, keeping her back to him so that he couldn't see her grin.

That was a mistake, for the dress had no back, or at least very little of one. "It's indecent," John spat out.

"It is not," Belle said, unable to work her voice into a properly protesting tone. "Lots of women wear gowns like this. Some even wear light fabric and then damp it to make it transparent."

"I will not have other men looking at your back. And that is final!"

Belle decided she didn't half mind his possessiveness. "Well, if you put it that way . . ." She darted from the room and made her way to her own chamber, where Mary was waiting with another freshly pressed gown. Belle had had a feeling she'd be changing her attire. But she had accomplished her goal. She'd gotten John's mind off of Spencer for a few minutes at least.

After changing, she headed downstairs, arriving just as the front door opened to admit Alex, Emma, Dunford, and Persephone. The quartet was chattering very loudly.

"What are you doing here?" Belle asked.

Emma looked behind her to ascertain that the front door was still open and yelled, "WE'RE TAKING YOU TO THE BALL TONIGHT!"

"You are?"

"OH YES!"

"But why?"

Emma saw that the butler was about to close the door. "Don't shut that yet," she hissed before turning to Belle and replying, "BECAUSE YOU ASKED US TO!"

"Oh, of course. How silly of me."

Lady Worth wandered into the hall. "What on earth is all the commotion?"

"I haven't the faintest idea," Persephone muttered, shooting an odd look at Emma.

"WE'RE TAKING BELLE AND JOHN TO THE BALL!" Emma bellowed.

"Fine. Be my guest, just stop shouting about it."

Alex shut the door quickly and said, "I've been urging her to get her ears checked. She's been doing this for three days."

Emma took Belle aside and whispered, "I just wanted to let our, er, enemy know that you're riding in our carriage tonight."

"So I gathered."

"He won't try anything with all of us in the carriage."

"He could always cut an axle or something like that. Then we'd all be in trouble."

"I don't think so. Too much of a chance that John wouldn't be the one to get hurt. He'll wait until later."

"What are you two whispering about?" Caroline demanded. "And what happened to your earache, Emma? I thought you could only shout. Come over here where it's lighter. I want to look in them myself. They probably just need a good cleaning."

Emma grimaced but allowed herself to be led off to the next room.

"I think I'll follow along," Persephone said. "She's been acting curiously all evening."

"Thank you," Belle said as soon as her mother was out of earshot.

"Don't mention it," Alex replied with a wave of his hand. "Although we've been having a devil of a time keeping all this from Persephone."

"She's very bright."

"So I'm learning."

"She's not going to let you pack her off to Yorkshire after having so much fun in London."

Alex shrugged his shoulders before turning to more pressing matters. "Where is your husband?"

"Upstairs scowling."

"Trouble in paradise?" Dunford asked with a quirky grin.

"Don't even think of taking joy in my distress, you wretch."

"Consider it a compliment. Nobody else's distress causes me nearly as much joy."

"I thrill for you, Dunford." She turned back to Alex. "He's a little irritated at having to go tonight. He doesn't think it's safe."

"It's not. But you can't remain a prisoner here forever. The Tumbley bash is probably the safest outing we could arrange. If Spencer tries anything we'll have a hundred witnesses. It will be easy to put him away."

"I tried to explain that to him, but he wouldn't listen. I think he's worried about me."

Alex smiled. "Husbands are supposed to worry about their wives. It's a lesson I learned very quickly. There's nothing you can do about it besides refrain from excessively stupid behavior, of course. Now, when do you think he'll be down? We really should be on our way."

"Any minute now, I should think."

As if on cue, John appeared at the top of the stairs.

"Oh good, there you are," Belle called out.

"Don't look so damned cheerful."

Belle offered her companions an apologetic look to try to make up for her husband's surliness. The two men looked heartily amused, and so Belle simply shook her head and waited for John to join them. Stairs always slowed him down. Once he reached the bottom, however, he moved across the hall with surprising swiftness.

"Ashbourne. Dunford." He greeted his guests with a quick nod.

"We thought it might be safer for you to come with us tonight," Dunford said.

"Good idea. Where's Emma? Isn't she coming?"

"She's off getting her ears checked," Belle replied.

"What?"

"It's a long story."

"I'm sure it is," he drawled.

Belle grabbed his hand and gave it a firm yank, pulling him to her side. "I'm getting tired of your attitude, John."

"Don't expect me to be pleasant for at least a

week," he hissed. "You know how I feel about this."

Belle clamped her mouth shut into a resolute line and turned back to Alex and Dunford. Alex was looking up at the ceiling and whistling to himself. Dunford was grinning from ear to ear.

"Oh, shut up," she finally said.

"I didn't say a thing!" This came from both Dunford and John.

"Men. I'm sick of the lot of you. Emma! Emma! I need you! Now!"

Emma came tearing out into the hall with amazing speed. "So sorry, Aunt Caroline!" she yelled over her shoulder. "Belle needs me." She didn't stop moving until she nearly barreled into Belle's side. "Thank the good Lord and you, too, Belle. I thought she was going to kill me."

"Shall we be off?" Alex said smoothly. "Where is Persephone?"

"She decided to ride with Aunt Caroline and Uncle Henry," Emma replied, taking her cousin's arm and leaving the men to fend for themselves. "She poured something hideous down my ears," she whispered. "Said they were filthy."

Belle smiled and shook her head. "She was just funning you. She hates it when people keep secrets from her."

Emma allowed Alex to help her up into the carriage. "Lady Worth could make Napoleon cry."

That comment elicited a loud grunt of agreement from John.

Belle shot him an irritated glance as she sat down next to Emma. John slouched into the seat across from them, but Belle was not fooled by his lazy posture. She could tell that every inch of him was on alert, ready to spring into action should it be necessary. John's vigilant attitude seeped into Alex and Dunford, and they, too, kept one eye on the doors and the other on the ladies.

Belle tried to avoid looking at the men; they were making her nervous, and despite the brave front she had put up for John, she was a little apprehensive about the evening. Luckily, Emma kept up a constant stream of conversation, and they chatted companionably as they rolled toward their destination.

"And the morning sickness is gone completely," Emma was saying. "At least I hope it's gone. I haven't felt ill for a week."

"That's good. Have you started to show?" Belle kept her voice low. The conversation really wasn't suitable for mixed company.

"A little, but these styles hide it quite well. And of course one can't see anything under this cloak, but—What on earth!"

The carriage lurched drunkenly to the right.

John was on top of Belle within seconds, moving instinctively to shield her from harm. "Are you hurt?" he asked, his voice urgent.

"I'm fine. I'm fine, just—Oh!"

They teetered a bit and then tottered to the left.

"What the hell is going on?" Alex demanded, moving from his position in front of Emma to the window.

"Alex, don't!" Emma cried out. "If we tip over, you'll be crushed!"

Alex reluctantly drew back inside. It didn't feel as if they were in extreme danger. The carriage was rocking and tipping, but in a manner which could almost be described as gentle. Finally, as if heaving a great sigh of relief, the carriage let out a loud creak and then fell toward the left, settling down at a slant that sent everyone tumbling toward the wall.

When it finally became apparent that they weren't moving anywhere else, Belle sent up a silent prayer of thanks that she had ended up at the top of the pile and set about unwrapping her arm from Alex's neck. "It appears," she said, crawling to the window, "that we've settled against a tree. That's why we haven't tipped completely over."

"Ouch!" Emma groaned. "You've bloody sharp knees, Belle. Watch where you're going."

"So sorry. It is rather close in here. Is everyone all right?" She looked beneath her. "Where's Dunford?"

"Mmmph grhrsmp."

Belle's eyes widened. Underneath all four of them? That couldn't be comfortable. "I, er, I'll get off right away. I think we're going to have to go out the top door. If we open this one, we'll all tumble out and hit our heads." She looked back out the window. "Actually, I don't think the door will even open wide enough to let us out. The tree's blocking the way."

"Just do it, Belle," Alex ground out.

"John, are you all right? You haven't said anything."

"I'm fine, Belle, just a trifle uncomfortable. There are three people above me."

"Brmmph thmgish," came Dunford's elegant retort.

Belle glanced down nervously at the tangled pile of angry bodies and crawled in the other direction, ignoring Emma's frequent grunts of pain and outrage. Her skirts kept tangling around her, so she finally gave up all pretense of modesty and hitched them up past her knees, inching her way up the slanted carriage seat until she could grasp the door handle.

"I've almost got it—there! Now if I can just

swing the door out . . . '' Belle turned the handle
and gave the door a shove. But gravity was working against her and winning. Every time, the door
swung back at her. "I'm terribly sorry, but I need
better leverage. I'm going to have to stand."

She moved off the carriage seat and set her right
foot down on the nearest object, which happened
to be Alex's head. Emma let out a little giggle,
which caused Belle to turn back. "Is something
wrong?''

"Nothing." This came from Alex, in a tone that
clearly said, "Get back to work."

Belle turned the handle again and pushed the
door with all her might. This time, it passed the
critical point and swung open. She let out a little
cheer and scrambled back up the carriage seat so
that she could poke her head out the opening.

"Oh, hello, Bottomley," she chirped, recognizing
Alex and Emma's driver. "What's going on?"

"Wheel came right off, milady. Got no idea what
happened."

"Hmmm, that's most odd."

"If you wouldn't mind continuing your conversation at a later date," John said from halfway
down the pile, "we'd like to get out of the carriage."

"Ooops. I'm sorry. Bottomley, would you catch
me if I slide down?" At his nod, she clambered
through the opening and slid down the side of the
carriage. "Wait there for Emma. I think she's next."
Belle darted around to inspect the damage. The left
wheel had come completely off and rolled down
the street, where a group of urchins had already
claimed it as their own.

"What do you see?" Emma came round the carriage.

"It looks like someone simply loosened the

wheel. Nothing appears to be cut or permanently damaged."

"Hmmm." Emma lifted her skirts and crouched down to take a look.

"Will you get out of the street?" Alex was the next one out of the carriage, and he, too, wanted to examine the carriage. He stuck one hand under his wife's arm and yanked her up.

"It appears we had a rather gentle assailant," Emma said. "Either that, or one who doesn't know how to use a saw."

John appeared around the corner, looking absolutely furious. "What did he saw off?"

"Nothing," Alex replied. "Just loosened the wheel."

John swore under his breath. "I apologize for placing you and your wife in danger. Belle and I will return home immediately, and I will forward you funds to cover the cost of the carriage."

Before Belle could protest, Alex held up a hand and said, "Nonsense. There is no permanent damage to the carriage. All we need is another wheel."

"What's this about a wheel?" Dunford finally emerged, looking rather crumpled.

"It came off," the other four said in unison.

"You needn't get so testy about it. I just got here."

"Sorry," Belle offered. "I feel like I've been standing here for an hour."

"You probably have," Dunford replied dryly. "You had the tremendous good fortune, if you recall, to have landed at the top of the pile. By the way, I sent Bottomley back to your place, Ashbourne, to fetch some help to clear this out. I shouldn't think it will take him long. We're actually only a couple of streets away from your home." He walked over to where the left rear wheel should have been. "I must say, Spencer did a rather poor job of it. If he wanted to crash a carriage, there are far more clever ways to go about it. He didn't even manage to break a single bone among the five of us."

Belle rolled her eyes. "You are so adept at finding the bright side."

John scowled and pulled her against his side. "I'm thankful that no one is hurt, but you'll pardon me if I don't see a bright side. I will not be the cause of any of your deaths. Let's be off, Belle. We're going home."

"So he can pick you off with a bullet as we walk back? I think not."

"Belle's right," Alex said. "You're far safer with us than without us."

"Yes," John replied acerbically. "But *you're* far safer without us than you are with us."

"Will you pardon us for a moment?" Belle said, pulling her husband a few feet away from the small crowd. "You must listen to me, John," she whispered. "Weren't you the one who told me that we cannot spend the rest of our lives dodging this man? He sounds just crazy enough to try something tonight at the Tumbley bash. If we catch him, we'll have hundreds of witnesses. He'll be put away for the rest of his life."

"Perhaps, but what if he succeeds? Or even worse, what if he misses me and gets you? Belle, I promise you that we will not have to run from this man all of our lives. I will deal with him, but I won't do it in a way that will put you in danger. You must trust me—this is not a man with whom any woman wants to be alone."

John clutched her shoulders tightly. "Belle, I can't live without you. Don't you realize he now has two targets? If he kills you, he might as well have killed me."

Tears pooled in Belle's eyes at his urgent words. "I love you, too, John. And you know how nervous I am for your safety. But I cannot live my life looking over my shoulder, either. And we're not going to get a better chance to trap Spencer than tonight."

"I'll go, then." He moved his hands to his hips. "But you're going home."

"I'm not going to wait in my room like a terrified little mouse," Belle said, her eyes flashing. "Together we can do anything. Alone, we're nothing. Have faith in me, John."

"I seem to recall your begging me not to take any unnecessary chances. Allow me the same courtesy. Go home, Belle. I have enough to worry about without having to keep an eye on you."

"John, for one last time, listen to what I'm saying. Do you love me?"

"Christ, Belle," he said raggedly. "You know I do."

"Well, the woman with whom you fell in love is not the kind of woman who can sit patiently at home when the man she loves is in danger. I think we can trap Spencer if we have enough people on our side. He's obviously not very bright. He couldn't even wreck a carriage properly. With all five of us working together, we can beat him. And tonight may provide the perfect opportunity."

"Belle, if something happens to you . . ."

"I know, darling. I feel the same way about you. But nothing is going to happen. I love you too much to allow it."

John looked down into her bright blue eyes, shining with love and faith and hope. "Oh darling," he said huskily. "You heal me. You make me believe that I actually deserve all this happiness."

"You do."

John placed his hands gently on her shoulders. "Hold still for a moment," he said softly. "I just want to look at you. I want to carry this picture of you with me for the rest of my life. I don't think you've ever looked as beautiful as you do right now."

Belle flushed with pleasure. "Don't be silly. My dress is crumpled, and I'm sure my hair is mussed, and—"

"Shhhh. Don't say anything. Just look at me. In this light your eyes look almost purple. Like black raspberries."

Belle laughed softly. "You must be in a state of perpetual hunger. You keep likening me to fruit."

"Do I?" John couldn't take his eyes off her lips, which he had just been thinking looked like ripe cherries.

"Yes, you once said my ears were like apricots."

"So I did. I suppose you're right. I've been hungry since I met you."

She blushed.

"Yoo-hoo! Young lovers!"

John and Belle finally tore their eyes off of each other and turned, blinking, to Dunford, who was walking their way.

"If the two of you can stop making verbal love to each other, we can be on our way. In case you hadn't noticed, the fresh carriage is here."

John took a deep and ragged breath before turning to Dunford and saying, "Tact, I take it, was not emphasized in your upbringing."

Dunford smiled merrily. "Not at all. Shall we be off?"

John turned to Belle and offered her his arm. "My dear?"

Belle accepted his gesture with a smile, but as

they passed Dunford, she turned and hissed, "I'm going to kill you for this."

"I'm sure you'll try."

"This carriage isn't as warm as the other one," Alex said with an apologetic smile. "I don't usually use it in winter."

In a few moments the entire crowd was settled into the carriage, and they were back on their way to the Tumbley winter ball. Belle and John huddled together in the corner, turning to each other against the cold. John laid his hand on hers, idly tapping his fingers against her knuckles. She felt warmed by his touch and looked up at him. He had been staring down at her, his brown eyes warm and velvety soft.

Belle couldn't help herself. She let out a little mewl of contentment.

"Oh, for God's sake!" Dunford exclaimed, turning to Alex and Emma. "Will you look at them? Even the two of you weren't this nauseating."

"Someday," Belle interrupted in a low voice, her finger jabbing at him, "you're going to meet the woman of your dreams, and then I'm going to make your life miserable."

"Afraid not, my dear Arabella. The woman of my dreams is such a paragon she couldn't possibly exist."

"Oh, please," Belle snorted. "I bet that within a year you'll be tied up, leg-shackled, and loving it." She sat back with a satisfied smile. Beside her John was shaking with mirth.

Dunford leaned forward, resting his elbows on his knees. "I'll take that bet. How much are you willing to lose?"

"How much are *you* willing to lose?"

Emma turned to John. "You seem to have married a gambling woman."

"Had I known, you can be sure I would have weighed my actions more carefully."

Belle gave him a playful jab in the ribs as she leveled a quelling stare at Dunford and asked, "Well?"

"A thousand pounds."

"Done."

"Are you crazy?" John's hand tightened considerably around her fingers.

"Am I to assume that only men can gamble?"

"Nobody makes such a fool's bet, Belle," John said. "You've just made a wager with the man who controls the outcome. You can only lose."

"Don't underestimate the power of love, my dear. Although in Dunford's case, perhaps only lust is necessary."

"You wound me," Dunford replied, placing his hand dramatically over his heart for emphasis. "Assuming I am incapable of the higher emotions."

"Aren't you?"

John, Alex, and Emma watched the interchange with considerable interest and amusement. "I had no idea you were such a formidable adversary, my dear," John said.

"You don't know a lot of things about me," Belle scoffed. She sat back with a self-satisfied smile. "Just wait until the evening is through."

A queer feeling settled in John's stomach. "I'm dreading every moment of it."

Chapter 23

"**M**erciful heavens!" came the hideous shriek. "What happened to you?"

Belle cringed. She'd forgotten about Lady Tumbley's distinctive voice, which was permanently lodged in the soprano register.

"A carriage accident," Alex said smoothly. "But we were so anxious to come tonight, we decided against turning back and changing. We're just a bit rumpled. I hope you'll forgive us."

Back in the carriage, it had been decided that Alex, as the highest ranking member of their group, should act as their spokesperson. His speech, which was accompanied by his most debonair smile, did the trick, and Lady Tumbley was soon preening most unattractively.

"Well, of course *I* don't mind, your grace," she gushed. "I'm so honored that you accepted my invitation. It has been many years since we've seen you here."

Belle noticed that Alex's smile had grown tight. "A mistake I must rectify," he said.

Lady Tumbley started to bat her eyelashes, a gesture which did not suit a lady of her years and girth. When she finally stilled her eyelids, she looked straight at John and said, "And who have we here?"

Belle stepped forward. "My husband, my lady."

"Your what?"

Belle stepped back. The screech had returned.

John took Lady Tumbley's hand and kissed her knuckles. "John Blackwood at your service, my lady."

"But Lady Arabella, my dear, I mean, Lady Blackwood, I just, well, I hadn't heard you'd been married. When did this occur? And, er, was it a large wedding?"

In other words—why hadn't she been invited?

"It was quite small, Lady Tumbley," Belle said. "Two weeks ago."

"Two weeks ago? An entire fortnight? And I hadn't heard?"

"It was in the *Times*," John put in.

"Perhaps, but I . . . "

"Perhaps you ought to read the newspaper more often," Belle said sweetly.

"Perhaps I should. If you'll excuse me." Lady Tumbley smiled awkwardly, bobbed a curtsy, and darted into the crowds.

"Our first objective has been fulfilled," Belle announced. "Within five minutes everyone will know that, one, our crumpled appearance is due to a carriage mishap, and two, I have married a most mysterious man about whom no one knows anything."

"In other words, everyone will know we're here," John said. "Including Spencer."

"If he comes," Emma said thoughtfully. "I doubt he's been invited."

"It's easy enough to sneak into such a large party," Dunford said. "I've done it a few times myself."

Emma looked at him oddly before asking, "What do we do now?"

"I suppose we mingle," Belle replied. "But we ought to try to stay in close proximity of each other. One of us might need help."

Belle looked around. Lady Tumbley had outdone herself this year, and the party glittered with candles, jewels, and smiles. The ballroom was one of the most distinctive in London, with a second floor gallery ringing the room. Belle had always thought that the Tumbley children must have spent countless nights up there peeping down at the elegant lords and ladies below. Belle sighed to herself, praying that she and John would get through this evening without harm, so that their children might someday be able to behave similarly.

For the next hour and a half, the quintet played the roles of innocent partygoers. Belle and John had no dearth of well-wishers, most of whom didn't bother to hide their insatiable curiosity about John and their hasty marriage. Alex and Emma stood nearby, their mere presence signaling their approval of the match. But more importantly, they were able to keep an eye out for Spencer while John and Belle were busy making polite conversation. Dunford acted as a roving spy, darting around the ballroom and monitoring the entrances and exits.

After nearly two hours, Caroline, Henry, and Persephone finally arrived and made their way immediately to Belle and John. "You wouldn't believe what happened to us!" Caroline exclaimed.

"A carriage accident?" John deadpanned.

"How did you know?"

"You had a carriage accident?" Belle said, horrified.

"Well, it was nothing dangerous. The left rear wheel slipped off, and we tipped a bit to the side. A bit uncomfortable, but no one was hurt. We did, of course, have to return home to change, however, and as a result we are extremely late." Caroline blinked a few times as she took in her daughter's slightly rumpled gown. "I say, that dress wasn't meant to be *crushed* velvet, was it?"

"We were the unfortunate victims of a carriage accident as well," John said.

"You don't say!" Persephone exclaimed, and then she made her way to a table laden with refreshments.

"That's odd," Lord Worth put in. "Very odd."

"Indeed." John's expression was grim.

Dunford appeared at their side. "Good evening, Lady Worth, Lord Worth. I must say, I had expected to see you earlier. Er, Blackwood, if I could have a moment alone with you."

John excused himself and met with Dunford a few yards away. "What's happened?"

"He's here. And looking furious. He came in through the side door a few minutes ago. My guess is that he wasn't invited. Either that or he's afraid the butler will call out his name. But he's in full evening dress. No one will look twice at him. He blends right in."

John nodded curtly. "He's going to try something."

"We need a plan."

"There's nothing we can do until he makes the first move."

"Just be careful."

"I will. Oh, and Dunford? Keep an eye on Belle,

will you?" John swallowed convulsively and searched his brain for the right words. "It would be very difficult for me should anything happen to her."

Dunford's lips curved into a tiny smile and he nodded. "I'll keep an eye on you, too. It would be very difficult for her should anything happen to you."

John caught his gaze. They didn't know each other very well, but they were bonded by their feelings for Belle, Dunford as her longtime friend and John as her passionately devoted husband.

John turned back to Belle and his in-laws, who were busily greeting a heavyset couple who'd come to offer congratulations on the recent wedding, expressing their sorrow that they hadn't been able to attend the actual ceremony. John caught the tail-end of the conversation, and had to bite his lip to keep from laughing as he watched Belle clenching her teeth, obviously trying hard not to point out that they hadn't been invited. Her eyes lit up when she saw him return.

"Our friend has arrived," he said quietly.

"Oh, who is that?" Caroline inquired.

"Just an acquaintance of John's from the army," Belle improvised, taking some solace in the fact that she wasn't exactly lying.

"You must go seek him out, then."

"Oh, I think he'll find us," John said archly.

Caroline's attention was then captured by a friend she hadn't seen since she'd returned from Italy, and Belle quickly turned to John and asked, "What are we going to do now?"

"Nothing. Just remain vigilant."

Belle took a deep breath and pursed her lips. She wasn't feeling especially patient. "Have you told Alex and Emma?"

"Dunford did."

"So we just stand here like sheep while he plots his nefarious schemes?"

"Something like that."

Belle grimaced and an extremely odd noise emerged from her mouth.

John looked to her in amazement. "Did you just growl?"

"I might have done."

"Good God, we'd better be rid of Spencer soon, or my wife is going to turn into an animal."

"A particularly vicious one, too, if I have any say in the matter." Belle sighed and looked around the ballroom. "John! Isn't that him right there?" She pointed discreetly at a blond man sipping a glass of champagne.

John followed her gaze and then nodded curtly, never taking his eyes off of Spencer. At that moment the cur looked up from his glass, and their eyes met. John felt an icy cold shiver run through his body, and suddenly he was more convinced than ever that coming tonight was a bad idea. He had to get Belle out of here. He'd have to deal with Spencer in his own way.

"He's coming this way!" Belle whispered.

John's eyes narrowed. Spencer had plunked his glass down on a nearby table and was making his way across the ballroom. John noticed that he was no longer looking at him; his gaze had shifted to Belle. Fury and fear raced through him, and his hand convulsively tightened around hers.

"Good evening, Lord Blackwood, Lady Blackwood," Spencer said mockingly.

"What the hell do you want?" John snapped. It was taking all of his self-restraint not to jump Spencer right there and then and wrap his hands around his throat.

"Now, now, Blackwood, why so surly? I've just come to say hello to you and your lady wife. That is what one is supposed to do at these events, isn't it? Of course my memory might be playing tricks on me. It has been so long since I've been to a London ball. Been out of the country as you know, for an extended period of time."

"Your point being?"

"It has been a long time since I have danced. I was hoping Lady Blackwood would do me the honor."

John yanked Belle closer to him. "Absolutely not."

"That's for the lady to decide, don't you think?"

Belle swallowed, trying to work some moisture into her throat, which had suddenly gone quite dry. "Your invitation is most kind, Mr. Spencer," she managed to say. "But I am afraid I have decided not to dance this evening."

"Really? How odd." Spencer's eyes glinted silvery-blue with malice.

"In deference to my husband," Belle improvised. "He does not dance, you know."

"Oh yes, he's a cripple. I often forget that. But I don't think that should stop you from enjoying yourself." He stepped forward and shoved a revolver against John's stomach, pushing it in and up to knock the wind from his body.

Belle looked down. Her stomach lurched with terror, and for a moment she thought she would be ill right then and there. The party was crowded, very crowded. No one would notice that one of the guests had just pulled a gun on another. If she screamed, Spencer would surely shoot John before anyone could wrestle the weapon from him. "I— I would love to dance with you, Mr. Spencer," she whispered.

"No, Belle," John said in a low voice.

"My husband," she tried to joke. "He gets very jealous. Doesn't like me to dance with other men."

"I'm sure he won't mind this one time." Spencer pulled the gun back, took Belle's hand, and led her onto the dance floor. John stood rooted to the spot, just beginning to get his breath back. His hands balled into fists, but he couldn't feel his fingernails biting into his palms. All of his attention, all of his energy, all of his soul was focused on the two blond heads on the floor. Spencer wouldn't hurt her, he knew that. Not in the middle of a crowded ballroom, at least. If anything happened to Belle in front of so many witnesses, Spencer would never get the chance to eliminate his true target. And John knew that Spencer wanted him dead.

"What happened? Why is Belle dancing with him?"

John turned and saw Emma, her face creased with fear and worry. "He pulled a gun on me, and asked Belle to dance."

"Did anybody see?" Alex asked.

John shook his head.

"Damn. It would be better if we had a witness outside the family." Alex grabbed Emma's hand. "Come on, darling, we're dancing too." With great speed and not so great grace, the Duke and Duchess of Ashbourne made their way onto the dance floor.

"What do you want?" Belle whispered, her feet automatically following the steps of the waltz.

Spencer flashed her a broad smile. "Why, just the pleasure of your company, my lady. Is that so incredible to you?"

"Yes."

"Perhaps I just wanted to make your acquaintance. After all, our lives have become, shall we say, entwined."

Belle felt anger building up within her, faster than fear. "I'd appreciate it if you would unentwine them."

"Oh, I plan to do so, have no fear. This evening, if all goes well."

Belle trod on his foot, then apologized prettily. She saw Alex and Emma dancing just behind Spencer, and she exhaled slowly, feeling much reassured by their presence.

"But I must admit," Spencer continued. "I am enjoying the look on your husband's face immensely. I don't think he enjoys the sight of you in my arms."

"I imagine not." Belle stamped on his foot, this time hard enough to cause Spencer to grimace.

"You seem like a nice enough chit," he said, once again ignoring her misstep. "I am sorry to inconvenience you by killing your husband, but there is nothing to be done about it."

Good God, Belle thought, the man was certifiably insane. She could think of nothing to say, so she slammed her foot down on his again, this time with considerable force.

"I see that the tales of your grace have been grossly exaggerated," Spencer was finally goaded into saying.

Belle smiled sweetly. "You shouldn't believe half of what the *ton* tells you. Oh my, is that the end of the dance? I must be off."

"Not so fast." He grabbed her arm. "I'm afraid I can't let you go just yet."

"But the dance is over, sir. Propriety dictates that—"

"Shut up!" Spencer snapped. "I'm going to use you to get your husband off into a side room. It wouldn't do to kill him in a crowded ballroom. I'd never escape the scene."

"If you kill him, you'll never get away with it," Belle hissed. "Too many people know you want him dead. You'll be arrested within minutes. And if you're not, you'll never be able to show your face in England again."

"Stupid female. Do you really think I think that I can shoot a nobleman and expect to live free and easy? I've been living in exile for five years. I'm used to it. Taking my place in society would be nice, but I'd rather have my vengeance. Now come with me." He yanked viciously at her arm, pulling her toward a set of doors that led to the rest of the house.

Belle acted out of sheer instinct. He wouldn't hurt her now. Not before he got John. She wrenched her arm out of his grasp and ran back to John, who was already advancing toward her. "Quick, we've got to get away from him. He's mad!"

John grasped her hand and started to weave through the crowds. Belle looked behind her. Spencer was closing the distance between them. Alex and Emma were behind him, but as a couple they couldn't move as quickly as he could alone. "This is too slow," Belle said nervously. "He'll get us before we reach the door."

John didn't reply. He picked up the pace, his leg screaming at the torture.

"John, we're not fast enough. We need to get over there." Belle pointed to the doors clear across the ballroom. Between them and their means of escape were a hundred dancing lords and ladies.

"And how do propose we get there? Dance?"

Belle blinked. "Why, yes!" With strength born out of fury and terror, she pulled John to a halt, planted her hand on his shoulder, and began waltzing.

"Are you crazy, Belle?"

"Just waltz. And lead us across the room. We'll be there in no time. Even Spencer wouldn't dare run across the dance floor."

John willed his injured leg into action and slowly began dancing, edging his way across the room with every step.

In her haste, Belle dug her fingers into his shoulder, trying to propel him further.

"Will you let me lead?" he hissed, followed by, "So sorry," when they bumped into another couple.

She craned her neck. "Can you see him?"

"He's trying to make his way around the perimeter. He'll never catch up with us. A superb plan, love, if I do say so myself."

They whirled frantically, their movements furiously off-beat, but a few moments later, they reached the other side of the ballroom. "What are we going to do now?" Belle asked.

"I'm taking you home. Then I'm going to the authorities. I should have done so long ago, but I didn't think they could do anything about verbal threats. But a gun in the stomach—that ought to put him away for some time, at least."

She nodded, following him to the door. "I can be your witness. And I'm sure Alex and Emma and Dunford can testify." She breathed a sigh of relief, glad that John wasn't planning to take the law into his own hands. If he killed Spencer, he'd be hanged.

They had just reached the cold night air when Dunford suddenly burst upon them. "Wait!" he yelled, stopping to catch his breath. "He's got your mother, Belle."

"What?" The blood drained from her face. "How?"

"I have no idea, but I saw him leave the room with her a few moments ago, and he was holding her very close to his side."

"Oh, John, we have to do something. She must be so frightened."

"I can't think of anyone more capable than your mother," John said, trying to put her mind at ease. "She'll probably have him tied up and ready for the constable in a matter of minutes."

"John, how could you joke about this?" Belle cried out. "This is my mother!"

"I'm sorry, love," he said, giving her hand a reassuring squeeze. "Dunford, where did they go?"

"Follow me."

He led them out a side door and down a dark hallway, where Alex and Emma were waiting for them.

"Do you know which door he went into?" John whispered.

Alex shook his head. "Emma," he said. "I want you and Belle to go back into the ballroom."

"Absolutely not!" came the heated reply.

The three men then turned their collective gazes on Belle.

"My mother is in danger!" she replied hotly. "As if I would abandon her now."

"All right," Alex sighed, realizing that a direct order was a waste of time. "But stay back!"

The two women nodded, and the quintet made their way down the hall, peeping into every doorway, taking care not to let the hinges creak whenever possible.

Finally they reached a room which was partially open. John was at the head of the group and immediately recognized Spencer's voice. He turned around and put his forefinger to his lips, motioning everyone to keep quiet. The three men wordlessly took out their guns.

"You silly man," they heard Caroline say disdainfully. "What can you possibly hope to accomplish by doing this?"

"Be quiet."

"I won't be quiet," came the imperious reply. "You've dragged me off from the party into a deserted room and pointed a gun at me which I can only surmise is loaded, and you expect me to be quiet? You are sorely lacking in intelligence, my dear man, and—"

"I said shut up!"

"Hmmph."

Belle bit her lip. She'd heard that tone before. If she hadn't been so terrified this might have been funny.

John, Alex, and Dunford exchanged looks. If they didn't make a move soon, someone would be dead, although they weren't necessarily convinced that the victim would be Caroline. John held up his hand and silently counted with his fingers. One. Two.

Three! The men burst into the room and spread along the back wall, their pistols trained on Spencer.

"It took you long enough," he sneered. He held Caroline's arm in a painful grasp, and his gun was pressed up against her temple.

"Your attitude is beyond surly," she scoffed. "It ill becomes you—"

"Mother, please," Belle pleaded, coming in through the door. "Don't provoke him."

"Ahhh," Spencer said approvingly. "You brought the ladies. What a treat."

Belle couldn't see John's face, but from the way he was holding his shoulders, she could tell that he was furious with her for not remaining out in the hall. "Just let my mother go," she said to Spencer. "She hasn't done anything to you."

"I might, if you'd be willing to trade places with her."

Belle took a step forward, but John's arm shot out like an iron band. "No, Belle."

"Really, Belle, don't be silly," Caroline said. "I can handle our lackwit friend here."

"I've had enough!" Spencer exploded. He slapped Caroline across the face.

Belle let out a little cry of dismay and rushed forward, eluding John's grasp. "Leave her alone!"

Spencer's arm snaked out and wrapped around Belle's waist, pulling her close to him. Her stomach turned over in dismay, but she swallowed down her fear and said, "Now let my mother go."

With a vicious shove, Spencer pushed Caroline away from him and she went tumbling to the floor. She opened her mouth to give him a scathing rebuke but then held her tongue, not feeling quite as brave now that he held her only daughter in his grasp.

In that moment, John lost the ability to breathe. It felt as if Spencer's hand were reaching out and squeezing around his windpipe. Belle was standing next to him, trying to appear brave, but John could see the fear and loathing in her eyes. He threw down his gun, put his hands in the air, and took a step forward. "Let her go, Spencer. I'm the one you want."

Spencer caressed Belle's cheek with the back of his hand. "Maybe I've changed my mind."

John's control snapped, and he would have jumped him right then and there if Alex hadn't reached out and grabbed the back of his shirt. "I said let her go," John repeated, his body shaking with fury.

Spencer's hand stole around to her backside and he gave it a little squeeze. "I'm still thinking about it."

Belle grimaced, but otherwise she did her best to remain silent. John's life was on the line here, and if she could save it by letting this man paw her, by God, he could paw her all he wanted. She just prayed he wouldn't try anything more intimate. The bile was already rising in her throat.

John's body was taut with rage. "For the last time, Spencer, let her go or I'll—"

"You'll what?" Spencer replied mockingly. "What can you possibly do? I have a gun. You don't. Furthermore, I have your wife." He let out a maniacal laugh. "And you don't."

"Don't forget us," Dunford drawled, jerking his head toward Alex. Their pistols were trained on Spencer's chest.

Spencer looked back and forth between his adversaries and laughed. "I cannot imagine one of you would do anything as asinine as to shoot me while I have a loaded gun aimed at the lovely Lady Blackwood. Still, she is not, after all, my main purpose in coming here, and I am afraid I am going to have to trade her in. Blackwood?"

John took another step forward. "Release her."

"Not just yet." Spencer yanked off his cravat and shoved it at Belle. "Tie his hands behind his back."

"What? You cannot mean . . ."

"Do it!" He raised his gun and aimed it at John's forehead. "I can't very well tie him up and keep my aim at the same time."

"Oh, John," Belle whimpered.

"Do as he says," John said. Behind him he could

feel Alex and Dunford tensing their muscles, getting ready to spring into action.

"I can't." Tears stung at her eyes. "I just can't."

"Tie his hands," Spencer warned, "or by God I'll shoot him on the count of three."

"Can I tie them in front? It seems so barbaric—"

"For God's sake, tie them any way you please. Just do it tight and be done with it."

With shaking hands, Belle wrapped the necktie around John's wrists, trying to tie it as loosely as possible without raising Spencer's suspicions.

"Step back," he ordered.

Belle took a baby step away from John.

"Farther."

"What are you going to do to him?" she demanded.

"You haven't figured that out yet?"

"Mr. Spencer, I'm begging you."

He ignored her. "Turn around, Blackwood. We're going to do it through the back of your skull."

Belle's legs grew weak, and she would have fallen to the ground if she hadn't crashed into an end table. Out of the corner of her eye, she saw Dunford slowly inching forward, but she had little hope he'd be able to save him. Spencer could see his every move, and there would be no way to surprise him. By the time Dunford could wrestle him to the ground, the fatal shot would already have been fired. Besides, the room was densely furnished; it looked as if the Tumbleys had shoved every stray settee, sofa, and table into it. Dunford would have to jump over two chairs and an end table if he wanted to take a direct route.

"You!" Spencer barked, jerking his head at Belle

without really looking at her. "Get back even farther. I'm sure you have a yen to play the heroine, but I will not have the blood of a lady on my conscience."

Belle moved sideways, as the end table was blocking her path. She sniffed. She smelled violets. How odd.

"Farther!"

Belle took another step back and thumped up against something solid. Something solid and . . . definitely human. She looked across the room. Alex, Dunford, Emma, and her mother were all in plain sight.

"Take this!" came a whisper.

Good God, it was Persephone! And she was pressing a pistol into Belle's palm.

Spencer raised his arm and aimed.

Belle felt herself dying. She'd have to shoot Spencer and pray that her aim was true. There was no way she'd be able to get the gun to John. Damn, why hadn't she let Emma teach her how to shoot properly?

John twisted his head around as far as he was able. "If I could have just one last wish?"

"What?"

"I'd like to kiss my wife goodbye. With your permission of course."

Spencer nodded curtly, and Belle hurriedly moved forward, concealing the gun in the folds of her skirt. With her free hand she reached up and touched John's face, making sure that Spencer could see her movement. John glanced down at his wrists, and Belle saw that he had worked his hands free of the loosely tied cravat.

"Oh, John," she whispered loudly, "I love you. You know that, don't you?"

He nodded. Give me the gun, he mouthed.

"Oh, John!" she wailed, figuring that the better show she put on, the more time they would have to plot. She moved her free hand to the back of his head and pulled him to her in a scorching kiss. She pressed herself as close as she could to John, praying that Spencer wouldn't be able to see what was going on in the narrow space between their bodies. She placed the gun in John's hands, quickly pulling the loosened cravat off his wrists as she did so.

"Keep kissing me," he whispered. She could feel his hand settling into the contours of the gun. Her tongue flicked out, tracing the outline of his mouth, savoring the slightly salty taste of him.

"Open your mouth, love," he said softly.

She did, and his tongue swooped in to deepen the kiss. Belle returned his passion with equal fire, all the while keeping one eye open and trained on Spencer, who was watching them with a fascinated expression. His arm had lowered slightly, and Belle knew that their kiss had pulled some of his attention away from his obsession to kill John. She resolved to distract him completely and moaned loudly with pleasure.

John began to trail small kisses along her jawbone, and Belle arched her neck to give him greater access. But she could feel that his attention was focused elsewhere. She felt him nod, and then from the shadows came a hideous, barely human shriek. The sound was terrifying. Belle felt sick to her stomach just listening to it.

"What the hell?" Spencer was jolted from his voyeuristic reverie, and he couldn't stop his head from turning toward the awful sound.

John abruptly let go of Belle, and before she realized what was happening, she pitched forward and tumbled onto the ground. John spun around, whipping the gun out and shooting Spencer's pistol cleanly from his hand. Alex and Dunford immediately rushed forward, tackling the stunned man to the ground.

Persephone stepped forward and folded her arms, a satisfied smile on her face. "Sometimes a little age and wisdom is a very good thing."

"Persephone, what are you doing here?" Alex demanded as he yanked Spencer's wrists behind his back.

"That's a fine way to greet me after I've gone and saved the day."

"Oh, Persephone," Belle said with great feeling. "Thank you!" She clambered to her feet and flung her arms around the older woman. "But what was that awful sound?"

"Me." Persephone grinned broadly.

Caroline raised her brows incredulously. "Surely that wasn't human."

"Oh, but it was!"

"It certainly did the trick," John said, joining the women after making sure that Spencer was tied up properly. "Although I must admit, I never dreamed you'd emit such a sound after I signalled to you to make a commotion."

"You knew she was here?" Belle asked.

"Only after I saw her hand you the gun. Well done, Persephone." John pushed his hair back and noticed that his hand was shaking. It would be a long time before the image of Spencer holding Belle hostage would fade from his mind.

"How on earth did you get in here?" Belle asked.

"I knew something sinister was going on. No one saw fit to confide in me." Persephone sniffed in disdain. "But I figured it out. I also eavesdropped a lot. And then I realized—"

"Excuse me!" Dunford called out.

Six heads swiveled in his direction.

"We might want to notify the authorities about him." He motioned down to Spencer, who was lying on the floor, bound and gagged.

Belle waved him off, too interested in Persephone's story. "He's not going anywhere like that."

Dunford raised his brows at her nonchalance but nonetheless planted his booted foot in the middle of Spencer's back, mostly just for the fun of it.

"If I might continue," Persephone intoned, thoroughly enjoying her role as heroine for the day.

"By all means," Belle replied.

"As I was saying, I overheard Alex and Emma discussing the ball tonight and realized that John and Belle might be in danger. That is why I insisted they take me along." She turned to Belle. "Now, I realize that I wasn't the strictest of chaperones, but I did take my position seriously, and I felt that I would be remiss in my duties if I did not come to your aid."

"For which I am extremely grateful," Belle felt compelled to interject.

Persephone smiled benignly. "I realized that you might need a secret weapon tonight. Secret even from yourselves. You were all so busy with your schemes you didn't notice that I disappeared the moment I arrived at the party. I went up into the balcony which overlooks the ballroom and watched. I saw this man accost you, Belle, and then force your mother out of the room."

"But how did you get in here?" Belle asked.

Persephone smiled craftily. "You lot left the door open. I just crawled in. No one noticed me. And the room is rather generously furnished. I simply darted between chairs and settees."

"I can't believe we didn't see you," John muttered. "My instincts must be off."

"It *is* dark in here," Persephone replied, trying

to reassure him. "And your attention was engaged at the time. I wouldn't worry about it, my lord. Besides, you were the first to notice me. After Belle, of course."

John shook his head in admiration. "You're a wonder, Persephone. A true wonder. I can't thank you enough."

"Your firstborn girl, perhaps," Dunford suggested impishly. "Persephone is a fine name."

Belle scowled at him. A fine name perhaps, but not for any child of hers. But then again—Belle's eyes lit up as an idea unfolded in her mind. An idea so perfect, so timely— "I must offer you my gratitude, too," she said, linking arms with the older woman. "But I'm not sure my first daughter is the right way to thank you."

"Whyever not?" Dunford's mischievous grin spread from ear to ear.

Belle smiled archly and kissed her former chaperone on the cheek. "Ah, Persephone, I have grander plans for you."

Chapter 24

$\sim\!\!\infty\!\!\sim$

A few weeks later John and Belle were curled up in bed at Persephone Park, enjoying their relative peace and quiet immensely. Belle was thumbing through a book, as was her habit before going to sleep, and John was sorting through a stack of business papers.

"You look very fine in your new spectacles," he said with a smile.

"Do you think so? I think they make me look smart."

"You are smart."

"Yes, but these give me a more serious air, don't you think?"

"Perhaps." John put his papers on a nightstand, then leaned over and dropped a wet kiss on one of her lenses.

"Jo-ohn!" She pulled the spectacles off and began to clean them against the quilt.

370

He plucked them from her hand. "Leave them off."

"But I can't see the book without—"

He took the book from her hands. "You won't need this either." The book slid to the ground, and John covered her body warmly with his. "It's time for bed, don't you think?"

"Maybe."

"Only maybe?" He nipped at her nose.

"I've been thinking."

"I certainly hope so."

"Stop your teasing." She tickled him in the ribs. "I'm serious."

He looked at her lips, thinking he'd like to nip at them, too. "What is on your mind, darling?"

"I still want a poem."

"What?"

"A love poem, from you to me."

John sighed. "I gave you the most romantic proposal a woman has ever had. I climbed a tree for you. I got down on one knee. What do you need a poem for?"

"Something that I can hold on to. Something that our great-grandchildren will find long after we're dead, and they'll say, 'Great-grandfather certainly loved great-grandmother.' It's not so silly, I think."

"Will you write me a poem?"

Belle thought about that for a moment. "I'll try, but I'm not as poetic as you are."

"Now, how do you know that? I assure you that my poetry is appalling."

"I never liked poetry before I met you. You have always loved it. I can only deduce that you have a more poetic mind than I do."

John looked down at her. Her face shone with love and devotion in the candlelight, and he knew he could deny her nothing. "If I promise to write you a poem, will you promise to let me kiss you senseless whenever I wish?"

Belle giggled. "You already get to do that."

"But in every room? Can I do it in my study and your sitting room and the green salon and the blue salon and the—"

"Stop! Stop! I implore you," she laughed. "Which room is the green salon?"

"The one with all the blue furniture."

"Then which one is the blue salon?"

John's face fell. "I don't know."

Belle bit back a smile.

"But can I kiss you in it?"

"I suppose, but only if you kiss me now."

John growled with pleasure. "At your service, my lady."

A few days later Belle was spending the afternoon in her sitting room, reading and writing letters. She and John had hoped to ride over to Westonbirt to visit Alex and Emma, but inclement weather had put an end to their plans. Belle was sitting at her desk watching the rain beat down against the window when John walked in, his hands shoved boyishly in his pockets.

"This is a welcome surprise," she said. "I thought you were reading over those investments Alex sent over."

"I missed you."

Belle smiled. "You can bring the papers up and read them here. I promise I won't distract you."

He dropped a kiss on the back of her hand. "Your mere presence distracts me, love. I wouldn't read a word. You promised I could kiss you in every room in the house, remember?"

"Speaking of which, weren't you going to write me a love poem in return?"

John shook his head innocently. "I don't think so."

"I distinctly remember the part about the poem. I may have to limit your kisses to the upstairs rooms."

"You fight dirty, Belle," he accused. "These things take time. Do you think Wordsworth just whipped out poems on demand? I think not. Poets labor over each word. They—"

"Have you written one?"

"Well, I started one, but—"

"Oh, please, please let me hear it!" Belle's eyes lit up in anticipation, and John thought she looked rather like a five-year-old who had just been told she might have an extra piece of candy.

"All right." He sighed.

"Fair is my love, when her fair golden hairs
With the loose wind ye waving chance to mark;
Fair, when the rose in her red cheeks appears;
Or in her eyes the fire of love does spark."

Belle narrowed her eyes. "If I'm not mistaken, someone wrote that a few centuries before you did. Spenser, I think." With a smile she lifted the book she had been reading. *The Collected Poems of Edmund Spenser.* "You would have gotten away with it an hour earlier."

John scowled. "I would have written it if he hadn't thought of it first."

Belle waited patiently.

"Oh, have it your way. I'll read you mine. Ahem. She walks in beauty—"

"For goodness' sake, John, you tried that one already!"

"Did I?" he muttered. "I did, didn't I?"

Belle nodded.

He took a deep breath. "In Xanadu did Kubla Khan a stately pleasure-dome decree—"

"You're getting desperate, John."

"Oh, for the love of God, Belle, I'll read you mine. But I'm warning you now, it's, well, it's— Oh, you'll see for yourself." He reached into his pocket and pulled out a much-folded piece of paper. From where she was sitting, Belle could see that the paper was liberally streaked with crossouts and heavy editing. John cleared his throat. He looked up at her.

Belle smiled in anticipation and encouragement. He cleared his throat again.

"My love has eyes blue as the sky.
Her warm, bright smile makes me want to try
To give her the world,
And when she's curled
Up in my arms where I can feel her touch,
I realize again that I love her so much.
My world has turned from black to white.
Kissing in starlight, basking in sunlight,
    dancing at midnight."

He looked up at her, his eyes hesitant. "It needs a bit more work, but I think I got most of the rhymes right."

Belle looked up at him, her lower lip trembling with emotion. What his poem lacked in grace, it more than made up for in heart and meaning. That he had labored so long on a task for which he obviously had no aptitude, and just because she'd asked him to—she couldn't help it, she started to sniffle, and fat tears rolled down her cheeks. "Oh, John. You must really, really love me."

John walked to her and nudged her into a standing position before gathering her into his arms. "I do, my love. Believe me, I really, really do."

MINX

Julia Quinn

Beautiful and feisty Henrietta Barrett has never followed the dictates of society. She manages her elderly guardian's estate, prefers to wear breeches rather than dresses, and answers to the unlikely name of Henry. But when her guardian passes away, her beloved home falls into the hands of a distant cousin.

William Dunford, London's most elusive bachelor, is stunned to learn that he's inherited property, a title – and a ward bent on making his first visit his last. Henry is determined to continue running the Cornwall estate without help from the handsome new lord, but Dunford is just as sure he can change things – starting with his wild young ward. But turning Henry into a lady makes her not only the darling of the town, but an irresistible attraction to the man who thought he could never be tempted.

978-0-7499-3914-4